PRINCE OF INK & SCARS
BOOK TWO IN THE WELSH KINGS TRILOGY

RAYA MORRIS EDWARDS

Prince of Ink & Scars

By Raya Morris Edwards

FIRST EDITION

Cover Design by @designsbycharlyy

Editing by Morally Gray Author Services & The Fiction Fix

This book is for Corinne, who loves Caden best.

AUTHOR'S NOTE

This book contains discussions and depictions of mental health issues in relation to OCD and ADHD. It is a fictionalized depiction of these diagnosis based upon my own experiences that is NOT intended to be a tool for educational use or to diagnose. Please reach out to qualified mental health professionals if you need help.

Content Tags & Trigger Warnings

Discussions of past child abuse and neglect (nothing on page)
Discussion of drug and alcohol abuse and overdose
Discussion of parental death
Some discussions of pregnancy
Explicit discussions regarding prescription drug abuse and addiction
Mental health issues regarding OCD and ADHD
Brief mention of rape (nothing explicit)
Discussions and depictions of action and violence and heavy use of weaponry including guns
Instances of misogyny
Discussions of physical violence including people fighting each other to the death in an arena
Head in a box

Explicit sexual content
Light breeding kink
Light daddy kink
Dirty talk

CHAPTER ONE

CIRCE

For the first time in forever, I was going out.

My best friend, Delaney, and her other best friend, Emmy, had talked about this for weeks. They'd been out a few times without me because I just couldn't make the time. I'd spent the last ten days working from six in the morning until seven at night on this new deal.

Three board members had to be convinced to sign one of the biggest deals of my father's career. My father said there was a lot resting on it, so it meant a lot that he assigned me to manage it.

Nothing was more important to me right now than work.

This was my first big test—could I complete it on my own without him at my side if things went wrong? Could I seal three complicated deals and walk away with exactly what I wanted?

My mouth was dry just thinking about it. It was incredibly flattering that he trusted me with something this important.

The only catch? He'd insisted I work alongside one of the other organization's people—a Welsh mafia soldier, to be exact. God, it made me roll my eyes every time I thought about it.

I didn't need some stuffy, boring guy who'd probably spend the entire time we were working together patronizing me. I'd worked with men for the last four years I'd spent in my father's business, and I knew the drill. Honestly, I was a little insulted my father wanted me on a team with one of *their* people—the Welsh organization owned our biggest competitor.

I was ready to do this on my own.

But that could wait. Tonight was Saturday, and I'd bought a new dress and shoes. For the next few hours, I was going to go out with my friends and have a drink. I'd be home by eleven, have a mug of warm lemon water, and take a long, hot shower before bed. I couldn't be hungover because, even though it would be Sunday morning, I still had to stop by the office.

In my bathroom, I put the finishing touches on my mauve lipstick. It was a pretty sheen, with some lip liner to keep it in check. Elegant and sophisticated, with my signature touch—silver and mauve glitter.

Something about those colors together gave me peace.

My earliest memory was being a toddler and waking up to the wind chimes outside my window—purple hummingbirds and silver bells, moving in the wind. I barely remembered anything else until kindergarten, until my father had to sit me down and explain why it was just me and him.

Death was a hard thing to explain to a child that young, but I remembered nothing of my mother. I was fortunate to have a father who loved me so much that he strove to fill both parental roles.

He put me in therapy. I talked through my thoughts. The therapist told my father I was remarkably well adjusted.

Ambitious was a better word. If my father wanted me to talk through my issues with a therapist and work through the exercises, I was going to be the best patient that therapist had ever had.

The same with gymnastics when I was seven.

Band when I was nine.

Dressage and polo when I was fourteen.

That phase stuck around for a while. My father moved in wealthy circles, and it was beneficial for him to rub elbows with the other fathers taking their daughters to polo matches. They all had money, lots of it.

Eventually, I went to college and was president of the polo team and the tennis club. On weekends, I drank strawberry mimosas at the country club with my father and filled the social void where my mother should have sat.

It was, after all, what was expected of me.

I pulled myself out of thoughts of strawberry mimosas, summertime at the club, and polo matches that stained my boots green, and looked around.

Where was my purse?

I left the bathroom with my towering heels clicking in my wake. Usually, I stuck to classic pumps, but tonight, we were going out to let our hair down, so I opted for chunky mauve platforms. They paired well with my daring little black dress.

Tonight felt different, and I wanted to dress for the occasion. Maybe tonight, I wasn't an overworked COO in training. Maybe I could be bold and sexy.

My phone rang as I descended the stairs, and I swiped it, hitting the speaker button.

"Hey, do you have a ride?" Delaney bubbled.

She sounded giddy, probably because she'd given up on hoping I'd actually stop working and go out with them for once.

"I've got an Uber waiting outside," I said, moving down the marble hall. "I just have to find my purse."

It could be anywhere in this enormous, old home. My father's house was a huge mansion outside Providence, in a private neighborhood. A thick apple orchard and a stacked stone fence kept us back from the road. The long drive was lined with glossed pebbles sunk into concrete and ended in a circular drive. To the right, at the edge of the orchard, was my koi pond. In the summer, I brought my thirteen ancient koi out to enjoy the fresh air and ample bugs. In the winter, I switched them to a tank inside. They were my only frivolous pastime. Everything else I did with my time made money for my father's company.

"I'll bet you left your purse on the hall table," Delaney said.

I glanced up and, sure enough, my little velvet designer bag was right there. I grabbed it, rifling through to make sure I'd included everything I needed for tonight—ID, credit card, painkillers, a mini water bottle, just-in-case tampons, and pepper spray.

"You're right. I got it," I said, tapping in the code to lock the door, holding the phone with the other hand. "Where are you coming from?"

"We just got here," she said. "Emmy had her brother drop us off. Do you think we'll be able to get a ride back?"

"It won't be that late. I'm sure there'll be an Uber somewhere to take us back," I said, stepping out onto the back porch.

It was warm, and the yard smelled of green apples and sunshine. A silver car waited by the garage—not an Uber; that part I'd lied about. My father was too protective to let me take taxis, so I was going to have our private chauffeur drive me and drop me off a block from the bar so no one felt awkward.

Delaney and Emmy had money, but not the way my father did. Not the way I would someday when I inherited the company.

Guilt twinged in my stomach.

I shrugged it back and slid into the back seat. Our driver, Louis, turned the air conditioning up and leaned back, putting the car in drive. He was about my age and had just started a few years ago. My father trusted him enough to let him drive me, but only after doing his first two years on our security team.

"Hey, Louis," I sighed. "How's your wife?"

"Ready to pop," he said, pulling onto the road. "She doesn't want my paternity leave to start yet. I think she wants me out of the house."

I smiled. "How long did my father give you?"

"Three months," he said. "That's all I asked for, and I'm coming back part time."

"Good. Just let me know if you need more," I said.

He dipped his head. "What's the plan for tonight?"

I chewed my lip, watching the stone fences and trees slip by. "I'm just trying to get out of my head. Emmy's birthday was yesterday, so we're going out to that new bar downtown."

"You need a bodyguard?"

"I'm good," I said.

He glanced at me in the rearview mirror from beneath the brim of his baseball cap. "I'm glad you're getting out. Not to get into your business too much, but you work hard, Circe."

I nodded. "I know. My father has a lot resting on me. I don't want to let him down."

"He'll still love you, you know," Louis said quietly.

For some reason, that hit me right where I was tired and tender. My lashes were suddenly wet, and I flipped down the mirror behind his seat and dabbed my cheeks.

"Damn it, Louis, don't get philosophical on me," I sniffed. "I just did my makeup."

He shook his head, smiling. "Sorry, ma'am. I'll make sure not to next time."

We both laughed, and I changed the subject to lighter things. The weather, the tourists that crowded the beach-side towns, the music festival he was planning on taking his wife to in Newport next year. A few minutes later, we pulled into downtown Providence, and he found a spot to park a block down from the bar.

I got out, and he rolled his window down.

"I'm going to watch you walk into the bar," he said, his voice firm.

"You don't have to," I sighed.

"I work for your father," he said. "And he pays me to keep you safe while I'm driving you."

I lifted my phone. "I'll call you right away if anything happens. But it'll be a crowded bar, and I'll be with Emmy and Delaney all night. Okay?"

He nodded, but he didn't budge. Sighing, I waved and started walking down the sidewalk. His car pulled out and slipped into traffic, easing along beside me until I pulled open the front door of the bar. I slipped inside and watched as he drove off.

For one beautiful second, I was alone, despite being in a packed room. Then, someone tapped my shoulder, and I turned to find Emmy bouncing with excitement.

I'd only met her a few years ago, but I understood why Delaney liked her so much. She was bright, always in a good mood. I envied that about her. She was also that one friend who always had her head in the clouds. I'd had to pull her out of traffic a half dozen times, and I'd pepper sprayed a man trying to convince her to get in his sports car, but she meant well.

She was one of the smartest people I knew, with two degrees in the sciences. She just didn't have an ounce of street smarts.

"Hey, you look amazing," she cried, throwing her arms around me.

"So do you, babe," I said, hugging her.

She pulled back, jerking her head towards the back of the bar as she dragged me into the crowd. "We have a table. Let's go."

She wore a short white dress with pink cap sleeves and matching stacked heels. Her blonde ponytail bobbed, and her gold jewelry glittered. The overall impression was of a pink frosted cupcake.

Delaney was at a standing table in the corner, talking to the bartender. He was a lanky man in a t-shirt that said EAT LOCAL in capital letters and *pussy* in tiny italics below it. I admired that; it took guts to show up to work in that shirt.

Delaney was giving him eyes and biting her lip. He was just her type, and I could tell he was into her relaxed aura. Her sundress hung off her slender frame, her nipples poking through the organic linen. She never wore a bra, which I admired but couldn't emulate. Tonight, she'd worn her hair up and her septum piercing with a blue bead to match her eyeshadow.

She glanced over as we approached. "See you," she said, her voice low as she fluttered her lashes at the bartender. He took the hint and vanished.

"So I take it you're not leaving with us tonight," I said, hugging her.

She shook her head. "Tonight is girl's night. No exceptions."

"Perfect," I said, hugging her. "What are we drinking?"

Emmy turned to the bar, stretching to look over the sea of heads. Even with stacked heels, she was short. "I ordered us all margaritas to start. Is that okay?"

"Perfect," I said.

"There they are," she said, stepping out of the way as the other bartender appeared with a tray.

I snagged one and took a deep drink, trying to get my tight shoulders to relax. It had been a long day of sitting in meetings. The sweet, salty margarita spread over my tongue, reminding me of how long it had been since I let my hair down and had a drink with my friends.

Weeks.

Maybe months.

Emmy started chatting about the boy she was talking to. He didn't sound like much of a catch to me, but she was excited, so I didn't say anything. Delaney was a lot harsher, giving the one photo Emmy had of him a cold glance and shaking her head.

"He looks like a fuckboy," she sighed.

Emmy turned the phone around, frowning. "Oh, maybe he does. I don't know. I didn't think about that."

"I mean, that's fine. If you just want him for sex," she sniffed.

Emmy blushed, shaking her ponytail back. "You know I'm not having sex."

"Not having it?" I asked. "Or *won't* have it?"

She shoved her phone back in her purse and took a deep sip of her drink. "Won't. I'm waiting for the right man with lots of money. This hair and these nails don't pay for themselves."

I laughed, knowing full well Emmy wasn't very money motivated. She had her first degree in a niche field of science that I didn't understand, but she spent a lot of time in a lab for less money than I thought she deserved. I mentioned helping her get a raise once, and she'd just giggled.

"No, thanks," she'd said. "I'm just happy to be here."

She still lived with her parents—we all did, except for Delaney, who had lost hers early on and lived with her older brother, Yale. None of us felt an enormous level of pressure to make money at this stage. The reason I worked myself such long hours had more to do with pressure and expectations.

We started talking about sex, then dating, and finally began picking through all the single men we knew. Delaney was involved through her brother with the Welsh Mafia organization, which I didn't know much about. It was a secretive, underground circle of extraordinarily wealthy men and women. I knew the head of it, Merrick Llwyd, spent a lot of time negotiating business deals throughout the city, some of which involved my father.

And then there was the other deal—the one I was supposed to be working on with one of their men.

The point of all that being, some of the men in that organization were *fine*. Delaney had tried to set me up with her brother a few times, but he was disappointingly obsessed with someone else. It was too bad; he was hot.

Speaking of hot men...my eyes skimmed over Emmy's head to the bar. The bartender with the pussy shirt was leaning on his elbows, talking with a tall, lean man with black hair.

Something about him held my attention.

He wore a dark t-shirt, and down his right arm were dark, heavy lined tattoos, like the curves of ancient architecture. They disappeared beneath his sleeve and reappeared to curl up one side of his neck, stopping below his jaw.

I dragged my gaze up his lean back, his long legs. A little bit of warmth stirred down below.

He was good looking—I could tell that before he even turned around—and I didn't say that about a lot of men.

But then, he turned around, and my heart screeched to a stop as a pins and needles sensation splintered through my body. His heavy lids moved over the rim of his glass as he lifted a beer to his lips. They met mine, glittering in the low lights.

We both froze.

A current of electricity sizzled between our bodies. Despite all the people between us, it felt like he was right here, burning me up with his blue eyes.

God, he was gorgeous.

Heat prickled down my spine, and I swore I was sweating beneath my bra. I tugged at my neckline and regretted it, hoping he didn't think I was trying to show my cleavage.

The corner of his mouth jerked up, and to my utter panic, he pushed off the bar and started towards me.

I whipped around, realizing I was alone. Where had Emmy and Delaney gone?

Heart thumping in my chest, I spun in a slow circle, trying to see through the people around me. It was getting darker outside. Inside the bar was dim, lit by lowlights wound around the periphery of the room.

I turned—there he was, a foot away. He had a strong face, a heavy nose with an aquiline arch, a thin, masculine mouth, and beautiful eyes, dark cobalt blue with long, black lashes.

"Hey," he said.

My lips were dry. "Hi," I whispered.

He held out his hand. I saw a flash of tattooed knuckles, and then he shook my cold palm.

"You look lost, sweetheart," he drawled.

"No, not lost," I said. "I have friends. They went to the...bathroom."

He took a sip of his beer, his throat bobbing. "Oh yeah?"

He had a deep, drawling voice with an accent. It took me a moment to place it because it had clearly faded, but it sounded English. It wasn't that stereotypical accent Americans always imagined. No, it was a little rougher and sat deep in his chest.

"I'm Cece," I lied.

"Caden Payne," he said.

My heart sank.

Oh no, I knew who this was, even if he clearly didn't recognize me. I'd seen his name on the paperwork. This was the mafia soldier I was supposed to complete my mission with, the one from the Welsh Mafia organization, my business partner in the deal my father had assigned to me.

I resented that my father thought I needed help to get the job done, so I'd been prepared to hate him on sight.

But he was too sexy to hate.

My head spun. His eyes dropped to my empty margarita glass, and he reached out and took it.

"Let me get you another."

There wasn't room to protest in his voice, and I found I didn't want to. I had a drink under my belt, and I'd just spent an hour talking about men with Emmy and Delaney.

And, in the broader perspective, I was also beyond horny from being celibate for the last five years.

Maybe it wouldn't hurt to just...talk to him. He clearly didn't know who I was, so what would it matter? Before I could speak, he took the glass from my hand and disappeared into the crowd.

My feet were locked to the ground.

The intelligent part of my brain told me to walk away.

The rest of me that was still tingling just from his presence told me to stay.

CHAPTER TWO

CADEN

I'd come to the bar for a sandwich and a beer. Not even ten minutes in, and I was already buying a drink for the absolute knockout standing on the other side of the room.

I'd promised myself I wasn't doing this anymore.

No risky sex. No abusing prescription medication. No being a dick for no reason. I was beyond that now; my responsibilities were too large.

A few years ago, Merrick had given me an opportunity to handle one of his biggest projects ever—constructing and running a training camp for his private security business. I'd secured Johansen Enterprises as our business partner despite them being our biggest competitor.

I was taking a huge chance, but I really believed this could work, so that meant I had a lot riding on this, both personally and professionally.

As soon as the ink was dry on the preliminary agreement, I went cold turkey and focused on nothing but work. I quit drinking except for social events, I wasn't self-medicating with anything I could get my hands on, and I forced myself not to get distracted.

This morning, I'd killed it at training. Lunch was a meeting with an international security agency to barter a deal for some of my men. During the afternoon, I worked out, cleaned my apartment, and ran some errands for training tomorrow. It was almost seven when I got back, showered, and realized my fridge was empty.

So, I took my Kawasaki down the street to a bar that had just opened a few blocks from my downtown apartment. The night was balmy and smelled faintly of the honeysuckle growing on the side of the shops by the bar. I walked across the street, fully intending on grabbing my favorite sandwich—a burger with only the bottom bun, the top just onions draped in cheese.

I got to the bar and, to my horror, it was packed. The bartender told me it would be a minute on the burger, so I ordered a beer and leaned on the counter.

Then, my eyes fell on her across the room.

Fuck, she was...indescribable. Her dark hair was wavy and fell down her upper back. She had brown eyes, a full mouth, and a gorgeous oval face. High cheekbones, a delicate, square jaw with a pointed chin. An elegant neck that flowed down to her shoulders, long arms that ended in ringed fingers and glittering nails.

Her lids fell, like she was shy, but I didn't believe that. She didn't look like a woman who doubted herself.

I couldn't look away. Nothing turned me on more than confidence.

I wasn't sure how it happened, but suddenly, I was refilling her drink, and she was waiting for me with wide eyes by the standing table in the corner. When I returned, she lifted her glass and took a deep sip. Her lipstick left a little purple half-moon behind.

Her cheeks flushed, and she looked down again. Was she flirting, or was she nervous?

"So what do you do?" I asked.

Her lids fluttered. "Small talk?"

"I can get right into the real talk if you want?"

"I'd much prefer it."

"Alright, when was the last time you orgasmed?"

Her jaw dropped, and I realized I was going to fuck up my resolutions tonight to stay focused on just work. Her lips parted and her dark brows arched, as delicate as a butterfly's wing.

God, she was pretty.

14

"That is too fast, sir," she said coolly. "I don't know you."

"You wanted to skip the small talk," I replied. "What do you usually talk about once you've discussed the weather?"

"Not...you know."

I felt my mouth curl into a smile. "Sex?"

She nodded, sending me a hard stare. I stepped closer, and she stepped back until we had moved into the far side of the room, until I had her slender body caged against a table on the back wall. The atmosphere was intimate, and she wasn't throwing off signals that she wanted me to stop.

In fact, she was leaning in. Her breathtaking face tilted up to mine like she wanted me to get my body closer. I leaned in, and a strand of soft, dark hair fell over her cheek.

A part of me wanted to run my fingers through it.

"Who are you?" I said quietly.

Her eyes widened. "What?"

"Why haven't I seen you around?"

She shrugged, stalling her answer by sipping on her margarita. It was effective, because I got completely distracted for a second. Her mouth was soft, firm, and painted mauve. My head spun just looking at it, wondering what it would feel like...wrapped around my...fuck, I needed to stop.

Why, though?

I dragged my mind back. "So where have you been?"

She shrugged, smiling. "Around. Busy."

"Who's your crowd?"

She cocked her head, giving me a strange look, like she was trying to figure me out.

"My crowd?"

"Who are you with?" I asked, lowering my voice. "You're not Welsh."

She shook her head, her eyes darting over me. "Are...you?"

"Welsh? Yes."

Her brows shot up. "Oh."

15

I leaned in, and this time, she leaned back in. Her body was warm, and I felt it through my shirt, like a siren luring me closer.

"Did you come here alone, Cece?" I whispered.

Her eyes darted over my shoulder, looking for something. "I had friends, but I don't see them."

"Are those your friends?"

She followed where I was pointing. The two women I'd seen her with earlier were in the corner, four empty glasses on their table.

She worked her lower lip, like she was debating going back to them. My eyes fell, distracted by her hands. Her fingers held the margarita glass elegantly, like she was having white wine in the country club. Unable to help myself, I leaned a little closer to her dark hair and inhaled.

Soft floral.

"Did you just smell me?" she whispered.

"You smell good," I said, unashamed. "Like flowers."

"Hyacinths."

My palm slid over her elbow, and she didn't pull back. "Do you want to stay with me? Or go back to your friends?"

She looked over her shoulder. The short, blonde girl giggled and waved at her, clearly urging her to stay. The other girl had her back to us, swiping her phone.

"It's supposed to be girls' night," she said.

"It looks like your friend is giving you a pass," I pointed out.

Her blonde friend waved more enthusiastically, like she was trying to shoo Cece away.

She laughed nervously. "Just a few drinks."

I took her hand, slipping my fingers between hers. She was pretty in a way that felt rare and ageless, like a painting or a statue from thousands of years ago, but fresh like her floral perfume.

And guarded. Her dark eyes were very guarded. I'd mistaken it for confidence at first, but now that I was up close, I saw she was out of her element.

I pulled her to the corner, drawing out a stool. She struggled up onto it, flashing her upper thighs. My cock twitched, and I turned towards the bar to hide my half-erection.

"Where are you from?" I asked.

She gave me a coy glance. "Here."

"This bar?"

This time, she rolled her eyes. "Yes, I live in the bar."

"You don't look like you live in a bar," I said.

She shifted, pinching her heels together for modesty. I couldn't help it—my eyes lingered at the little tanned valley where her thighs pressed together. Her skin glinted in the low light. Was she wearing body glitter? I was a sucker for body glitter, especially on naked thighs barely covered in short skirts.

I glanced up, and our eyes locked.

"Um...are you looking at something?" she said hoarsely.

My dick twitched.

"Do you want the honest answer?" I leaned a little closer.

She bit her glossed lip, lightly so she didn't mess up her makeup. "Maybe I do."

I let my gaze tumble over her curves. My eyes moved back to her face, and her soft mouth parted, the tip of her tongue just visible past her teeth.

Fuck.

"Honestly, you're beautiful," I said quietly.

She giggled, twirling a little bit of dark hair around her manicured nail. There was something so electric about the sound; she didn't look like the sort who usually giggled. She had a serious shell around her...but it was starting to come undone.

Our bodies were so close, I could feel the electricity thrumming between them. "Do you want to get out of here?"

"Like...to fuck?"

My brows elevated, and she cocked her head.

"Yeah, I guess. To fuck."

She emptied her glass and reached for her purse, taking her time applying her lip gloss. She popped the cap back on. Her throat bobbed.

"I don't know. Do you?"

My eyes skimmed over her face, just below mine. Her dark gaze glittered in the lights. She wanted me to be the one to make the first move.

"Yeah, I'd like to take you home," I said.

She smiled primly. "Okay, Caden, you take me home."

Her voice was low, husky, and it shot right to my dick, making it twitch. Before she could change her mind, I took our glasses and her hand and went to the bar to close out my tab.

She bit her lip, chewing hard, but when I glanced back, she just gave me a sultry glance.

Fuck, I'd let this woman step on my face and thank her for it.

I paid and pulled her through the crowd. We stepped onto the hot pavement, and she stumbled in her clunky heels, falling into me. I caught her in my arms.

"Let me take your shoes off," I murmured.

She shook her head, laughing. "No, I don't want to step on the dirty sidewalk."

"I'll carry you."

She blushed, shaking her head. "I'll let you take them off later."

That was fine with me. I guided her with my hand around her waist to the Kawasaki. Her eyes widened as I unfastened my helmet and fitted it over her head.

"You'll mess up my hair," she whispered.

"If we crash and you're without it, it'll be really messed up," I said, strapping it under her chin.

For a second, I was tempted to reach down and kiss her, to bite the pout right off her mouth.

Instead, I got on my motorcycle and helped her settle herself behind me. Her arms wrapped around my waist and her hands locked. Her helmeted head rested on my back as the engine purred and we pulled out onto the street.

Her fingers unlocked then, the nails digging into my stomach and chest, sending heat pulsing down my stomach to my dick. It was already waking up, but now, it was ready to go. She was going to see how much I wanted her the minute I stepped off the bike.

A few minutes later, I pulled into the garage below my apartment and cut the engine. She hopped off, her heels loud on the pavement. I dismounted, but she was too busy trying to get the helmet off to notice the ridge beneath my pants.

"Here, let me," I said.

She tilted her chin up, and my fingers brushed her skin as I unhooked it and pulled it free.

"Does my hair look silly?" She smoothed it back, running her fingers through the tips.

I shook my head. She pursed her lips, and I wondered if right now was the time to kiss them.

"Do you want to...go upstairs?" she whispered.

"Fuck, yes," I said, reaching down to take her hand. She clearly wasn't used to having her hand held, because she tensed like the sensation was unfamiliar each time.

But then she melted, letting me lead her up the stairs to my front door.

"Why do you have all these locks?" she asked.

I glanced over the padlock and the little metal bar above it. "It's just two."

"Two plus the deadbolt."

"Maybe I'm a criminal," I said lightly.

She narrowed her eyes. "Maybe criminals are my type."

I pushed open the door, and she gave me that sultry look from beneath her lashes as she passed me. Her pointer finger trailed across my abs and slipped lower, to just right above my belt.

Heat shocked down, and my dick throbbed hard.

She stepped inside, ass swaying. My head was empty as I followed her in, but not enough to forget to lock the door behind us and check it. She moved to the kitchen area and turned, leaning back against the counter.

19

"Well, I'm here now." She tilted her head innocently. "What were you thinking?"

I set my keys aside. "Lift your skirt."

My lips parted as her long fingers flipped the very edge of her hem, tugging it up an inch.

"I feel like you're not a very good man," she whispered.

"Why? Is it the neck tattoos?"

She pointed above her at the chandelier made of animal bones, at the long row of collectible weaponry over the fireplace in the living area.

"That's weird," she whispered.

"It's ethically sourced," I said, taking a step closer. "The bones, anyway."

Her eyes widened, her hands sliding behind her back as I got even closer and bent over her, pinning her up against the sink.

"I think it's the tattoos," I breathed.

"I have a tattoo," she whispered.

I scanned her body quickly. "I don't see it."

She lifted her hand and turned her middle finger to the side. Tucked away was a little purple butterfly. For a micro tattoo, it was incredibly sharp, and I wondered if it was new.

Without thinking, I lifted her hand to my mouth and gently bit the butterfly, making her gasp.

"Lift your skirt," I ordered.

This time, she tugged it up to reveal a silky pair of mauve panties. Arousal flooded me in a surge, and I forgot everything. My mind went empty, and there was nothing left but the driving need to drop down and taste between her legs.

My knees gave way and hit the ground. Her eyes widened as her fingers wrapped around the edge of the sink.

"What are you doing?" she gasped.

Her thighs were so soft—fuck, they felt so good. I ran my palms up, shoving her skirt to her waist. She moaned as my fingers grazed her ass and slipped beneath her panties, her head falling back when I peeled the silk from her pussy and let it fall around her heels.

She was pierced.

Curiosity roused, I lifted her thigh and draped her knee over my shoulder. She was beautiful, cleanly shaved, with a faint blush over her sex. I ran my fingertip lightly over the seam, wetting it so I wouldn't hurt her when I parted her pussy to reveal her clit.

There was a tiny silver bar through the hood, and clipped onto it was a mauve gem.

It wasn't the first time I'd seen a clit piercing, but it was the first time I saw one on the most perfect pussy I'd ever laid eyes on.

Without thinking, I bent and licked it. She gasped, and my entire body tingled as her sweet taste spread over my tongue. Dick hard as a rock in my pants, I licked over her again, rubbing up against her piercing as I went.

Her hips lifted as my tongue came away, hungry for more.

"Oh God," she whispered. "You're good at that."

Right then, I realized I didn't care if I got any satisfaction tonight. I wanted to make this woman come and come again until the wetness dripped down my chin and her hands were tangled in my hair and she had to pry my face from between her thighs.

So I did. And even though she was so fucking proper and pretty, she let me turn her into a mess over my kitchen sink.

I forgot her name. Maybe she forgot mine.

It didn't matter, though, because she gave up after the first orgasm and just let me eat her out until her pleasure moved in waves, until it slipped down her thighs and soaked into my shirt, mixing with my sweat.

We lay on the kitchen floor for a while, and she played with my hair and ran her elegant fingers over my face, exploring the tattoos on my neck.

I left her in the kitchen with some ice water while I showered all the sweat and pussy off my neck and chest. Then we made out on the kitchen floor for another hour. No sex—just touching, kissing, letting our bodies ebb and flow together through our rumpled clothes. My dick ached, but I was so drunk on the taste of her mouth that I barely noticed.

She left around three because she couldn't keep her eyes open and I had work in the morning. A car came to pick her up, probably an Uber. I could only see the headlights in the road. I pinned her against the garage wall and kissed the side of her neck as she moaned, hips rubbing up against my groin.

"I want to see you again," I said.

"You will," she gasped.

I bit her neck and pushed my phone number into her pocket. She walked away with a pink mark on her skin, giving me a heavy-lidded glance over her shoulder as she slipped into the dark.

Like she really intended to see me again.

CHAPTER THREE

CIRCE

I woke late, a little slower than usual. My neck cracked loudly as I dragged myself out of bed and searched for my phone on the floor. I snatched it, swiping the screen to reveal a barrage of texts from my group chat with Emmy and Delaney.

My stomach flipped as the memories of last night came flooding back, sending heat curling through my stomach and making my clit pulse.

He'd touched me—no one had touched me in years.

My skin was deliciously raw, like I could still feel his fingertips on my thighs and his tongue on my pussy.

Flustered, I vaulted out of bed and ran into the bathroom, pulling the curtain back to let the sunlight flood the room. In the mirror, my naked body stared back at me.

My fingertips skimmed over the pink marks on my skin. At first, the memories felt good, like a sweet secret only I knew. But the longer I stared at those fingerprints, the more I was torn on what I'd done.

One part of me was elated all it had taken to make him fold was for me to giggle and twirl my hair once. He'd be easy to work alongside. I could get in, make the important deals, and get out before he knew what was happening. I could take all the credit and prove to my father I didn't need a partner for this deal.

The other part of me dreaded having to face him now. Had I fucked up the mission?

We were scheduled to have our first meeting within the week, and he was going to realize who I was as soon as I walked in.

And he was going to know I'd known.

Heart thumping, I flipped the shower on and stepped in, letting the hot water wash him away as I scrubbed until my skin glowed. Normally, I worked out before I showered, not after.

But I needed to be clean right now.

It was sinking in that I'd messed up before we'd even started. My hands shook as I toweled off and lined up my vitamins, filling a glass with water.

In the fridge in my bedroom, I grabbed the last green juice and poured it into one of my crystal glasses. Even the slightly bitter acquired taste couldn't make me feel like myself again.

I was used to order, neatness, being pretty, wearing pearls, sitting with my ankles tucked properly.

I didn't go home with tattooed mafia soldiers.

He'd thrown me off my game. I needed to get back on track, or he was going to wipe the floor with me in that meeting, and I couldn't have that.

Plus, I was annoyed.

For some reason, it was pissing me off that he'd gotten me to cave so quickly. Yes, I had seduced him, but he'd done a lot of seducing himself before we even agreed to hook up. All he'd done was buy me a drink and have sexy tattoos.

Clearly, that was enough for him to get my panties down around my ankles.

Wrathfully, I brushed my teeth. I might not feel like myself, but no one needed to know that. By the time I'd slipped into my yoga set, I was feeling a lot better.

Everything was back to how it should be. Equilibrium was achieved.

I grabbed my juice and headed into the mini gym off my room. Soft meditation music on the timed speakers drifted through the morning air wafting in through the window. I rolled out my mat and slid into a gentle downward dog, letting my muscles sink and rest.

Usually, I enjoyed the gentle stretch I did after my shower. Today, it gave me a little twinge between my legs. I frowned, noticing for the first time that my pussy was sore. Rolling onto my back, I extended my calves and ankles, letting my hand drift down and skim over my sex through the cloth.

There it was—a little twinge where he'd worked his magic.

I flipped over and slid into a pigeon pose, glaring up at the ceiling as I extended my spine.

Five times.

Last night, he'd made me come *five* times. That should be illegal or something.

I cracked my neck and switched legs.

Who was he anyway? All I knew about him so far was that he worked for Merrick Llwyd, the head of the Welsh Mafia organization. My father hadn't briefed me any further than that, so I was going into his office the minute I had a chance to uncover the rest. I'd have to be casual about it—my father could never know what had happened last night.

I wasn't sure how he'd react, but I knew it would be negative. He was always trying to point me in the direction of nice young men who graduated from Harvard who wore checkered button ups.

My father had a specific idea of who he wanted me to be and who he wanted me to marry. I had to be pretty and perfect like a doll, a flawless representation of his business with an ideal son-in-law at my side.

I frowned, trying to center my focus. I did yoga every morning, but I'd never had this much trouble with it.

Caden was everything I wasn't allowed to have. Maybe that was why I'd caved so fast and let him bring me home, not because there was anything special about him.

Just because he had tattoos, hard abs, and a motorcycle. Not because he had the most beautiful eyes I'd ever seen.

Frustrated, I got to my feet and turned off the speakers. I hadn't even broken a sweat, so I changed into my work clothes and did my makeup. My outfit for today was typical—a cream pencil dress, white gold accessories, mauve lipstick.

I fixed my hair, grabbed my purse, and went downstairs to face the day.

My father stood in the front hall. He was a stoic man who was always perfectly dressed in a light-colored suit, his gray flecked hair slicked back from his hard lined face. He glanced up from sorting a pile of mail, fixing his steel gray eyes on me.

"Morning, honey," he said. "Heading into the office?"

"Just to drop some paperwork off," I said, standing on my toes to kiss his cheek.

He sent me an approving look, setting the mail on the hall table. The front hallway was one of my favorite places in the entire house, huge with a curved ceiling and stone walls that led the way to the double doors with glass panes. As a girl, I'd ridden my tricycle up and down these marble floors for hours.

"Do you want brunch?" he asked. "It's in the garden."

I considered skipping and picking up something on the way to work but decided against it. This might give me an opportunity to find out more about Caden without my father suspecting anything.

"That sounds nice," I said, setting my purse down.

We went out into the garden. It was a large, well-manicured part of the lawn with stone pathways, trimmed hedges, and pale wicker furniture. Around the side was the open gazebo, already set with breakfast. I sank down into my usual chair and kicked my heels off, tucking my feet in. My father sank down, reaching for the coffee.

"How was your night with Emmy and Delaney?" he asked.

Guiltily, I held out my cup and let him fill it with coffee. "It was good; we were out late."

"I saw Louis had someone go get you at three," he said. "Did your friends make it home alright?"

I glanced down at my phone. From the barrage of texts, they'd gone to Delaney's and spent the night speculating about what I was doing.

"Yeah," I said. "It was nice. We all had fun."

I'd definitely had more fun than I'd ever had with anyone in my life. My father nodded, distracted by his phone pinging. I cleared my throat and stirred my coffee, gazing out over the garden.

Why did it feel like this changed everything?

Plenty of people hooked up. I hadn't even had sex with Caden. Surely, we could hit the reset button and pretend nothing happened? It was in his best interest, just like mine, to not mention what had happened. He didn't seem like the kind of person to be reckless.

My mind wandered back to his apartment. It was intimidating. Everything was minimal and clean, but there were so many strange things here and there, I wasn't sure if I liked it. The weapons on the walls. The chandelier made of bones. The rug in the living area printed like a medieval tapestry.

All the ink curling on his skin.

Those heavy eyes that seemed to hold back something, like if I fell into them, I might fall through space until there was nothing left but sweet darkness.

I shivered.

"You alright?" my father asked.

I nodded. "Yeah, sorry. Is there anything you want from the office before our meeting tomorrow?"

He shook his head. "I have a report on your partner for you to take a look at. It's in my office."

A little twinge of irritation went through me. I was beyond flattered that he was trusting me with it, but why did I need Caden to help?

Frankly, it was a little insulting.

I took a breath, composing my face. "Are you sure a partner is necessary?"

He gave me a level stare. "Trust me on this."

"I'm just saying, I can do this alone," I protested.

"Circe," he said, not unkindly. "You're my daughter, but I'm also your boss. Don't argue with me about your assignments."

His voice was firm. I squared my shoulders and committed to pretending it didn't matter. If I could lie about having hooked up with Caden last night, I could lie about this.

"What's his name again?" I asked casually.

"Caden Payne," my father said. "He's Merrick Llwyd's most trusted soldier. From what I can tell, he's been transitioning him into right hand duties the last few years and transitioning his old commander into other roles. I looked into it, and it seems it started around the time Caden made contact with me about funding the Wyoming base."

"Which means?"

My father glanced up, pale eyes glinting. "You tell me."

I chewed my lip. "Caden is important. The Wyoming base is the biggest deal Merrick Llwyd's ever made, so he'd only put someone he trusted in charge of it. So maybe Caden was...working on something else before? And now he's getting switched?"

My father nodded and shook his head. "Yes. No. He's important. But why?"

We'd done this so many times before. He'd push me, make me learn to think like him. I was good at it after all this time, but this one stumped me. I closed my eyes and thought back over Caden last night, studying his image in my mind's eye.

"He...worked on something illegal before," I said. "Important, but secret."

"Not bad." My father poured another coffee, taking a sip. "But no."

Frustrated, I closed my eyes again. Sometimes, I felt like my father could be a little patronizing.

The image of Caden's dark blue gaze and heavy lids appeared in my mind. He looked wary, guarded, like he had a secret.

My eyes snapped open.

"He's someone to Merrick," I said. "He's personally important outside of work."

"Excellent."

"Who is he replacing within the Welsh organization?"

"Yale Bennett," my father said. "He trains their soldiers alongside Caden, but recently, Caden has been pulled into the spotlight and given the Wyoming Project."

"So he's not dirty," I said.

"Oh, he's dirty," my father said. "But on paper, he's clean. Yale's the opposite, which is why he didn't get the Project, since it's all legal."

I stared across the garden to my koi pond. "So who is Caden Payne?"

My father set his phone down, and I leaned in, glancing down at a photo on the screen. It was Merrick Llwyd at a statue unveiling, with Caden standing in the background, looking like a bodyguard with sunglasses and tattoos up his neck.

I brought the phone closer, squinting. Merrick was tall, almost six and a half feet, and Caden was an inch or two shorter. They both had lean, muscular builds and handsome faces. Their hair was dark, almost black, and Merrick's eyes were turned to the camera, dark blue with heavy lashes.

My brows shot up.

"Caden is related to Merrick," I said.

My father leaned back, taking a packet of organic cigarettes out. I always scolded him for having one, but today, I was too distracted. The lighter flicked, and I ignored it, too busy staring at the two men.

"He is," my father said. "I suspected when he was assigned to this mission that there was something more going on. He's incredibly talented; don't underestimate him. Merrick is clearly trying to mold him into a right hand."

"Against his will?"

"From what I can tell, yes."

I handed the phone back. "Merrick is how old?"

"Forty-seven."

"And Caden is...thirty," I said slowly. "Merrick's either his father or his uncle."

"From what I can tell, Merrick had an accidental pregnancy with someone he didn't know well when he was a teen," my father said. "I tracked down who I think was Caden's mother, and she was in the States nine months before his birth, in Rhode Island."

I stared into the distance, trying to absorb this information. Things were changing fast. Last night, I'd gone to the bar for a girls' night and ended up with the son of the Welsh *Brenin's* tongue between my legs.

Oops.

This was a lot more complicated than I'd realized.

"Interesting," I said lightly, getting to my feet. "Alright, I'm going into the office, and I'll grab the report off your desk later. It was good to have breakfast. See you tonight."

I kissed his cheek and left him in the garden, scrolling his phone. In the hall, I grabbed my purse and hit the garage door button in the foyer. Across the driveway, it lifted to reveal my topless convertible, white with mauve trim and vegan leather seats.

I drove into the city with fluffy pop blasting from my speaker. In the parking lot of Johansen Enterprises, I parked in my designated spot and pulled out my phone. Last night, on the way home, I'd saved his number.

But I hadn't texted him.

I stared down at the name: Caden Payne.

It sounded like a nice name for a nice boy I could take home to meet my father, not like the man who'd eaten me so well that he left fingerprints on my hips. Arousal fluttered, and my finger hovered over his name. With a sudden surge of what could only be described as bravery, I tapped it, brought up my messages, and typed quickly.

Hey, this is Cece.

Heart thumping, I hit send.

It went through. There was a second, and then I could tell he'd read it.

No, it's not.

Frowning, I texted: *Is this Caden?*

Don't fuck with me. You want to talk, bring that ass over. You know where to find me, Circe Johansen.

Heat poured through my body as my heart thrummed. I sat there for a solid ten minutes, just staring down at my phone. Then, three typing bubbles appeared and rolled. My jaw dropped.

Get the fuck over here, Circe.

No one talked to me like that, not even my father. Rage flooded me, and I blindly typed and hit send.

I don't even know where you are, and you're really rude.

You know my address. Have your driver bring you.

Furious, I threw my car into drive and pulled out of the parking lot. How dare he talk down to me like that? I hadn't done anything to him; we'd both mutually agreed to hook up.

Not that it was a real hook up, of course.

I barely remembered the drive into downtown or parking on the street and flouncing through his open garage to the entrance. My heels clattered on the stairs as my nerves thrummed. I knocked once, and he jerked open the door.

Damn it. He was all sweaty and, in the light of day, he was even sexier than last night, if that was physically possible.

He was a big man, but his build was lean, so he didn't seem bulky. He wore black fatigues and boots, his t-shirt soaked through, sticking to his ridged abs. His wet hair was slicked back like he'd just run his fingers through it. The sunlight cut through his window, making his eyes glitter like sapphires.

"What happened to you?" I asked.

"I was teaching a bunch of kids self-defense," he said. "No rest for the wicked and hungover."

I stared at him, trying to pull my thoughts together. He smelled good—sweaty and salty like the ocean, but good. Between my legs, against my silk panties, arousal woke, warm like pooled lava.

My mind ran away from me, feeding me images I had no business entertaining. The animal part of me I clearly hadn't constrained with hot yoga, herbal tea, designer dresses, and manicures roared to life, and it wanted Caden to slam me against the cupboards and fuck me hard.

I swallowed as my cheeks radiated heat.

"Can I come in?" I asked.

He considered it. "No thanks."

I gasped. "You're so rude."

"Not the first time I've heard that."

"Clearly you didn't take it to heart."

He shrugged, leaning in the doorway. "I'm not letting you in because you're a liar. You went home with me knowing who I was. I'm also not letting you in because now that I know who you are, I know I've got no business sending the heiress of Johansen Enterprises back to her daddy with my handprint on her ass, which is what I'll do if you put a foot into this apartment."

My entire body burned. The air crackled between us, and his lips parted, though his heavy eyes stayed blank.

He was so arrogant, so sure of himself.

I cleared my throat, trying to get my temper reined in. "I didn't mean to deceive you."

"Well, you did."

"It wasn't personal," I said, tilting my chin. "I thought you looked like a good time."

"I am a good time, but I come with baggage you can't handle."

I glowered—he was probably right. He stepped over the doorstep and crossed his arms, towering over me. I forced myself to stand straight and not back down.

"We're done here," he said. "No one will hear about last night from me."

Maybe deep down, I'd been afraid of that all along, because those words drained some of the tension. Our eyes met, and I swallowed back my pride.

"I think that's for the best," I said.

"I need to get ready for my afternoon shift."

His eyes were hard. It was slowly sinking in that maybe I couldn't work Caden the way I did businessmen. Maybe he wasn't swayed by my usual methods. It was also dawning on me that he was a lot smarter than I'd anticipated.

"How did you know who I was?"

He pointed at the doorway. "Night vision security cameras and facial recognition software."

I swallowed. I'd been one step ahead last night. Now, he had me on defense.

"Maybe I didn't know," I said.

He sighed. "You wouldn't have lied about your name if you didn't know who I was."

"I don't use my first name with any strangers," I snapped. "You're not special."

"I know," he said before he shut the door in my face.

CHAPTER FOUR

CADEN

I peeled myself off the mat and grabbed my phone. The three recruits, both in their third year, looked up from where they were practicing grappling. I lifted a hand, waving at them to continue. My phone beeped, letting me know I'd missed a call.

My father's name appeared. Two missed calls from Merrick.

I worked my jaw. Sometimes, I struggled with working so closely with him. I was a fully grown adult when I met my estranged father, already shaped by the world and resentful of what it had done to me.

Then, along came Merrick, the head of the Welsh organization and my biological father. He was charismatic and successful. If I'd had the chance to grow up with him instead of my mother, I'd be a different person. I wouldn't have tasted fear and pain so early or so thoroughly.

I couldn't even blame him. Merrick had no idea I existed until I walked into his office, dropped my backpack on the ground, and let him know I was his son.

My phone rang again, and I answered it.

"Hey, I'm teaching a class," I said, running a hand over my forehead to clear the sweat.

"I have three new soldiers coming in this afternoon," Merrick said.

"From where?"

"They're graduates."

"So they're eighteen, done with school. What's the goal here? Ship them out to Wyoming for security training?"

There was a short pause, and Merrick cleared his throat. "I'd like you to evaluate them."

I frowned, stepping further from the grappling mat. "For what?"

"For the arena."

I stopped in my tracks. The Welsh organization liked to pretend they were so much more civilized than other mafia groups, but when it came down to picking a new king, a *Brenin*, we were right back in ancient Rome, fighting each other to the death in an underground arena for the throne.

My father had done it. He'd trained as a teenager and taken down twelve men in hand-to-hand combat in the arena before his twentieth birthday. He'd proved his worth.

A little part of me envied how simple that must have been. I'd fought for every ounce of respect, sometimes to blows and blood. Merrick had walked into the arena a boy and came out a man, all his suffering finished in one day.

We weren't all so lucky.

I cleared my throat. "Okay, when are they coming?"

"Yale's supposed to bring them in about an hour," he said. "We've got three more years before I announce I'm retiring. There's one recruit in there I think has a shot."

"A real shot?" I didn't believe it.

"Yes, he's good," Merrick said. "You call me when you're done evaluating them and let me know what you think."

"What's his name?"

"You'll know who I'm talking about," he said. "And if you don't, he's probably not the one. Call me later. Thanks."

He hung up, and I shoved my phone in my bag and clapped my hands once. The soldiers on the floor jumped to their feet, falling into a line with their hands tucked behind their backs and eyes straight ahead.

"That was good. We're cutting it short today," I said. "Next Thursday, I want to see some improvement, so make sure you're working hard. Yes?

"Yes, sir," they echoed.

"Alright, at ease. Get the fuck out," I said, waving at the door. "The rest of the day is yours."

They fell out of stance, talking amongst themselves as they headed for the showers. I cleaned the room up and left for the locker room, hoping for a hot shower before the evaluation.

The locker room was empty, so I tossed my things in the office and pulled my shirt off. I laid my phone on the desk and paused. The memory of when she'd texted me over lunch flooded back, this time with a hint of regret.

I'd been a dick, but maybe she deserved it. If I'd known who she was, I never would have taken her home. Pulling off this deal successfully would make or break my career. It was about proving my worth, because I'd missed the boat, and I was too old to fight in the arena.

I worked my jaw.

Fuck, last night had been so good.

My head fell back, and arousal sparked, running down my spine and making my dick wake up. It felt like it had a hair trigger on it. After being celibate for the last year, it was getting harder to control myself. I needed to jerk off a lot more to keep from getting hard in awkward places.

I'd come off a little aggressive, telling her to get her ass over to my apartment. While I'd waited, I'd flip-flopped between fucking her until she apologized for lying or telling her to go to hell.

I was proud of myself for not caving, especially when my bedroom was so close—and *especially* because now I knew that between those long legs was the prettiest pussy I'd ever had my mouth on. She'd tasted like pure desire, like being starving and eating my fill at the same time.

My mind wandered as I stripped down and went into the shower stall. The hot water rained down, washing the sweat away, but I could still taste her on my tongue.

She wasn't my type. I liked women at least fifteen years older, liked dominating women a lot more powerful than myself. She only checked one of those boxes. Maybe it was because I knew none of those women wanted me for longer than a night.

That kept me safe.

She was complicated, with so much to prove. I could taste that on her words. Maybe we were too alike in that aspect.

Maybe I resented her so much because she was who I could have been if I'd known Merrick from the beginning. I could have grown up with a rich father to protect me. Instead, I was covered in ink I'd never wanted because it was better than the scars underneath.

She was out of my league. No scars, no shitty tattoos like I had. Body supple, waxed, and soft from flowery lotion. No flaws, just that little purple butterfly tattooed on her glittering finger. Clear, trusting eyes framed by lashes worth more than my rent. Jewelry hanging off her body that definitely cost twice my paycheck.

Maybe a selfish part of me wanted to make her dirty.

Maybe I was jealous.

Or maybe I just wanted to ruin something beautiful because I was chronically destructive. Maybe all my work on myself in the last few years meant nothing.

I winced. Between fantasizing about her body or beating myself up over my failures, I picked fantasizing about her and beating myself off instead. The locker room was empty, and I was in a private shower, so my hand slid down and wrapped around my cock.

It thickened, my mind going back to last night, back to her slender legs wrapped around my head. Her glittering fingers in my hair as she rode my face. The memory of her pussy dripping down my neck until it soaked my shirt.

My head fell back.

My jaw tightened until it hurt.

My hand slid over my cock, palming the head until the silver ring there cut into my skin. She had pretty hands, and I wanted them on my dick, stroking me, running the pad of her thumb over the tip of my cock. I wanted her big, dark eyes looking up at me as she licked all the way up my length.

My cock jerked.

That was fast.

I was clean and in my fatigues, waiting in the arena, when the hour struck three. We didn't usually use the arena for recruits, but I wanted to see this group out here and gauge if it intimidated them. I walked the wide oval, my boots making tracks in the sand. The stone walls stood over ten feet tall, and beyond them were the stands.

Merrick had fought here. His blood had stained the sand.

Guilt stirred. I would never do that.

I'd never be the Welsh Prince.

If I'd been less stubborn, maybe I could have started training the minute I got to Providence, but I hadn't. I'd let myself steep in resentment and drugs and sex with strangers. I was so angry with the world that I rejected my birthright.

And now, it was too late. Twenty was the cut off to join the training program.

Maybe that was the real reason I didn't want anyone to know Merrick was my father. Not because I worried about nepotism accusations, but because everyone would know I'd rejected who I was and missed out. Merrick was descended from Welsh kings; his ancestry could be traced back to the earliest memories of our ancestral leaders.

I had that blood in my veins.

And I'd chosen to silence it.

Maybe, despite how good of a soldier I was, deep down, I wasn't worth following in his footsteps.

The door on the far side made of steel bars swung open, and Yale walked through, three figures at his heels as I waited at the center of the arena.

"Line up," Yale said.

I glanced at him as they obeyed, and he nodded, stepping back to give me space. They were all eighteen, still practically children. The first was broadly built, with pale beige skin and dark gray eyes. I studied him as he kept his eyes ahead, arms tucked at his side.

He was nothing exceptional.

I moved on, studying the boy beside him. He was thin with a gaunt frame, like he'd hit puberty, and it stretched him without filling him out. His eyes were lowered. I circled him slowly. He looked scrappy, like he'd had to fight to keep his head above water.

That was a bonus. Maybe he was who Merrick was talking about.

"What's your name?" I asked in Welsh.

He glanced over his shoulder. "Sean, sir," he responded in English.

I moved back around. "When I speak to any of you, you'll answer in kind."

"Yes, sir," he said, going pale.

I frowned, dragging my eyes from head to foot. "You don't speak Welsh?"

"Not well, sir, but I can, sir," he said, his voice cracking.

"Then speak it," I said, looking him in the eye.

He was shaking. I glanced over my shoulder at Yale, and he shrugged. I wasn't trying to be a dick to this kid, but I needed to know what they were made of. Apparently, this one wasn't as scrappy as I'd initially thought. Not wanting to push him further, I moved on.

The last young man in the line had his chin lifted, his eyes straight ahead, focused on the far arena wall. I scanned him, picking over his appearance. He was slender and lean, but he looked strong. His dark hair was shaggy, falling over his startling blue eyes. His complexion was pale beige, and down his right cheek ran a jagged, silver scar.

I circled him. He stayed completely still.

When I paused before him, his stare broke, and he glanced at me, just for a second, but I saw something flicker in his gaze.

Blue fire. My scalp prickled.

"Where are you from?" I asked in English.

"Providence, sir," he said.

39

I frowned. "I've never seen you before. The others, I think I've seen around town. What's that accent?"

"Welsh, sir," he said.

"I got that," I said impatiently. "Is that Neath?"

He nodded once.

"Where did you get that scar?" I asked, switching to Welsh.

"There was an incident at my school the other year, here in the States. I got jumped by some classmates, and they cut me up," he said, answering me in the cleanest Welsh I'd heard from anyone other than Merrick.

"Why?"

He lifted his eyes to mine, and I saw simmering anger behind them. Fuck, he reminded me a lot of myself.

"They were fucking with me, sir, so I beat the shit out of them, and they came back for me with a knife."

"Did you beat the shit out of them again?"

"I did, sir."

"Good," I said. "Who are your parents?"

"They're dead, sir."

"And your name?"

He cleared his throat, like he was proud of it. "Maelon Boaughan."

"That's a good name."

"Yes, it is, sir."

I raised a brow, impressed. He was holding his own, showing a little teeth but keeping it respectful. I glanced back at Yale, and he nodded, his brows lifted. I needed a moment to confer with him before I set up a meeting with Merrick to talk over the next steps.

"Alright, you three, head back to the barracks," I said. "Training starts at seven sharp tomorrow."

They nodded, and Yale pointed them back through the door. The gate clanged shut, and I turned to him.

"What do you think?" I asked.

He shrugged. "He's got a lot of spirit, but we need to see if he's got any raw talent."

I ran a hand over my face. I'd slept like shit last night because Circe had left at three, and I'd had to jerk off twice before my dick calmed down enough to let me rest. Even after that, I'd laid awake thinking about her for an hour.

"Why was he in Wales?"

Yale's mouth thinned. "His mother took him back to live with her distant family."

"And his father?"

Yale cleared his throat, his voice dropping. "He lied about his parents. His mother is still alive; she lives outside Providence. She was an assault victim."

My stomach turned. "So she doesn't know the man who attacked her?"

He shook his head. "He was American, that's all we have. I read the report. I think she wanted to run away after that, so she fled to Wales when he was about eight, and he finished school there."

"Why wait that long?"

"I don't know. Maybe money." He shrugged, glancing at his watch. "Listen, I have to go. I have a class, but I'll send Maelon to you tomorrow for his paperwork."

I felt sick as we split in the hallway and headed back to the locker room to grab my things. My scalp prickled. The back of my neck was cold. Every part of me wanted to recoil, because this boy was like looking in a mirror, and I wanted to turn and run so I didn't have to face myself all those years ago and admit I'd failed. That so many people had failed me.

But I couldn't. This was my chance to go back and save the boy no one had bothered to save all those years ago.

CHAPTER FIVE

CIRCE

Two days after the fiasco on Caden's doorstep, I got home to find the house empty. My father had left a note that he was out, having dinner with a friend. I texted to let him know I was eating at home and going to bed but didn't pry into what he was doing. My father dated often, and I stayed out of his business.

I wished he would extend the same courtesy to me. Sometimes, he could be a little overprotective. Every time he got wind of a potential suiter, he ran a background check before I had a chance to even go on a date.

I'd learned my lesson about sharing my love life over the dinner table.

Slipping my heels off, I padded into the kitchen and dropped them and my handbag on the chair by the door. In the fridge, I found two premade deli sandwiches our chef had left yesterday.

I grabbed a sandwich and vegan chips and piled them on the island counter. The clock struck eight. My eyes fell through the window to the koi pond, glittering in the early moonlight.

I always felt bad when I ate before my fish.

I snagged the fish food and let myself out the side door in my bare feet. Dew covered the grass like a net of diamonds. The landscaper had mowed early in the day, and little bits of grass stuck to my skin.

A sense of peace settled over me. I leaned on the edge of the koi pond and sprinkled the food over the surface. My biggest, oldest fish, Percy, bobbed to the surface, and I touched his cold, slippery nose.

A smile broke over my face before it vanished as I realized someone was watching me. My body went cold, and I drew back, stumbling and grabbing the stone wall to break my fall.

My heart thumped. Then, my vision cleared, and I realized who was standing at the edge of the driveway.

"Caden," I whispered. "What the fuck are you doing in my yard?"

He was in a suit, but it looked like he'd put it on in the morning and gotten impatient with it throughout the day. The jacket was gone, his sleeves rolled to his elbows, and his collar was open, showing a suggestion of his chest tattoos.

He had one hand in his pocket, head down, eyes up and fixed on me like an animal in the shadows.

"I came to see you before our meeting this week," he said.

I glanced around, mouth dry. "Did you drive?"

"I walked."

"We're two miles from town."

He shrugged, moving closer. "I run several miles a day. It doesn't bother me."

"You're so fucking weird," I said. "How did you get through the gate?"

"You left it open."

Guiltily, I realized I had. I'd been so distracted, I'd driven right through, and it was after hours, so security hadn't been there to fix my mistake.

"Don't mention that to my father," I blurted out.

"Don't worry, I'm not telling him I'm here," he said.

"Well, you shouldn't be."

He lifted his head, the moonlight glinting across the sharp bridge of his aquiline nose. He was pretty like a statue, pretty like a painting of an ancient god, and handsome like he could kill without a second thought and get away with it.

The problem was his personality.

"What do you want?" I whispered.

He looked down at the koi pond, and there was a long silence as his jaw tightened. "Do you ever wonder what it would be like to stand in one of the Wonders of the World?"

I stared. "What?"

He took another step, moving closer until he stood beside me, looking down at the silvery water dotted with orange fish. He looked down at me, and his eyes lingered on my mouth.

"Sometimes, I dream that I walk to the temple of Aphrodite in the early morning when it's still cool," he said softly. "I stand in the doorway and watch the incense rise from the cold floor."

He was so close, I felt his warmth kiss my skin. Was this an intimidation tactic to start talking about bizarre things? Was he trying to get me confused?

I cleared my throat. "Are you fucking with me?"

His hand came up and brushed back my hair. His palm was warm, but it didn't linger. "Do you ever want things you can never have, butterfly?"

My dry lips cracked. "Butterfly?"

His tongue flicked out. "On your finger."

I spread my hand, looking down at the tiny purple butterfly.

"That's right," I whispered.

He leaned in, eyes glittering. "In another life, I'd fuck you in a temple, on the cold stone, as an offering to the goddess. But unfortunately, we're stuck in the twenty-first century, so I think I'll just torment you instead."

His voice changed, dropping the silky tone. There was something dark, like desire, in it. Anger flared, and I stepped back, grabbing the box of fish food. He laughed softly as I turned on my heel and began striding across the driveway. His footfalls followed me until I got to the door and spun around, holding up my hand.

"Go away," I snapped. "You're fucking rude."

"It wasn't all a joke," he said, mouth thinning. "I would fuck you."

"That's not what you implied when I stopped by your apartment."

"I'm trying to be a good boy."

"Well, you're not succeeding."

He shrugged. "I never do."

I jerked open the kitchen door and stepped inside, but his hand shot out and braced it wide. I glared up at him, running my eyes over his lean body. Why did he have to look so good?

"Can I come in?"

"Why?" I glared.

"I'm hungry."

"Sounds like a personal problem."

"I'll trade you an orgasm for a sandwich."

My jaw dropped. What had happened since our last encounter that made him change his tune? I cleared my throat, ignoring his heavy gaze boring into me.

"No thanks. I have a vibrator," I said coolly.

He laughed aloud, a rich, deep sound. I hated to admit it, but I liked it. *A lot.*

"Let me in. Tell me about your day," he said, his tone firm.

For some reason, I let him into my kitchen. Maybe it was how good he looked with his rumpled dress shirt, or maybe it was that I could faintly smell his scent, a clean, cool smell, and it reminded me of being in his kitchen. *That* reminded me that he'd made me come five times the last time we were alone.

I set the fish flakes aside and crossed my arms.

"What do you want to eat?" I said, keeping my voice casual, as if my heart wasn't pounding.

"Whatever you want to feed me." He crossed his arms and leaned against the counter.

We stared at each other. Outside, an owl cooed from the orchard. I cleared my throat and broke my gaze away, going to grab the sandwiches. The back of my neck tingled as I cut them up and slipped vegan chips between the bread. I liked a little crunch in mine. I didn't really care if he did or not.

"Here," I said, handing him one.

He took a bite and nodded. "It's good."

"Thanks. Courtesy of our chef," I said. "What were you trying to do?"

"How do you mean?" His brow cocked.

"You said you dreamed you went to Aphrodite's temple in the early morning," I said, my voice hoarse. "And watched the smoke rise from the ground."

"Incense," he corrected.

"Whatever," I said. "Why did you say that?"

He shrugged, heavy eyes shrouded in the dim light. "Because it's true. You reminded me of it."

My mouth felt dry. Did I want to get philosophical with him? He seemed like the kind of person who could pull me into a labyrinth of strange new thoughts I might not be prepared for. The problem was, I *was* a bit curious.

"Why?"

His eyes flicked down. "You have a butterfly on your hand," he said. "Butterflies are representations of the soul. The goddess Psyche is associated with butterflies. She was so beautiful, they said she was mistaken for Aphrodite."

My stomach twisted. Was he calling...me beautiful? Or was this a manipulation tactic?

"Where did you go to college?" I asked.

His eyes narrowed, and he took a bit of his sandwich and chewed. Finally, he cleared his throat. "I don't have a formal education. Failed out when I was fourteen."

That caught me off guard. "Oh? Where did you learn all this stuff?"

"Libraries are free, butterfly."

"Don't call me that," I whispered. "I know what you're trying to do."

He set the crust of his sandwich aside and brushed off his long fingers. "What am I doing?"

"You're trying to mess with my head," I said. "I know we're both being forced to work together. Neither of us want to be babysat, but this deal between our companies means a lot for our reputations, and we need to look like we're getting along—so stop messing with me."

He crossed his arms, lip curling. "Your reputation is bulletproof. You'll always be the Johansen heiress."

He didn't understand, but I hadn't expected him to. I tilted my chin.

"This is my first big business deal," I admitted and wished I hadn't.

He didn't say anything, but his brow stayed crooked, like he was thinking deeply. My eyes moved from his face and slid down his neck, studying the ink down his neck. It was thick, dark lines, curving and curling like the engravings in an old door or church pew. There weren't images I could recognize, just curves, swirls, lines, and shapes. The effect when seen at a glance was stunning.

My eyes moved lower.

Down to where his shirt tucked into his pants. His belt buckle glinted silver.

"My eyes are up here," he drawled softly.

Heat washed over my face. "You're so full of yourself," I whispered.

He laughed softly but didn't reply. That part bothered me. I was good at withholding my opinions in work meetings, but outside of that, I had a tendency to word vomit.

The way he smiled and stayed silent was the ultimate weapon.

It was armor I couldn't break down.

"Why do you dream of dead goddesses?" I asked impulsively.

He cocked his head. "Not sure. I think there are some people who live in the thin parts of the world."

"The what?"

His jaw worked. He had this stupidly sexy jaw muscle that made me ache downstairs.

"Do you ever get this longing for something you've never had, something complete...something better?" he said, his voice dropping. "Someplace you've never been but hope to go?"

My stomach pitted. Yes, I knew what that was, and I'd always called it nostalgia. I nodded, wordless.

"Maybe in another life, I did fuck you in a temple," he said. "In the early morning, when the air is still cool. Maybe your hair smelled like incense. Maybe that's just a shadow...or we're a shadow of what we could have been."

Something about his words made me want to cry. My throat felt lumpy and cold. I sniffed and cleared it.

"You're a bit strange," I said.

"I hear that a lot," he said. "It doesn't bother me. Anyway, that feeling...my people call it *Hireath*."

"Nostalgia?"

"No, a longing for what could have been. A place you'll always want but never get."

"Well, that's depressing."

He shrugged and pushed off the counter, coming to the island where I stood. "Enough about me. Let's talk about things you missed out on."

His eyes glittered, and I had a feeling I knew where he was going to turn the conversation. Like clockwork, his eyes dropped, and he came closer, caging me against the island.

My heart picked up.

"I'd like seconds," he said. "I changed my mind."

"You changed your tune," I whispered. "Oh, how the tables have turned."

His throat bobbed. Lean, tattooed fingers brushed my hair behind my ear. A raw heartbeat flared between my thighs. Quickly, he lifted me onto the counter and bent in, brushing a kiss against the side of my throat.

Oh God, my body was on fire.

My nipples hardened. My bare toes curled.

I took a deep breath.

"This mission is my test," I whispered. "My father wants me to take over for him, and if I do this right, I'm ready. I'm not fucking that up, even for a man with an Adonis belt."

His head fell back, and he laughed aloud.

"I wouldn't fuck that up for me either, butterfly," he said.

My hands curled on the edge of the counter. He bent and kissed my neck, letting his hot mouth linger. When he pulled back, I swore my heart was beating so hard, I could hear it.

"This mission is important to me too," he said. "May the best man win."

"Or woman."

"What is this? A little private rivalry?"

"Yes, maybe. I'm not worried you'll outperform me."

"I might."

"Doubt it."

He smirked, holding out his hand. Without thinking, I shook it. When he pulled back to look at me, his eyes flickered like blue flame.

"The mission starts later this week," he said. "If we're being technical."

I shook my head, even though it took all my willpower. "I'm not sleeping with you, Caden Payne."

He bent in again, breath hot against my mouth.

"I'll bet you taste so good," he said, his accent thickening. It usually sat deep in his voice, like he was on his way to forgetting it most of the time. But tonight, it bobbed to the surface.

And I liked it.

I shook my head. "I've been working all day. I need a shower."

The corners of his mouth went crooked. "I kinda want to taste that."

God, he knew how to wrap me around his little finger. What would it hurt anyway? He'd already gone down on me once before...and our mission didn't start until later. I bit my lip, chewing hard.

"Fine," I whispered.

He exhaled, kissing that burning spot on my neck again. At this rate, he was going to kiss it raw before morning. His hand slid up and pushed me onto my back on the counter. I caught myself on my elbows, looking down, cheeks burning as he pushed my skirt up my thighs.

"Are you wearing that diamond on your clit again?" he murmured, mouth brushing my knee.

I nodded, speechless.

He groaned, biting my thigh and sending pain shivering up to my pussy. My eyes followed his tattooed fingers as he shoved my skirt up to my thighs, revealing my white thong, a little silver bow on the waistband. He licked and sucked up my leg, leaving my skin burning from his touch.

One finger grazed my clit as he pulled my thong aside, making my legs jerk. His head bent, dark hair glinting.

The front door slammed, and my heart stopped.

"Stop, stop, get out!" I gasped, shooting upright. "My father's home."

Lightning fast, he licked me from pussy to clit, his hot tongue sending a wash of ecstasy through me for the barest second before he straightened.

"Still got what I was promised," he said, snapping my thong back into place.

I jumped down, shoving my skirt over my hips. "Go, get out," I hissed.

He seemed unbothered. "I'll see you later."

I waved a hand, trying to get him to hurry. My father's footsteps rang out in the hall, and he called my name.

"Caden, get out of here," I begged.

He yanked the side door open and stepped out, the house shrouding him in shadow as I followed. For a second, I saw him like a vision, eyes glittering, head cocked, the base of his throat still flushed with arousal. My gaze dropped and, for a flash, I saw a hard ridge beneath the front of his pants.

Then, I slammed the door. Hard.

CHAPTER SIX

CADEN

I had an early meeting the next morning, but all I could think about was Circe. In the main hall of the training center, I set up the meeting table before anyone else was there. Everything was ready, the projector was set up, but I was still in a haze when eight rolled around.

The little details stuck to my brain. The way her ass nestled in her thong. The little diamond on her clit. Her long, oval nails and the feeling of them in my hair.

The more innocent details were even harder to get out of my mind. How she licked her lip gloss with the tip of her tongue, like she was checking if it needed touched up. The little crease that appeared by her right brow when she was mad.

The door swung open, and Merrick entered, Daphne at his heels. I hadn't seen Daphne, his aunt by marriage, or Ophelia, her wife, in a while—by choice. A few years ago, I'd allowed Merrick to tell them I was his son. Now, they spent all their time tiptoeing around me or staring longingly when they thought I wasn't looking.

I understood why. I was their one chance for a grandchild, and I'd pushed them away.

"Hey, Caden," Daphne said, giving me a warm smile. She was short with dark hair and wore a linen shirt, shorts, and boating shoes. Her eyes were kind, and her face was lightly lined. I wasn't

51

sure how old she or her wife were, but I guessed they were nearing their late sixties.

"What brings you to the training center?" I asked.

"Merrick thought I should take a look at Maelon," she said. "And I'll sit in on the meeting."

She had every right to be here. Before the arena and Merrick's formal training, Daphne had trained him from an early age. She was the first to see his raw talent as his adoptive parent, and she nurtured it.

It was her training that had produced the greatest *Brenin* in our history. It didn't bother me that she was sitting in on the meeting, but I did sometimes feel like Merrick pushed Daphne and I together on purpose, like he was trying to get me to follow in her footsteps somehow.

I admired Daphne; she was a titan of the last generation, but I wasn't sure being a kingmaker was up my alley.

My father poked me in the side, handing me a folder. "Can you do a rundown of the deal with the Johansens? Just for Daphne and anyone else who isn't up to speed?"

"Sure," I said, moving to my spot at the head of the table.

Daphne sank down beside my father. I glanced at them from the corner of my eye as Daphne said something in his ear, and they both laughed. She gave him a side hug, squeezing his shoulders.

My chest hurt, just a little. I didn't have any room to complain when Daphne would have lavished all her affection on me if I just knew how to receive it.

I laid my paperwork out, trying to pretend I didn't care. Merrick fixed his attention on me, and I felt it burn, like he could read my thoughts. He had his arms crossed and his legs tucked under the table, the same way I sat. Sometimes, I thought he was just a better version of me. We both shared blue eyes and dark hair, our facial structure, our height, but he was a kinder, softer, more noble man.

Deep down, I knew he was a better man too.

"You ready?"

I turned to find Yale loitering behind me and nodded. "Yeah, I've got to go over the Wyoming base for Daphne and a couple of the others first. Then, we can hit the rest."

He nodded, sinking down into the chair at my left. Almost every chair was full with Merrick's soldiers, so I rapped on the table to let everyone know we were starting. They fell silent.

"First, I'm starting with a rundown of the Wyoming base so far," I said, clearing my throat. "We lost funding from the Cardiff family a few years back. I was assigned securing new funding."

What I didn't add was that it was my father's fault we'd lost the funding. The Cardiff's son, Osian, was engaged to Clara, my father's wife, up until the point he put his hands on her. Merrick had lost his shit and beat Osian to death.

Needless to say, the deal was off.

"What's the funding for?" Daphne asked. "Like, what specifically?"

"Infrastructure," I said. "It's a huge base that takes up a lot of space. It's expensive to train private security, so we need a benefactor to foot the building costs."

"Makes sense," Daphne said, giving me a grandmotherly smile.

I composed myself. She and Merrick were making me feel like I was doing a school presentation. I shifted, keeping my back to him, and started pacing.

"The total costs are in the multimillions," I said. "I struggled to find anyone willing to invest, but Lukas Johansen agreed, so long as his board signs off on it, because he is our direct competitor, and he benefits if he can also train his private security with ours."

"Risky," said Merrick, "but brilliant. We've tied our success together."

"Thanks," I said. "That's the general idea. Questions?"

I glanced around, waiting. Everyone was quiet.

"Alright, we're in phase two now that we have a deal signed," I said. "Lukas Johansen needs three of his predominant board members to sign off on this deal. He's so confident that we both already have men out at the Wyoming base, training together.

Because he stands to lose just as much if he can't convince the board, I feel confident this next phase will be simple."

"We're working alongside one of Lukas' people to secure the funding," Merrick said.

Daphne leaned close to my father. "Is she pretty?" she whispered.

Merrick glanced to the side. "What?"

"I just thought, because Caden is single, it could be like a meet cute."

Yale snorted.

I cleared my throat. "I know you're both whispering, but we can all still hear you. Please."

Internally, I made a note to never, *ever* run a meeting with my father and great aunt present again. Daphne mouthed an apology and folded her hands, looking down as Merrick tried not to smirk.

On autopilot, I moved on, working through everything on the list until I reached the end. We had a short discussion about the day's training between the commanders. Then, everyone split up and dispersed to their offices and classrooms.

My father lingered while I sorted my papers.

"Can I talk to you outside?" he asked.

"I have training in a minute, but yes," I said. "Alone?"

He nodded. "Daphne will be here for the rest of the day. I have to be in the city for a meeting with the hotel architect."

I left my folder on the table and followed him through the hall and out the front door. It was sticky out today, the humidity making Merrick's wavy hair tighten into curls and sweat trickle down my back.

"Sorry if Daphne made you uncomfortable," he said.

I shook my head, remembering that I was a brand-new version of myself, a more patient, more professional version.

"She's fine. I get it," I said.

Merrick slipped on his aviators. "Clara and I are going out to dinner if you'd like to join us."

He used to have a note of hopefulness in his tone when he asked me to spend time together outside of work. Now, he said it like he already knew the answer.

"Sorry, I need to work," I said. "Maybe another time. Was that what you wanted to talk about?"

He shook his head. "No, I just wanted to caution you about this mission. I trust your judgement, and I think Lukas will hold up his end of the deal. But just...be careful about getting too involved."

I stared at him for a long time.

"You can just say 'don't fuck the daughter'," I said.

"Okay," Merrick said, shrugging. "Don't fuck his daughter."

I put my own sunglasses on, and we looked at each other from behind the protection of tinted lenses.

"I know what I'm doing," I said. "I got this deal, and I can close it. I promise."

He nodded. "I believe it."

I jerked my head back at the building. "I need to get going."

He hesitated, like he wanted to say something else. Instead, he nodded, reaching down to pull open the door to his Audi. "Let me know when you leave for the first leg of the assignment."

I nodded. "I will, but I've got this under control."

His engine revved and whined into silence as I moved back to the front door. Instead of going inside, I decided to sit on the curb and have a rare cigarette.

I was shaken, but not by anything Merrick or Daphne had said.

No, I'd just gone through a meeting that should have bothered me. It would have bothered the old Caden, but all I could think about was last night, in her kitchen, the soft skin of her thighs touching my face.

The little snap as I released her thong.

The faint scent of her lotion.

And the realization that I'd never told anyone in the world about the temple of Aphrodite.

Yet, I'd told her, like she was someone I could trust to hold all my deepest secrets.

CHAPTER SEVEN

CIRCE

The morning after he'd shown up in my garden, I went upstairs to my home office instead of heading to the city. When I joined the board of Johansen's Enterprises, my father had surprised me with a fully renovated space where I could work from home.

I stepped inside and let the door fall shut. Everything was quiet. The curtains fluttered, revealing the balcony lined with blooming hyacinths. My desk sat in the center of the room, facing the far wall covered in bookshelves, so I had a good view of the double doors and the balcony that looked out over the orchard and koi pond.

There was a space in the yard beyond the rose garden not visible from down below. It was a rounded hilltop with a flat, grassy top. I blinked hard at it because...for a second, it looked like there were pillars rising into the sky.

What was wrong with me?

Maybe Caden and his talk of sleeping with me on a temple floor was getting to my head. No doubt that was exactly what he wanted.

Annoyed, I yanked the curtains shut. My heels clacked across the floor. Everything smelled faintly of hyacinths, the familiar scent calming. I settled myself into the cream swivel chair and flipped open my laptop to reveal a long list of emails waiting for me.

I sighed.

I was so grateful for everything I had. Not many people had a father who doted on them the way mine did or had a job set up for them as soon as they graduated. I'd worked so hard, putting in long hours, to feel like I deserved a small portion of what life had handed me.

But I was still tired sometimes.

I cracked my neck, startled by the crunching sound. My fingers tapped over my keyboard, answering the first set of emails on autopilot. They were easy, just approval for some raises.

It felt like it took much longer than it should have. This morning, I was dragging, and I needed to do something to get my head in the game because, unfortunately, I had a date later.

The first date I'd been on in years.

Rubbing my eyes, I rose and made an espresso at the kitchenette in the corner. As I waited for the creamy coffee to fill the cup, I tapped my foot, trying to keep my mind from going back to that night at his apartment.

Trying not to remember how his tattooed fingers dug into my hips.

How the muscles rippled down his stomach as he fucked me on the stone floor of Aphrodite's temple.

Wait, what?

Damn it, he'd successfully messed with my head.

I grabbed my cup and sat down at my desk. My fingers hovered over the keyboard again, iridescent mauve nails glinting as I flexed my joints. Maybe I should get them done this afternoon after my date—something I wasn't looking forward to but that I'd let Delaney push me into. I kicked my heel absently against the leg of my chair and started picking at my thumbnail.

My computer pinged. It was a reminder from my phone that my date was coming up. I needed to leave by eleven-thirty to get there by twelve. I glanced at my white gold watch—ten-fifteen.

I got up and finished my espresso, grabbing my phone and heading to the balcony. Outside, the air was warm and smelled of roses from the garden below. I swiped my screen, hit call and speaker. It rang once, and Delaney answered mid-yawn.

"Hey, what's up?" she grumbled.

"I have a date with that guy," I said. "At twelve. Feeling kind of bleh about it, so maybe I can just cancel?"

"No, you promised to date a little this year."

"I will, just maybe not him."

I heard her roll over, and I knew she was still in bed. "You promised. Just give him a chance. He's a nice guy...I think. His dad does stock market stuff."

"Yikes," I murmured.

"Not like that kind of wall street. He goes to church."

"Where?"

"Um...I think he's a Presbyterian," Delaney said.

"Well, I'm not. Look, we're doomed to fail."

I heard her get out of bed and the shower turn on in the background. "Listen, you're not looking for someone to fulfill you. Circe Johansen needs a man to kiss her goodbye on the way to his job that you don't know or care about so you can focus on your company. He just needs to give you good head and not talk too much."

"Why's that?" I laughed.

"You have everything else. What is a man going to do for you?" she yawned. "Except the good head part."

My mind flashed with that arrogant smirk, cobalt eyes glittering like sapphires. Lids heavy with desire. Tattooed neck with sweat etching down between his collarbones. Tongue dragging over my clit as he held eye contact with me. My stomach flipped.

He wasn't my type. He was all muscles and tattoos and a chip on his shoulder about everything, the antithesis of the man I was about to meet up with.

I sighed again, but this time louder. "He's a total prep, Delaney."

"Babe, go look at yourself in a mirror."

"Okay...I'm elegant."

She laughed. "Hey, I have to go, but text me if you really, really need me to get you out of the date. Have fun and give him a chance!"

"What was his name again?"

"Oh God. I'll send you his profile."

"You're the best." I tapped my phone, hanging up. It was almost eleven, so I left the office and headed back to my room.

It took me a half hour to find something to wear I felt comfortable enough in for a first date. In the end, I picked a mauve sweater, cropped jeans, and heeled shoes. Then, I grabbed my purse and headed downstairs and out the door. The front door security system beeped as I hit the remote, and the detached garage slid open, revealing my white and silver vintage convertible.

It was an eighteenth birthday gift from my father, and I practically lived in it when I wasn't at home or the office.

I sank into the leather seat and pulled my heels off, tossing them on the floor. Barefoot, I pulled down the drive, flipping the radio on high. Warm sunlight fell in golden dapples over me as I headed into town, music wafting behind me.

It was the perfect day. Too bad I'd agreed to go on a date—I really should have been in the office by now.

It was twelve on the dot when I pulled up outside the Vengeful Mermaid on the other side of the river. Contrary to the pub-style name, it was an upscale, modern restaurant with an ocean view. Everything inside was airy and light, and the decor reminded me of a butterfly wing or a fish scale in iridescent greens, blue, and pinks.

I parked and stepped out, shielding my eyes. The parking lot was full, but there was a man standing by the door who I was pretty sure was my date. I swiped my phone and hit the link Delaney had sent.

Damian. That was easy enough to remember. I pushed my phone in my purse, arranged my face so I didn't scare him off, and moved across the parking lot. He looked up and broke into a pleasant smile. He was nice looking, with dusky brown hair, gray eyes, and a wide, triangular grin.

He looked like he had a membership to a country club and called his mother every weekend. Very safe, very nice. My father would have loved to talk politics or business with him over a glass of scotch.

I drew near, feeling myself slip into my work persona, sweet and modest.

"Damian?" I asked.

He nodded. "Circe?"

"Yes, that's me."

He gave me an awkward side hug, and I saw his eyes run over me but stop before they got to my breasts. God, I was going to feel so bad when I turned him down. I could already tell he was sweet.

He led the way inside and even pulled my chair out. We were seated in the far-left corner with a stunning view of the ocean. Down below, I could hear waves crashing against the rocks. Even inside, it smelled faintly of the sea.

Salt, fresh air, and freedom.

Damian took a seat, and I offered him a smile.

"So what are you up to today? Other than this of course," I asked brightly.

He shrugged. "Oh, you know, I had some work earlier. But today, I only did a half day because I have a meeting with your father. Our business sometimes crosses."

"Who's your father again?"

"Charles Galt."

I frowned, trying to figure out why that name sounded familiar. "Oh, is he related to Vincent Galt who works with Merrick Llwyd?"

"Yeah, Vincent is my uncle."

The waiter appeared, and I ordered a white wine, hoping he wouldn't be put off by me having a glass in the middle of the day. He seemed fine with it. I sat quietly while he scanned the liquor menu and finally ordered a lite beer, something fancy with citrus in it.

My mind shot right to the first time I saw Caden, his eyes locked on me as he put his cheap beer to his lips, tatted throat bobbing as he swallowed.

God, he had no right being that confident.

I forced my eyes back to the man sitting before me. He had a kind face, but it was so clean cut. I wondered if he measured the half centimeter of stubble on his square jaw, or if it just stopped growing when it was the perfect length.

I glanced over my shoulder, catching my reflection's eye.

I gave myself a once over. Perfectly manicured nails, holding my menu at the proper height. Napkin folded properly. Feathery false lashes shading my eyes. Mauve lipstick, perfectly in the lines.

Was I so different than him?

I swallowed past the dry lump in my throat and plastered my pleasant smile back into place, the one I used when I sat in boardrooms full of men. Damian leaned back in his chair, and I forced myself to give him the once over, trying to appreciate his looks and failing.

God, what was wrong with me? He *was* handsome.

"So, you have quite a resumé, Miss Johansen."

My mind was blank. "I do?"

Damian was clearly having some reservations about me. His brows drew together in a polite, inquiring frown.

"Your job," he said. "At your father's company... I thought you were training to take over for him. Aren't you the COO, or you will be?"

"Oh, yeah, sorry," I said, waving a hand.

For some reason, the ring on my middle finger—which was the correct size and never slipped—flew off my hand and smacked into the window. Mortified, I whipped around and cracked my knee on the table leg loud enough that the entire restaurant *had* to hear.

"Oh—fuck," I swore, biting my lip as the word slipped out.

I clapped both hands over my mouth. Damian jumped to his feet and chased after the ring. It rolled down the middle of the room and clattered to a halt. I followed it with my eyes, face burning, as he scooped it up.

Then, my eyes moved higher.

My stomach twisted.

Caden was at the bar, Yale at his side, his back to me. They were deep in conversation, but those cobalt eyes were locked on me over Yale's shoulder. His mouth curved in a short smile. Not a mocking one—no, this was much worse. There was a little pity in his gaze, like he was thinking *poor girl, what a mess.*

I swallowed, turning around and sitting down hard. This was officially the worst date ever, and it had nothing to do with Damian. He appeared at my side and chivalrously slipped the ring back onto my finger.

I released a short sigh as he sank down.

"You're probably wanting to leave right now," I said lightly.

His shook his head. "You're not what I expected, but let's give it a shot. We haven't even ordered."

I glanced over my shoulder. Caden cocked his head, and his eyes ran over Damian, looking at him like he was nothing more than a minor inconvenience. That pissed me off enough that I turned back around and offered him a sweet smile.

"I'd like that," I said.

Caden Payne was going to sit there and watch me have a nice date. That was his punishment for that pitying smirk.

"Maybe our next date should be to the jewelers," Damian said.

My eyes widened. "What?"

His brows shot up. "God, I meant to get your ring resized. I'm so sorry, today is not my day either. It was meant to be a joke."

I reached across the table and patted his hand, which seemed to surprise him. "Still not more embarrassing than me flinging my ring at a window."

He laughed, his shoulders relaxing. The waiter appeared, saving us, and I ordered a salad with steamed fish on the side. Damian got the pasta with mussels, and the waiter left us alone in agonizing silence.

I had a gulp of white wine. It was starting to hit my veins, making me bolder. I fluttered my lashes over the glass, and he cocked his head, clearly a little confused.

"So tell me what you do exactly," I said.

He launched into an explanation of stock trading that made my face melt from boredom. I had to listen to this kind of talk all day long at work. I was sorry I asked, but I didn't stop him, because he lit up talking about it.

Then, I had another glass of wine.

The second glass was a bad idea. My body swayed as I stood up and allowed him to kiss my cheek. He paid and put his hand on my elbow, leading me out into the hallway. Unwilling to let him walk me to the car, I paused, glancing down the hall.

"Hey, I'm going to the bathroom," I said. "But thanks so much for the date. I'll text you."

We hugged awkwardly and parted. I watched him stride into the parking lot. My shoulders sagged, and I let out a sigh of relief as he drove away. That was the worst date I'd ever had with such a nice person, and I felt terrible about it, since I was *not* doing that again.

I straightened my sweater and strode down the hall. In the bathroom, I fixed my lipstick and pulled my hair into a ponytail to get it off my sweaty neck. The wine had me feeling warm. I needed to go sit at the bar and have a glass of ice water to make the room stop spinning.

And call an Uber. My father could pick my car up later.

I strode out of the bathroom, heels clicking, and ran right into a solid chest. Warm, firm hands clamped on my upper arms to keep me steady as cobalt eyes swam into view.

Caden.

Damn it.

"I thought you left," I snapped, more aggressively than I intended.

"I was in the bathroom," he said, gaze flicking over me. A crease appeared between his brows. "You can't drive like this."

I pulled back, narrowing my eyes. "Of course not. I'm calling an Uber."

"Yale drove me here," he said. "Let me drive your car back."

"No, my father will pick it up."

The corner of his mouth jerked. "No, I'll drive your car back with you in it."

I chewed my lip. To my surprise, he actually seemed genuine. I picked absently at my nail, staring past him at the hostess stand. It would be an inconvenience to have the car picked up later, and I'd have to explain to my father that I'd had too much wine at noon. He'd have questions, since I rarely drank during the day.

I wasn't dying to explain my bad date to my father either, especially because Damian Galt was exactly the sort of man he wanted me to eventually marry, the kind of person who could be part of our company someday.

I sighed. "Okay, fine. You drive me home."

The corner of his mouth twitched again. He had a way of smiling that was so arrogant, like nobody ever got the better of him. I fucking hated it.

He held out his hand, like he intended on escorting me, and I glared. I could hear his faint laughter as I strode out into the parking lot, heels clacking on the pavement. He followed me, walking easily with one arm hanging at his side.

He sank down in the cramped driver's seat. He was in excellent shape, and I couldn't help but sneak a glance as I climbed into the passenger side. He wore black fatigues and boots. His t-shirt rode up a little when he sat down, flashing some ink on his lower abs.

Rock hard abs, a little trail of dark hair going up. Heart sparked, and I plopped into the passenger side, slamming the door.

My body was a traitor.

He adjusted the seat, making room for those long legs, and hit the key fob. The engine purred, and the radio started playing. I glanced over again, watching as he searched the dashboard for something.

"What are you looking for?"

He ignored me, hitting the volume button to silence the music.

"Um...why did you do that?" I asked.

"Because it's shit," he said.

My jaw dropped, and he let out a sigh as his hand flexed on the wheel. There was a long silence as he pulled the car out onto the street.

"I'm trying to be less of a dick," he said finally. "Or at least learn to filter myself."

"Why are you a dick in the first place?" I shot back.

His throat bobbed, jaw working. "Because if you hang around dicks long enough, you turn into one. Not everyone was born with a silver spoon in their mouth."

64

He was driving fast, one lean arm hanging on the top of the wheel. I glanced out the window, trying to absorb his words. I knew he'd arrived in Providence about ten years ago; I'd read his file, but I'd assumed his life hadn't been vastly different before that.

Maybe he had a reason for those hard eyes.

I glanced back at him. He was tapping his other finger against the windowsill fast, in little motions. I wondered if it was a nervous movement. Otherwise, he seemed totally relaxed.

I pulled my eyes away. My brain was just finding excuses to look at him.

We were both quiet for the drive. It was warm out, and the air smelled faintly of flowers. Summer in Providence was my favorite time of year. Despite the booming tourism industry, it was peaceful in our neighborhood. The trees hung heavy over the road, dappling the car with sunlight as we passed below.

I sighed involuntarily. He glanced over, his hand flexing on his thigh.

"Alright there?" he said.

I shrugged. "Fine. Just don't want to go back to work."

"Me either." He nodded. "Don't forget about our meeting later this week."

I nodded as he pulled up the front drive and parked by the koi pond. He put the car in park and shifted to face me. He cocked his knee, making my eyes flick down before I had a chance to jerk them back up, taking in the faint rise under the front of his pants. Or maybe it was just a crease.

Thank God he was looking away.

"I know," I said. "I don't forget meetings."

Caden yawned, stepping out of the car. He stretched, and I saw a flash of a gun holster on his belt, hidden beneath his shirt. I pushed open my door and got to my wobbly feet.

"Is your father home?" he asked.

I shook my head. For some reason, I felt a crackle of tension, like a bit of static electricity. There was a long silence. My nails dug into my purse. Why was it so awkward to face him?

Was it because of what we'd done? Because I was going to keep pretending like I did that all the time and it meant nothing.

"I wasn't going to ask you in," I said.

He cocked his head. "I wasn't going to come in."

"I'll call you an Uber."

His heavy eyes scanned the lawn, glancing up at the sky. "I'll walk. I walked here the other night when you threw me out on my ass so your father wouldn't find out what a bad girl you are."

His words curled, taunting me. My temper flared, emboldened by the alcohol.

"Do you have a problem with me?" I snapped.

He shrugged, lids heavy. "Maybe. What about it?"

"Okay, what's your problem?"

"I don't want you on this mission with me," he said flatly.

"I don't want you here either."

Our voices were loud, echoing in the orchard. The tension buzzed over the top of the car, but this time, it wasn't sexual. Or at least, not on my end. I was pissed at how mean he was—I hadn't done anything to him.

Other than let him go down on me without revealing my identity.

Not one of my finer moments.

I swallowed guiltily. In retrospect, I shouldn't have done that. I took a deep breath and tried to steady my swirling head. The facts were simple. Neither of us wanted the other there, but we had no choice. Our success hinged on working well with each other, and we both wanted this mission to succeed.

"That's not your fault," I said.

"What?"

"That you got assigned to work with me," I said. "And it's not my fault I have to work with you either."

He cocked his head, and I thought his eyes softened.

"Alright," he said finally. "Let's just get through this."

He circled the car, coming towards me. In my tipsy brain, I couldn't tell what he was doing, but he was getting closer. The warmth of his body spilled over me, and I backed up against the car.

66

Then, he reached out and dropped the keys in my purse.

I sighed, my shoulders falling.

"What?" he said.

I shook my head, mouth dry. My eyes dragged down over his shirt, getting a guilty look at the way it hugged his abs, showing a trace of the V disappearing below his belt. I swallowed and forced them back to his face. He was watching me quietly, his expression unreadable past those heavy lids. They were a shield between him and the world.

"So we're not in competition?" I said.

"Oh, no, I'm going to walk all over you when it comes to getting this funding. Eat my dust, butterfly."

"Okay. Goodbye," I said primly. I wasn't letting him get a rise out of me again.

"See you later," he said, not moving.

The wine made me a lot bolder than usual, so I darted around him, only pausing at the bottom of the stairs to turn around. He was watching me, squinting under the afternoon sun.

"I'm not sleeping with you," I said. "Now or ever."

The corner of his mouth turned up.

"Yeah, okay."

My teeth gritted and anger flared, but he was already walking up the drive. I stood on the porch and watched him until he turned the corner and disappeared past the gate.

CHAPTER EIGHT

CADEN

I woke up a second before my alarm blared, rolling over and tapping it. The automatic window shades rose, revealing the city below. It was six, and the sun was just over the horizon. I swung my legs onto the floor and stretched, cracking my spine.

Ever since I'd decided to get my life together, every morning started the same.

Wake up and shower.

Head to the training center.

Run until my legs were water.

Teach morning class.

Hit the gun range with Yale.

By then, it was eleven, and I was ready to get started with the day's meetings. This morning, my body protested. Maybe it was how far I'd walked going back and forth to Circe's house, but I doubted it.

I cracked my neck, stepping into the bathroom. I flipped the knob and adjusted, letting the warm water trickle over my open palm. Everything was exactly as it had been for the last decade, so why did the world feel so new and different?

Was it just because this was the biggest project I'd ever worked on and it all began today?

Or something else?

I stripped my sweatpants off and stepped under the shower. The mirror across the room caught my eye, and I paused, narrowing my eyes. I'd lost a little weight in the last six months, probably from all the neurotic running. I turned my arm, studying the cover up tattoos.

None of my shitty ink was visible when my clothes were on. All anyone ever saw was the expensive, carefully planned cover ups. They never saw the scrawls, the scars, the burns.

Into my mind burst the memory of a scent I could never shake. Sweat, body odor, cigarettes. The feeling of sneaking through the hall on the sides of my bare feet. Hoping, praying, begging any deity who would listen that I could get to my room unnoticed.

Freak.

My neck snapped to the side. Crack, pop.

A rush of anxiety moved through my chest, and I rotated my neck again, cracking it.

I shook my head hard and turned the water cold to clear my brain. Shivering, I washed up and stepped out, shaking my wet hair out. From the closet, I pulled on my training pants and shirt and boots. My gym clothes were already packed in a bag hanging behind the door in the kitchen. I'd shower again at the training center after my workout was done.

My fingers tapped against the counter, my foot jiggling as my espresso machine dripped coffee into my thermos. The second it was done, I shoved the canister in my bag and left my apartment.

Flip the locks. Check the deadbolt twice. Tap the door with my middle knuckle on the left, right, and center portion.

Quick, so I barely noticed. If I did it too slowly, it had to be done all over again.

My car was parked on the street, and behind it sat my sleek Kawasaki Vulcan. The morning sun glinted off the black paint as I threw my leg over and revved the engine, letting it purr to life. I'd bought the Kawasaki after I'd found out Merrick wasn't going to station me out west, a little treat to make myself feel better for having to spend another winter waiting for something to happen on the Wyoming Project.

Cool morning air whipped through my hair as I moved through the city. When I pulled up outside the training center, Yale was already waiting at the door, phone to his ear, pacing like he would rather not be having a conversation.

I strode up the walkway and send him an inquiring glance. He rolled his eyes and shook his head.

I already knew who he was talking to. Yale always had some kind of woman drama going on, and it was always with the same person. Candice Roberts. I barely knew her, but since Merrick had married Clara, we'd crossed paths a few times because they were best friends. Candice struck me as sharp, a little insecure, and very sheltered. I struggled with that last aspect of her character.

Nobody had sheltered me. It made me resentful of people who had the luxury of being protected, and Candice was heavily protected by both her father and Yale, despite them being not being official.

I stepped into the training center and turned left to head to the gym. Yale's boots clattered behind me, and he fell into step at my side. His face was thoughtful, eyes narrowed.

"Did you fuck up again?" I asked.

He shrugged. "No, she didn't get in."

I pulled the gym doors open. "Into what?"

He followed me inside, keeping up as I moved into the locker room. It was mostly empty. Morning training had already begun, and the second round wouldn't start for another hour. I stripped my shirt off and opened my bag.

"Law school," said Yale.

He was already dressed in his workout clothes, his chest drenched in sweat. He usually ran the early AM classes, except on Fridays when I took over so he could have a day off.

I paused, staring at him. "Why the fuck was she trying to get into law school?"

He shrugged. "I guess it's just something she wanted to do."

I could tell he wasn't telling the truth, but I wasn't about to pry.

"Okay, so what does that have to do with you?" I pulled on my sweats and shirt, sitting down to grab my sneakers.

"I told her she couldn't be a lawyer because her tits were too big," he sighed. "I feel like I really fucked up. Maybe that was what got her confidence down."

I paused, staring at him for a long moment as I gathered my thoughts. Yale was smart, but he had a tendency to let his mouth move faster than his brain.

"That was a weird thing to say," I said lightly.

He ran a hand over his face. "It made more sense in context."

"Okay," I said, raising a brow to let him know I didn't believe him.

"This was a while ago. We were in a shouting fight," Yale admitted. "I told her I meant to pursue her, buy her engagement jewelry, maybe ask Merrick what he thought about us being together and get his permission."

No matter how long I lived in the Welsh organization, their customs around engagements still surprised me. Instead of a ring, Yale would be expected to buy an entire set of diamond jewelry and present it to Candice, piece by piece, until she accepted the last one, which was, shockingly, an intimate piercing for her clit.

But before any of that, Yale would have to ask Merrick what he thought about it. Merrick, as *Brenin* and keeper of the organization, would weigh the situation. He'd inquire about Yale's financial status, his future plans. If he approved the potential match, Yale would go to her father as her financial guardian and present the match on paper.

If he said yes, then Yale could buy the jewelry and offer the first piece to Candice.

If she refused, he was out several grand.

It was weird, but I liked it. The process was complicated, but if my mother had been protected the way our women were, maybe she'd never have met my stepfather.

"So she said she wasn't interested?" I asked.

We headed down the hall to the gym. I started warming up on the treadmill, and Yale draped himself over the armrest beside me and sighed mournfully.

"She said she still had things she wanted to do before she got married," he said. "I asked what. She didn't know, so she got mad and said I was putting her on the spot. It escalated, and I told her she wasn't the type to be a lawyer because she'd struggle to get respect from the organization's male lawyers."

"She asked why, and you said because she's got big tits," I guessed.

He sighed again. "It was more roundabout than that, but yeah. And I'm not wrong; she would have been up against a lot."

"But it wasn't your place," I said. "Some things need to be found out in their own time."

"No, I should have encouraged her. Taken her side. Not just told her that her body would have made it harder for her to do what she wants."

I tapped the screen to set the treadmill. "You're not wrong. Merrick likes to think we're so evolved, but it would have been hard for her to be the first female lawyer in the organization."

"I don't want her to get hurt," Yale said quietly.

I snapped my earbud in. "Then protect her. If you want her, act the part."

He straightened. "Says the guy who's been single for ten years."

"When I find someone worth it, I'll let you know."

His jaw worked as he stepped off the treadmill. "You're changing, Caden."

I paused, my other earbud in my fingers. It was the first time anyone had said that to me since I'd decided to be less of an asshole. A flicker of triumph started between my ribs. I rarely gave myself the luxury of feeling good about myself. Pride was a new experience.

"Thanks," I said shortly.

He left, and I pushed my earbud in, turning my music up too loud, trying to drown out the last part of our conversation where he'd said I'd been single forever and that I was changing. I'd wanted to change, to be a completely different person for so long, but it felt strange to hear it spoken aloud.

Like my efforts had finally produced something real.

I had to change—I felt soiled, like all the bullshit I'd gone through and done before I got to Providence had tainted me forever. It didn't matter that I'd worked my way up to become Merrick's right hand. Inside, I was just a kid with shitty tattoos, cigarette burns, and scars on my knuckles.

It wasn't until I met Merrick that anyone cared.

I swallowed, increasing my speed. Why couldn't I just let him love me? Why did my walls go up when he called me his son?

I had taken my time accepting my heritage, and now I regretted not signing up to train for the arena when I first arrived. I was too old now, already thirty. All the trainees for the arena were just hitting eighteen. And if I somehow won against a bunch of twenty-year-old kids, what was the point? To be *Brenin* for fifteen years before we had to hold another competition to choose my successor?

No, I'd missed the boat.

Now I was stuck training men with more potential than myself forever until I aged out of that too.

I would never be the man my father was. I was a Grade A fuck up, raised by strangers in strange houses on strange streets. I'd never be a warrior like Merrick, never taste the primal fear of fighting in the arena, never stand covered in blood and listen to the roar of triumph from the crowd before I ascended to the most coveted seat in our world.

I'd come to accept I'd always live with that regret, but the question I couldn't answer was the one that came after resignation.

What now?

I'd held that question so long, wrapped in my hands, shielding it so no one ever saw my doubt, like a tiny flame always in danger of going out and leaving me in resignation.

My brain was tired and overloaded when I finished my run. My body felt exhausted as I dragged myself through the rest of my workout and headed back to the shower. It was nine, right on the dot.

I showered again and got dressed in my black training fatigues. Instructors wore black, students wore gray. I tossed my bag in the locker and strode from the training center, taking the Kawasaki uptown. Johansen Enterprises was on the other side of the river, sitting on the hill over the city.

I took the bridge instead of the ferry, the warm wind whipping through my hair. The traffic was heavy because it was lunch time, but I managed to find a parking spot on the other end of the lot outside the building. It towered over me, made of sleek silver and iridescent windows that reflected the sky overhead. They probably had a lot of birds smash themselves on those.

I made a mental note to bring it up to Circe just to torture her later. Then, I made a second note *not* to do that, because I was trying to be less of an asshole.

There was a man in a sharp gray suit standing on the other side of the door, loitering in the atrium. He had to be a security guard or something, because I instantly detected the shape of a gun under his jacket. When I entered, he sent me a suspicious stare.

"Can I help you?" I said, forgetting my resolution not to be an asshole.

"Are you Caden Payne?" he asked, looking me up and down.

"Yeah, why?"

He stepped back, beckoning me across the room. I followed, boots clipping on the polished white floors. Overhead, hanging from the second story balcony, were strands of wisteria. Turning in a slow circle, I absorbed my surroundings like a soldier.

Lots of exits. Open space. A positive and a negative.

A woman had helped decorate this place, and I had a pretty good idea which one. It wasn't utilitarian in the way I'd expected. It was...beautiful. Airy windows that let the light in, spacious communal areas. The furniture all matched the logo—a pale mauve and silver against a cream backdrop. After seeing Circe for the last few days, I knew those were her signature colors.

I paused behind the guard as he swiped a card to let me through the revolving gate.

"Straight ahead, turn left. The boardroom is on the forty-eighth floor, but there's a personal assistant at the top who can guide you," he said.

"Thanks," I said.

I heard him grunt as I strode away. People milled about, doing a lot more standing around than working. I narrowed my eyes as several of them gave me strange looks. My black fatigues stood in stark contrast to their sleek suits and pencil dresses.

It was all clean, soft, and feminine.

Just like her.

Stepping into the elevator, I adjusted my helmet under my arm. The elevator was glass and looked out over a quad of green grass and flowers. Purple hyacinths.

It occurred to me as the ground dropped away, the flowers dwindling into dots below me, that I was looking at a visual representation of something I'd grown up without.

Parental love.

Fuck love—Lukas Johansen *adored* his daughter. His business was a monument to that. I swallowed, realizing that, deep inside, I was envious of what she had.

And that made me want to hate her a little.

I straightened my shoulders. I'd been dealt a different hand. It wasn't that fucking deep.

The elevator stopped, and the doors slid ajar. Directly across the hall was a black and white photograph of Circe, sitting primly with some kind of award in her hand, smiling her demure smile, not a hint of arrogance in her eyes.

She was humble, especially for someone who'd grown up being fed with a silver spoon. Even I had to admit that.

"Can I help you, sir?"

I turned on my heel. At the other end of the hall was a slender, silver haired woman sitting at a round desk. The air smelled faintly of flowers, the diffuser on her desk puffing as elevator music played.

She smiled serenely, waiting for my answer.

"Caden Payne," I said, striding across the hall and pausing by her desk. "I have a meeting in five minutes with Lukas and Circe."

She nodded, hitting the intercom on her desk. It beeped, and Lukas' voice came through, deep and lightly accented.

"Is Caden here?"

"Yes, he just got in, sir."

"I'm ready."

She tapped another button on her desk, and the door to our right slid open. I gave her a quick nod in thanks and stepped through, entering the boardroom. It hissed shut behind me, and I had to blink to adjust my eyes.

The boardroom was decorated like the rest of the building. The long table sat on a soft cream rug, surrounded by silver chairs. In the center was a bouquet of...of course, purple hyacinths.

No surprises there.

Lukas rose, buttoning his suit jacket. He crossed the room, extending his hand. I shook it, sizing him up. He was a tall man, maybe an inch shorter than me, and he had broad shoulders. There was an elegance about him I found interesting, in the way he moved, spoke, even in his expressions. He was tempered and proper to his core.

I found that dangerous.

It was a mask, and I didn't trust it. He might be partnering with us on the Wyoming Project, but he wasn't my friend. He was our most aggressive direct competitor in the private security business. Outside of this deal, our families weren't friendly.

Right now, it served us to work together, but I had no doubt that the second it didn't, he'd go back to being my enemy.

"Have you eaten?" he asked.

I shook my head. "No, but I don't eat till two."

He pushed his hands in his pockets. "Is that a...custom?"

"No, I just train all morning," I said. "Don't feel hungry until later."

"Hmm, well I suppose that's why Merrick does so well in the security business," Lukas said. "He works you hard."

I nodded once. "I work my men and myself hard."

He gave me a tempered smile and crossed the room, flipping the button of his suit open and sinking down. I followed, taking the seat across from him. Through the window, the city and the river glittered in the afternoon sun. I squinted, thinking I could see the top of the training center.

"Where's Circe?" I asked.

"Circe is on her way; she was at lunch," he said.

On cue, the door at the back of the room slid open. Apparently, they couldn't have normal doors that unlatched and swung in. No, they had to hiss and slide into the wall like we were in a sci-fi movie.

My thoughts came to a complete standstill as Circe walked in.

She was talking to someone, her back to us. As the door shut, she turned with a smile on her face. Her dark waves bounced and fell around her shoulders. Her slender body, made taller by a pair of towering heels, was covered in a white pencil dress. On her ears, throat, and wrists glittered silver jewelry.

Her mauve lips pulled back in a smile, flashing perfectly white teeth. Time slowed as those dark waves settled on her shoulders and bare upper arms. Her lashes were curled up, highlighting her dark eyes, narrowed with laughter.

Then she saw me and sobered, going professional.

I shifted in the chair, and to my absolute horror, I was halfway hard. She floated by me, sending me a coy look through her lashes, and sank down beside her father. Luckily, I didn't have to stand to shake her hand.

Otherwise, this meeting would have gotten incredibly awkward.

Pull yourself together.

I cleared my throat and laid my helmet on the table. Circe looked at it for a second and cleared her throat too. Our eyes connected for a brief second, and I knew exactly what we were both thinking.

The kitchen sink.

The kitchen floor.

Down below, my dick twitched. Fuck, why did she have to be a knockout? It was just my luck that the woman I had to work alongside was so stunning, I accidentally hooked up with her before I knew who she was. Because of course I did.

I was a fuck up.

Involuntarily, I cracked my neck.

"You alright?" she asked.

"Sore from training," I said. My dick was going down slowly, so I stretched my legs out and crossed my ankles, folding my arms over my chest.

"Alright, what's the agenda?" I asked.

Lukas rose and pulled a briefcase from under the table, setting a pair of laptops on the table. He removed a remote control and hit a button. A screen came down on the far wall and the lights dimmed, shades sliding over the windows. It all felt very theatrical.

"Your job together for the next few months is to get the approval from two men and a woman on my board. First up, we have Tennessee Galt."

"Galt like Vincent Galt?" I asked.

Lukas shook his head, walking closer to the screen. "Well, sort of. He's a second cousin by marriage, but his name being Galt is a coincidence."

"Tennessee is a woman's name," I said.

Circe's dark, perfect brow arched. "It can be a man's name."

I shrugged, tapping the table with my thumb. "Alright, where is he going to be?"

Lukas paused in front of the screen, hitting the remote again. A picture of a map appeared, but it was too bright for me to make out the words.

"The lodge in New York where Vincent Galt hosts work retreats is being rented out for one of the biggest meetings of real estate investors in the area. You two will attend and, by the end of it, I want his name on the consent forms."

My eyes met Circe's, and I looked away fast. Her mouth pursed, like she didn't like the idea of traveling with me. Of course, I didn't either, so I didn't fault her for her reaction.

"How long is the retreat?" I asked.

"A week," Lukas said. "I'll provide you everything you need, transport, and so on. If you get the forms done early, you can come home whenever you like."

"When is it?" Circe piped up.

"Next week." Lukas paced the floor, pausing to lean out the door. I heard him murmur something to the woman in the hall. The door hissed shut, and he circled back to the screen.

"Any questions?" he asked, facing us and bouncing lightly on the balls on his feet.

Circe's mouth pushed to the side as she chewed the inside of her cheek. I leaned forward, tapping my thumb harder.

"And I'll get a file on Galt?" I asked.

Lukas nodded. "I'll send everything over tomorrow."

There was a knock at the door, and Lukas rose, stepping around my chair and disappearing into the hall. The door hissed shut, and Circe whirled, sending me a pointed look.

"Can you stop that?"

I stared. "What?"

She pointed at my hand with one mauve nail. "You're tapping like crazy. Are you nervous?"

Embarrassed, I went still at once and pushed down my emotions. I'd learned to disconnect when people said things like that. It was part of the reason I was so fucking guarded.

I hadn't even noticed I was tapping.

I lifted my eyes to hers, remembering I was trying to rebrand.

"It's not on purpose," I said coolly.

She looked taken aback, and a flicker of regret passed over her face as she leaned back. Before she could speak, the door hissed open again, and Lukas stepped in with a tray in his hands.

He set it down, revealing a pot of tea and three glasses of sparkling water. My brow rose, but I bit back the urge to say something. Lukas Johansen was a proper, straitlaced person, and when they were together, so was his daughter.

The corner of my mouth turned up. When I was with her, she'd been anything but proper—unless rubbing her pussy on my face, her perfectly manicured nails wound in my hair to keep my head still, was proper. Unless the little burst of arousal that followed her orgasm, the one that trickled down my chin, was appropriate behavior.

I glanced over at her profile, pert nose lifted, full mouth parted.

I had a feeling I could get the picture-perfect princess of the Johansen Empire to do all kinds of things that weren't proper. I narrowed my eyes without meaning to. Maybe I just wanted to fuck her because she was gorgeous, but I suspected it had a lot more to do with the negative feelings I had, the ones that made me want to get her good and dirty.

Make the perfect makeup run down her cheeks.

Fuck up her lipstick. Make her choke on my dick.

"Can I get you anything?"

I shook my head, Lukas coming into focus. Now that I was seeing them together in a work environment, the perfect façade his daughter kept up made more sense. Lukas was, for lack of a better term, anal. In my experience, most high producing people like him were.

My eyes shifted. I'd met people like him before, a lot of him in my line of work, and I knew there was always a second. Normally, it was a son, but there was always a successor, someone groomed to be exactly the same.

In this case, interestingly enough, it was Lukas's daughter.

I could see his mark in everything she did: the way she sat, back ramrod straight, elegant hands with manicured fingers folded, face rested in a pleasant smile. She was a doll. For Lukas' purposes, she could have been made of porcelain and paint, and he would have been just as proud.

I had a feeling, if I could find the right pressure point, I could tap once and shatter her like fine glass.

She sat there like that until her father finished the meeting and promised to send over the files. He shook my hand and excused himself. She got to her feet and started gathering up the cups.

"What are you doing?" I asked.

Her brows creased. "Cleaning up. Just because I'm somebody important at this company doesn't mean I can leave a mess for others."

I didn't point out that her father had walked out without cleaning anything up. She snapped the laptops shut, and I brought the tray out to her assistant. Without speaking, she walked me down to the atrium.

"I'll be by your house the day we leave," I said.

She nodded once, keeping her eyes focused through the window. "You'd better go then," she said crisply.

"You're in a hurry to get rid of me."

"What? Did you think we'd get lunch together?"

"Not lunch. Maybe a quickie in the bathroom?"

Her dark eyes flashed. "Get out."

I laughed, and before she could spin and go, I leaned in quickly enough to whisper, "You're thinking about it right now, aren't you?"

Her cheeks flushed pink. "I'm not fucking you."

"I never said anything about fucking," I murmured. "But I'd be happy to let you ride my face in a bathroom stall anytime you want, ma'am."

Her mouth popped open. I wasn't sure where that had come from. I was supposed to be her business rival. Here I was, practically begging her for an orgasm—hers, not mine—and it was getting embarrassing. I was letting her get the upper hand, and I couldn't do that.

I slung my helmet over my shoulder, walking backwards to the door. "You'll fuck me," I said. "Just you wait."

She was speechless, so I left her there, perfect mouth hanging open, staring at me from her ivory tower as I crossed the parking lot and swung onto my Kawasaki.

CHAPTER NINE

CIRCE

That Saturday, I packed my bags in the afternoon after a hot yoga session that left my legs watery. For some reason, I couldn't get any of my clothes to look good on me.

Maybe I was just nervous about going on a trip with Caden.

Frustrated, I tore apart my closet, trying on every pair of jeans I owned. Everything was too tight or too loose or the wrong color. Finally, I settled on a cream yoga set with a fuzzy cropped sweater. Then, I grabbed my rolling suitcase, pushed on my sneakers, and strode down the hall.

Sometimes, when I walked like this, I could feel my father's influence on me. Long stride, back straight, confident steps.

Like I owned the world.

My father was still at work when I'd said goodbye to him that morning. I knew he'd call me tomorrow, but part of me wished he was here to wave goodbye. Maybe it was because this was my first business deal of this size, maybe because the stakes were so high.

I just needed a little reassurance.

In the distance came a low hum, and I hit the button to open the detached garage just as a black Kawasaki screeched around the corner, Caden aboard. He wore the same clothes he always did— black fatigues and boots.

Something sparked downstairs.

I shook my head as he dismounted the bike. He pulled the helmet off, tucking it under his arm. There was a wet spot on his t-shirt from sweat. For some reason, it made me think of the perfect, starched button up Damian had worn. I doubted he ever got sweaty the way Caden did.

My forehead scrunched in a scowl. Was that a good thing or a bad thing? I wasn't sure anymore.

His cobalt eyes fell on my suitcase, and a muscle twitched in his jaw. "That won't fit on the Kawasaki," he said.

I stared, trying to figure out what he meant. "I'm not riding that thing all the way to the lodge. Are you kidding?"

His gaze narrowed. "Well, I'm not letting you drive me."

"I'm a good driver."

"Highly doubt."

I forgot all about his sexy, sweaty t-shirt and decided I'd much rather flip him off instead. So I did, with one freshly manicured finger.

"Nice," he said.

"Thought you'd like that."

He sighed, snatching my suitcase from my surprised hand. The gravel crunched under his boots as he crossed to the open garage. I paused, wavering until he stopped and glanced back.

"What are you doing?"

"Putting your shit in the trunk of your car," he said.

"You're not driving my car," I snapped.

He tossed the suitcase into the back seat and lifted his hand, my keys hanging from his middle finger. "Come on, we're burning daylight."

When had he taken my keys?

He'd gotten the upper hand—I'd give him that just this once. I joined him in the garage, arms crossed tight. He reached across and opened my door—like the gentleman he usually wasn't—and I sat down, tossing my ponytail to make sure he knew I was pissed.

He laughed softly, and the engine purred as we backed into the lawn. He parked and jumped out, leaving it running while he put his Kawasaki into the garage and hit the button to shut the door.

Then, he settled himself in the front seat and drove my car out onto the street. The sun was just beginning to set over the trees. I kicked my sneakers off and curled up, ignoring him pointedly. It wasn't very satisfying, because he was ignoring me back.

I snuck a peek from beneath my lashes. He was settled in, long legs stretched out, one hand draped lazily over the wheel. I followed the lines of dark ink up his forearm to where they disappeared beneath his shirt. They reappeared on the right side of his throat, extending to his sharp jawline.

Forgetting I was trying to be subtle, I let my gaze wander over his face.

He had a nice profile. A strong nose with a little arch in the middle. Sleek black hair so dark that it reflected the light like a raven's wing.

But those heavy-lidded eyes with dark lashes were what had been my downfall that night in the bar. I never, ever hooked up. I'd slept with my high school boyfriend a few times, but I'd never had sex with a stranger.

I'd definitely never let one take me home and go down on me without asking for anything in return.

Why was he so obsessed with eating me out anyway?

God, this was so embarrassing.

Why did it have to be him? Why did he have to be so physically perfect but such an asshole otherwise?

The sun was finally creeping below the horizon when he rolled the top of the car up. I'd shifted to my side, curled up with my eyes closed. The radio played softly in the background. I had to admit, it was cozy. He drove fast, but he was careful. And, I admitted begrudgingly, I felt safe with him behind the wheel.

We drove in silence on the highway for about an hour. He had the car on cruise control and his knees were spread. I cracked my eyes and found my gaze lingering on the zippered front of his pants.

There was a faint rise, but maybe it was just the way the fabric bunched.

Or maybe not.

I swallowed, my throat oddly dry.

The car slowed, and the turn signal clicked. I lifted my head, looking around.

"What—why are you stopping?" I asked, my voice hoarse.

He guided the vehicle down the off ramp, the lights of a state border rest stop flickering ahead. "Need to take a piss. You want anything?"

I frowned, straightening and grabbing my shoes. It bothered me how vulgar he could be; he could have just said he needed the bathroom.

"I'll use the bathroom too," I said primly.

The corner of his mouth turned up, the streetlamps flickering in his eyes. He stepped out of the car, unfurling those long legs as I moved after him. It was dark, and there were a group of men standing by the door. One glanced at me, giving me a slow, up and down stare.

Instantly, I curled up inside and my steps faltered.

Right away, Caden was beside me, one hand on my waist. My heart thrummed. I glanced up at him for a second, but he was steering me inside like he did it all the time, like it was normal for him to guide and protect me with a hand on my hip and his body as a barrier.

Inside, he released me outside the restrooms, turning to push the door to the men's open.

"I'll be right back," he said.

Why had I frozen up like that? Heat crept over my face, and I turned without speaking, pushing into the women's bathroom. It was sickly hot inside and smelled of bleach. I paused before the mirror, grabbing a handful of paper towels to run under cold water.

There was a reason my father had our house outfitted with the best security system money could buy. There was a reason he had a tracking chip in my car and I let him have my phone location most of the time.

Except for when I'd been with Caden.

My neck prickled. I dabbed it with the sopping towels, my heart slowing.

You're safe.

I breathed in through my nose and out through my mouth. Hands steady, I gathered up my hair and tied it in a messy bun on my head to keep it off my sweaty neck. Caden would be wondering what was taking so long.

I used the bathroom, washed up, and stepped out into the main area. He was standing by the vending machines, and when I drew near, I swore I could feel the heat radiating off his body. Maybe that was just a part of me that wished he'd put his hand on my back again.

"What do you want?" he asked.

I shrugged. "A diet soda."

He raised that sharp brow. "I thought you only drank tea and sparkling water."

"And diet sodas."

He gave me a look, a slow, thorough look that reminded me he'd seen between my legs. A shiver made its way down my spine, but I ignored it. People acted professional all the time with people they'd slept with, and I hadn't even had sex with him.

"I want gummy worms too," I said, drawing myself up. I usually tried not to eat sugar, but sour gummy worms were my weakness.

He leaned in, swiping his card and hitting the button. "Whatever you want, sweetheart."

My stomach flipped. The way he said it, like there was no H, scratched an itch, like he was curling his tongue around that word and flicking the way he had on my clit.

I turned abruptly and left the main area, stepping out onto the sidewalk. The men were gone as I walked to the car and waited, arms crossed, for him to appear. He did, holding our snacks, his heavy eyes devoid of expression.

Good; a blank stare was better than a smirk.

He dumped everything in my lap and started the car. He'd gotten himself two energy drinks and a bottle of water. I put them in the center console and popped the lid of my coke, promptly cracking the tip of my acrylic. A little flicker of pain moved down my hand and wrist.

Involuntarily, I gasped, and his gaze swung around as he pulled back on the highway.

"What?"

"Nothing," I said.

His thigh tensed as he accelerated. "Tell me."

"Fine," I sighed, defeated. "I broke a nail. Go on, make fun of me."

His expression didn't change. He shrugged once, reaching for his drink. "There's a salon at the lodge. Get it fixed tomorrow."

I'd expected him to tease me about being upset over a nail. Confused, I settled back and peeled off my sneakers again. There was a fuzzy mauve blanket in the back seat, and I grabbed it, spreading it over my legs.

"Comfortable?" The wry note was back.

"Very," I said, ripping open my gummy worms.

He laughed softly, running a hand over his chin. He hit the radio, and a soft rock song filled the car. I dug in the bag and pulled out a gummy, biting the blue side off. It was my favorite; unfortunately, the red side was my least.

I put that back in the bag. He yawned and took a drink.

I glanced over, watching a muscle in his jaw twitch. I hated to admit it, but he was so attractive in everything he did that I was a little jealous. I worked hard to make my father proud, to be pretty and perfect. Caden just walked into the room, and every head turned.

He crushed his empty drink in his fist and set it in the trash compartment in the console. I bit off the blue side of another gummy, stretching it out, not taking my eyes from him.

He narrowed his eyes. "Are you only eating one side of that?"

I nodded. "Blue is good. Red is gross."

He laughed again, just once. I liked his laugh when it wasn't mocking. It was pleasant and sat deep in his chest.

"Give me the rest," he said.

I did a double take, sure I'd misheard him. My hand froze halfway in the bag, sugar sticky on my fingertips.

"What?"

"Give me the half you don't want," he said, extending his palm.

A little stunned, I bit the blue part off and laid the rest in his hand. He tossed it in his mouth, and that sexy muscle worked in his jaw. I turned, staring ahead, tingles running through my body.

"What's the matter?"

I cleared my throat. "Nothing. I just didn't expect you to not mind swapping saliva with me."

"I didn't realize you were sucking on them first."

"I'm not," I said, scowling.

"Then contamination is minimal."

In retrospect, I should have let it go. He was pointedly ignoring the electricity in the car crackling quietly between us. If I hadn't pushed, he would have just fallen quiet.

"It's a couple thing to do," I blurted out. "That's why it's weird."

He yawned. "I ate you out for two hours straight, so I think we're beyond that boundary."

My jaw dropped.

"Gummy," he demanded, offering his palm.

Obediently, I bit the blue half off and gave him the rest. The highway rushed by outside, and neither of us said another word.

Not even when the bag was empty and I stuffed it in the trash.

He dusted off his hand and popped open his second drink. I finished my diet coke and curled up under the blanket.

Sleepily, I mulled it over. Ever since he'd insisted he drive to the lodge, something felt different, like my need to control everything was...not gone, but less annoying. Maybe it was because he'd gotten off that motorcycle and told me exactly what was going to happen.

Maybe I was just tired of having to run things and desperate for someone else to do it for once.

That had to be it.

It wasn't like I trusted him or anything.

CHAPTER TEN

CADEN

It was one in the morning when we pulled up outside the lodge. Circe was dead asleep, her cheek smashed against the seat. I pulled up beneath a pine tree and pushed open my door. The soft scent of the woods wafted across my face. I'd been up to the lodge a few times, and it was pleasant, set deep in the woods away from the noise of the city and highway.

I circled the car, getting our bags out. When I returned, she was still asleep, snoring lightly, her hair fluttering.

It was strange, seeing the picture-perfect Circe Johansen snoring.

I shook her shoulder, and she hiccupped, bolting upright.

"What...are we here?"

"We're here," I said. "Let's go, I'm tired."

She nodded, rubbing her eyes and smearing her mascara in the process. Deep in my pants, my dick jerked. Not a lot, but just enough that I felt it. Grabbing the bags, I let her lock the car and hurry to catch up to me.

We entered the quiet lodge. It was a large building that had been recently renovated. The last time I'd stayed here had been less than ideal. It was a relief that they'd stripped the floor and walls and filled the space with light wood and plush, plaid furniture.

We crossed the floor, and the woman behind the front desk lifted her head from her phone. Her eyes ran over me and lingered on Circe's smeared makeup as she popped her gum and tapped her keyboard.

"You're Caden and Circe," she said. "I was told we had a late check-in."

I dropped the bags, getting my wallet out. Circe rubbed her face, noticing she had mascara on her palm. She scowled and licked her fingertip, rubbing it away.

My dick did that thing again at the sight of her tongue—not quite a twitch, just a quick check in to let me know it saw something it liked.

"Can I see your ID?" the woman drawled.

I jerked back to reality. "Yeah, here you go."

She took it between two long nails and studied it for a second. "Okay, let me find you in our system."

She handed the ID back and tapped loudly. My jaw twitched, annoyed by her attitude—not that I had a leg to stand on when it came to being sarcastic. I'd done my time in that area. She typed for a long time and then sat back, reaching into the key compartments.

"Okay, I got you checked in," she said, dumping the keys on the desk. "You're next door to each other on the second floor. You can unlock the door between the suites if you want."

"I do *not* want that," said Circe.

The woman gave her a slow blink and picked up her phone again. I grabbed up our bags and strode across the room towards the hall, leaving Circe to catch up. She ducked into the elevator beside me, tugging her hair out of its messy bun. It tumbled down her shoulders in a dark cascade.

Fuck, why did she have to be pretty?

I didn't usually do pretty. I liked sexy, liked older and experienced. I didn't like good girl heiresses who did hot yoga, drank oat milk, and only ate their vegetables steamed.

At least, not until now.

The elevator doors slid back to reveal the dim hall. I could hear her soft footfalls behind me, striding lightly and confidently. She had a lithe footstep that reminded me of a cat when she wasn't in those clunky heels.

I paused between our doors, turning back. "Right or left?"

She took one of the cards, flipping it. "Left."

I swiped my keycard, pushing the door in. I wasn't sure why, but after seeing her freeze up outside the rest stop, it felt like I should make sure she got in safely. Just because we were on a mission together. Not for any other reason.

She slipped inside, sending me a confused glance. "Goodnight," she said slowly. "See you at breakfast."

I jerked my head and slipped into my suite. It was spacious and smelled fresh, like the pine trees outside. The window was cracked and thick, warm air wafting through. I dropped my suitcase inside the bedroom, pushing open the door to reveal a king bed outfitted with thick quilt. It was a relief it looked nothing like it had during my last stay.

I stripped to my boxer briefs and turned on the shower. This time, unlike at the training center, I managed to keep my hands off my dick.

It was early morning when I woke. The lodge was just starting to come to life, so I knew I had a few minutes before I ran into an onslaught of people I barely knew. I slipped on my running clothes and moved down the hall to the side door, kicking it open and stepping into the fresh mountain air.

Everything was washed clean. Water dripped from the pines. The ground smelled faintly sweet and dark.

I moved down the road and turned off onto the dirt trail that ran through the forest. It was a ten-mile loop of flat ground, so I could do it pretty easily before breakfast. Usually, I didn't have any trouble turning my brain off when I ran, but today, I just kept running.

First, it was Circe.

Then, it was Lukas.

Then, it was Merrick.

And of course, it bounced right back to Circe. Realistically, even if we decided to give into the obvious attraction between us, we would never be anything but quick fun. She had everything—money, connections, a pick of anyone she wanted to date.

I had money, but not the way she did.

That didn't matter. It wasn't like I wanted her to be my girlfriend. No, I just wanted her to eat the blue end of gummy worms in my bed. I wanted to listen to her talk about koi fish. I wanted to watch her hair tumble down in the shower, to dig my hands into it, lather soap down her shoulders, play with her body until her pulse quickened and her pussy grew slippery.

But I didn't really *like* her that much.

I slowed to a brisk walk. Up ahead, the trail turned and headed back to the lodge. I followed it, trying to focus on anything but my thoughts. The breeze swept through the trees, shaking dew off in a soft shower.

My feet slowed and stopped as I leaned back, taking a deep breath and expelling it.

I'd needed this—a chance to get out of the city, to fix my head before training and this mission started in earnest.

By the time I got back to my room, it was almost nine, and I was feeling irritated at my own brain. I managed to control myself in the shower again, washing up without incident. I got dressed—not in my usual fatigues, but a white button up and gray dress pants.

I stepped out into the hall, rolling my sleeves up. Circe's door was shut; she was probably still sleeping, so I headed to the dining room alone.

Scratch that—she was already seated by the window. I crossed the room and sank down in the empty seat opposite her. She jumped, dropping her phone on the table.

Her eyes widened slightly and ran over me. I returned the favor, taking in her tight yoga set. Why did she always have to wear such skintight clothes? At least this morning, the material was thick, but the coral fabric still hugged her curves. I had a hard time dragging my gaze away.

"Just wake up?" I said, sitting back.

"No, I've been at hot yoga," she said.

"Of course," I said. "I ran. Can't take a break."

"Old habits die hard," she said. "Once a neurotic high achiever, always one."

I didn't reply. I'd assumed she'd still be sleeping, but here she was at nine in the morning, already worked out and showered, a cup of steaming tea and poached eggs before her. She'd even found time to brush out her hair and pull it into a sleek ponytail.

"I'm just used to training daily," I said.

The waiter appeared, and I ordered steak and eggs. She had a little plate of fruit to go with her eggs and some wheat toast. When they brought coffee, I poured a cup and sat back, watching her cut her egg into fourths, the steam rising in delicate spirals.

"It's nice up here," she said. "This is my first time."

The corner of my mouth jerked. "I come up here a lot. The mountains help clear my head."

"Well, that's good, because we have our first meeting with Tennessee Galt for lunch," she said.

The waiter set my steak down, and I cut into it, revealing the perfect amount of blood. Circe looked faintly disgusted as I started eating.

"I was thinking I'd take this meeting alone, just this time," she said.

I lifted my brow. "Oh really?"

She squared her shoulders. "Yes. I think I'd be a better candidate for it."

"Why's that?"

"Because I'm less abrasive," she said.

The corner of my mouth tugged up. "You mean your neck isn't tattooed, and you've got a rich father."

She rolled her eyes, fluttering her lashes in the process. God, if I wasn't irritated, I'd enjoy that sight.

"I think I should go in and soften him up," she said primly. "And you can seal the deal later if you need to."

"Like I did with you?"

I wasn't sure why I'd said that. She went still, her fork slipping to the table. There was a long silence, and then she sighed.

"Please don't bring that up again," she said firmly.

I cocked my head. "Why? It happened. Almost twice."

Her dark eyes blazed. "Just because it happened doesn't mean we need to talk about it."

"Is it bothering you?"

She shook her head hard. "It will never happen again."

I put a piece of steak in my mouth, but I didn't reply, even after I'd swallowed. She wanted me to back her statement up—I could tell— but I kept silent. It was bothering her so badly, I could see her vibrate in her chair.

Finally, she turned her narrowed eyes back on me.

"It won't," she said quietly.

I shrugged. "You look like you could use some stress relief."

"I'll stick to my vibrator," she said. "I like to end my night with an orgasm."

I laughed. She was quick, smart, and it woke my dick up under the table.

"Which would you pick? If you had to choose," I said, as if we were talking about the weather. "Vibrator or tongue?"

Her lips parted and the tight front of her shirt heaved. "Tongue, but not yours."

"Ouch."

Her slender, dark brow arced. "Please. You probably have people lining up outside your apartment to sleep with you."

"Why's that?"

She fumbled, squirming. "I mean, look at you."

"I wish you would."

It took her a second to recover, but when she did, she was back to her graceful, poised self. "Don't lie and say you don't know you're good looking with...all those tattoos."

"The tattoos are cover ups," I admitted, pretending I wasn't elated by her compliment.

She chewed her lower lip. "For what?"

"Shitty tattoos I got when I was younger," I said. "I don't want to be reminded of everything I did as a kid."

"Why is that?"

I sighed. "Because not everyone has a father who loves them."

She faltered. "What...what were the tattoos before?"

I unbuttoned the top two buttons of my shirt and pulled it aside, revealing the faded ink on the top of my left pectoral. She leaned in, and for some reason, a flush moved up her neck. Her mouth parted, and I found my gaze lingering on it.

"What is it?"

"A tire iron," I said. "Technically, two of them."

She shifted back. "I don't understand."

I buttoned my shirt, going back to my steak. "Don't worry about it. I'm going to get it covered later."

There was an uncomfortable silence before she cleared her throat.

"Alright, fine," she said. "You can go to the meeting with me."

"Thank you," I shot back. "I'm in your debt."

She rolled her eyes and took a bite of her toast. There was a little butter on her lower lip, but she didn't notice, so it sat there, holding all my attention, making me wonder if it would cause a problem if I just...leaned across the table and kissed it away.

The thought of kissing her roused the memory of that night...of kissing her on the floor after I ate her out.

And how good it had made me feel to give her five orgasms in a row.

I wasn't naturally good at anything, all my talent boiled down to bullheadedness and hard work. But there was one thing I did well without trying, and that was eating pussy. I never questioned myself when I was on my knees.

She cleaned her plate and dabbed her mouth. It was disappointing to see that butter go, but it was probably for the best. I checked the front of my pants to make sure I wasn't hard and rose.

"I'm going downstairs," I said. "Need to make my rounds."

"Your what?"

I tapped the table once. "I know you think I'm not equipped for diplomatic work, but I was the one who got the deal with your hardass father. It took two years of working over rich assholes, so maybe give me the benefit of the doubt when I say I know how to do my job."

I hadn't meant for it to come out that aggressively—I really was trying to be less of a dick—but it was honestly insulting that she thought, just because I looked a certain way, that I couldn't do my job.

A flicker of anger moved through her dark gaze. "I'll see you later then," she said coolly.

I nodded, not wanting to antagonize her further, and left.

CHAPTER ELEVEN

CIRCE

Back in my room, I did my makeup slowly with the TV on in the background. It was a mindless show, a reality competition that played often in the gym at home. I needed something, anything, to think about that wasn't the way my heart had done an unexpected flip when Caden walked up to my table.

He had no business looking that good in a button up. All those tattoos should have clashed with dress clothes, but they didn't. They looked sinfully good, and all I could think about was how Damien's clothes had worn him and Caden's did the exact opposite.

That wasn't fair. Damien hadn't done anything to deserve being brought up in my head every time Caden turned me on. He'd done nothing but be the kind of man my father wanted me to end up with.

I sighed, meeting my gaze in the mirror. My hair was pulled back in a French twist, a curl grazing my neck. I touched it, running my fingertips over the bare skin to my bra strap. No one had ever touched me gently, the way men did in books and movies, coaxing my body to respond to their caresses.

And God, I wanted that. I was twenty-five, and I'd only had sex a handful of times with my first boyfriend.

After five years of coming home at night and watching movies and shows packed with romantic clichés, getting up in the morning in a bed by myself and going to work like it didn't matter... I knew I was young, but watching Emmy and Delaney go through all the normal things, like getting ready for first dates, gossiping about men, and recapping what they'd done the night before, hit hard.

I'd given up a lot to be the perfect daughter.

I loved my father, but he'd never let me have traditionally feminine wants or dreams. I was doomed to sit, pretty and demure, in the empty spot left by a mother I never met.

A doll in a display case.

My throat felt lumpy. I ran a glass under cold water and took a sip. My phone beeped, reminding me I needed to hurry up because our meeting was in thirty minutes.

I jerked back to reality, grabbing my dress from behind the door. It was pale mauve—no surprises there—and simply cut. I zipped it up the back, wriggling to get the tight fabric into place. The neckline dipped deep enough to show my white gold necklace and a trace of cleavage.

I slipped on matching heels and dabbed on my signature lipstick, blotting it with a tissue. My phone pinged, and a text from Caden popped up. My fingers clenched, crushing the tissue hard.

Ready?

My hand tingled as I swiped it aside. What was wrong with me? My mind drifted back to every flip of my stomach or rising pulse I'd experienced since we'd left Providence.

They were getting more frequent and harder to dismiss.

Did I want *him*?

Or did I just want to *sleep* with him?

Those were two very different things. If I just wanted to get under his clothes and feel that lean, inked body for a night, that wasn't...completely out of the question. He'd made enough blatant comments for me to know he'd be happy to blow off some steam together.

I cocked my head, ignoring a second text letting me know he was outside my door waiting.

I was a twenty-five-year-old woman on birth control, tested, and perfectly able to sleep with another consenting adult.

So why were my palms drenched?

I flipped the sink on, letting the cool water run over them before a sharp knocking sounded.

"Come in," I called. "It's not locked."

My heart was in my mouth as the door creaked. I grabbed a washcloth and ran it under the icy water and dabbed my neck. I was sweating between my breasts, but there was no time to get that.

He appeared in the doorway. His brow cocked, and his eyes did that thing that made me feel naked: a quick drop, a little linger, and then a slow drag up my body. His jaw worked as he met my eyes in the mirror.

"You were a bit mean this morning," he said coolly.

My jaw dropped. "What?"

He shrugged once. "You were pretty rude."

My defenses shot up. "I was not."

"You tried to oust me from the meeting because you think I'm shit at my job," he said, his voice even, though there was a hint of anger behind it. "I thought you were humble. My mistake."

I spun, stepping back until I hit the sink. He had a hand in his pocket, that lean body rising easily a foot over me. Why did he have to be so tall? It made everything he said seem so much more important than my protests.

A crease appeared between his brows. "Anyway, let's go."

He stepped back and disappeared into the living area. I gave myself a shake, unsure what I felt. I'd expected to be angry, but I was shocked more than anything. No one ever spoke to me as directly as Caden did.

"We need to leave," he said, his voice level.

I flicked the light off, grabbed my purse, and sailed past him into the hall. He followed me out and the door slammed shut. I didn't wait for him; I just strode quickly ahead, with him following at an easy pace.

Our meeting was upstairs in one of the conference rooms. There was a fake fire roaring in the hearth and a platter of coffee waiting on the round, cherry wood table. I sank down at the end, and Caden kicked the chair beside me back, folding his long body up in it. He barely had room to tuck his legs under the table.

I scowled.

He glanced over. "What's up?"

"Nothing," I said primly. "But you're being pretty rude, and it's ruining my Botox."

He laughed, that rich sound echoing. A little bit of the tension eased.

"Well, stop scowling and you'll be fine," he said.

"Stop making me scowl."

He shifted and his cobalt eyes, heavy with dark lashes, fixed on me. "What if I just made you come instead?"

The door burst open, and two men in suits, chattering to each other, entered. I was frozen to the spot, barely able to offer them more than a glance. The corner of his mouth jerked up, and I noticed he had the faintest dimple on that side.

He swiveled, rising and offering his hand to the first man. "Tennessee Galt," he said, his voice switching from husky to all business.

I had a feeling deep inside that he reserved that husky tone for special circumstances.

Like trying to get his co-worker to fuck him.

Oh God, I needed to get those thoughts out of my head. I brushed back my hair, rising and offering a warm smile. Tennessee was a pleasant-faced man in his early sixties, his white hair brushed back and his blue eyes calming. I'd met him many times before during board meetings. He'd always been respectful to me, even when I'd first started.

"Circe, looking wonderful," he said, hugging me. "How's your father?"

"He's busy as usual," I said brightly. "Everything's been great. Numbers are strong this year."

Tennessee nodded, stepping aside to reveal the second man. He was maybe fifteen years younger and had a broad, handsome face and wide shoulders. When I shook his hand, his grip was like iron.

"This is Clay Maxwell," Tennessee said. "He's my new financial advisor. I wanted to bring him along to get a fresh take on all this."

For some reason, I got a strange vibe from Clay Maxwell. Maybe it was because his eyes lingered on me too long, or that he just looked like someone who was waiting to point out the fact that I was—yes, shockingly—a woman in a high-ranking position.

Palm itching from contact with his, I sank back down. Caden stepped in between us and shook his hand. The muscles in Caden's forearm flexed, and I glanced down, noticing he'd changed his demeanor. His back was straight, shoes planted firm. Like he was making a subtle show of strength.

I sank down at the table, crossing one knee over the other. Caden sank down beside me, but he kept his knees spread and his back straight.

Like he was trying to send a message.

The only message it was sending to my brain was a prompt to remind me that, under the zipper of his pants, he had a dick, and I was devastatingly horny and had been for a while.

Inwardly, I sighed. Not even bothering to scold myself anymore.

He was gorgeous, and I hadn't gotten laid in five years. Desire was bound to happen while working in such close proximity, but I wasn't going to give into it.

"Alright," said Clay, his voice booming over the table. "Let's hear it."

I leaned in before Caden had a chance to speak. "I'll walk you through it and get you up to speed on everything. Are you familiar with the Wyoming Project?"

"It's Merrick Llwyd's business venture," Clay said, eyes lingering a little low on my face. "His training grounds for a private international security force for hire. I believe your father is training security forces there as well, is he not?"

I nodded. "The deal on the table between my father and Merrick Llwyd isn't complex. They share training space, Lukas funds half the expansion via Johansen Enterprises, and everyone gets a long-term payout, including investors."

Clay lifted a brow, like he didn't believe it was that simple. And truthfully, it wasn't, but that wasn't unusual. Our investors needed business to be easily understandable with a promise of a big check at the end. That was all they cared about.

Caden crossed his arms. "It's a rock-solid venture, so much so that Merrick Llwyd has already started building before securing funding. And he is one of the most well-respected businessmen in Providence."

Clay glanced at Caden, who met his stare with confidence. For a second, I felt a tremor of tension between them, like they weren't meshing, which was a bad sign for this meeting.

"Let me go over some numbers with you both," I said, taking a folder from my bag and offering Clay a sweet smile, the one I used with men like him.

The tension in his shoulders eased. "Alright, I'm all ears."

Tennessee was quiet for the first several minutes while I moved through the building and business plan for the Wyoming Project. He perked up when I handed them sheets of projected numbers, and I could tell he was warming up to the investment.

Caden stayed as he was, giving off the energy of a watchdog, waiting for permission to attack.

My jaw ached from talking an hour later when we finished. I shook Tennessee's hand, and he promised to get back to me by the end of the day tomorrow. Caden slipped in at the last moment and caught him in the hall, engaging him in conversation.

I waited, polite smile glued on. Clay gathered up his things and circled the table, stepping out into the hallway. The door banged shut behind him and suddenly, he was very close, his broad body filling my vision.

"Are you new to Johansen Enterprises?" he asked.

I glanced over at Caden and Tennessee several yards away. "No, I'm the chief operating officer."

His brows rose. "Really? You look young."

Inside, I sighed. Outside, I kept my polite smile going.

"I am," I said. "My father owns it."

If he was surprised, he didn't show it. His gaze drifted down...down to my gold necklace and the hint of cleavage.

"Are you free later?" he asked, his voice dropping. "Outside business, I'd like to take you to dinner."

My brows shot up. "That's bold, Mr. Clay."

He moved a step closer, and I took a tiny step back and into the wall. If I'd been attracted to him, I might have found his flirting attractive, but he had an abrasive presence that turned me off.

"You're used to being treated well, I can do that," he said, shrugging.

"Oh? What does that mean?" I tilted my head up, giving him a challenging stare.

He waved a hand. "There's a world-renowned restaurant at the hotel a few miles from here. Let me take you out tonight. I'll wine and dine you the way you're used to. Maybe, if you're pleased, we can talk about the deal more. In a less...formal environment."

My stomach sank. "What exactly do you mean?"

I'd found being direct and forcing men to explain themselves was the best route in these situations. He faltered but recovered fast.

"Let me make you feel good, Miss Johansen," he said, his voice dropping even lower, going a little husky.

"That won't be necessary."

We both spun. Caden stood directly behind me with an expression like he was going to haul back and punch Clay in the face. His narrowed gaze crackled, and despite the pleasant smile on his mouth, his knuckles were white.

His hand hovered over my lower back.

"We have an early meeting," he said firmly.

A crease appeared between Clay's brows, and he took a step back. His eyes raked over Caden, who met his gaze with a stone-cold glare. Maxwell was physically bigger, but I had no doubt that, in a brawl, Caden could beat the shit out of him.

And we couldn't have that.

I offered Clay the sweetest smile I could muster and put my hand on his arm. "Thank you. I'm very flattered, Mr. Clay, but Caden is right; we have an early meeting. Maybe another time."

I bit my lip and batted my eyes up at him, patting his arm and giving it a little squeeze. All the anger drained from his face, replaced by a slight flush. He was, as I'd suspected, predictable.

"Fine," he said. "We'll talk tomorrow."

Relieved, I watched Clay and Tennessee walk off until they disappeared around the corner. Then, I turned on Caden, who was staring after them with a heavy, ice-cold stare.

"You need to stay out of my business," I whispered.

He looked me dead in the eyes. "If anyone is going to fuck you, it's going to be me. And if I see him trying to pin you up against a wall again, I'll make sure he gets to watch when I do."

He was a fucking psycho. Heart hammering, I attempted to speak, but my mouth was dust dry. He rummaged in his pocket for a second and came up with a crushed pack of cigarettes.

"Going to have a smoke," he said.

He strode off, looking so sexy and angry that I couldn't even be annoyed. Deep down, I had to admit that his jealousy was flattering.

And if I thought I was horny before, it was nothing on what I felt now.

CHAPTER TWELVE

CADEN

I went down for dinner around seven, but she was nowhere to be seen. What had happened back in the hall had probably scared her off, but that didn't mean I regretted it. Clay Maxwell was on my immediate shit list the minute he walked through the door. I knew men like that, the kind who liked fast cars and women too young for them, and it pissed me off.

When I'd heard him proposition her, my blood went white hot. Maybe I shouldn't have said the thing about fucking her in front of him. That was over the line.

But I stood by the rest.

I ate and had a bourbon at the bar before going back to my room. My eyes ached, and not even taking a hot shower helped it. I pulled on a pair of sweatpants and stepped out onto the balcony, feeling vaguely guilty about the pack of cigarettes in my pocket.

The air was warm, a hint of coolness wafting from the pine forest. I flicked the lighter and inhaled.

After I'd left the UK, after Merrick and I first met, he'd given me space to work through the news that I had a father who was the billionaire head of a mafia organization. That one had taken a few swallows to get down. For an entire month, I'd stayed at the lodge, running ten, sometimes fifteen, miles a day.

Smoking heavily. Crushing Adderall on the sink. Trying to wrap my head around the realization that my entire life could have been different.

I could have avoided all the pain. The violence. The horrifying shit I'd done just to get by.

I glanced behind me at the cozy lodge room. It was probably good they'd renovated it. I swore I'd memorized every nook and cranny of mine during those four weeks.

The lodge had been a haven outside Providence for me while the truth sank in, but it didn't heal me. I'd dragged all the shit I'd carried back with me. Not even Merrick knew how miserable I'd been for the first several years, and he didn't know that, until five years ago, I'd been a serial abuser of prescription drugs.

Crushed pills to get me going in the morning. Alcohol to pull me out of it at night. A hundred million lies about why I bit the inside of my cheek, why my nose bled every time I showered, why my entire body ached like a motherfucker from locked muscles.

He'd be so disappointed.

I sighed, releasing the smoke and snapping my eyes open.

"Hey."

My scalp prickled, and I swung around. On the balcony beside mine sat Circe, wearing a silk dressing gown. It was big on her, loose enough that it draped over her body and trailed on the ground.

The neckline hung on her shoulders, exposing her collarbones. Two delicate lines, like a stag's antlers, bone white in the moonlight.

Out of nowhere, a deep hunger moved through my body and settled in the pit of my stomach.

I had to have Circe Johansen tonight.

Fuck everything else until the morning. Yes, I'd sworn to Merrick I wouldn't fuck this mission up. Yes, he was counting on me. Billions of dollars hung in the balance. But nothing felt real anymore except the feral craving in my veins to have her for the first time.

I blew another stream of smoke. "Hey."

She licked her lips. They were a pale pink instead of mauve. She'd taken off her makeup, and I could make out the natural shadows

106

beneath her eyes. The only things left were her lashes, but they were much sparser without makeup.

I liked how naked she looked.

"Did you have dinner?" She cleared her throat.

I nodded. "Where were you?"

She sighed, a long, musical sound. "Honestly, after our meeting, I needed some alone time. I ordered room service."

I knew she meant that as a reference to my behavior earlier, but I ignored it. Her eyes followed me as I stepped forward, into the light cast from her open door.

Electricity crackled between us, and the air felt thick. Her eyes moved over my body. I'd looked at her like this before, but she'd never dished it back until now. In my sweatpants, my cock woke up. This time, I didn't try to keep it down. She was welcome to look if she wanted.

Her glittering eyes moved lower. Her brows shot up and her full mouth parted.

"Oh my," she whispered.

I wasn't wearing anything but sweatpants, and I was at full mast, every part of me visible through the fabric. There was nothing to be done about it—trying to cover up would only make things worse.

Instead, I sighed and took another drag off my cigarette.

"It's got a mind of its own," I said lightly.

She swallowed, slender throat bobbing. God, I wanted to get my teeth on that. Bruise up her perfect skin, maybe hold the soft flesh between her neck and shoulder with my teeth while I fucked her from behind.

She was perfect, draped in satin, and I wanted to fuck her up tonight.

I leaned on the balcony railing until we were a foot apart. Below us, the lodge staff moved about, getting things ready for the night. She glanced over the edge and bit her lip.

Then, she bent forward. I couldn't lean in any further, but God— I'd do anything to just get a taste of her mouth.

Recklessly, I reached out, touching her chin and running my touch down her throat and up again. Heat shot through my arm and tingled down my spine. Her breasts heaved, and the outline of her nipples appeared.

Her heart had to be pounding. I could make out the pulse of a vein beneath my fingers. Our eyes locked together like magnets, and I couldn't pull away.

Her chin dipped as she gently nuzzled her face into my palm.

Fuck me.

I was going to come in my pants from her touching my hand.

It was my turn to have a heart pounding out of control. Her lashes fluttered, those dreamy, dark irises flashing up at me. Then, she turned her head, and her soft lips touched my fingertips.

They parted. Hot breath seared my skin.

The soft wetness of her tongue enveloped my two fingers, pulling them in to the first knuckle. My vision flashed—I was having some kind of out of body experience, not unlike the one I'd had when I first touched my mouth to her pussy.

Her tongue was so soft as it wrapped around my fingertips. Her hand came up and encircled my wrist, keeping me still as she pushed them in a little further. Our eyes locked, and she started sucking them like she had my cock in her mouth—gentle, dipping her head, even pressure, using that sweet tongue up the underside of my fingers and curling it around the tips.

"Stop," I managed.

She paused, blinking up at me.

"Unlock your fucking door," I said, straightening.

She froze, breasts heaving. I stabbed out my cigarette and walked into the room, pulling the doors and curtain shut behind me. I turned the handle of the door between our suites, and it swung open. She stood on the other side, eyes huge.

I was sleeping with this woman tonight.

Fuck the mission, fuck everyone's expectations. For one night, there was going to be nothing in the world but these two rooms and the door that connected them.

"Your bed or mine?" I said hoarsely.

"Yours." Her voice was barely audible.

My hand snaked around her waist, and she gasped as I pulled her inside, slamming the door with my foot. Then, she was in my arms, her legs around my waist as I carried her across the floor and fell with her onto my bed.

Her hair pooled dark around her face. Her breasts heaved, the only sound our heavy breathing.

I ran my hand over her body, barely grazing her skin. She moaned softly, and her hips rose, working in a hungry gesture beneath me, begging me to get my tongue between her soft thighs.

"Are you on the pill?" I whispered, tangling my fingers in the silk.

She panted something I didn't hear, but honestly, I wasn't listening. I pulled aside her gown, exposing the most perfect breast I'd ever seen: full and teardrop shaped, big enough to rest comfortably in my hand.

Her skin was pale beige, green and blue veins spreading out like little rivers. I bent and flicked the tip of my tongue over her pink and brown nipple, tasting the floral bittersweetness of her body lotion. It left a little shimmer on her breast that mingled with the wetness left behind by my mouth.

God, she was so everything I wasn't. That feral desire to dirty her up returned with a vengeance.

"What did you say?" I murmured, dazed.

"I said, I'm on the pill," she moaned as I licked her nipple again.

"Just for tonight, we're gonna pretend you're not."

I pulled the other side of her dressing gown, exposing her other breast, as perfect as the first. She gave a little whimper. I lowered my mouth and sucked in slow pulses, getting it hard with the tip of my tongue before grazing it with my teeth.

"What does that mean?" she whimpered, writhing with each flick of my tongue.

Her nails dug into my shoulders, raking down my chest. I didn't bother to lift my head; I just kept licking and nipping her breast.

"It means I like pretending you're not," I murmured between bites.

"You like pretending you're trying to get me pregnant?" she panted. Her hand came up and wound in my hair, nails piercing my scalp.

"Yeah, what's the problem?"

"There's no problem," she moaned. "I just didn't see that one coming."

I sank my teeth into her soft flesh, and she yelped, her palm contacting my forehead, pushing my face off her breasts. Our eyes locked, and triumph flooded through my chest.

This was the same, demure woman who'd sat opposite me in the meeting room today, elegant shoulders straight, not a hair out of place.

Now, she was on her back, naked down to her navel, wet hair splayed on the bedspread, no makeup and dark eyes glittering with desire.

I shifted, getting on my hands and knees over her. Her gaze flicked over me, and she bit her lip hard.

"I've been tested," I said.

"Maybe you should wear a condom anyway," she whispered.

I reached down, tugging aside the rest of her clothes, leaving her body completely exposed from her teardrop breasts, down the line of her abdominals, to the little V where her thighs clenched to cover her pussy.

"Maybe I shouldn't," I said distractedly.

"Oh God," she moaned softly. "You're so hot when you're horny."

I bit back my laughter as her hips rose, seeking friction. I shifted lower, and her naked pussy pushed against the ridge of my cock. The only thing between us was the thin fabric of my sweatpants.

Recklessly, I reached down and shoved the waistband below my cock. She froze, and our eyes locked.

"Is it out?" she whispered.

It took everything I had not to laugh. She was nervous, I could see it in how she gnawed at her lower lip, biting it raw.

"You can look, butterfly," I said softly.

She pushed herself up on her elbows, and her pink tongue flashed, wetting her mouth as her eyes stayed glued to mine.

"You know you want to," I whispered. "Go on."

CHAPTER THIRTEEN

CIRCE

I hadn't realized how horny I was until I looked down and saw him on his knees over me with his cock out.

God, he was gorgeous, every tattooed, muscled inch of him. His cock was big—much bigger than I'd expected for some reason, maybe so big it looked a little painful. The dark hair on his groin was neatly trimmed. I skimmed my eyes up his length, and my brows rose as I got to the tip, hard and slightly curved upwards.

I blinked. He had a...well, that was unexpected.

"What's that?"

He ran his lean fingers down to the head. "It's a piercing. Why so surprised? You've got one."

I shook my head, a tingle going all the way down to my clit. His piercing looked so different from mine—mine was tiny, just big enough to clip a charm onto. His was a thick ring running through the opening of his dick and out the underside, the perfect place to hit my G-spot. It was so distracting I barely noticed the tattoos around the base and under the hair on his groin.

My stomach swooped.

I'd wanted to feel him inside so badly, I couldn't keep myself from rubbing on him, but now, I needed to explore him more than anything. I pushed myself up on my knees and reached out...hesitating and looking up for approval.

"Go on," he said.

His cobalt gaze churned like dark water. The lean muscle down his stomach quivered and tightened. I swallowed—was my mouth watering? When my hand wrapped around his hot base, his head fell back.

A soft groan escaped his lips, and knowing I was the cause of it sent a rush of heat down my stomach to my thighs. My hips shifted, and a bit of wetness slipped down the inside of my left thigh. For some reason, that sensation jerked me out of the moment.

"Caden," I whispered.

He lifted his head, meeting my eyes. The air between us felt fragile, like fine blown glass threads connected our bodies. Like if we made the wrong move, we'd shatter something precious.

"Should...we do this?" I managed past my dry throat.

"It's just sex," he said, his voice oddly hoarse.

For some reason, I didn't believe him. It wasn't just sex for me—it was that first night in his kitchen, all the times I'd glanced at him and he was already looking at me. It was the way he'd driven me home when I couldn't drive myself and walked back to the city. It was the way he'd grabbed my waist the second he felt my fear outside the rest stop.

It was the way we were somehow tuned into each other without meaning to be.

He was everything I couldn't have.

The exact opposite of who my father wanted me with.

And yet, I couldn't deny that the moment I'd laid eyes on him in that bar, my carefully curated world started to crack.

But I couldn't admit that to him, not when we were both at odds, on either side of two worlds that could never intertwine.

So, I shook my head. "Just sex," I repeated.

He leaned in, gently pushing me down onto my back. His lower body settled over mine, his hard cock digging into my thigh as his hot breath washed over my face.

My heart increased, far faster than when I'd seen his dick. He was going to kiss me with that perfect, sculpted mouth.

My eyes fluttered shut.

His lips brushed mine. They parted...and oh God, the heat and taste of him spilled through my mouth.

The rest of the world evaporated. His mouth pressed to mine, opening to let me moan into it. My hand slid up his smooth back and gripped the hair at the nape of his neck. My legs curled around the backs of his thighs and pulled him close.

The tip of his tongue swiped mine, tasting like the possibility that he could ruin my entire life. I opened my mouth, too drunk on him to do anything but invite him in. Not one brain cell was working in my head, but every other part of my body was alive, welcoming him in for more, begging him to ruin me.

I had to have him.

"Inside," I gasped, snapping my eyes open.

He kissed the side of my throat. "What?" he murmured.

"Explore later," I panted. "Just put it in now. Please."

I wasn't sure how this was going to work. He was huge, and I hadn't had sex in a while, but that wasn't stopping us. He trailed kisses down to my collarbones, lifting his hips so he could reach between our bodies. The hot head of his cock pushed against my soaked opening. The muscles in his lower back rippled, and a little spark of pain moved through my hips.

"Hold on," I gritted.

He paused, dark gaze flicking over my face. "You're not...you've done this before?" he asked hoarsely.

Heat washed over my face. "Yes, I'm just...out of practice."

"How out of practice?"

"Five years," I admitted.

"I don't have lube," he said. "I wasn't expecting to have sex."

I shook my head. "I'm very wet. I just need patience."

He bent in, nuzzling my neck. "I can do that."

His hips moved closer, and the head of his cock stretched me a little more, then more...until it slipped inside.

We both gasped, our bodies going perfectly still. Something sparked very far off in my mind—or my body. It was hard to tell, like a part of me had been in the dark for a long time and his touch lit a match.

"You...." I whispered.

"Yeah," he said.

"It's just...."

"I know," he said huskily.

There was no extra room, but it didn't hurt. Pure electricity ran through where our bodies joined, like a live wire. He pushed deeper, and I felt the piercing slide up my sensitive muscles. Not precisely; it was more a general feeling of there being something inside me that felt good.

My clit throbbed as he settled in me, sheathed to the hilt. There was definitely some pressure up against my cervix, but not enough that it hurt. Or maybe he was keeping some of his weight off me.

My body tingled and buzzed. My acrylic nails dug into his back until the muscle in his jaw twitched. He pulled back an inch and thrust in slowly. To my surprise, I loosened, and my stomach swooped.

Oh, that felt good.

He swept his eyes over me, lifting his hand and cupping my breast. His thumb had a little tattoo on it I'd never noticed before now. I couldn't tell what it was, because he started using that thumb to circle my nipple and I forgot all about it. Pleasure surged, and I clenched down on him.

The corner of his mouth jerked up. This time, it wasn't arrogant.

"That's a good girl," he said, voice low.

My jaw went slack. Something about the way his heavy-lidded eyes fixed on me as he said it—cock still buried deep inside—felt so...honest. Like for the first time since we'd met, there wasn't any bullshit between us.

My lips cracked, and my hands skimmed down his side and around his chest, resting on his firm pecs where he had a smattering of dark hairs. My thumb lightly caressed the faint raised ink of his tattoos.

"Say that again." My words tumbled out in a rush.

"Good girl?" He cocked his head.

I nodded, pushing down my embarrassment. He shifted his hips, withdrawing almost all the way. I tensed involuntarily as he pushed back in despite how soaked I was. My spine arched, and his hand came down, gripping my upper thigh and lifting my hips to give his cock more room.

He bottomed out, and my eyes rolled back.

"Fuck, that's a *good* girl," he said, voice rasping.

"Oh God," I whimpered.

He braced his other hand on the bed and his abs rippled. He was in ridiculously good shape, and the control he had over his body amazed me. Even as someone who did yoga every morning, I didn't think I could hold myself up with one hand, someone else's hips with the other, and thrust with perfect precision.

His lips parted, elation moving through his eyes as I gasped. He knew what the fuck he was doing, there was no doubt about it. I'd expected that to some degree, but not like this.

I'd never guessed it would feel like this.

I bit my lip, the desire to be loud overwhelming me. When I was dating my first boyfriend, he'd dropped an offhand comment that I made too much noise in bed. After that, I was sure to keep it down to ladylike sighs and a little moan here and there. The last thing in the world I wanted was for Caden to tell me to be quiet.

"Does it feel good?" he panted, withdrawing halfway.

I nodded, eyes rolling back as he pushed in again.

"Can you take it hard?"

His heavy eyes were hungry, taking over my body, lingering on my breasts, my hips, down between my thighs to the wet ring on my clit.

I nodded, although I wasn't sure.

How hard was hard for him?

He pulled out and flipped me over, so hard and fast that the wind was knocked from my lungs. Before I could manage to protest, he gripped my wrist and placed my hand on the headboard. My heart skipped a beat.

Oh, this wasn't sex. I was getting *fucked.*

His breath burned the back of my neck. He released my hand, and I started to draw back, but he clicked his tongue.

"Better keep that there, sweetheart," he said.

There was an undercurrent of darkness in his voice, so I obeyed, face flushed. He slapped me hard across the ass, sending a jolt of pain that went all the way to the soles of my feet, making my toes curl.

"You'd better fucking behave, Johansen," he growled.

Arousal surged between my legs, and I swore, I dripped down my leg. No one talked to me like that. No one ever handled me like this—rough, like he knew I could take it.

He pushed in, and I could tell he was holding back.

"Fuck, you're soaked," he hissed from between his teeth.

I started to nod, but he gripped my hips with both hands and slammed into me. My mouth fell open, and I forgot to be quiet. A yelp followed by a moan burst out, and he purred, like a growl deep in his chest.

"That's more like it," he said, working his hips. "Don't hold back. I'm going to make you fucking scream."

He slammed into me again, the force shoving the bed into the wall. Whoever was on the other side of the wall could definitely hear us. I just hoped they couldn't hear the embarrassing whimpers coming from me, or his heavy breaths and the low moans rumbling through his chest on the instroke.

His long, tattooed fingers slid up my side and ran down my lower belly, slipping over my clit until he found the little silver piercing. He groaned, sinking down until his other hand covered mine on the headboard. His lean stomach curved against my back, his warmth heavenly.

We both froze as he explored my clit with his finger and thumb, feeling the piercing all slippery with my arousal.

"Why'd you have this done?" he breathed.

In my delirious state, it didn't occur to me to lie. "I wanted to rebel, but it had to be a secret. It's silly, but I like it."

He hummed, pumping his hips just enough so the steel bar rubbed my front wall, and my eyes rolled back.

"Not silly," he said. "It's sweet."

Sweet wasn't the word I'd expected. "What do you mean?"

His fingers moved over my clit, stroking it so gently, I felt every rotation. My thighs shuddered and my knees almost gave out, but his grip on my hand tightened, keeping me in place so he could pump into me as he plied my clit.

"I noticed the charm on it the first time," he breathed. "I remember pulling your panties to the side and thinking it was sweet."

I'd turned that memory over and over in my head. I'd caught my breath as he dropped to his knees, hooking his thumb under the wet fabric of my panties.

The muscle in his jaw had twitched. He'd cocked his head, lips parting.

Like he saw something he liked.

Breathlessly, I'd watched as he leaned in and curled his tongue around the little bow charm and sucked.

All at once, it was too much.

I jerked back to the present, where I was drowning in him. The gentle caress of his piercing. The memory of his mouth between my legs that night. The smell of him, the lean hotness of his body against mine, inside me.

My pussy tightened, and I felt something roll in like a storm, less of a rumble and more of a volcanic eruption.

"Oh God," I burst out. "I'm going to—oh!"

My body shuddered as an orgasm hit me like a tsunami. My legs gave way, and he caught me and sat back on his heels, still inside me, still holding me against his chest. His hips pumped slow and steady, rubbing that steel bar up against my G-spot as I came.

"Fuck, that's it," he moaned. "That's my girl."

His lean hand ran up my stomach, between my breasts, and clenched around my throat, applying even pressure to the side of my neck as his hips worked, rubbing that exact spot. I couldn't move even if he wanted to let me. I just lay against his hard chest and shook.

Something ran down the inside of my thigh. He moaned softly as he rode my orgasm out, not speaking, barely breathing, just fucking me through it, holding me close until the last ebbs of pleasure were wrung from my body.

He shifted, withdrawing and pushing all the way back in. "That's good, fuck...you did so good for me."

My brain was a clean slate. My mouth made a spent, desperate sound, like a strangled moan. He pulled free, releasing a gush of wetness onto the bed. Mortified, I stared down at it.

I had done that.

No, he'd made me do that.

His tattooed fingers tightened, his mouth dragged down the side of my throat, and against my thigh, his cock twitched.

"Gonna fuck your pussy hard now, butterfly," he murmured.

I whimpered. He didn't stand on ceremony. Before I could react, he flipped me onto my back and pushed a pillow under my hips. His eyes burned, his throat flushed. A trickle of sweat etched down the hard line of his abs. My thighs trembled as his fingers dug into them, pulling me close.

He pushed back inside, and I cried out. My pussy was so sensitive from my orgasm that I could feel every inch of his cock as he entered me. He seated himself, bracing his hands on either side of my head. Our eyes locked, his dark and dangerous, mine stained with tears.

"My pussy," he rasped.

Shock moved out like a ripple as my dry lips parted. "Not...yours."

"Tonight it is," he said, his voice dropping until it was almost a growl. "Tonight, you're my slut, Circe, and I'm going to fuck you until you're pregnant."

Heat moved like a wave over my face. Prickly sweat broke out between my breasts. Was it bad that I was turned on by that?

"What?" I whispered.

He struck my thigh, sending pain stinging down to the sole of my foot. His eyes were serious. "I'm going to fill your tight cunt up with my cum, get you knocked up. Make you mine."

Never in a million years did I imagine that Caden Payne had a breeding kink. I was aware of what that meant, but not what it would look like in action. I swallowed hard, my throat dry, and nodded once, unsure what I was signing up for.

He pumped his hips, pressing me back against the bed. My hips bent back over the pillow, giving him the last bit of space. He was so deep, it hurt, but it was a sweet, pleasant ache that made me feel so full, I had to bite my tongue to keep quiet.

He dragged his cock out and thrust. "That good, sweetheart?"

I nodded, my fingers digging into the sheets. He bent, and his lips grazed mine.

Fuck, he tasted so good that any shreds of reservation melted. I parted my lips for him and let him consume my breath, kissing me like he'd never tasted anything as good as my mouth and tongue.

A ripple moved through his body as his heavy lids fluttered.

"You're going to take my cum," he breathed. "You're going to be a good girl and take it all in your pussy."

I couldn't do anything but whimper, but that was enough for him. His hips sped up, rutting into me so hard, the bed shook. The distant, heavy expression he always had in his eyes disappeared. Replacing it was hunger, sharp, like a predatory animal.

"Fuck," he gasped.

His spine arched, and my legs locked around his lower back, instinctively pulling him into my deepest point. He groaned and collapsed, catching himself at the last minute. His face buried against my neck, and his hips shuddered.

I felt it—I felt the distant warmth, the twitch, inside me.

The world spun around us. My fingers smarted from digging at the sheets.

He released a slow breath, pushing himself up so he could look me in the eyes.

"Honestly," he said hoarsely, "I usually last longer."

We both laughed awkwardly, breathlessly. He disengaged his hips and pulled from me, sending a little hint of pain through me. I started to push myself up, but he planted his hand on my stomach and pushed me back down.

"No, you keep that inside," he said firmly.

I wasn't sure if I was turned on or mortified. He peeled himself from the bed and grabbed the cigarettes from the desk by the window. His pants were on the floor, and he put them on before unlatching the balcony door. My head felt light, my legs made of water.

He lit a cigarette and stood in the open door, that heavy stare back in place, lean body looking like a Greek sculpture in the doorway. I turned my head, and our eyes met. The air crackled between us, and the silence felt loud.

"I'm...I guess I should go," I whispered.

He took a slow drag, expelling the smoke through his nose. "You hungry?"

Surprisingly, I found I was starving. I pushed myself up against the headboard, and this time, he didn't stop me. Between my legs, I felt his cum trickle out and soak into the bed.

I hoped, in the depths of my soul, that my birth control held up.

"Yeah, I could eat," I whispered.

He stabbed out his cigarette and went to get his shirt. I couldn't keep my eyes to myself as he pulled it on, drawing it down over that lean stomach. The faded crossed tire irons flashed at me before he adjusted his neckline.

Those meant something to him. I could tell.

"Where are you going?" I asked.

He paused by the door. "I'm getting you something to eat."

I bit my lip, confused. "Why?"

A line appeared between his brows. "Because I fucked you. I might be an asshole, but I'm not going to fuck you and kick you out without at least feeding you."

I nodded, still so stunned, I couldn't formulate a full sentence. He left, and I heard his footfalls die away in the hall. Slowly, I got to my feet and went to the bathroom.

I was a mess, damp hair tangled. There must have been some mascara left on my lashes, because it was smudged under my eyes. My lower lip was pink with a little bite mark.

I grabbed a handful of tissues and braced one knee on the edge of the tub. Wetness was smeared on the inside of my thighs. It smelled like him. Gently, I reached down and ran my finger over it. There was no one to see me, so I could do exactly what I wanted.

Quickly, I licked the tip of my finger.

Salty, clean, a little soapy.

Between my legs, my pussy pulsed, and more of him slid down my thigh. My stomach swooped and my heart fluttered. There was something so primal, so satisfying, about having part of him inside me.

I bit my lip, letting my head fall back.

This man was going to be my downfall.

CHAPTER FOURTEEN

CADEN

My pulse was going crazy as I walked back to my room with a to-go bag. The bar only served pub food this late, so I ordered two burgers with griddled onions and an extra-large serving of fries. Hopefully, the Johansen Empire heiress would deign to eat greasy food like the rest of us plebeians.

She was sitting in bed, wrapped in her dressing gown again. Her dark gaze darted to my face, like she was trying to gauge my mood. She lifted her hand and chewed nervously on her thumbnail. I'd never seen her look shy before, and it was strangely attractive.

So she did have some vulnerability behind her perfect armor.

I set the boxes on the bed, pushing a throw blanket beneath. She tentatively reached out and flipped the lid open. Her brows arced.

"Not good?" I asked.

She shook her head hard. "No, I just haven't had a burger in ages. I'm so fucking hungry."

The words came out in a desperate rush. I pulled off my shirt and sank down beside her.

"If you want a burger, just have your private chef make you one," I said wryly. "You can have anything you want."

Her brows scrunched. "I'm not a spoiled asshole, for your information."

"And I'm not an incompetent dick," I said.

Her jaw went slack. "What?"

"At breakfast. Remember, you said I wasn't equipped for meeting with Galt?" I said.

"You're still hanging onto that?"

"It was presumptuous."

She was so flustered, she couldn't speak. A little bit of triumph flickered in my chest as she picked up one of the burgers and flipped the top. Her stomach growled audibly, so I reached over and closed the bun, pushing it towards her mouth.

"Eat the food," I said. "You earned it."

Her brow cocked. "I earned it?"

"Yeah, you were a pretty good girl."

She was speechless. Without thinking, I leaned over and kissed her, right on her open mouth. And because I was already fucked, I went all in and gave her some tongue too, swiping it against the tip of hers, forcing her to taste me.

I pulled back, but her hand shot out, gripping my jaw to pull me back to her lips. My stomach flipped, my dick going rock hard. The dark hunger that had flooded me the first time I tasted her came roaring back.

I slid my hand up her neck, not a thought in my head, and gripped her in place, tightened my fingers until she gasped into my mouth.

God, I wanted to leave my teeth marks on her silky skin. I wanted to send her back to her desk in her ivory tower with my handprint on her ass.

Our lips broke apart, and her eyes glittered, dark and wide.

"I'm...I'm wet," she whispered.

Her words went straight to my groin. "I know, I just came in you."

She shook her head once. "No, I'm just wet. I need to be fucked...again."

The covers rustled, our feet hitting the ground. Our bodies collided against the wall as the lamp beside the bed swayed and crashed to the floor. My frantic fingers tore at her dressing gown, shoving it off her shoulder and baring one perfect breast.

She pushed the front of my sweatpants down, her hand wrapping around my cock, and my hips stuttered as she stroked me hard and fast.

"Fuck, you're so big," she panted. "Inside me. Now."

The corners of my mouth jerked up. "Yes, ma'am."

Her legs wrapped around my waist, and I thrust all the way in, sliding my sensitive cock into the soft heat of her cunt. Her nails raked over my shoulders, breaking the skin on my upper back. Our eyes locked, and I slammed her up against the wall so hard she yelped.

"You can take it, sweetheart," I murmured. "You wanted fucked. I'll make sure you're fucked."

Her arms wrapped around my neck and her spine arched against me. "God, yes," she panted.

I thrust hard, and our bodies thumped against the wall, probably giving our poor neighbors entertainment they hadn't requested. Right now, I'd have fucked her on the balcony in front of everyone if it meant I could make her feel like this again.

Fuck all the back-and-forth bullshit. I could put up with a lot, working with this woman, if she let me fuck her like this at night.

The wall shook. Our panting breaths filled the space. Neither of us had the presence of mind to say anything. I sank against her and pushed my fingers between us to find her swollen clit. Her lips trembled, and her stomach quivered as I stroked her, teasing and fucking my cock into her until she gave a short, hoarse cry.

"That's right, come on my cock," I breathed.

"Fuck—Caden," she wailed, hips shaking as her pussy pulsed around me.

My brain went beautifully quiet. It never went quiet like this—it was always loud and messy and chaotic. But when she cried out my name, all the static and bullshit turned off like a light switch.

My body slowed.

I was fucked. I couldn't stop doing this, not when it made me feel like I was healed. I couldn't skim a little off the top and be satisfied.

No, I needed to drown in her, to sink to her deep end and break the surface reborn.

The problem was, we were co-workers, with more than a little rivalry mixed in. This shouldn't have happened.

I'd fucked up when I ate the red half of her gummy worm. We'd both felt the air crackle between us. And now, I was balls deep inside her, hand on her throat, with nothing in my head but the desire to spend forever right here.

"Caden," she whispered.

We both went still, our faces almost touching.

"What?" I whispered back.

She shook her head once, gnawing on her lip. "You just went somewhere for a second."

"No, I'm right here," I said, my voice hardening. I thrust once, hitting her against the wall. "In your cunt."

Her nails dug in, and I fucked her deeper. My orgasm sparked and chased down my spine. A groan worked its way from behind my teeth as I came again. I worked my hips, trying to get it all into her deepest point. I wanted her wet with it, sore from it.

Our bodies went slack.

Her eyes were wide as she reached down, and my dick twitched when she touched the base, stroking over me with her soft fingertips.

"You still hungry?" I whispered.

She nodded. "Starving for food, but otherwise satisfied."

"Glad I could accommodate."

I set her down, pulling free of her soaked pussy. She walked with a little hitch in her step back to the bed and sank down. Her hair was a mess down her back, and I ran a hand over mine, slicking it back with sweat. Her eyes lingered on me as I tugged my sweatpants up and sat down beside her again.

"Go on," I said.

She picked up the burger. "Sorry if I gross you out. It's hard to eat a burger and be clean."

I laughed. "Why the fuck do you care, sweetheart? I just fucked you raw and came in you twice. Who cares what either of us look like?"

Her eyes narrowed, and she sank her teeth into the burger. Sauce dripped down her chin as her lids fluttered and she groaned, shoulders sinking. She chewed, swallowed, and shoved another large bite into her mouth.

Fuck, she was hungry.

"Don't eat a lot of burgers?" I said, reaching for my fries.

She shook her head, taking another bite as I ate my food in silence. It was good, but not the best I'd ever had. When we got back, I'd probably do something reckless, like take her to my apartment and make her a burger. Maybe fuck her in my bed once or twice before dinner to make sure she was satisfied all around.

My head wasn't quiet anymore. It was roaring, whirling with confusion.

She finished her burger and started eating the fries, dipping them in the sauce pooled in the bottom of the box.

"You're hungry," I said quietly.

She froze, lifting her head. "What?"

My mouth felt dry. "You're hungry from being kept in that ivory tower. You need food, a lot of it, and to be fucked until you can't walk."

Her lids lowered like she was disdainful, but her expression didn't match the pink flush up her throat.

"I suppose you think you're the person to feed me," she whispered.

"I could."

"But?"

She tensed as I leaned in closer. "Sweetheart, I can feed you so good, you'll never be hungry again."

She didn't know what to say to that, but I saved her from trying to figure it out by cupping her right breast, sliding my hand under her dressing gown and stroking her hard nipple. Her hips jerked, and her lids flickered.

"You want to feel something, sweetheart?" I murmured.

127

Her eyes rolled back. "Yes…I think so."

My fingers curled in silk, crushing it, ripping it open.

"Nobody has to know." My hand skimmed down her side and gripped her hip, kneading the soft flesh hard enough to bruise. "You can still be all pretty, perfect, sit in your office with your flowers and shit."

"Hyacinths," she whispered.

"I know what they are," I murmured. "You can be pretty and perfect all day, but after you're done with meetings, after you lock up that boardroom, I want you in my bed."

She was too distracted to speak. Her eyes followed my mouth, entranced.

"That's just not realistic," she said.

Considering what we were doing right now, it seemed pretty realistic to me.

"I mean it, Circe," I said.

She shook her head. "No, thank you."

I bent in, kissing the side of her soft neck. "Tell me that again after I fuck you through this mattress one more time."

CHAPTER FIFTEEN

CIRCE

I slept better than I had in years. Around nine, I woke with a tender ache between my legs. My fingers skimmed down and stopped on my lower belly, pressing just enough to feel that I was sore inside too. It was no wonder he was proud of himself; he'd railed me so hard last night, I would be feeling it all day.

My stomach churned. Last night was an enormous mistake. That was clear to me now, but I couldn't get myself to feel regret. The listlessness I was so used to that it felt like a permanent fixture had eased when I was with him. Maybe it was just hunger, and finally eating something heavy had satisfied it.

But I doubted that.

I dragged myself naked out of bed and swayed on my feet. A little trickle etched down my thigh, clear and smelling faintly of him. My face went hot even though I was alone. My fingers traced over it and up to my breasts, rubbing it on my nipples.

Arousal flared and burned, quickly followed by shame that all it had taken was the sight of him shirtless on the balcony to make me cave.

If I didn't get it together, I was going to fail this mission.

I had to keep my eye on the prize.

Resolutely, I showered and washed away the traces of him from my body. I scrubbed my hair because his fingers had dug into it, and my body because his hand touched it, and between my legs because he'd marked me with his cum.

I had a meeting with Tennessee Galt in an hour, one that Caden didn't know about. I was going to seal the deal and have his approval for the Wyoming Project by noon.

In the dining room, I noticed something through the window the minute I sat down. Down in the yard, overlooking the forest on the south side, stood two figures—Caden and Tennessee Galt.

Caden was in his fatigues, arms crossed over his chest. His stance was different, relaxed and easy, the way I saw men converse in meetings or work parties.

The way they talked when I wasn't part of the conversation.

My body froze, my fingers on the back of the chair. Down below, I saw Galt laugh, and Caden held his hand out. They shook hands, and I sank into my chair, not wanting to see anything else.

He'd tricked me.

He'd fucked me so hard that I woke up late, feeding me the heaviest meal he could to keep me down even longer. Then, he'd gotten up early and sealed the deal without me.

Asshole.

Rage flooded my chest. The waitress appeared, and I barely remembered ordering breakfast, but it arrived. Scrambled egg whites, green juice, an oat milk latte, and a halved grapefruit. Wrathfully, I ripped the grapefruit open and began cutting it into smaller pieces, imagining I was doing the same to Caden's perfect, pierced dick.

He'd gotten the upper hand this time, but never again. I didn't need him to complete this fucking mission. We had two more signatures to get, and I was scoring both of them.

At that moment, my phone rang. My father's name appeared on the screen, and I lifted it to my ear.

"Hey, what's up?"

It sounded like he was in the kitchen. There was a faint echo. "I'm sending you the info about the next target," he said briskly. "How's this mission going?"

"Almost signed, sealed, and delivered," I said. "Where are we going next?"

There was a faint scuffle on the other end. It sounded like my father was covering the phone and talking to someone else.

"Are you busy?" I asked. "You can call me later."

"No, it's just the...bug exterminator," he said. "I'm at home."

I frowned. "We have bugs?"

"I thought maybe we did—I mean, we do, but not anymore," he said, his accent getting stronger.

It hit me all at once. Oh no, he had someone over at nine in the morning. "Hey, uh, just email me that info, okay?" I said quickly.

"Alright," he said. "Just please keep me updated."

I hung up with lightning speed and set the phone aside. Of course, I knew my father wasn't celibate, but he usually stayed in the city on nights when he took women out. That way, we never had any awkward moments where I walked into the kitchen and found a woman wearing his shirt. It was our unspoken rule.

Well, I was out of the house. He had every right to take his dates home. The thought that he wasn't alone at the house warmed me through the mortification. My father had been a widower for twenty-five years; he deserved his second chance at love.

Soft footfalls sounded, and I glanced up to find Caden slipping into the seat opposite me. My jaw went tight, and I sent him a hard stare.

"What?" he drawled.

"You made me sleep in," I snapped.

The corner of his mouth jerked. "No, you fell asleep in my bed at nine-thirty with a fry in your hand."

Humiliation made my cheeks pink. "You knew I'd sleep in."

"I did not," he said.

He sank down and crossed his arms, stretching his long legs out under the table. The toe of his shoe hit the toe of mine, and for some reason, that set off a flood of rage. I shot to my feet, grabbing my oat milk latte, spun on my heel, and flounced out.

I was almost in my room when I heard his footsteps. I whirled, blood boiling.

"Just fuck off," I said. "I know what you're doing."

He was standing with his arm at his side like he always did. I wondered if that was because he kept his gun strapped to that hip and he was a soldier through and through, always thinking of potential threats, or just because it made him look like an utter douchebag to always have one hand in his pocket.

"I am not sabotaging you," he said sharply. "You are wet behind the ears, Circe."

His voice rung out and, all at once, I knew why he was in charge of training soldiers. His stance was rock solid, cobalt eyes narrowed and unwavering. Even his jaw was cut like stone. He looked so fucking good, but I had no interest in that right now.

"What?" I gasped.

The muscle in his jaw worked. "Tennessee Galt went to a party last night. He's unmarried; he went home with someone, but he doesn't drink, so no chance of a hangover. She left early, he went golfing. It's a nice day, he just got laid—I struck when the iron was hot. You didn't. So swallow it and move on."

No one had ever spoken to me like this. Part of me wanted to lash out.

The other part wanted to release frustrated tears.

"How could you possibly know all that?" I snapped.

He took a step closer. "He divorced amicably ten years ago. That's easy to look up. I did some digging online and discovered he doesn't drink. Then, I paid off the bartender to text me if he left the party with someone. You were sleeping when I got up this morning, so I did a loop past his door, saw her leave, then saw him leave and head for the golf course. I got dressed and joined him, sealed the deal before the first round."

My fists clenched. My heart thumped, but this time with rage and embarrassment. He moved closer until he stood directly over me and bent, lids heavy and dark lashes stark against his cheekbones.

"I'm not cheating at this game, Circe," he said softly. "It's possible that I'm just more experienced than you."

He sidestepped me and kept going, disappearing down the hall and leaving me in shock.

I went into my room and slammed the door.

He didn't appear for the rest of the day. I wasn't sure where he was—probably off celebrating his victory somewhere. I ordered lunch, purposefully getting something he'd hate: steamed vegetables and fish. Then, I went down to the gym and took the three o'clock hot yoga class.

Every position stretched muscles he'd thoroughly used the night before, and when I stripped off later to shower, I noticed I had bruises on my hips and thighs. When had that happened? I couldn't remember. Wrathfully, I put on a sweatsuit and settled down to watch a movie for the rest of the afternoon.

My phone pinged. I swiped the screen, and a text from Delaney popped up.

You ignoring me?

Frowning, I swiped back. She'd texted me eight times about a dress I'd borrowed around eight-thirty last night, while I was getting my insides rearranged by the man I'd sworn up and down I hated. Guiltily, I typed out a quick answer.

Sorry, fell asleep early. Had a heavy dinner.

It only took a second for her to text back.

You? I doubt that.

Frowning, I typed: *I had a burger.*

I don't believe it. Were you having sex?

No. Of course not, why would you ask that? Who would I have sex with here anyway?

Her line of dots rolled for a solid minute. Then:

Idk, maybe Caden. I heard you were paired up with him for a work trip.

I frowned, typing rapidly. *How do you know Caden?*

He's best friends with Yale?? Hello, do you ever listen to me?

Sighing, I texted back: *Yeah, sorry, I forgot.*

133

He's hot, you should hit that, she texted.

My stomach flipped.

Absolutely not. Gross.

Gross?

Yeah, gross. He's got a massive ego.

I'll bet he's got other things that are also massive.

I rolled my eyes and laid aside my phone. I was so used to telling Delaney everything that if I kept texting her, I might spill the truth, and I didn't want anyone finding out that he'd fucked me.

Dinner time came and went, and I stayed in bed, wrapped in my plush comforter with another reality show droning in the background. I wasn't sure why I felt so depressed about this morning.

Maybe because he was right—I'd been presumptuous.

Maybe a little arrogant, and definitely dismissive.

He was good, I knew that now. He knew what he was doing, and he was efficient. Maybe he wasn't just an annoyance.

There was a quiet knock at the door between our rooms. I cleared my throat, glancing across the room at my reflection in the mirror. My eyes looked tired, my hair piled on my head, and I'd showered off all my makeup.

"Come in," I said wearily.

The door swung open to reveal Caden in sweats and a white-shirt, a brown paper bag in his hand.

"You didn't come down to dinner," he said.

I shrugged, staring past him at the TV. "I'm not hungry."

"Not even for a sandwich?"

I sighed but kept my eyes averted. His weight made the bed sink, and a flicker of annoyance moved through me that he was sitting beside me without asking. He sat there, completely still, waiting for me to break.

Finally, I couldn't stand it anymore—I reached out and peered in the bag. Inside were two white cardboard boxes that smelled amazing. My stomach flipped, and I glanced up, falling into the deepest blue gaze. There wasn't a trace of the stern anger I'd seen earlier when he'd given me a verbal dressing down.

"Is this a peace offering?" I asked.

His heavy lids flickered. "Think of it more as a pregame. I'm trying to get lucky."

I frowned. Of course he was just trying to get laid. I balled my fists and pushed myself up against the pillows, sending him a sharp glare. He ignored me, taking out a box and flipping the lid open. Inside was a grilled cheese and warm potato wedges. My stomach growled loud enough that he could hear.

Smirking, he picked up a wedge and put it to my lips.

"Open," he said quietly.

My lips parted, because it gave me a secret thrill when he talked like that. The taste of butter and parmesan and warm, fried potato filled my mouth. It took everything I had not to moan the way I had last night when I bit into that burger.

Mindlessly, I took a bite and chewed. The corner of his mouth jerked up, like he was so fucking pleased with himself. Fine, he could have this victory too. I took the box from him and burrowed into the blankets and pillows. He shifted so he was facing me and started eating.

"It's not bad to be green," he said.

"Green?"

"Inexperienced, wet behind the ears."

Brimming with quiet rage, I bit into my sandwich.

"I'm going to tell you something, and if you tell anyone, I will end you," he said.

That sparked my attention. I turned, taking in his stark gaze. He really was so handsome. He had big eyes, a beautiful facial structure with sharp cheekbones and a cut jaw, and the prettiest lashes I'd ever seen on a man. For the first time, I wondered if he knew it.

It was starting to dawn on me that there was more to him than met the eye.

"I'm good at people," he said finally. "I had to be. Things were pretty rough growing up."

I studied him, hoping he wasn't tricking me again. His face was completely serious, and that muscle in his jaw was tight, like he was struggling with something.

"What...happened?" I asked.

He shrugged once. "My mother didn't want my biological father in my life, so she never told him about me. My stepfather was a piece of shit."

I stayed quiet, afraid I'd fuck up and tell him I knew that Merrick Llwyd was his father. He set the sandwich down, pulling his knees up and resting his elbows on them. His shoulder muscles tightened, apparent beneath his thin shirt, and I swallowed, trying not to stare.

"I went to prison, the UK's version of juvie," he said after a long time. "Got out and was out for a month, just long enough to turn eighteen and get sent back for two years."

I hadn't expected that. For some reason, I'd assumed that because Merrick was wealthy, Caden's mother was privileged as well. Maybe he was right; maybe I'd judged him too harshly and too soon.

"You want to ask why?" he said softly.

I nodded, mouth dry.

The corner of his mouth jerked, but this time, it was just grim. "I beat my stepdad's ass."

A shiver tingled up my spine. "What...do you mean?"

"He put his hands on my mom constantly growing up," he said, his voice freezing over. "She died, overdosed when I was around fifteen. My stepdad was a piece of shit, but I didn't have a choice except to live with him. He swung at me one too many times one night, so I hit back."

My jaw was on the floor. "I'm so sorry," I whispered.

Darkness seeped into his eyes, like ink spilling into water. I felt his pain, like a silent chord reverberating deep inside him.

"That's when they arrested me," he said. "Then I got out, went to go get my stuff a month later. He was there, and he started...saying all this fucking shit about my mom. He pulled a gun. We were in the garage, and I just...I just flipped my shit. I was just done being his punching bag. I barely remember it, but I decided only one of us was going to walk away."

My heart thumped. My stomach felt raw.

"What did you do?" My voice came out in a croak.

He lifted his eyes, narrowed and dark. "I beat him with a tire iron until he didn't move. Then, I left."

The silence was so intense, I could hear the air conditioning units whirring outside.

"You...killed him?" I whispered.

He sniffed. "He died, yeah."

My stomach churned. I knew that the Welsh Mafia organization had different rules and ideas around killing, but it was just different staring the reality of it right in the face.

"You only got two years?" I managed.

"There were cameras in the garage; that's how they found out it was me," he said. "They caught him pulling the gun on me, and the judge ruled it self-defense but gave me two years because I had a record. It was confusing."

"If it was self-defense. There should have been no jail time, right?" I said.

He shrugged. "Honestly, it worked out. Prison was rough, but I had nowhere to go. I had a bed and three meals until I got my head together."

My hand was shaky as I reached out and hesitated, wondering if it was alright to touch him. He didn't lift his head, so I pulled back, tangling my hands in a knot.

He ran a hand over his face. "Anyway, that taught me to read people really well or risk getting the shit kicked out of me. So count yourself lucky that you can afford to be green."

He turned, shaking his head once, like he could just flick off those memories and move on.

"Anyway, eat before it gets cold," he said with a huff.

Obediently, I bit into my sandwich. His gaze fell to my mouth, and I had to force myself not to squirm. I wasn't used to being vulnerable in front of anyone. I rarely even let Delaney or Emmy see me without makeup. But here I was, with my hair in a messy knot, tired eyes, and a grilled cheese in my lap.

And he was looking at me like he was starving.

I swallowed hard.

"Sorry for assuming things about you," I whispered.

"It's fine," he said.

"You should...eat too. It's good."

His eyes stayed on my mouth. "I could...eat."

My heart was thumping so hard, I could hear it. "Eat what?"

His chest heaved. "You want me to make you feel good? You apologized for being presumptuous. Let me apologize for snapping at you."

Between my legs, my clit tingled.

"I'm not your friend," I managed. "We work together."

He set his food aside, shifting closer. "I'd like to maintain a good working relationship, even if you are a little...condescending."

"I am not."

"Tell that to yourself."

I gasped, and his hand shot out and gripped my hip, sliding quickly under my waistband to my bare skin beneath. With his other hand, he set my box aside and moved closer until he had me cornered against the headboard.

His eyes burned. "Let me eat your cunt, butterfly," he said. "I'm hungry for you again."

He had the dirtiest mouth, and I didn't have the presence of mind for a comeback. So I just nodded, and he dipped in close, his lips inches from mine.

His lids flickered before he leaned in and kissed me, hungry and moaning in his throat as our tongues brushed. His tattooed fingers pushed boldly under my sweatshirt and pulled it over my head, baring my breasts to the cold room.

He bent, flicking his tongue across my nipples as my eyes fell and locked on the faded tire irons.

Fuck.

How many more horrifying tattoos had he covered up?

I didn't have the time to think about it, because he pulled my sweatpants off, leaving me in a skimpy thong with a little pink bow on it.

Which he was...oh God, he was biting down on it and dragging my panties off my hips with his teeth.

I wriggled my thighs as the fabric dragged down, keeping them locked together to cover my sex. The tips of his fingers skimmed my calves, and goosebumps rose in their wake. My panties came away in his hand, crushed by his fist.

The same fist that had beat someone to death with a tire iron.

I swallowed hard.

That was self-defense. He'd protected himself.

His eyes locked with mine as he slid his palms over my knees. A bit of dark hair fell over his forehead. I hadn't noticed up until now, but the irises of his eyes changed color like the sky. Cobalt blue one minute, then drenched black with desire the next.

He bent and kissed my knee, and his lips burnt like a brand.

"Open up for me, sweetheart," he said softly.

Head empty and pussy even emptier, I obeyed. Why did I always want to obey him without question when he was like this? All broody and hungry and dominating. It turned my head and made me forget my own name.

It didn't hurt that I could see all those dark tattoos through his white shirt.

His lean fingers slid up my thighs, digging into the soft flesh. He kneaded gently as he went, and my muscles eased. My hips slid back, and he spilled me onto my back. The air left my lungs, the ceiling spun overhead, my thighs tensing as I hesitated. Then, I let his rough palm slide between my knees and open me to his gaze.

He'd seen me there before, but not like this.

Not with all the time in the world.

"Fuck," he said softly.

I let my eyes fall shut. The tension in the room from our earlier disagreement was replaced by a different kind of tension, the kind that had his breath moving fast enough that I heard it. That made me feel the soft sheet against my back, my hair tickling the back of my neck. That made me remember the pattern of the ceiling overhead and hear the soft rush of sprinklers outside my window.

He bent, and warmth washed over my sex. Then, so gently I barely felt it, he kissed the inside of my thigh.

My toes curled—I'd forgotten how good he was with his mouth.

My head spun. My fingers moved down of their own accord and slid into his black hair, stroking gently, my fingers guiding his mouth closer to the place where I ached for it most.

He paused, and disappointment welled in my chest. My eyelids cracked open, and I peered down. He was laid out between my legs, one arm under my thigh and the other braced on the bed. Instinctively, I brushed aside the hair on his forehead.

His eyes glittered. "I get to do this as long as I want. That's your punishment for doubting me."

That didn't sound like much of a punishment to me. If he was going to eat me, maybe I'd doubt him even harder next time. My mouth dry, I nodded, and his mouth cracked in a smirk.

"You hold on, sweetheart," he murmured. "I'm gonna put you to sleep again."

"You're awfully confident," I gasped, his mouth grazing just above my clit.

He didn't answer; he just curled his tongue over my clit and licked, long and slow, before pressing his mouth closer and sucking gently. My vision flashed, and my hips strained against his chin.

Oh God, I was right on the edge already.

He laughed, so deep in his throat that it was just a vibration. His tongue ran over my entrance, gathering all the wetness I couldn't hold back. He moaned lasciviously as he did, like I was the best thing he'd ever had.

My head fell back.

He touched the entrance of my pussy, and my head spun as the tips of two fingers eased inside me. I was still tender from what he'd done to me last night, and it made his touch all the sweeter.

His mouth brushed my thigh as his fingers slid deeper, giving me time to adjust.

I'd never imagined Caden Payne could be so gentle.

Heart fluttering, I reached between my thighs and slid my fingers through his dark hair. He dropped his mouth to my clit and moaned as I stroked him. His fingers moved, flipping so he could caress my front wall.

My eyes widened as they alighted on that spot.

"That's good," I gasped.

He moaned again, this time with a hint of desperation. It hit me that he liked this more than I'd anticipated. His fingers moved slowly and with even pressure as his tongue lapped over my clit, hitting the perfect spot to make my hips rise.

"That's it," I gasped. "Right there."

He loved it, I could tell in the way his other hand tightened on my hip like a quick reflex before it moved up over my lower belly and pushed gently, sending a surge of pleasure through my sex.

My orgasm coiled and burst. My spine locked, lifting me up so violently, he had to push me back down to keep me still. His fingers and tongue never stopped, and my breath came in short gasps, my head spinning, vision flashing. When I came down to earth, my entire body felt like water.

He lifted his head, nuzzling my inner thigh. "Ready for the next one?"

All I could do was whimper. I caught a glimpse of his smirk as he lowered his head. Then, it was happening all over again—the buildup, the rhythm of his tongue and fingers pushing me towards the edge, the explosion of pleasure, the whimpers, the sweat dripping from his forehead to my lower belly.

God, it felt beautiful and primal.

Like standing in a temple. In the still-cool early morning.

Watching the incense rise to the sky.

In my haze, I thought I felt what he longed for—a place that belonged only to the two bodies wound together in this bed. No fear, no pressure, no painful memories, no secrets.

Just two bodies, two souls.

The night wore on. He only resurfaced when I was so exhausted, I could barely speak. Then, he slid between my legs and into me. His beautiful body moved in a slow beat like a drum, washing against me like a wave on the shore, taking and giving with every stroke.

He finished and rolled me into his arms, keeping his cock inside me as we fell asleep tangled in the sheets.

CHAPTER SIXTEEN

CADEN

She got up early the next day—maybe just to prove she could—and I stood in the doorway between our rooms and watched her get dressed.

It felt incredibly intimate, but she didn't tell me to go.

Her cheeks were pink as she slipped on her yoga set. It looked so good on her, hugging her curves. I tilted my head and enjoyed the way she fussed with it in the mirror, tugging the bra and adjusting the waist, turning in a circle to make sure it laid flat.

She put on her sneakers and grabbed her suitcase, but I closed my fingers over the handle, pulling it from her grip. She froze, inches from me, dark eyes wide.

"I'll get that," I said.

She didn't protest as I walked her out to the car, and she didn't say a word when I opened her door and guided her in with a hand on her lower back.

Why was I feeling like this? Like she was mine or something? Maybe because it had been so long since I'd spent the whole night with a hookup. Or maybe because...she didn't feel like a hookup.

She felt like so much more.

We both kept quiet on the drive back. What we'd done the last two nights was a palpable presence, like a silent specter in the backseat.

Neither of us said a word when we parted.

I took the Kawasaki home, and Circe went to drop the report off to her father. It was late when I got back to my apartment after stopping by the empty training center to get my workout in. My body was still tense when I got on my Kawasaki to head home. Inside, I was coiled and restless, a caged animal.

I thought about staying up to watch TV, but my eyes were starting to ache. So I went home, took a sleeping pill because I didn't need a sleepless night thinking about Circe, and collapsed into bed.

The night felt like it was a hundred years long. I rolled fitfully. My feet hurt, my body ached. Slowly, I became aware I was waking up, but it was different than usual, like swimming through water towards a bright light.

My eyes opened, and my entire body went rigid. I was on a couch with a blanket that smelled of sweet perfume over my body. The ceiling overhead was unfamiliar.

I sat upright, heart thudding. I wasn't in my apartment or my bed anymore. Instead, I was on a couch in the center of an expensive, minimalist apartment that smelled faintly of flowers. To my left was a woman with her back to me, steam rising in a cloud from a glass teapot.

Circe?

No, not Circe. She turned around, and my jaw dropped. It was a slender, middle-aged woman with silvery blonde hair and slightly feline features.

"Gretchen Hughes?"

Somehow, I was in the living room of Merrick's therapist, the same one he'd begged me to start seeing for the last ten years. The same one who I used to tell Merrick I was going to fuck just to see him get riled up, back before I embarked on my mission to be less of a dick.

She offered me a motherly smile, leaning back against the counter. "How are you feeling, darling?"

My mind churned. I looked around, at a loss for what to think. "Did you—what the fuck is happening? How did I get here?"

She laughed, a tinkling sound. Then, she sobered and picked up the tray with the blooming tea and crossed the room. She laid it down before me and dusted her hands while I stared blankly at the tea and toast.

"Uh, what's going on?" I repeated.

She sank down on the coffee table, tucking her ankles. "You showed up at my door at three in the morning last night."

My stomach flipped. "I sleepwalked?"

She shook her head, pursing her lips. "You drove your motorbike here, darling. In your sleep, in just your sweatpants. So I put you to bed, but I haven't called Merrick, since I wasn't sure what you wanted."

"Fuck." My stomach dropped. "Fuck, that's not good."

She shook her head. "No, it's not."

We sat there in silence. The steam rising from the blooming smelled faintly of jasmine. Warm, pale sun fell through the windows. I'd never been in Gretchen's home office because, despite Merrick pleading with me, I'd refused to go to therapy.

But some part of me must have wanted this, deep in my subconscious, or I wouldn't be here.

Gretchen reached out and patted my knee. "I canceled my morning appointment. I think maybe we should talk."

I didn't protest this time. How could I when I'd just driven a motorcycle through Providence in my sleep? Clearly, I needed some kind of help.

"Eat your toast, darling," she said, standing and clicking across the floor in her heels.

I pushed aside the blanket and sat up against the back of the couch. Still numb, I obeyed. The toast wasn't bad, the bread tasting like it was fresh from the bakery, crunchy and buttery.

Gretchen returned, sinking down on the far end of the couch. She crossed one leg over the other and laid a legal pad on her thigh.

"You're not my therapist," I said.

"I'm giving you a freebie," she said, unbothered. "Take it like a good boy."

I laughed, my shoulders easing. "Yes, ma'am."

She smirked and fixed her eyes on me. "Alright, let's talk. I know Merrick has been trying to get you to come to therapy. I'm just not sure why he cares about you so deeply. It's more than just a work relationship. Are you willing to talk about that?"

My stomach froze.

I never told anyone I was Merrick's son. Maybe because I wasn't good at letting people love me, and everyone would see how I'd kept him at arm's length.

Or maybe because they'd doubt everything I'd done. They'd say the way I'd pulled myself up from rock bottom was nothing.

But more likely, it was because, deep down, I didn't think I deserved Merrick's love, and I wasn't ready to say that to myself, much less to anyone else.

So, I fell back on the nepotism card.

Merrick hadn't offered me my position as his right hand and training commander because I was his son. He'd offered it because I was top of every single class for the first five years, because I could beat the shit out of everyone in combat training, and because I knew weapons and was good at getting what I wanted.

I'd learned two things quickly growing up—how to read people and how to defend myself.

"Caden?"

My lips parted. "This is confidential, right? Even if it's just a freebie?"

She nodded. "Nothing you say goes anywhere. I will never share anything about you to Merrick or vice versa."

I cleared my throat, eyes on the floor, staring at the tip of her beige heel.

"Merrick's my father," I said hoarsely.

She made a note. "I thought so. Either that, or your uncle."

"Why?" I frowned.

"I've been his therapist for a long time. Your faces move the same."

I sighed, running a hand over my face. "I think sometimes people can tell, but they don't want to be the first to say anything."

She folded her hands, flicking the pen absently. "Why don't you want people to know?"

"I want to earn what I have," I said.

"I see," she said skeptically. "Do your peers respect you?"

I nodded.

"The men you train?"

"It seems like it."

"And you don't think that work you put in to earn respect will have staying power?"

I sighed. "I don't know."

Gretchen made a note. "Tell me how your childhood was in three words."

I didn't have to think about it. "Lonely. Painful. Violent."

Gretchen was a true professional. Nothing changed in her face—I could have been talking about the weather. "Can you tell me who the culprit was?"

I cleared my throat, and she pursed her lips.

"You'd like coffee instead of tea?"

"I'm more of a pour over and espresso guy."

"Like father, like son." She rose and busied herself in the kitchen. In minutes, the rich scent of coffee filled the sunny apartment. When she returned, she handed me a cup and sat back down, this time in the chair opposite me.

"Alright," she said briskly. "Who was it?"

"Stepdad," I sighed. "Mom, maybe some. I don't know. How do you blame an addict for their disease?"

"Many people do."

I shook my head. "I...can't."

"You love her," she said softly.

I cleared my throat again. "I loved her. She's gone."

"You love her even though she hurt you." Gretchen's voice felt thin, like fine threads.

I nodded, wordless.

There was a long silence. Then, Gretchen made another note. It bothered me that she kept writing down things about me, but that was her job, so I resolutely kept my mouth shut.

"Let's pivot," she said. "Have you ever received any formal diagnosis?"

I flexed my wrist. "I have some nerve damage in my left hand. Did physical therapy for it."

She smiled. "I meant a psychiatric diagnosis."

"No," I said firmly.

"I'd like to run you through a pre-evaluation test," she said. "Or two."

My eyes narrowed. "Why?"

She chewed her lip, thinking for a minute. "Has your father ever talked about his own mental health to you?"

I nodded. "I know you diagnosed him with adult ADHD and OCD. Also, I'd rather you called him by his name and not...by what he is to me."

"It's called exposure therapy, darling," she said, making another annoying note. "Anyway, Merrick's diagnosis is genetic. Your chances of inheriting ADHD are high, and even higher if your mother had it."

"Well, that fucks me, doesn't it?"

She nodded. "Forewarned is forearmed."

I laughed, but the sound was dry. "Alright, I'll take it."

My phone dinged, and I realized I must have put it in my pocket in my sleep. I pulled it out, and an email popped up from Gretchen. It was a single link, which revealed a thirty-five-page evaluation, single spaced.

"Holy shit," I said.

"Better clear that schedule today," she said brightly. "Now, I'd like to see you back here in a few days. How does Monday work?"

I stared down at the first question. The entire world went quiet— except for all the roaring I always had in the very back of my mind. The very first line stared back at me like it was the only thing in the world.

How often do you feel like you're a car in park with your foot pressing the gas all the way down?

I knew the answer to that: every minute of every goddamn day.

How likely are you to engage in risky behavior such as using drugs, driving too fast, or engaging in unsafe casual sex?

Ouch.

I lifted my eyes to Gretchen, who had a knowing look on her face.

"Monday works," I said grimly.

She rose and moved gracefully to the kitchen again. There was an iPad on the counter, which she swiped on to reveal a calendar. I got up too, adjusting my pants. I was a little uncomfortable that I was in her kitchen naked except for my sweatpants. Apparently, my sleepwalking brain hadn't considered underwear a necessity.

She turned around. "Would you like some steak and eggs?"

"Fuck, yes," I said. "I'm fucking starving."

She took a pan out, flipped it, and laid it on the stove. "Sleepwalking works up an appetite. Now, tell me what you think your worst trait is."

I balked. "Um...how can I pick just one?"

"Do your best." She took a pack of meat and an egg carton from the fridge. "Let me guess...you're a little on the rare side of medium rare?"

"Yeah," I said.

"Anyway, answer me, please."

"Are you asking my worst trait, or what I hate the most?"

"The latter, I suppose."

I blew out a breath. "I'm self-destructive. Anytime something good happens, I just get this urge to fuck up. I have to hurt myself or lose the thing that's making my life better."

"Why do you think that is?"

"Maybe I fucking hate myself, I don't know," I said. "Maybe I don't deserve good things."

She laid the steaks out, the pan sizzling. "But you know you're Merrick's best."

"I do," I said, touching my temple. "In here."

149

"You never thought to seek therapy for this," she mused. "Do you think you're addicted to your own pain? That you run off the fumes of it like an adrenaline high?"

My stomach twisted. There was an annoying lump in my throat. "I don't have anything else to drive me."

"You think your best comes from feeling like you're not enough," she said softly. "That's not an uncommon train of thought."

I swallowed. The steaks sizzled as she flipped them. "Can I smoke on your balcony?"

She nodded, reaching into the drawer by the stove and removing a pack of cigarettes and a lighter. I took them without speaking and crossed the room, pulling aside the glass doors. It was a balmy day outside, around nine in the morning. A dove cooed from the church rooftop down below, and the ocean glittered on the horizon.

I lit the cigarette and inhaled, holding it. Into my head came the last time I'd had a smoke: on the balcony, the most beautiful woman I'd ever met laying naked in bed behind me.

Circe.

In the distance, I could see the faint smudge of Johansen Enterprises. She was sitting in her office right now in a mauve pencil dress, the fabric hugging her body, with those tall fucking heels that I wanted over my shoulders tucked under her desk. There was probably soft harp music playing, and everything smelled like hyacinths.

My dick woke up at the mental image of her face. I glanced down, trying to think of anything else.

"Caden, how do you like your eggs?" Gretchen called.

"Over medium, please," I said. "Thanks."

Luckily, it took long enough for her to make the eggs for my dick to go back to sleep. I ducked back inside once it was behaving then stubbed out the cigarette in the sink and tossed it. She laid a plate in front of me, and my stomach twisted at the sight.

"Do you exercise obsessively?" she asked.

I glanced sideways, frowning. "You have an interesting style of therapy."

"It works for me."

"Why do you ask?"

She glanced over. "You're very lean."

I cut my steak, a little blood pooling on the plate. "Hitting on me, Gretchen?"

She laughed. "If I recall, you used to hit on me at parties, and I'd turn you down cold."

"Yeah, well," I said. "I turned over a new leaf."

I bit into the steak and my brows rose. She nodded, smiling.

"It's good," she said. "That's always a favorite with some of my late-night clients. Do you prefer sleeping with women older than yourself?"

I took another bite of steak, chewed it. "Yeah, I started fucking my neighbor when I was around eighteen. She was in her late thirties."

"What's your cut off?"

"I don't have a cut off, more like a preferred age. Maybe forties to fifties."

"Well, we'd never have worked. I like them older too."

"I think I was mainly trying to antagonize Merrick by hitting on you. I respect you, Gretchen."

The words felt forced, but I was really trying to be more honest, with myself and everyone else. She cut her steak primly but didn't answer for a moment.

"Do you need an apology for my past behavior?" I asked dryly.

She shook her head, giving me a look. "No. I'm just thinking about you because you're an interesting case. I haven't had anyone as complex as you in a while."

"Really?" I said. "Who was the last one?"

She took her time, eating a piece of steak and patting her lipstick with a napkin. Finally, she sighed. "Your father."

That wasn't what I wanted to hear. She could tell; I knew it because neither of us spoke while we finished eating. Then, she cleared the plates and brought me a plain white t-shirt and a pair of men's sneakers. I eyed them warily.

"Are these...from your ex or something?" I asked.

She shook her head. "I ordered them from the store when you showed up in just your pants. You can keep them, darling. Now, you have to go; my next appointment will be here soon."

I pulled the shoes and shirt on and left. She watched me from the door, her eyes narrowed in thought. I sank down on the Kawasaki, surprised to find I'd worn my helmet and hung it on the handlebar.

"Caden," she called. "Did you take a sleeping pill before you went to sleep last night, darling?"

"I did, actually."

"I'd say that's what happened, but don't sleep alone until you can figure this out," she called. "Call your father; he's got a spare room."

The thought of asking my father to watch me and make sure I didn't wander off sounded like hell. I nodded once, fitting on my helmet and kicking off the ground. I could feel her eyes on me, and it wasn't making me feel better that she hadn't had a case like mine since...Merrick.

Back at my apartment, I pulled the Kawasaki into the garage and headed upstairs. I'd shut the door but not locked it, which made my scalp prickle. I was meticulous about locking my front door.

I showered quickly, changed into my fatigues, and did a round of the apartment. Everything was in perfect order except for one thing: the back burner on the electric stove was on low.

My heart thumped, increasing in speed.

Fuck, I was going to set my apartment building on fire or wreck my motorcycle if I did this again.

I stood in the middle of the apartment staring blankly at the wall.

My phone rang, and I swiped it off, ignoring Yale's message asking where I was. He could wait. Right now, I needed to figure out how to get my ass safely through the night.

Maybe it was time to swallow my pride.

CHAPTER SEVENTEEN

CIRCE

The world felt different.

The morning after we returned from the lodge, I woke up with a start and lay on my back, just watching the ceiling with the strangest excitement in the bottom of my stomach.

I had slept with him.

It was *beyond* good, and I'd discovered a completely different person beneath all his armor.

Giddy, I sat up and padded to the window to push it open. The air was warm, the sun shone, birds sang in the orchard. For one, glorious moment, I forgot there was no world where Caden and I worked. Maybe one where we fucked in a montage, ate in bed all summer, swam in the ocean forever, but worked? No.

I shook my head hard.

There was no way we worked out.

I dressed, feeling especially beautiful in my short pencil skirt, towering heels, and blouse that showed off my bracelets and necklace. My stress was gone, wrung out by his tongue and fingers. The knots I usually had in my shoulders had dissipated.

It was a miracle. He'd fucked all the tension out.

I turned in a circle in the mirror. Relaxation looked good on me.

Down in the kitchen, I practically sailed through and grabbed a banana and a granola bar. My father was making himself an espresso and reading a file folder. I clipped past him and snatched his cup, taking a sip.

"Hi, I'm heading out for breakfast," I said. "Then I have some documents to file. I left all the paperwork in your office."

He sent me a long stare, a crease between his brows. "You're very chipper this morning."

I tossed my hair. "I'm always chipper."

"Not like this."

I shrugged, grabbing my things and emptying the espresso. "I'm just glad we got through the first part of the mission, and it went well."

He gazed at me thoughtfully. Why was he staring at me...like he wanted to say something else, but he was biting his tongue?

Was I missing something here?

"You okay?" I asked.

He nodded, pulling me in for a hug. I curled against his chest for a second, his chin rested on my head.

"You're doing great, honey," he said quietly. "And I need you to keep doing great, even if things change with this mission."

I pulled back. "What do you mean?"

He shook his head. "I just mean that sometimes, things change. I need to know you're always on my team."

Guilt surged through me. My mind went back to the two nights I'd spent with Caden. Technically, I hadn't done anything that was actual betrayal. I hadn't spilled company secrets or anything like that. All I'd done was have a little adult fun with a consenting, gorgeous, man.

It wasn't important that he was the son of my father's biggest competitor. I was perfectly capable of compartmentalizing.

"Well, I need to get going," he said. "You be careful."

"I always am." I kissed his cheek, and he gave me an affectionate squeeze before gathering his things and leaving.

Still a little guilty, I drove into the city and pulled up at the Vengeful Mermaid. The last time I'd had a meal here was...that awkward date with Damien.

Oops, I'd never texted him back. But then, he hadn't reached out either, so it must have been a mutual choice.

I stepped out of my car and clipped into the restaurant. Emmy and Delaney sat out on the balcony, both looking airy and made up in sundresses and aviators. Emmy waved as I crossed the room, and Delaney nodded. She seemed a little off.

I sank down. "I only have a few minutes."

Emmy rolled her eyes. "You always only have a few minutes."

"Enough for a mimosa?" Delaney cocked her brow, smiling for the first time.

"Maybe just a sip," I said.

We ordered, and Emmy started talking about her work, which I had a hard time following. I was better at strategy and business than science. But it lit her up, so I nodded and asked all the right questions. After a while, Emmy got up to use the bathroom, and it was just Delaney and me.

"You okay?" I asked.

She tilted her chin and adjusted her sunglasses. "Yeah, I've just been kind of stressed."

"About?"

She pursed her lips. "Yale's putting pressure on me to consider getting married in the next few years. He wants to start the engagement process."

I'd been friends with Delaney long enough that I was familiar with the Welsh organization's engagement process. It was long, involved, and cost a lot of time and money. It wasn't Delaney's style.

"How do you feel about...what was his name?"

"Trystan," she whispered. "I don't think he's a bad guy."

"You just don't want to marry him."

She nodded, her jaw working. "He's hot, I guess."

"How old is he?"

"Thirty-eight."

"Well," I said, gesturing, "you do...like...older guys. Maybe if you get to know him, you would warm up to him."

She sighed, taking off her sunglasses. Her eyes were puffy and right away, I felt terrible for her. She didn't pull away when I took her hand and gave it a squeeze.

"Yale won't force you to get married," I said.

"No," she sighed miserably. "But it's the pressure of not doing the thing that everyone expects you to do that is hard to handle."

My mind shot back to my last night with Caden. Maybe I knew exactly what Delaney was feeling. I wouldn't be forced into an arranged marriage either, but if I wanted to keep my life as COO and representative of Johansen Empire, I had to marry someone my father approved of.

And he wouldn't approve of Caden.

Emmy reappeared, and we finished breakfast. Delaney seemed lighter after talking. I gave her an extra hug when we parted, and she pushed her aviators up quickly, like she was trying to hide her eyes.

"Hey, let me know if I can help with the whole Trystan thing," I whispered. "Just text me whenever you want."

She nodded, ducking into her car. I watched her and Emmy drive away with a sinking feeling in my stomach. I worked too much, and I was missing my best friends' lives. It made my stomach twist with guilt every time I had to decline an invite. If she did marry Trystan, I'd probably be late for their wedding.

I slipped into my car and, for a second, I considered driving to Caden's apartment downtown.

Something was changing; I was never like this. I didn't want to work today. I wanted to get fucked through a mattress and eat take out in bed.

Or...maybe I just wanted that with Caden.

My knuckles turned white on the steering wheel.

This was a fantasy. There was no world where Caden Payne and I worked. I wasn't sure I wanted it to work out long term anyway. It wasn't like I felt something for him other than lust, right?

I needed to get myself together, complete this mission, and go back to my normal life of boardrooms and business.

Deflated, I drove straight to the office. My eyes were wet, although I wasn't sure why, as I took the elevator to the top floor. My father's office was closed, which wasn't unusual. He usually took meetings around eleven.

I slipped into my office and locked the door. For some reason, everything was too bright today. Maybe I shouldn't have had that mimosa. Taking a deep breath, I turned my computer on and sank down, crossing my legs.

The screen flickered on, revealing the search engine I'd left up the last time I'd worked from the office. For a second, I just stared at it. Then, quickly, I typed in something that had been in the back of my mind for days.

Temple of Aphrodite at Ephesus.

I glanced over my shoulder even though I was alone and stole a glance back at the screen. That was what I'd thought. Most of my classes in college had to do with business, but I'd taken a few history courses. When I'd thought about it, I'd realized that the Temple of Aphrodite wasn't one of the seven wonders of the world.

That was strange. He didn't seem like the type to get that wrong.

I closed out of my search and opened my email, turning myself on autopilot. Maybe none of this mattered. Maybe he'd made a simple mistake, but I had a feeling he hadn't. I worked through my emails, looked over a handful of project proposals, and ordered lunch a few hours later.

The afternoon wore on.

I ate my chicken breast and steamed vegetables. I sat up straight in my chair, my heels tucked under the table. I moved through my afternoon meetings. But in the back of my mind, I couldn't stop thinking about him.

Every time I closed my eyes, all the dirty things he'd said tumbled through my mind. I thought of the heavy expression in his gaze when he'd looked down, his cock buried in me, like he wanted to eat me alive. But most of all, I thought about our bodies on cold stone.

Wrapped up, entangled and buried in each other.

Moving in the cool of the morning with the scent of incense in the air.

It was a relief when the clock hit five. My pulse was thrumming as I headed out and drove directly home. To my relief, my house was empty. I pulled my heels off and ran upstairs, shutting my door and locking it. My hand hovered over my purse as I debated pulling my phone out and texting him.

I couldn't...and yet, I needed him.

No, I had to control myself. Frustrated, I tossed my things aside and went into the bathroom, turning the shower on, feeling oddly embarrassed because I was never this horny. With a sigh, I pulled my little box of sex toys from the cabinet. In the corner was a velvet bag, and in it was a clear rubber dildo I'd never actually used.

Normally, I just slid my fingers or my discreet vibrator under the covers and did what needed to be done before falling asleep.

I bit my lip, debating. What did it matter? No one would ever know.

My hands moved of their own accord and grabbed the dildo and a little bottle of lube. In the shower, I turned the shower head towards the wall and sank to my knees. If I didn't just do this, I was going to lose my nerve. So, I pressed it onto the floor between my thighs and sank down on it.

Disappointment twinged. I was full, so full it hurt a little, but it wasn't the same as him. He was warm and alive. His pulse had beat with mine as his hands roamed over me, urging my pleasure to climax. Resolutely, I closed my eyes and rode it gently, the way I might have on top of him.

It felt good, but it didn't hold a candle to him.

The least I could do was work the tension out so I could get some work done in my home office before bed. Planting one hand on the wall and sliding the other over my clit, I moved my hips slowly. My mind drifted back to him, to how he'd touched me.

To how he'd put his mouth between my legs like he was worshiping me.

My spine arced. An orgasm swept through me and left me shaking, holding onto the shower railing. The only thought in my head was how triumphant he'd be if he ever found out I'd gotten off to the thought of him.

CHAPTER EIGHTEEN

CADEN

I knocked on the door with a bag over my shoulder and my Kawasaki parked in the front around seven. Maybe I should have called. Merrick's car wasn't in the open garage, but Clara's pink and cream topless car sat out by the fountain.

I knocked again. Footsteps pattered, the lock whirred, and Clara's round face appeared around the door.

"Caden," she said, pulling it all the way open. "What are you doing here?"

I cleared my throat. "Can I spend the night?"

Her jaw dropped. "Um...of course. Come in."

I followed her inside. She was a few years younger than me and looked it. Her dark hair was piled on her head, tied with a berry pink band. She wore overlarge sweats, the waist rolled up, and a cropped tank top. There were little green pieces of rubber under her eyes that I knew had something to do with makeup. Maybe skincare. I wasn't sure what.

I followed her down the hallway and into the kitchen. She turned, a crease between her dark, arched brows.

"What's up?" she said. "Do you want something? I have wine? Or hot chocolate? Or Merrick has some really nice bourbon I can get from the cellar?"

I sank into the stool, setting my bag down. "Dealer's choice."

She pursed her lips, studying me. "You look like you could use the bourbon."

She disappeared down the stairs and appeared a moment later with a bottle. "I hate that room so much. It's creepy," she said absently, breaking the seal and taking down a crystal glass. She set it before me, grabbing something from the freezer and dropping it in.

I stared down, watching the pink, heart shaped whiskey stone sink to the bottom.

"Cute," I said.

She smirked, leaning on the table. "I bought them for Merrick for Valentine's Day the other year. He likes them."

I took a sip, letting the bourbon soothe my whirling head. Probably not the best idea, but I was here in Merrick's house, and my first meeting wasn't until noon tomorrow. And...I hated to admit it, I felt safe.

Clara absently chewed at the inside of her cheek. "So what's up?" she asked.

I had another sip. "Does it bother you? Living with all of Merrick's mental health issues?"

Her brows arched. "No. It's worth it. I just learned the things that bother him that he can't change and figured out how to work with it. Or I give him space to do things how he needs to."

My throat felt dry. "And it doesn't bother you?"

She shook her head. I had a hard time letting that sink in.

"Does it scare you?"

Her lips parted for a long silence. "It did...or it has before. Not the ADHD, that feels manageable for me, but...um...there was a week about a year after we got married when he was under a lot of pressure from work, and he had some issues. That scared me."

My chest twinged. "What kind of issues? Can I ask?"

"Yeah, I mean, he's pretty open about this now," she said, her voice hoarse. She cleared her throat. "He has a lot of intrusive, OCD-related thoughts."

My mouth was dry. "What kind of intrusive thoughts?"

She sighed. "Not nice ones. People think intrusive thoughts are about impulsive behaviors, but I learned really quickly it's not that."

Curiosity rose in me. Was it possible that some of the darker parts of my mind weren't my fault?

"His intrusive thoughts are tough," she said softly.

"What are they?" I pressed.

She gave a little shrug. "The worst one...he was struggling with this recurring thought that he...um...stabbed me in my sleep. Like, he knew he didn't, that he wouldn't, but he'd get so afraid of going to sleep beside me that he wasn't sleeping at all. So...so we had separate beds for a while until he got it under control."

My stomach turned. "What did you do?"

She sniffed. "I sent him to Gretchen once a day for a week. She had him on a low dose of anti-anxiety meds until it stopped. She's licensed again."

"Wait...Gretchen wasn't licensed?"

Clara waved a hand. "Not important. She renewed it recently."

"So Merrick's issues...stopped?" I asked.

"It took work. Usually, he gets symptoms because there's stress from an external factor," she said, sounding a bit like Gretchen. "Once that anxiety is gone, he can handle the symptoms. So work eased up, he did some really intense therapy, and then he got it together after a month or two."

I rolled the whiskey in the glass as she pushed off the counter and poured a glass of red wine from the fridge. Her gaze burned into me as I stared into my cup.

My stomach turned. I knew what the usual prescription was for an ADHD diagnosis. I'd snorted twice the dose enough times—off my car, off the back of a toilet, off my hand. I'd taken it just to feel that high thirty minutes later, to feel like a million dollars for an hour and a half. I still tasted the alcohol I burned through to deal with the plunging low as the drop hit.

I'd learned a hard lesson from it.

I was hardwired to be an addict. Maybe that was why I'd been so adamant not to touch anything harder. That would have been the kiss of death.

Every upper and downer I could get my hands on, I'd abused. Sleeping pills, really any prescription medication with a pleasant side effect—I'd run through them all.

It was the reason I barely took Tylenol, why I was trying to cut out cigarettes, why I tried to only drink socially.

My brain was hell-bent on self-destruction.

No, I knew medication wasn't the right solution for me, I'd just abuse it. I'd burned that bridge a while ago. I just wanted time and patience.

"Merrick tried meds before," I said quietly.

She nodded. "He prefers not to be medicated, but he also knows sometimes, it's what needs to happen."

I looked up, remembering that sometimes, I could just be honest. I didn't have to make snarky remarks. I didn't have to put up my defenses.

I took a quick breath.

"My father is very lucky to have you," I said.

She gave a small, confused smile. "Thank you. Are you okay?"

"I don't want you to have to deal with my bullshit."

"Caden, as weird as it is, you're my family."

It was a bit weird. She was younger than me, and she felt more like a friend than anything else., but she was right; in a modern way, we were family. I ran a hand over my face, leaning in to balance the glass between my fingers. She crossed the room, sipping her wine, and climbed onto the stool opposite me.

Her dark, sharp gaze was piercing. "Talk to me. Please."

I met her stare head on.

"I turned my stove on and drove my Kawasaki through town in my sleep," I said quietly.

Her hand clapped over her mouth, giving me a preview of how Merrick was going to react. There was a long silence, and then she cleared her throat.

"Okay, were you on sleeping meds?"

I nodded. "I went up to the lodge for a few days to work on securing the funding for the Wyoming base. We came home early, and everything was normal. Took a pill, went to sleep and woke up on Gretchen Hughes' couch."

"Okay," she said, pulling her expression together. "Alright, people sleepwalk all the time, especially if they have a bad reaction to sleeping medication. Did something happen at the lodge that was keeping you from sleeping?"

Into my head flashed the image of Circe with her thighs wrapped around my head, her mauve tipped fingers stroking my hair, evoking feelings I wasn't sure I was capable of feeling until that point. Part of me—the part that was light from bourbon—wanted to spill it all to Clara and get her perspective on the situation. But she was Merrick's wife before she was my friend, and I couldn't expect her to keep secrets from him.

And he couldn't know I'd slept with Circe.

I shook my head. "No, just in and out. Regular work shit."

Her eyes narrowed. "Hmm, not sure I believe you."

"Well, believe it."

She cocked her head. "There's the old Caden I was expecting."

"I'm trying to be less of a dick, but you have to take what you get."

She laughed, draining her wine. "Want another drink?"

I nodded, and she refilled our glasses. The conversation turned towards the living room remodel she was overseeing in her spare time. She took me on a tour of it and showed me the 3D mockup she had on her laptop. I listened to her chatter, grateful for the distraction, but in the back of my mind, all I could think about was the soft scent of hyacinths.

We went back into the kitchen. Clara said she was hungry, and I'd skipped both lunch and dinner, so she dug through the fridge. I knew she wasn't much of a cook, but I wasn't picky.

In the nick of time, the front door opened. Merrick's footsteps sounded in the hall, and he appeared in the doorway. He'd been at work; he was still in his black dress pants and dark maroon button up. His hair was messy, like he'd driven with the top of his Audi down.

His brows rose as he looked at me sitting on the counter and Clara boiling linguine noodles with a wine glass in her hand.

"What's this?" he asked.

Clara moved to him, and I politely glanced away while she kissed him. "Caden's staying the night."

Merrick sent me a sharp, concerned glance. I just shrugged, not wanting to get into it anymore tonight. He set his briefcase and jacket down by the door and started rolling up his sleeves.

"What are you making, *cariad*?" he asked brightly.

"There's shrimp in the fridge, so I was hoping for seafood pasta," she said, poking the boiling water. "But I don't have the sauce done yet."

He picked up her wine and pointed to the counter. "You keep Caden company, and I'll figure this out."

She climbed up to sit on the end of the counter and started chattering about something she and her best friend, Candice, had done earlier that day. I zoned out, watching my father move around the kitchen. There was a dull ache in my chest, maybe a hint of jealousy.

Was this what being happy looked like?

And if Merrick could have this, why couldn't I?

Clara left her seat and joined Merrick, hovering at his elbow. She oversaw him like she knew what she was doing, offering suggestions and laughing at his quick retorts.

A sudden warmth stole over me, chipping away at the ice inside. The kitchen smelled like cheese and pasta and good wine. The window was open, and through it came the soft sound of the sprinklers. Frogs chirruped from the pond at the edge of Merrick's yard.

It smelled, sounded, and felt like a home.

The home I'd never had.

A home I could have if I could stop self-sabotaging and believe that I deserved it.

It hit me right hard that the only thing stopping me from doing this more often was me. Merrick practically begged to have me in his life. No doubt, right now, he was concerned but also over the moon that I was staying the night.

So why was I punishing myself because I hadn't had him all along?

I had a family, ready to welcome me. The past was just a shadow, and the future was waiting for me to reach out and grasp it.

So why couldn't I?

Gretchen's words glimmered in my head, silvery and cool, like a spider's web built into the back of my mind.

Do you think you're addicted to your own pain? Do you run off the fumes of it, like an adrenaline high?

My throat was dry as I set the glass aside.

Yes, maybe I was addicted to my pain. It was all I'd ever known.

"Caden."

I snapped back to reality. Clara stood before me with a glass of water and a wide bowl of pasta sprinkled with cheese and fresh basil. I stared down at it, stunned. As far as I could remember, outside of a restaurant, no one had ever cooked me a meal.

"Do you want to eat on the back porch?" she asked.

I nodded, accepting the plate. Merrick stood in the doorway, holding the door open. He jerked his head, and I moved past him and stepped onto the desk. I could tell Clara had helped decorate it, because the railings were strung with lines of glittering pink lights, and the table in the middle was a soft rose color.

We sat down, Merrick stretching out his legs. Clara leaned into his space, like a moth to flame. There was a noticeable difference in her when he was around. Her shoulders relaxed, her body always bent towards him.

She trusted him. Completely.

Until I saw them together, I'd never been around a healthy couple.

It had always just been abuse and rage, fear like blood in the back of my mouth.

My head was light from bourbon, but it started receding as I ate. Clara asked me about work, and I gave her the safe answers I knew

Merrick preferred. He didn't like her knowing the details of what we did.

At some point, my shoulders felt less tight, and my mind started to wander. My two nights with Circe felt like they'd rewired my brain. Maybe that was why I'd gotten up to roam Providence in my sleep. Maybe, deep inside, I'd tasted something more, and now, I had to have it again.

This evening felt like having a home. We were eating together without abuse, without fear—it was a new feeling.

And I'd felt it with Circe at the lodge.

I wanted to let myself imagine having that every night, but that felt dangerous. Being alone was a safer option.

But was being safe enough anymore?

I decided right then that I wasn't getting into what had happened with Merrick tonight, not when I wasn't sure if it involved sleeping with Circe.

Instead, I let the evening wear on. We had a little more wine, and Clara brought out more pasta. We talked about everything and nothing. Clara didn't mention anything I'd told her, and Merrick and I steered clear of work. Instead, we talked about Merrick's new hotel chain I had some stock in. We talked about the economy until we noticed Clara had fallen asleep against Merrick's arm.

He carried her upstairs as I cleaned the counters and loaded the dishwasher. When I turned around, my father stood in the doorway, his eyes soft.

"Clara told me you sleepwalked," he said.

"I thought she was asleep."

"She woke up for a minute when I put her in bed," he said, sinking down at the table. "Caden, you need to start seeing Gretchen."

I swallowed, setting the towel aside. It was scrunched into the shape of my fist.

"I am," I said finally. "I have an appointment."

His shoulders sagged, and relief moved over his face. "Good."

He wanted to say more, but he was afraid to. I'd pushed him away one too many times, and now, he was worried I'd shrink back. It made me feel like shit that he was afraid to speak plainly.

"I'm good," I said. "Maybe I've had a lot on my mind, but I'm good."

"Good."

"Yeah."

He cleared his throat. "What's your opinion on Maelon?"

Grateful he was throwing me a rope, I shrugged. "He has it, but whether he's willing to be trained is another story. Then, even if he is, it's hard to get trainees to sign up. I won't push him into anything. Knowing the stakes, it has to be voluntary."

Merrick's lids lowered. "I'm thinking of changing that."

"What?"

"I might introduce a proposal to change that," he said more firmly. "No one should have to die. We're not gladiators."

I was quiet for a moment, letting that sink in.

"We were," I said. "Maybe."

Merrick sighed. "All the old gods are dead. Maybe there never were any."

My mind went back to the fantasy I'd had a long time ago. I'd walked along a dirt path and paused in the doorway of a stone temple to Aphrodite. I could still smell it, could feel the cool air vividly. A little part of me that wanted more pretended that dream meant something.

Then, I found out historically, it was a temple to Artemis, not Aphrodite.

I was hyperfixating on a place that never existed. It was a dream, nothing else, just like my hope of being in a place where I could rest and heal from everything.

It was a place that never could be. Maybe that was why I fantasized about fucking Circe there. Being with someone like her...that was just a dream, no more solid than incense rising to the sky.

I cleared my throat. "Wasn't the point of the arena so that our leader experienced violence firsthand so he would only use it as a last resort?"

Merrick leaned back and rested his head against the wall.

"Am I a good *Brenin*?" he asked quietly.

I felt the weight of his words and my reluctance to open myself up to him. For the first time, I actively fought it. I pushed back my fear of opening myself up.

"I would go to war for you, sir," I said. "But only because I know you'd never ask that of me."

His lashes fell and his jaw worked. There was a long silence, and then he nodded once.

"Maybe the men who built the arena were wiser than I am," he said. He ran a hand over his face. "Or maybe I just need to go to bed."

"Maybe just go to bed," I said. "It's late."

He jerked his head down the hall. "The guestroom is made up. There's soap and towels."

"Thanks," I said.

My vulnerability was all used up for the night. He nodded goodnight, and I listened as he climbed the stairs and walked down the hall to his bedroom. An uncomfortable feeling filled my chest.

Was it...envy?

I swallowed it down, but it bubbled back up as I strode down the hall and shut the guestroom door behind me. Maybe I wanted to come home to someone the way Merrick had tonight. Have dinner with her on the porch and hold her until she fell asleep. Carry her up to bed.

Why couldn't I have that?

I closed my eyes and tried to visualize coming home to my apartment after a long day. There was a woman standing at the counter, still in her dress and heels. Her hair fell down her shoulders in dark waves. My mind's eye followed the lines of her familiar body as she turned.

Circe.

My eyes snapped open.

No, I had to stop thinking about her like this. It would only lead to more bitterness and heartbreak.

CHAPTER NINETEEN

CIRCE

Later that week, I met up with Delaney and Emmy, this time for coffee downtown. I dodged Emmy's questions about what was going on in my life and turned them back on her. She didn't mind; she loved any opportunity to talk about her job. Delaney was withdrawn. She stood with one arm around herself, sipping her latte while Emmy chattered.

"Are you alright?" I ventured.

She offered a tight smile. "Fine, just tired."

"What's making you so tired?" Emmy teased. "You have a boyfriend?"

She frowned. "What? No."

I nudged Emmy. There was a serious note in Delaney's voice, like there had been at the restaurant. I gave her a pointed look, and she shook her head, clearly not willing to talk about it.

We parted ways, and I made a mental note to check back with her tomorrow. A little part of me was sad, watching them walk off. I sighed and got in my car and turned the key.

"Hey."

I jumped out of my skin, almost hitting my head on the car roof. It took a second, but my eyes focused on the lean figure spread out in the passenger seat.

My heartbeat exploded.

"Goddamn it, Caden," I gasped. "What are you doing here?"

He looked me over, unashamed. "You left the door unlocked."

"It auto locks after two minutes."

"I got in one minute after you left."

"And you've just been sitting here this entire time?" I stared at him, horrified by his audacity.

"I had a lot of business calls to make, and your car is comfortable," he said.

I just stared at him, speechless. He sent me a heavy-lidded stare, one that felt more indecent than being naked in front of him, and got out. He walked around the car and opened the door. Confused, I got out, and he took me by the waist, ushering me to the passenger side of my own car.

What...the hell?

He slid into the driver's seat and adjusted it back to make room for his long body. Then, he made the engine purr and pulled out onto the street.

"I beg your pardon," I said, finally pulling myself together.

He rested one hand out the window, the wind whipping his dark hair. "No need, you're fine."

I turned in my seat. "*You* are not fine. Where are we going?"

He glanced over from beneath those dark lashes. Something about him was different. There was a faint aura of desperation about him that I hadn't seen since the night...well, since he'd gone down on me at the lodge.

I swallowed past my dry throat as my hands twisted together in my lap.

The air crackled. He dragged his eyes back to the road.

"We're fucking, aren't we?" I whispered.

His knuckles tightened on the wheel.

"Yeah, we're fucking," he said.

Maybe it was his confidence, just showing up and taking the wheel out of my hands. Maybe it was him and his tattoos, all hell bent on getting me in bed. Whatever it was, my body responded like he'd lit a match and put it to gasoline.

One minute, I wasn't remotely thinking about sex. The next, I had a rerun of everything he'd done to me in the lodge going through my head at a hundred miles an hour.

A barrage of images. His tongue, his teeth, his body, his tattoos.

His dark hair falling over his forehead as he looked up from between my thighs.

It was so easy; *I* was so easy. He'd just aimed, fired, and *bang*, he had me on my back with my legs open.

My fingers dug into the hem of my skirt. I was wearing a pale pink seersucker dress that clung to my body. My hair was done; I'd just washed it. I smelled like flowers, like the perfume I'd dabbed on my wrists. If he was going to fuck me, today was the day for it.

I glanced sideways.

He was in his fatigues and boots, all black against dark ink on his arms and the side of his neck.

Down below, my pussy pulsed. It was achingly empty for the warmth he'd filled me with at the lodge. I was wet just watching him drive, knowing what he was about to do to me.

He parked around the back of his apartment. My fingers dug even harder at my hem as he cut the engine. Silence fell as I dug at my dress, fraying the stitching. His hand flexed on his thigh, and I glanced at him from beneath my lashes as he stepped out, unfurling his body. The front of his pants had a faint ridge under his zipper.

I swallowed, almost choking.

I'd been tender after he'd fucked me, and he'd been gentle both those times.

I had a feeling he wasn't in a gentle mood today.

He pulled open the door, and his palm filled my vision. Waiting for me to let him help me from the car. Gently, because I wasn't sure of myself, I put my fingers in it. He lifted me from the car, and I glanced up at his face.

There was something in his eyes that startled me, buried beneath the roaring inferno of blue fire, but I had no idea what to call it.

"Let's go," he said, his voice low.

My heart thumped like we were being pursued. He slid his fingers through mine and pulled me across the street, ducking into the stairwell. I hurried after him, my heels clattering on the stairs.

His locks clattered.

He yanked me into the apartment and shut the door, whirling me and slamming me back against it. Before I could react, he dropped to his knees and ripped my dress up the front, all the way to my waist.

A gasp burst from my lips. How dare he? This was designer.

He yanked my panties off, shredding them, and buried his face between my legs. The groan that sounded in his chest was desperate, like a starving animal finally finding food. The panties were designer too, but suddenly, I didn't care.

He was eating me like I was his last meal, like he didn't care about anything other than getting the taste of my pussy on his tongue. My thighs clenched, and he growled, knocking them open with his head.

"Keep them open," he snapped. "I'm fucking busy."

"I'm falling," I gasped, sliding down the door. "Please, take me somewhere else. Not the kitchen."

He caught me, his hands fumbling with the straps of my heels. They fell to the ground, and he picked me up, carrying me across the room. My heart, which was already pounding, was trying to jump out of my chest.

We were going to his bedroom.

That felt serious.

He kicked open the door, and I saw a flash of the room. Plain, a big bed with pale gray sheets, a wide window that looked out over downtown Providence. He tossed me, and I let out a little shriek as I hit the bed. He fell over me, panting on his hands and knees. I saw a flash of dark, hungry eyes as he ripped the rest of my dress from my body, leaving me in just my mauve lace bra.

"My clothes," I whimpered.

"You look better naked," he murmured, dragging his mouth up the inside of my thigh. "Fuck, you're so pretty."

His voice was thick, almost drunk. A little part of me wondered if he'd ever talked to other women like that.

Part of me hoped he hadn't.

His mouth slid, hot and hard, up my hip and then withdrew. Quick as a flash, he flipped me onto my hands and knees before him. His hand came down on my ass, and a sharp crack split the room. I gasped, and the pain was a delicious shock down my thighs.

My pussy throbbed, instantly soaked.

My spine arced as I lifted my head and met my eyes in the mirror on the far wall. Right away, my brain started running with images of him with other women in front of the mirror, but I stopped it.

We weren't together. He could do what he wanted.

Why was I so jealous anyway?

He lifted his head, and our gazes locked. Then, he spat on his palm and slapped my ass—a lot harder this time. My pupils blew wide as my mouth fell open. I whipped around to protest, but he dropped to his knees behind me, one hand buried in my perfect hairstyle, ruining it, the other hooking two fingers in my mouth and dragging my face back to the mirror, smearing my lipstick over my cheek.

Oh my God.

Something slipped down the inside of my thigh.

His narrowed eyes met mine. "You gonna be a good girl?" he asked.

He was using that low, husky tone he'd used at the lodge. My stomach quivered, but I couldn't nod. He was holding my head firmly in place.

"Say yes," he ordered.

Confused, my eyes darted from side to side.

"Go on, do your best, butterfly," he murmured.

His palm left my hair for a second, just long enough to crack across my ass so hard, my eyes flew wide. Then, it returned, hauling my head back. God, I was going to have bruises tomorrow, and I loved it.

"If you don't do as you're told, I'm going to make you crawl," he threatened.

Right now, I was absolutely positive he would make good on that threat. Feeling silly, I sniffed and gagged on his fingers, trying to answer him, but the only sound that came out was a muffled moan.

He didn't back down, his eyes still locked on mine in the mirror.

"Five," he said.

Wait...what?

"Four."

A little rebellious spark ignited. What would happen if I let him finish?

"Three." He cocked his head.

My toes curled, my heart thumped.

"Two."

I made big eyes at him. His fingers tightened, sparking pain down my neck.

"One," he whispered.

Panicking, I did my best to answer him. The word was muffled and gagged by his fingers, but it was enough to spark triumph in his eyes.

He released me, and I froze, watching as he hauled his shirt over his head. His gun went on the holster by the bed, his boots came off. Then, he returned in just his pants and grabbed me by the ankle, hauling me back and flipping me so hard, the air burst from my lungs.

He moved fast. One moment, he was standing, and the next, he was on his hands and knees with his face inches from mine.

"What's your net worth, butterfly?" he breathed.

Confused, I stared up into the blue depths of his eyes.

"Um...I don't know," I whispered.

"Millions?"

"Something like that," I squirmed uncomfortably, but he kept me still.

His eyes roamed over my face. "Is that why everyone treats you like you're made of glass? Pretty, perfect, locked up in a tower. I think you want to be fucked like you aren't breakable, like you aren't a million dollars' worth of pretty glass."

My chest ached. How did he look at me and just know? Was it so obvious that I was desperate to be let out of my cage?

A whimper worked its way up my throat, and the corner of his mouth jerked up. He sank down over me, the front of his pants grazing my naked pussy. His hips worked, rubbing the hard ridge under the fabric over my clit as my eyes rolled back.

"You're gonna have to do something for me," he said softly.

I swallowed. "What?"

He bent, kissing my mouth, flicking his tongue so I tasted it, just for a second. My body ached as I felt that touch in every corner.

"You're going to call me daddy," he said. "Just this once."

My jaw dropped. "Wh—what? No, I will not."

My mind raced. Maybe I'd gotten in over my head. The problem was, even though I was horrified by his words, my body was having the opposite reaction. My nipples pebbled, brushing against his shirt. My pussy clenched. The sweetest shame trickled through my body.

"Open up for me," he said, leaning in.

I hesitated. His hand clenched on my thigh, sending a little jolt of pain up through my hips. Swallowing, I hesitantly parted my lips.

"Wider," he ordered.

I cracked my lips. His two fingers came up and corrected me, spreading them and pushing on my tongue until it was fully extended. He dipped them deeper into my mouth, and I gagged. My brain thrummed, basking in the humiliation of what he was doing to me.

He pulled them out. "You're sensitive," he said. "I'll have to work on that."

My cheeks burned. I wanted to squirm, but I kept still with my tongue out, waiting for his next instruction.

I'd always been strong willed. It was one of my best traits when it came to running the business. I was confident, I knew what I wanted, I liked winning. So why was I soaked at the idea of being obedient to him? Why did I want him to make me do the most embarrassing things he could think of?

Was there something wrong with me?

Was I losing my confidence?

I didn't have time to think anymore, because he bent in and licked my tongue before he spat into my mouth.

My body tingled. My lips snapped shut, and I swallowed without thinking about it. The corner of his mouth curled.

"Good girl," he praised.

Those two simple words made my eyes roll back in my head. He picked me up again and flipped me onto my hands and knees. His hand slid up my back and flicked open my bra. It slid down, baring my breasts.

He hummed in his throat. "Fuck, you're pretty," he murmured, kissing up the back of my neck.

I whimpered, head empty.

He adjusted my hips, and I heard his zipper hiss. My eyes widened as I felt it—the hot, hard head of his cock press against my soaked opening, that metal ring against my sensitive pussy, rubbing over my entrance as he eased the head inside me.

My pussy stretched until it burned. My thighs shook.

His mouth grazed my ear as his abdominal muscles clenched against my back and his cock thrust all the way to the hilt, not giving me time to adjust.

My head spun.

My God, he was big. Too big for me.

"Who's your daddy?" he said, voice dropping to a growl. "Who's going to fuck your tight little cunt until you cry?"

All my resistance melted. The walls I'd put up to get me through meetings with men who scared me, the forced smiles, the barricades I'd built around my feelings so I could be tough and mean and get what I wanted—those all vanished.

Suddenly, I was naked, inside and out.

Wrapped up in his arms, his cock inside me. Urging me to let go and be safe.

I lifted my eyes, noticing how my mascara was smudged on my cheeks, how he'd smeared my lipstick when he hooked my mouth.

"You are," I whispered.

"Call me it, just one time."

My lips quivered. I turned my head and his lips brushed over my cheek, so close to mine. I shuddered, taking a breath, my lips grazing the corner of his mouth.

"Daddy," I breathed.

His lashes flickered, stomach tensing. Then, he thrust hard, hitting the perfect spot, one that made my body shudder from my head to my curled toes.

"Fuck," he growled. "That's my *good* girl."

My head spun, light as a feather. "Say that again."

He laughed, thrusting rough and deep. He gathered me against his chest, lifting me back onto his lap as he sat on his heels. My eyes shut, trying to block out what I knew was a pornographic reflection of us in the mirror. I wasn't sure if I was ready to see where we joined together.

That felt too real.

His other hand came up, cupping my breast. His scarred, tattooed thumb circled my nipple, rolling it between his fingers.

"Fuck, pretty girl," he breathed.

I peeled my eyes open and froze. He was behind me, pants pushed down below his groin. I was in his lap with his cock shoved deep inside, filling me so full, it stretched me uncomfortably and pushed up against the deepest point.

He was everything I wasn't.

The antithesis of me.

My eyes tumbled over our bodies—hard, inked muscles against my untouched body, tattooed fingers rubbing gently over my pink flushed nipple, kneading my breast in his rough fingers.

I whimpered. He bent, kissing the nape of my neck. The hair on my neck rose. His hips sped up, taking me harder as little waves of pleasure built between my legs. My hand drifted down and found my clit, pinching it and rubbing my piercing gently as he rode me.

Oh God, that was—*oh*.

My stomach tightened. My lids flew open, and my body went stiff in his arms. His eyes flashed, and his hips sped up, angling. The pierced head of his cock hit my G-spot, sending delicious waves of pleasure through my body, down to the soles of my feet. My toes curled hard.

"That's a good girl," he panted. "Come all over this cock."

I fell apart, spine snapping and locking, head falling back against his shoulder. He slid his forearm across my throat and pinned me against him, gripping my hip so he could fuck me hard.

He was like steel, so hard that it hurt. My eyes streamed, dragging my makeup down, incoherent whimpers tumbling from my lips.

He went faster. My orgasm throbbed, still going strong. My nails raked across his forearm, and he swore through gritted teeth. Then, we fell forward, onto our hands and knees. His hips shook as he pushed me down into the bed, plunging his fingers into my hair to pin me to the bed. My spine arced as he slammed into me, fucking me so hard, I swore I saw stars.

"Gonna fill this pussy with my cum," he panted. "Gonna get so deep in you, it won't matter if you're on the fucking pill."

My brain buzzed. I'd forgotten about the part where he liked fantasizing about getting me pregnant.

He bit me—he fucking bit me out of nowhere. I yelped, my hair rising. His teeth sank into the soft flesh where my shoulder met my neck, one hand on the bed, one still in my hair. I cried out, pain splintering through my pleasure.

His hips slammed into me. My nose was dripping, smearing on the bed. There were black mascara stains on his sheets. His teeth left my neck, the place where he'd bitten me smarting.

"Beg for it, you pretty slut," he growled.

I hiccupped, biting back a wail. "Please, please."

"Try harder."

The last tiny shreds of my dignity dissolved.

"Please," I cried, my voice muffled. "Please...come in me. I want your cum in me. Get me pregnant."

Those were the magic words. He went so hard, I saw stars. He needed to finish or pull out and cut his losses, because he fucking hurt. I was soaked and turned on and he was still too big for me. I was a second from collapsing when a shudder moved through his body and he groaned under his breath.

Deep inside me, he twitched.

He stopped thrusting, and I froze so I could feel everything as his hips rode his pleasure out against me until they were spent.

He exhaled a heavy breath. Gently, he pulled out and fell onto his back on the bed, taking me with him so my cheek rested in the crook of his arm. Overhead, the ceiling fan whirred. Outside, cars moved by in the distance. Someone rang a doorbell on the first level.

"Fuck," he sighed.

I nodded. My body was so weak, all I could do was lay beside him and try to catch my breath. It took a moment, but a slow, anxious feeling started creeping in.

My stomach turned.

I'd done it again. I'd slept with the enemy.

I was failing my mission. My father would be horrified if he found out.

"I should go," I whispered, sitting up.

He stayed as he was, on his back with the front of his pants still open. His groin was soaked, and his dick was still hard. I turned away, his gaze burning into the back of my head.

"Why?" he murmured.

I ran a hand under my nose. "I have work."

He sat up. "Fuck work for one afternoon."

"I've already fucked work today," I managed. "I spent the morning with my friends, and now I've spent the last hour with you. I have to work."

To my surprise, his warm palm slid up my spine. It rested on the nape of my neck, and his fingers started kneading gently. No one ever touched me like this, not with such calm and confidence that he could take control.

My entire body ached with guilt. I wrapped my arms around my knees and dropped my forehead.

"Hey," he said quietly.

"What?" My voice was muffled.

"Did you eat breakfast?"

I shook my head.

"Lunch?"

"No."

He sighed. "You're staying here until you eat."

I made to stand, but his hand shot out, wrapping around my wrist and pulling me back down. His cobalt eyes were deadly serious.

"I'm feeding you," he said flatly. "And you're going to sit here and eat. Understood?"

My jaw dropped. "You need to take it down a notch."

He rose and tucked his dick in his pants. "What are you going to do? Walk out on me?"

"Maybe," I snapped.

"In what?" he said. "Just your bra? You don't have anything left."

I looked around, defeated. He was right; I was naked and he had me right where he wanted me. I narrowed my eyes. He was good at strategy, and I didn't doubt he'd had this plan going the entire time.

The question was...why did he want me to stay in his bed so badly?

Confused, I scowled at him. He bent, lifting my chin. For a second, I fell into endless deep blue, and then he kissed me slowly and thoroughly. When he pulled back, I was dizzy.

"Make yourself comfortable," he said. "I'm going to order food. If you're good, I'll get something for you to wear later."

CHAPTER TWENTY

CADEN

When I returned, she was in the bathroom. I stripped and pulled on a pair of sweatpants. Neither of us were going anywhere. I had the folder with the info for our next mission in my inbox. There was no reason we couldn't look it over together. It would save us a meeting later.

Really, she should thank me. I was just being efficient.

The bathroom door creaked open, and I glanced up, my eyes falling on her naked body. My stomach swooped.

She was so stunning.

I beckoned her and, to my surprise, she came, pausing at the edge of the bed. I laid my palm on her thigh and ran it up, over her stomach, to her soft breast. A flush crept over her cheeks.

She was different when she was naked, especially this time. There was an unexpected vulnerability in her dark eyes that I hadn't expected.

I ran my middle finger along the faint line of her abdominal muscles down to the seam of her pussy. Her thighs tightened, but she stayed perfectly still, watching me.

"We have to stop doing this," she whispered.

My fingers lingered over her pussy. It was so warm and soft, and she'd tasted so good when I ate her out. My chest tightened.

No, I didn't want to stop doing this.

I shrugged. "Why?"

"Because even though we're working together, we're technically business rivals," she said. "We don't even like each other anyway. It's starting to feel a little...Romeo and Juliet, but without the...feelings."

"Says who?" I slipped the tip of my finger into her pussy, and her lashes fluttered. I could feel the warmth of my cum inside. "Says you?"

She rolled her eyes. "Whatever. I'm trying to be responsible."

My finger slid in further until I could feel her clench.

"Are you sure it's not because your father doesn't want his princess sleeping with someone like me?" I murmured. "Or is it because you're ashamed of it?"

She bit her lower lip. "Why would anyone be ashamed of sleeping with you?"

"I'm not exactly one of your Harvard grads," I said. "Not like that man I saw you out with before."

She rolled her eyes again, shaking back her hair. "You're gorgeous and you know it," she said, a little bite to her voice.

"Oh, am I?" My finger curled, hitting a spot that made her gasp. "Is that enough? I can't play polo, I don't wear seersucker. I somehow think my face isn't a get out of jail free card."

"Can you please take your fingers out of me?" she whispered. "It's so distracting."

I stroked that spot, gently, in slow circles. Then, I pulled them free and lifted them to her mouth. She balked, her cheeks flushed pink.

"Taste us," I urged. "Maybe you'll change your mind."

Her soft lips parted. I slipped my wet fingers through, and she moaned, her lids fluttering. Her tongue moved, cleaning me off.

"That's a good girl," I breathed.

My fingers slipped from her mouth with a little pop. The air between us crackled, and my other hand gripped her hips, yanking her closer. The soft skin of her lower belly was sweet when I kissed it, licking between her hipbones, circling her navel with my tongue.

She was so soft, so sweet. So everything I wasn't.

The doorbell rang. We both went still.

"I'm naked, so you'll have to get that," she whispered.

I ran my tongue up her body as I stood and finished by kissing her mouth. She still tasted like us together, all salty and sweet. I licked us off her mouth and left her standing there panting, her fists clenched.

When I returned with the food, she was sitting up in bed, propped up on the pillows against the window.

"I hope you can't see up into your apartment," she said. "I assumed they were reflective on the outside."

I sank into bed beside her. "They are. I wouldn't let just anyone see you naked, butterfly."

She didn't like that word, but I wasn't sure why. And that made me want to call her butterfly more, to push her until she admitted why it made her purse her lips.

We were both quiet as I unpacked sandwiches, a salad so she could feel like she was being healthy, and chips. She cracked the top of her water bottle and took a sip, letting out a sigh.

"Getting fucked made me thirsty," she said.

"I imagine you're starving," I said, passing her a chunk of sandwich. She was already reaching for the salad, but I moved it away. "Eat this, and then you can have that."

"You're bossy." Her brows raised.

"I thought I was your daddy," I said, bending to kiss the side of her neck quickly.

"Caden, that was for sex only."

"Not to me. Eat."

This time, she sat back and pulled the sandwich into her lap. It was a grilled panini with mozzarella, basil, tomato, and balsamic dripping out the sides. I'd tried to order something with vegetables so she wasn't totally out of her element.

"Can I wear your shirt?"

"Why?

"I don't want to spill on my bare skin."

"I'll lick it off you."

She rolled her eyes, but I saw a tiny smile before she bit into the sandwich. That little moan returned, and her lids fluttered.

"It's good," she managed.

We ate in silence, me unable to take my eyes off her. There was something about getting her out of a professional setting and stripping her bare that fascinated me. It felt like discovering a new world. I wouldn't have been surprised if I was the first man to see her naked and eating in bed.

She set aside her empty plate and sank into the pillows. "I'm so full, I might be sick," she whispered.

I laughed. "Just sit still. You can sleep here if you want."

She shook her head. "I can't."

"Why?"

"Because I have my contacts in," she said.

"Your what?"

She blinked hard. "My contact lenses. I can't sleep in them."

My dick jerked. "You wear glasses?"

She nodded. "Just at night. Or my days off, but I haven't had one of those in a while."

"How come I've never seen them?"

"Because I've always worn my contacts around you. I don't like wearing my glasses in front of people, so I take them out literally the minute I go to sleep."

I frowned, sinking down beside her. "Why?"

She shrugged. "It feels more professional to wear contacts. I don't know why."

I brushed back her hair from her breasts. My fingertips skimmed her nipple and it tightened. "Okay, go home and get your shit and your glasses. You're sleeping here tonight though."

She chewed her lip. "I can't. Someone will see us."

"No, they won't," I said. "You park around the back. No one can see that unless they're in the parking lot, and I don't know anyone in this building."

She hesitated, so I bent in and took her nipple in my mouth. It was soft and hard all at once as I rolled it against my tongue. Her fingers came up and buried in my hair, holding me to her chest.

"Fuck, you're so good with your tongue," she sighed.

I pulled back. "Sleep with me tonight, and I'll show you I can be so much better."

She groaned, rolling over and grabbing her phone. Her brows drew together as she swiped the screen.

"That's weird," she said. "My father's not coming home tonight."

"So that makes it easy," I urged. "Go get your stuff. Get your ass back to my bed."

"He's been staying out a lot lately," she said, texting rapidly. "I think he's got a girlfriend or something."

"Yeah?" I yawned, rolling onto my back.

She shrugged, laying her phone back. "He dates a lot of women at the country club. Probably one of them. Anyway, just this once, I'll give you what you want, but only if I can work here this afternoon."

Triumph rose in my chest, and I sat up. "Perfect. I'll take you home."

She shook her head. "No, you run to the boutique a few blocks down and grab me a new dress. You owe me that much. I'll be back in an hour."

I gripped her by the throat and kissed her, dragging my mouth down her throat, nipping at her collarbones as her nails pierced my ribs. Then she pulled back and pointed at the door, her brows arced so there was no room for argument.

An hour later, she was gone, driving down the street in her topless car wearing a plain sundress with no panties underneath.

I sat my laptop on the table and went to get my phone. It had fallen on the floor, and when I swiped the screen, I realized I had two missed calls and a text. One call was spam, the other from Yale, and it had a voicemail of him asking if I was still going to be at training tomorrow. The text was from Merrick.

I hope you're being careful with this mission. I have a lot riding on it.

Frowning, I answered:

Of course. Why? His reply appeared immediately.

Lukas Johansen is going to be livid if he finds out my son is fucking his daughter. Get your head on straight.

My heart sank. I set my phone aside, unwilling to answer it. It wasn't like Merrick to be so brusque, so I knew I'd hit a nerve. Probably because I'd promised not to fuck this up at the beginning.

How had he found out?

Annoyed, I went to the kitchen and sat down at my laptop. I had paperwork from my time at the lodge to catch up on. My hands moved of their own accord, filling out the endless pages that documented everything we did. Merrick was a stickler for bureaucracy, especially after some of the things Yale and I had done over the years. At one point, we'd both been wild cards.

A lot of things had changed since then.

An hour passed as I mulled it over, then another. It was settling in that she'd lied and run off when there was a soft knock on the door. In a second, I had it open.

She stood there in jean shorts, cropped to show her long legs, sandals, and a plain white t-shirt. She'd showered and redone her makeup, and she had a pink overnight bag in her hand. I took it and pulled her inside.

"I thought you'd changed your mind," I said.

"I almost did," she whispered.

Fuck the paperwork. Fuck everything but the indescribable feeling of being in bed with this woman. My hands moved over her body as her clothes littered my floor. I lifted her and carried her into the dining area, laying her on the table there.

Her fingers buried in my hair, playing with it as I bent over her. My tongue grazed down her stomach and found her clit, sucking gently on that silver ring. Her thighs clenched, keeping my head right where I wanted it.

The only thing better than afternoon sex was morning sex, and I was planning on having that tomorrow.

She stroked my shoulders and played with my hair.

I ate her out until she came once, twice, three more times. Until she left a wet spot on my table. We made it back to the bed, and I pushed her down on her back and slid inside her pussy. Her eyes widened as she took me, like it hurt a little, but she didn't push me off. She just lay in a satisfied haze and let me have my way with her.

"Good girl," I whispered, my mouth on her neck.

She moaned, that breathy sound that drove me crazy. I fucked her thoroughly, keeping the head of my cock moving against her G-spot. She looked up at me from between her legs on my shoulders and whimpered.

We didn't get any work done. I just wanted to fuck this woman until she fell asleep in my bed.

Around five, I ordered burgers from the bar where we'd met— grilled to perfection, only the bottom bun, onions piled on top, cheese sauce drenched over everything. She ate hers with her fingers, a towel spread over her lap. We showered after that, and she let me wash her hair, gently so I wouldn't tangle the waves.

Then, I went to the bistro down the street and got a tub of ice cream. She insisted I get dairy free because it was healthier, and I didn't care, as long as she was happy. We ate it naked, and I flipped her on her back and licked it off her nipples. It melted in the dip of her navel, and I lapped it up. My head was dizzy, maybe because the blood never left my dick.

It was late when we finally got to the email.

I turned her on her stomach and pushed a pillow under her hips. She flipped my laptop open and clicked on the email, downloading the file. I spat on my hand and touched her clit, playing with her pussy as she attempted to bring the document up.

"Caden," she whispered, turning to look over her shoulder. "I'm sore."

I kissed the back of her neck, tasting the sweetness of her skin.

"I'll be gentle," I whispered, lifting her knee to spread her pussy. She made a noise in her throat as I pushed inside her, and her inner muscles clenched. She was soft, so fucking tight, so perfect. Like she was made for my dick.

My chest felt strange. Deep inside, it ached.

I pushed my face into the nape of her neck, breathing in the sweet scent of her hair. My hips worked. Distantly, I heard her trying to read the file aloud, but my brain could only focus on one thing.

I had feelings for this woman. Real feelings.

And if I didn't fight them back, we were going to have a problem. We weren't friendly with the Johansens. As soon as this deal was done, we'd go back to being rivals. The son of the Welsh *Brenin* and the daughter of the Johansen Empire were like oil and water.

There was no world where we worked.

At least, not on paper.

In another world...one that felt like a distant memory, maybe we were lovers. Maybe she held my hand in the cool of the morning. Maybe she kissed my mouth beneath the stars. Maybe we were free to be nothing more than two people who wanted each other.

Instead, we were caught up in all this bullshit. In emails and feuds and money. In tax brackets and missed opportunities and regrets.

Instead, I had to pretend I didn't really want her that badly.

That this was just fun.

Every time I slept with her, I knew that wasn't true. Every time I kissed her body, I knew I was fucking myself. I knew it was going to hurt so much when this was all over.

But I did it anyway, because just a taste of her was worth weeks of agony.

CHAPTER TWENTY-ONE

CIRCE

I read the email aloud and couldn't remember a single word of it because, after he finished fucking me, he put his head between my legs. Finally, I gave up and just let him do as he liked.

Almost an hour later, he resurfaced for air and a glass of water. Drunk on sex, I wandered into the bathroom to wash up and came out with my hair in a messy bun and my plastic framed glasses on. He'd come back to bed, sitting propped on the pillows.

He gave a low whistle, patting his lap once. "Come here."

I climbed aboard. "What? You have a glasses fetish or something?"

He ran his fingers up my neck, touching a flyaway curl. "No, you just look good. I like it...having you in my bed like this."

My chest ached. His hand closed around my throat as he pulled me in, kissing my mouth. He still tasted like my pussy, sweet with a little tang. When he pulled back, he had that drunk expression in his eyes.

"Do you feel like you wasted your time then?"

"What?"

"You said earlier you should be working," he said. "Do you think I made it worth your time?"

Our afternoon tangled up in his sheets flashed through my mind in graphic detail.

"Yeah," I admitted.

His mouth jerked. "You want me to go back down?"

"No," I said firmly. "I can't come anymore. I need a break."

His jaw worked as he glanced behind me at the TV mounted on the wall. "Want to pretend we're normal and watch a movie together?"

I climbed off him, nestling against his side. "Sure, let's see what Caden Payne likes to watch."

He started working the TV off his phone, bringing up all his recently watched movies and shows. I wasn't sure what I'd expected, but every single one of them was something to do with an ancient civilization. He swiped through dozens of documentaries and movies about ancient Rome, Greece, Egypt, and more. Finally, he got to the end and sighed.

"Probably not anything you'd want to watch," he said.

"Let's watch your favorite show," I said.

His brow lifted. "Alright, you asked."

He turned on a miniseries about ancient Greece that started with a graphic battle scene. I coiled up tight against his side, watching from the corner of my eye. His hand drifted down and slid between my thighs, resting up against my pussy, like he just enjoyed the warmth.

This felt so good.

Deep down, I'd doubted I'd ever feel anything this normal. My life up until meeting him was work during the day and going to parties that involved work at night. Oftentimes, I'd even spend weekend mornings at the country club so my father could network.

But this...neither of us got anything out of this other than pure enjoyment.

I pulled myself back to the present. The fight scenes had stopped, and now the main character was back home and getting it on with his wife in a tent. Dramatic moonlight pooled over them, which didn't match the furious pace he was jackhammering. My brows rose, and I swung my gaze up to Caden.

"Are you uncomfortable?" he asked.

"After the places you put your tongue today, I don't think I could be," I said. "I'm just glad you're more skilled than that guy."

"I rearranged your guts," he said, yawning. "I just have more precision. And I made sure you were wet."

"He did kind of just skip that part," I remarked.

"Maybe if I demonstrated—"

I gave him a look. "Caden, it's a movie. I'm too sore to go again tonight."

He kissed the side of my neck. "I could just lick it, make it feel better."

"I've never met a man who liked eating pussy as much as you do," I said.

His eyes narrowed. "How many other men have eaten your pussy?"

"Just my ex," I admitted. "I only have one ex. But, you know, people talk."

He sighed, sinking back. "I've slept with a fair amount of people, but I've been celibate for the last little while. I'm trying to...sort of get my head on straight. Get focused."

That was enough for me. I didn't need the graphic details of all the beautiful women he'd had in his bed over the years.

"Well, you're good in bed," I said, shifting the subject.

He paused the TV and flipped onto his stomach, resting his head in my lap. The action surprised me—it felt somehow more intimate than sex. Slowly, I reached down and smoothed back his hair.

"You're good in bed too," he said.

I didn't reply. I was too distracted. There was a soft, warm sensation in my chest when I looked down at him, and it made me want to cry. I opened my mouth and shut it again. My fingers stroked through his hair, playing with it, running my touch over the tattoos on the side of his neck.

He cleared his throat.

"I've been staying at a friend's house," he said quietly.

My fingers faltered.

"Why?"

There was a short pause. "I...I had an incident where I got on my bike while I was asleep."

My jaw dropped. "You drove a motorcycle in your sleep?"

193

He shifted onto his back, head still nestled in my lap. "Yeah, I turned the stove on. It was like everything you shouldn't do, I did. So I've been staying at a friend's and having them lock me in to make sure I don't wander."

"That's scary." That was an understatement, but I wasn't sure what else to say.

He looked up at me, studying my face like he was hesitating. Finally, he cleared his throat. "Will you make sure I don't wander tonight?"

My insides melted. For some reason, this was the most romantic thing anyone had ever said to me. He trusted me to keep him safe. Wordless, I nodded.

He got up and disappeared in the closet. I waited, confused. When he reappeared, he was carrying a pair of black leather handcuffs. My brows shot to my hairline.

"Um...what is that?"

The corner of his mouth jerked up. "Relax, it's just to keep us together...at least this time."

He knelt on the bed, taking my wrist and locking one cuff to me and the other to him. There was a foot of space between them, but he clearly didn't intend to keep space between us, because he got into bed and pulled me down to lay against his chest.

I inhaled, dizzy. He smelled so good, I wanted to bury my face against his chest.

So I did, pressing against his warm skin. He felt the shudder move through my body, and his hand slid up, drawing my thigh around his waist. His chin rested on the top of my head.

"Go to sleep, butterfly," he said quietly.

I swallowed the dry lump in my throat. "What are we doing?"

His voice was thick and sleepy. "That's a problem for tomorrow."

My eyes fluttered shut. He was right; I could deal with all the new, softer feelings coursing through my veins in the morning.

CHAPTER TWENTY-TWO

CADEN

I woke up to no one at the other end of the handcuffs.

And the smell of bacon.

Sitting bolt upright, I blinked to bring the world into focus. She'd opened the shades, and early sunlight was spilling through. Faint golden rays split through the buildings down below. The bedroom door was ajar, and I could hear her in the kitchen. She was quiet, but her feet pattered on the floor and the espresso machine whirred.

She was making breakfast.

For the second time, someone was cooking for me. Was this what being domesticated felt like?

I pushed back the covers just as she walked in the room holding a tray, and my jaw dropped. She was gorgeous. All she wore was the t-shirt I'd discarded on the floor yesterday. Tangled waves were piled on her head, little bits falling around her shoulders.

My eyes ran over her body, eating up the sight of her bare thighs and the peaks of her nipples showing through my shirt. They rested on her big, plastic framed glasses, perched on the bridge of her nose.

God, this side of her made me rock hard.

The other sides did too, but there was just something about seeing her with her guard down that did things to me. Absently, I pried the handcuff off and pushed myself upright, sitting back against the pillow. She crossed the room and set the tray loaded with bacon, eggs, toast, and espresso on the bedside table.

I snatched her waist, pulling her onto my lap. Her soft thighs clenched as I took her gently by the throat and pulled her down for a kiss.

"You made me breakfast," I said.

She shook her hair back, tilting her chin up. There was a hint of the combative Circe I'd gotten used to in her eyes.

"I'm hungry," she said. "You fed me last night. Fair is fair."

"I'm not complaining." I ran my hand from her throat, down over her breasts. "You're so fucking beautiful."

She flushed, struggling off my lap and tumbling to her side of the bed. "Let's eat," she said briskly.

I'd gone too far, let last night cloud my judgment, and now I'd made her uncomfortable. Casually, I set the tray between us and tried some of the espresso. Her brow arced, waiting on the verdict.

"Good, but not as good as my espressos," I said.

She rolled her eyes. "Not likely."

For a moment, I thought about telling her I'd learned to make good coffee at a café near my house growing up. The owner was a woman in her seventies who'd never had children. She saw me loitering in the street one day, and I told her why I didn't want to go home. After that, she let me sit in her shop when school was over and do my homework.

She passed away six months after we met. For those six months, I had the best grades I'd ever had.

It just went to show how much someone giving a fuck would have made a difference.

I glanced up, feeling her eyes on me. My chest tightened.

Circe Johansen, the daughter of one of the wealthiest men in the States, was in my bed, and it made no sense. And yet, I'd told her all those unsavory things about myself, and here she was, making me breakfast after we'd slept handcuffed together.

"What's wrong?" she asked.

I shook my head. "Nothing. Are you working this morning?"

She nodded, taking a piece of bacon and nibbling on it. "I'll get ready here and go to the high rise. I can't afford to lose more work time. This mission is taking a lot of time away from my regular tasks."

"Surely the COO of Johansen Enterprises can do what she wants," I said.

She bit her lip, working it. "You would think."

"You can't?"

"My father has high expectations," she said flatly. "He's giving me responsibility over the thing that he cares about the most. I have to respect that."

I emptied my espresso cup and set it aside. "And he cares about this...more than you?"

She lifted her chin. "I'm not a thing."

I was tempted to make a comment about how she liked being treated like an object under the right circumstances, but I bit my tongue. Not every raw emotion needed to be deflected with humor.

Sometimes, it needed to be laid out and just...sat with. That was an uncomfortable truth I'd learned in the last few years of trying to clean my life up.

Deflection was the enemy of healing.

"No," I said. "You're not."

Her eyes stayed on me as she bit into her toast. I ate quickly, knowing I needed to be at the training center soon. She was still eating when I was done, so I went to shower. Halfway through, the door opened, and she slipped into the steamy space.

My stomach flipped.

Her hands slid around my neck. Right away, I was rock hard and lifting her in my arms, pressing her to the wall and reaching down to slide myself inside her pussy. There was the strangest ache in my chest as I fucked her, and I'd lost the urge to be rough.

I wanted to be so fucking gentle with her, even though it felt dangerous.

My hips worked as she buried her face into my neck. I made her come, and when I was finished, she kissed me, but she didn't meet my eyes as she got dressed for work. Then we went down to the back parking lot, and I opened her door and helped her in.

Her hands gripped the wheel as she glanced up through her lashes.

"Bye," she said. "Back to being co-workers."

I didn't say anything, but that word really got me. It wasn't wrong; we were two people working alongside each other. But after the things we'd done last night, co-worker felt laughable.

A little broken, I took the Kawasaki to the training center. Yale was already gone, so it was just me and my first class. Numbly, I moved through the motions. In the shooting range, I stayed back and let the upperclassmen work with the younger men. It wasn't like me to skimp on training. But truthfully, my social battery was low.

Maybe just dead.

I felt dirty, so I showered again. Then, I was halfway through putting my clothes on when the compulsion to shower again hit me. This time, I couldn't resist it, and I found myself scrubbing my skin raw under uncomfortably hot water.

My head spun. I hated this, hated being this way.

I wanted out of this body, out of this mind that tortured me.

But the only path to relief was a hard one. I needed to keep my promise to Gretchen and fill out the evaluation. My brain knew that, but the other part of me just couldn't make myself do it.

Head fucked up and skin tingling, I forced myself out of the shower and pulled my clothes on without drying. I needed to get out of here, or I'd be stuck scrubbing myself for the next few hours.

Trying to wash away all my imperfections until my skin bled.

Heart thudding, I grabbed my things and strode down the hall and out of the training center. I needed her again, but I couldn't do that. If I could have my way, I'd go to her office and take her away. I'd rent a hotel far away where no one could find us, and we'd stay in bed for days, just fucking and talking and eating.

She was the only person who made my brain quiet, who centered my system that was stuck in fight or flight.

She was the stillness in the eye of my hurricane, as soft and clear as an early morning, standing on stone steps, watching incense rise to the sky.

But she wasn't mine.

So, I drove until I ran out of road. Merrick had a chain of hotels that were being built along the coast. I took the Kawasaki out to one of the construction sites I knew would be empty today. The path wound up the mountains and ended at a flat, stone foundation that overlooked the sea.

There, I lit a cigarette and sank down to let my legs hang over the edge.

It was late when I stood up, body stiff, and went home.

CHAPTER TWENTY-THREE

CIRCE

I left Caden in the back parking lot and went to work, but I should have just gone home. My mind was restless. My body ached in the sweetest places from what he'd done to me. I couldn't focus on anything with a constant replay of last night going through my head.

Finally, around five, I left the office and went home.

The house was quiet. My heels clicked loudly down the hall as I walked into the kitchen. I'd half expected my father not to be home, but to my surprise, the side door was open, and I could see him standing in the garden.

Frowning, I set my purse aside and stepped outside.

"Hey," I said softly. "You good?"

He turned, arms crossed over his chest. I knew him well enough to realize instantly something was off.

"We need to talk, Circe," he said.

My heart skipped a beat. Had he found out what I was doing and who I was doing it with? Shame rose in my chest and I found myself working my hands together. Rubbing my white knuckles.

"Is everything okay?" I whispered.

He turned to face me. "I haven't been truthful with you when it comes to my intentions with the Welsh Mafia."

That wasn't what I'd expected.

"Okay, what...what does that mean?"

He cleared his throat. "I don't trust them, and I never intended on seeing this deal to the end."

My stomach dropped like a stone. "What?"

"The base Merrick has built is costly and it's vulnerable," he said. "My men are out there, being housed alongside his. All it would take is a little uprising, quick and clean, and I'll own all the infrastructure."

For the first time in my life, when I looked at my father, I didn't see the man who'd raised me, the safe, paternal one who'd tucked me in at night and kept me safe. Sudden revulsion rose in my throat, and I had to swallow it back.

He wasn't just my father. He was a man, a powerful one.

And he was hungry for more.

"Dad, that's...not right," I whispered.

He shrugged, his face hard. "It's not a lucrative deal for me unless I can train private security candidates at the same rate as Merrick. He's not giving me a fair shake."

"But you agreed to this," I protested. "You knew exactly what he was offering."

His eyes flashed and he strode past me to the doorway. "I never intended on honoring this agreement. Don't get soft on me. These people, this organization, they're not good people. They'd do the same to me."

He turned and disappeared inside. Into my head swam every second of last night with Caden, the nights we'd spent together in the lodge.

My blood turned to ice.

My father could never know I'd slept with the Welsh *Brenin's* son. I would be a traitor, and I knew exactly how Johansen Enterprises dealt with anyone who crossed them. I would be a public disgrace. I couldn't let my father know what I'd done, or I would lose everything.

I had to pretend I didn't care.

How could I when the world had shattered? Sickness rose in my chest, not from fear, but from disgust. My fists balled as I strode after my father, ducking into the dim kitchen. He stood at the island countertop, pouring two glasses of wine.

"Have a drink with me," he said.

Numbly, I obeyed. The wine touched my lips, acrid on my tongue.

Judas.

The word turned over in my head.

Who was the betrayer? Me or my father?

Or both of us?

"Your real mission is not to get approval from the board members, but to monitor Caden Payne closely," my father said, swirling his wine once. "He's the one person I'm worried about stopping me."

"Why did you keep this from me?" I whispered.

"What?"

A little spark of rage flared deep in my chest. From the beginning, I'd thought he'd assigned me the deal with the Welsh organization because I was capable. Because I'd given him years of my life. I'd gotten a degree for him. I'd sat there like a fucking porcelain doll in board meetings to make him proud.

I'd built my entire life around what he wanted.

And...he didn't have the courtesy to tell me the truth.

"Why did you keep this from me?" I said, my voice shaking.

His lids lowered, like he was ashamed. But that only lasted a moment before his cutthroat businessman mask slipped back on, and then he was back to being the CEO of Johansen Enterprises.

"Because you're a good person," he said. "And you wouldn't have done it."

My heart broke.

I'd always thought that was a metaphor, but I swore, I heard something crack in my chest. My insides were tender, pulsing with my heart like a wound.

Like a knife to the back.

Sick, I took a deep breath and tried to gather myself. He was staring at me, not like I was his daughter, but like I was his colleague.

"And why are you telling me now?" I whispered.

"Because it's time," he said. "Caden trusts you enough now, his guard is down. After this week, we'll only have one board member left. I need to cut things short before we get to the board meeting and hold the vote on this."

There was a long, painful silence. From my oldest memory, my father was the safest person in the world. But now, I wasn't so sure. He was looking at me like I didn't have a choice, which made me wonder what the consequences would be if I said no.

I swallowed hard. I needed to be very careful right now. My hand shook as I lowered my glass. My father's pale eyes dug into me.

"Does he mean something to you, sweetheart?" he said, his voice soft.

Immediately, I shook my head.

His brow raised.

"He means nothing to me, Dad," I whispered. "I work for you. I don't have to agree with what you're doing to carry out your wishes."

A muscle in his jaw twitched. "Why don't you agree with me?"

"I wouldn't do it," I said. "But I'm not in charge."

He stepped forward and put his hand on my cheek. I swallowed, biting back my tears, trying to keep my emotions hidden. That was what he wanted after all. He wanted me to be good, obedient, and fight for his company without ever questioning him.

"I love you," he said.

I nodded. A tear slipped out from my lashes, betraying me.

"What is it?" he pressed, taking my hand.

I shook my head, wiping my cheek. "Nothing, I can handle this. It's just a big task. That's it."

He took my face in his hands, and for a second, I thought he would comfort me. But he just turned it up so I was looking him in the eyes and held me there. My heart thudded, wondering what he saw in my eyes.

Did he see my guilt?

Finally, he bent and kissed my forehead. "I love you, Circe. You're my best asset."

I sniffed. "Thank you."

He released me and took up his wine, draining it. "Tomorrow, I want you to go see Caden Payne. I'd like you to bug his apartment so I know when he's there. He's the only one who can stop me, and I need him in Providence when we take the base."

Numb beyond belief, I nodded. He reached into his pocket and took out a little plastic case. I stood there, staring down at it, thinking about all the things Caden had done to me in that apartment, all the things I'd felt within those four walls.

My hand closed over the case—or rather, my father closed my hand over it. I cleared my throat to keep the tears back.

"I expect it to be live by the end of the week," he said. "You've got your work cut out for you."

"Yeah," I whispered. "I can do that."

He patted my arm and set his glass in the sink. "I have a long day tomorrow, so I'm going to bed. You'd better get your rest too."

He disappeared upstairs. I threw the rest of my wine in the sink and cleaned the kitchen, taking care to wipe down everything, stalling for time before I had to lie down and face reality. Finally, I turned off all the lights and dragged myself to my room.

I lay on my back for hours, staring up at the ceiling. Too stunned to feel. Too hurt to realize that deep down I was angry.

My father, my rock, had betrayed me.

It was early when I finally woke, my eyes swollen. I wrapped myself in a soft dressing gown and practically crawled to the kitchen for a glass of ice water and a coffee. There was a note from my father on the counter.

I'll be gone until tomorrow, but I will see you for our meeting. Love you. Make sure to finalize the paperwork for this leg of the mission. And keep your eye on the ball, sweetheart.

I knew what that last part meant—do what I want even though I lied to you and set you up. Guilt flooded me at the thought of what my father's plan required of me. I'd just slept in Caden's bed—not that it mattered. When I put a knife in his back, he'd never look at me the same way again.

We would be over.

For the first time in years, I went upstairs to my bedroom and cried like a baby. Hard, curled up in the shower, water streaming down my face and mingling with my tears and snot. The last thing I wanted to do was betray Caden.

I had a horrible feeling this was the real thing.

It took me an hour and a lot of rolling with a frozen jade stone to repair my puffy face. My phone had a million unanswered texts. My heart hurt as I skimmed over all the people I was ignoring because I couldn't tell them the truth.

The truth was...I was falling for Caden Payne. But he was the last person in the world I could end up with, especially after what my father had asked of me last night.

We were doomed for heartache.

Miserably, I took my birth control and swallowed it down with a green juice. I was still wet between my legs from how much he'd come inside me. Hopefully, the pill held up, because the only thing that could make this mess worse was if he got me pregnant.

I took a test, just to be sure, because my emotions were all over the place. I had a few in the cabinet that Delaney had left last year when she'd had a scare.

Negative.

I wasn't pregnant, I was just devastated.

But there was no time to lick my wounds in peace. I did my hair and makeup and slipped on a pale mauve pencil skirt and a white blouse. The skirt was a little short, but I didn't care. If anyone looked my way, I was in the perfect mood to rip them to shreds.

My office at Johansen's Enterprises was quiet. My personal assistant, Stephanie, had it set up with flowery diffusers that bubbled quietly. My avocado toast and tea sat on the desk beside my laptop. I sank down and rubbed my eyes. Carefully, so I didn't mess up my makeup.

Despair seeped in, moving through my veins like blood.

This wasn't enough anymore.

My father should just cover me in plastic wrap, put me in a display case, and let me rot there forever. It would be more honest than what he was doing now.

My calendar pinged. I tapped my laptop, and the screen appeared.

I had a meeting with Caden. Of course, before everything had gone down, we were supposed to meet in the boardroom with my father before the next mission started. I hovered over my phone.

Maybe I should tell him not to come.

There was a light tap on the door, and Stephanie popped her head in. "Um...you have a visitor," she said.

I frowned, hoping it was Caden and hoping it wasn't.

"Who? Do they have an appointment?"

"No, but I thought I should let you know," she said.

"Who is it?"

She leaned in and mouthed something. I stared, confused.

"Who?"

She slipped inside and shut the door. "Merrick Llwyd."

My stomach dropped like a stone. My palms went instantly clammy, and my hands twisted in my lap. What was the Welsh *Brenin* doing here, in my office? What did the father of the man I'd just fucked senseless want with me? Had he found out?

I adjusted my face. No one could know how I felt.

"You can send him in," I said primly.

She chewed her lip for a second, hesitating. I nodded firmly, and she slipped out, pulling the door open. She darted to the side, and a tall man in a dark suit strode through my door.

It was the first time I'd met Merrick in person. My stomach twisted as we looked at each other over the desk.

He was handsome, like Caden, but ranging more into the silver fox area. His dark hair was brushed back, his cobalt eyes bigger than Caden's, framed with the same heavy, dark lashes. He had a strong jaw, a heavy nose with a flatter bridge than his son, and the same thin mouth.

He sat down, smiling politely.

"Hello, Miss Johansen," he said, his dark, rich tone curling like Caden's but without the accent.

I held out my hand. He shook it, flashing the wedding band on his other hand as he adjusted his jacket. I knew his wife a little bit; we'd exchanged a few pleasantries in the women's bathroom at the country club. She was a lot younger than him, and she was always well dressed and covered in diamonds.

I knew what that meant for men from his organization.

"Can I help you with something, sir?" I asked, keeping my voice casual.

"I'll be here for the meeting with Caden and your father," he said. "I thought I'd stop by early."

"Oh?" I rose and moved to the coffee and tea bar. "Can I get you anything?"

"Unless you have a pour over, then no thank you," he said.

"I do, actually," I said, opening the cabinet.

He had an overwhelming presence, and I could feel the combativeness. There was no world in which he didn't know I was more than just co-workers with his son. My stomach twisted as I made him a coffee and brought it over. He dipped his head, not taking his eyes from me as I sank down.

"Did you have something you wanted to ask?" I said.

His brow arced. "How well do you know Caden?"

I leaned back, crossing one leg over the other.

"I know he's your son."

His face didn't change. "Who told you that?"

"My father guessed," I said. "You look a lot alike."

He crossed his leg, mimicking me. His head cocked, and there was something in his eyes that made them dark, a little dangerous.

"Are you fucking my son?" he said, his voice low.

My jaw went slack as heat poured up my spine and washed over my face.

"Excuse me?" I gasped.

"It's an easy question. Are you sleeping with my son?"

"Caden doesn't need you to defend him," I snapped.

"I don't trust you."

"And yet, you're willing to take money from my company."

"Your father gets a satisfactory cut of the profits. He'll walk away happy so long as you keep your end of the bargain." His face remained as still as stone. His eyes burned softly, like his fuse was lit but not yet an inferno.

A chill went down my spine.

"Are you trying to bully me?" I said.

He cocked his head. "I don't bully women. We have a strict policy against hurting women at all in the organization. Your father is fair game, though. How much do you love him?"

I faltered, caught off guard.

"How dare you?" I whispered.

"If you're fucking him to mess with his head, to betray or hurt him, I will gut your father like an animal," he said softly. "I'll drain your empire from the inside and leave you with nothing."

Anger flared, washing away the guilt. Maybe my father was right not to trust the organization. I'd never seen anyone with such intense hatred in his eyes, like he really could disembowel my father without a second thought.

"Please leave," I said, keeping my voice steady.

"I'd rather not," he said.

"Or what?"

He leaned in. "Or I'll make good on my threat. Do you want to know what happened to the last person who hurt someone I loved?"

"What? You canceled their loan?"

His eyes flared. "I tied him to a chair and beat him to death with my hands."

The silence was deafening. My stomach roiled, and the peppermint tea on my desk suddenly smelled disgusting. Sickness washed over me, coupled with fear. I was under too much stress, torn up with guilt, and Merrick was scaring me to death.

"Get out," I whispered.

Sweat broke out over my face and down my back. My stomach churned as the realization hit me that I was in over my head. This mission was supposed to be my test, but my father had overestimated my abilities in pulling me into his scheme to betray Merrick.

I wasn't prepared to be caught between three of the most powerful men in our city.

I was twenty-five years old and green—Caden was right about that.

I definitely wasn't equipped to face off with Merrick Llwyd.

He frowned, and I stood up abruptly, turning towards the bathroom. My head swam, my knees buckled, and suddenly, I was on my knees on the ground with Merrick crouched before me. He lifted me gently, setting me back in the chair.

"Are you sick?" he asked, reaching for a paper napkin. He poured a little ice water onto it and applied it to my wrists.

"No." I shook my head, mouth dry.

He glanced up and back down. "How long have you and my son been together?"

I cleared my throat. "I'm not pregnant."

Was that a hint of...relief? It was hard to tell. His mouth thinned as he pressed the wet napkin to my inner wrist. It felt like it was working—my racing pulse was slowing down.

"Do you scare your wife like that?" I said weakly.

He laughed, looking up at me with a softened expression. My heart ached. It was paternal, not dissimilar to how my father looked at me.

"I feel sorry for the women involved with men like us," he said finally. "Your father should be ashamed to put you at the forefront of his business instead of protecting you. Over my dead body would my wife be put in a situation like this."

I bristled. "What does that mean?"

He sighed, releasing my hand. "My organization is traditional. We're making strides, but we still have firm beliefs we'll never change."

"Like being a misogynist?"

"It's not misogynistic to protect your wife or daughter," he said quietly. "Your father put you on a platter and served you to the wolves."

"I can handle myself," I snapped.

"I'm trying to make you understand how vulnerable you are." He rose and sank down to sit on my desk. "Your father isn't looking out for you."

I sniffed, unsure if I was angry or confused.

"My son isn't thinking straight," he said. "Your father is hungry for power. It's the only reason he signed that deal."

God, if only he knew. Sickness roiled in my stomach.

"And you?" I ran my hand under my nose, still shaking. "What do you want with me?"

"Just to warn you."

"So you're saying that, because I'm a woman, I'm disadvantaged?"

He nodded. "Yes, you are."

I frowned. "That's a horrible thing to say."

"It's not if it's the truth," he said.

My mouth felt sticky, and my eyes burned. "Okay," I said wearily. "Consider me warned."

He stood and buttoned his jacket. "My wife would like to meet you," he said, his voice going abruptly back to a pleasant tone, like we'd never had this conversation.

"Why?"

"Because we'll both be there for the opening weekend of my hotel," he said. "I know your next target will be there, so you'll be busy part of the time, but she'd love to grab a drink with you the first night."

I got to my feet, forcing my body not to shake. "Is this your way of fucking with me? Using your wife?"

His eyes flashed and his mouth thinned. "Unlike some others, we don't use our women as shields or weapons."

"Don't insult my father," I said firmly.

Merrick inclined his head. "As you wish. Maybe his intentions are purer than I anticipate."

Guilt surged. He was right; my father had less than pure intentions with the Welsh organization. But he wasn't using me as a weapon—he thought he was giving me an opportunity. He was trying to prepare me for the real world where I'd be running his empire, and that involved making hard choices. I stayed silent as Merrick went to the door, pulling it open.

He paused, looking back. "If you find yourself in trouble, call me."

"I don't have your number," I said coldly.

"I'll leave it with Stephanie."

"Don't bother."

He dipped his head, and the door swung shut. I heard him talking with Stephanie on the other side of the door as I sank down. My laptop screen stared back at me as emails piled up, messages sitting at the corner of the screen.

I wanted to scream and smash it.

Instead, I picked up the phone. The ringtone buzzed twice.

"Hey," Caden said.

"Hi," I said, keeping my tone bright and professional like I was dealing with a client. "I'd like you to head to my office and fuck me over my desk. Disrespectfully, please. Does twenty minutes from now work for you?"

There was a short, shocked silence.

"Uh...okay," he said. "I'm at training right now."

"And I need you to blow my back out before this meeting," I said. "So wrap up whatever you're doing and be here in twenty."

He laughed quietly. "Yes, ma'am."

I set my phone aside and went to the window. Merrick stood in the parking lot next to a fancy black Audi. He had his aviators on, and he was smoking, staring up at the sky like nothing bothered him.

My fists clenched. I was tired of being fucked with.

No one came in here and talked to me like that without consequences.

CHAPTER TWENTY-FOUR

CIRCE

He showed up twenty minutes later, on the dot. Stephanie let him in, a crease between her brows. She was probably wondering why I had a trail of men who looked vaguely like each other going in and out of my office.

Caden looked like a million dollars in dress pants and a white button up, open at the collar. I ushered him inside and locked the door, hitting the button to lower the shades.

His cobalt eyes glittered, not unlike his father's. Anger simmered as my fingers moved down the buttons of my blouse.

"Couldn't wait?" His brow crooked.

"It's complicated."

My blouse fell to the ground, and he picked me up, shoving my skirt over my ass and yanking my panties down, and set me on the desk. I pushed my laptop aside and spread my legs.

"Don't be too loud," he murmured, kissing up the side of my neck.

"Why?" I gasped, reckless for the first time in forever. "Who cares if I get laid in my office? I'm the chief operating officer; what are they going to do to me?"

He smiled against my throat. "I like it."

He reached between us and unfastened his belt, lowering the front of his pants. He was hard and gorgeous, pierced and ready to slide into me and scratch that itch. I pushed my hips close hungrily, running a hand over his shoulders.

"You know, you'd look good with a buzz cut," I panted, dragging my nails through his hair. "You've got such a good face; your hair kind of takes away from it."

"Oh yeah?" He laughed, spitting into his hand and rubbing it over my pussy.

"Better do it if that's what I want," I teased.

He gripped my thigh and yanked me down onto his cock. Pain split through my hips as my brain went blank. Euphoria followed the discomfort as I adjusted to his hard, veined length. His lids drooped, eyes flooding with lust.

"Fuck me, that first thrust is always so good," he murmured.

I worked my hips. "So good," I breathed.

He braced his hand on the desk, bending me back slowly until I was flush against the desk. His face and broad chest, half covered in a white shirt, filled my vision.

"I don't care if you run this empire," he said quietly. "When my cock is in you, you're nothing but my whore."

He pumped his hips once, stroking the piercing over my G-spot, making my eyes roll back in my head and an undignified whine slip out. He lifted my leg and slapped my thigh. Pain splintered beneath his hand, and my pussy ached.

"God, you're just the worst," I gasped.

"You wanted disrespected, I'll give you fucking disrespected," he said, leaning in. His fingers pressed my lips apart so he could spit onto my tongue. Obediently, I swallowed. "I'm going to fuck your pussy and come down your throat."

"Don't ruin my makeup," I begged.

He pulled out and flipped me, bending me over the desk in front of him and spreading my thighs with his knees.

"I won't ruin your makeup," he said, shoving his cock into me. "Can't make any promises about your pussy, though."

He fucked me in the most deliciously disrespectful way. Hand on the nape of my neck, keeping my head down. Other hand on the desk so he could brace himself and slam into me again and again. At some point, the friction of my clit and piercing against the desk sent me over the edge.

Shaking hard, I came, biting my mouth until I tasted blood to keep quiet.

He slapped my ass, the sound like a whip cracking. Then, he pulled out, right when I was about to tap out, and sank down into my chair, but not before locking the wheels. His hand snagged my wrist, yanking me into his lap.

"Sit on my cock, butterfly," he panted, midnight blue eyes burning.

For some reason, that name didn't bother me this time. Obediently, I climbed into his lap and reached between us to grip his hot length. Our eyes met as I sank down onto it, wincing. His hips worked, getting me acclimated to taking him from this angle.

"Ride me," he ordered.

My nails pierced his chest through his shirt. His eyes glittered and his lips parted. Sweat etched down his chest, catching in the dark hair between his pecs, leaving glittering trails down his tattoos.

His big, lean hands gripped by hips, guiding me as I began shifting gently back and forth. I didn't want to admit it, not even to myself, but I didn't really know what I was doing on top. I'd done this once, maybe twice, and that was years ago.

"Feeling okay?" he murmured.

"Yes," I gasped. "You're just big...but don't get cocky about it. It's a lot."

The corner of his mouth jerked up. "I'd rather not hurt you. But I like seeing you struggle to take it."

My pace quickened and he groaned, his fingers clenching on my hips. It hurt, but not much. His fingers slid down between us and found my clit, stroking it with his thumb.

"Come for me," he breathed. "It'll give you more room."

I was so turned on, it wouldn't take much. He slid his other hand up and pulled my bra down around my waist. My breasts fell out and his lids dropped. He had that clouded expression he got when we fucked. Heavy lids over lust drenched eyes. His lips parted, showing

214

a sliver of bottom teeth. He leaned in, still playing with my clit, and caught my nipple in his mouth.

"Oh God," I whispered, burying my hand in his hair.

His hips rose and fell, fucking up into me. My orgasm sparked, growing and tightening in my core as he moved me closer and closer. My head fell back. Heat surged down my spine and thighs. My toes curled.

He sucked my nipple, grazing it with his teeth.

I came, so hard that all I could do was shake in his lap, helpless. He groaned, keeping the same pace until the last bits of pleasure were wrung from me. Then, he lifted me off his cock, and I sank to the ground at his feet.

He shifted to the edge of the chair. "Come close," he ordered.

I obeyed, head empty. He slid his hand under my jaw and guided my head into his lap. In my heels, my toes curled. There was something so deliciously degrading about letting him fuck my mouth in my own office. I parted my lips, and he slid into my mouth, tasting slightly sweet and salty, like lust. His other hand gathered my hair in his fist.

He pushed, and I gagged.

"All the way for me, butterfly," he breathed.

He pressed his hips in, and the head touched my throat and I gagged again. Instead of easing up, his hand slid down my throat, gently caressing it, distracting me from the sensation of having his cock forced into such a sensitive part of me.

"Breathe through your nose," he murmured. "Relax your throat for me."

I obeyed, and he groaned softly, fingers stroking over my neck. Everything in me fought the intrusion, but he just kept going, making my head spin.

"Swallow," he ordered.

Had he finished already? Confused, I swallowed, and my gag reflexes flared as the head of his pierced cock touched the back of my throat.

"Go on," he said, voice hushed. "A little more for me, sweetheart."

I swallowed again, fighting to stay relaxed as he went deep.

"I'm going to fuck your throat," he said, his voice low and gentle. "Hit my leg if you need out."

I couldn't respond, not even to nod. But I didn't want out; I wanted to stay on my knees and let him use me like his own personal sex toy. So I just moaned, and he gasped, his hips working gently, fucking with short strokes.

His phone buzzed on the desk. And to my horror, he picked it up and put it to his ear.

"Lukas," he said, his breathing suddenly even. "Is this about the meeting?"

Heart pounding like a drum, I stayed perfectly still with my eyes locked on him, his cock halfway down my throat. He ran his fingers through my hair, taking care not to mess it up. The side of his knuckles stroked my cheek.

God, this was wrong. I wasn't even sure if I recognized myself anymore. Old me would have never done anything so scandalous.

"I'm not sure why she didn't pick up," Caden drawled. "I'm not with her. I assume she's in her office, as we have a meeting in a few minutes."

His hips adjusted, fucking me with tiny strokes. I gagged, and saliva slipped from the corners of my mouth. His hand closed on the back of my head, keeping my face in his lap.

"That's fine, we can push the meeting fifteen minutes," he said.

There was another silence.

"Merrick said he was already there," he said. "Alright, that's fine. Same place as usual works. See you then."

He hung up, tossing the phone aside. I sent him an inquiring look, but he shook his head. He was so hard in my mouth, I could feel the throb of his heartbeat.

"Suck," he said, his voice firm.

My pussy throbbed; my nipples ached. Obediently, I started sucking him, curling my tongue along his length as I went. His hand slid back under my chin, and I wondered if he could feel his cock through my throat. But I didn't have time to dwell on that, because his thighs stiffened.

"Fuck, butterfly," he breathed. "Take all of me."

He spilled into my mouth and down my throat, salty and tasting like Caden. My hand dug into his legs as I let him come, sucking him gently through his pleasure. Finally, his body relaxed, and he pulled me back, letting me sit on my heels.

I looked up at him, waiting.

He leaned in and kissed my mouth. "That's my girl."

CHAPTER TWENTY-FIVE

CADEN

I already had a hard time concentrating, but sitting in a meeting with Lukas, after what I'd done to his daughter? Keeping my focus was impossible. She sat on his other side, all proper with her spine straight and her hands folded. Like I hadn't just bent her over and fucked her before making her swallow my cum on her knees in her own office.

Merrick sat beside me, a distinct aura of disappointment around him.

He knew, I'd known that since he'd texted me. But we hadn't spoken about it yet.

We moved over the information for the upcoming weekend. Our target, Raine Forge, would be there on the second day. He'd stay from Friday to Sunday morning. He'd bring his wife and college-age son. Circe and I had two full days to make him feel at ease over this deal and sign his name on the paperwork.

I was confident I could do it.

I just had to keep from getting distracted.

That might be hard. I glanced sideways at Circe, but she was as motionless as a doll propped up in a chair. There was a discreet smile on her face, eyes glazed over.

She was a far cry from the woman I'd fucked last night.

I wanted to see her like that again. Totally bare, nothing between us.

On her back on the cool stone in the early morning. Naked thighs trembling. My cum spilling from her pussy like an offering. Her soft moans rising like incense into the sky.

I snapped back to reality. I was disassociating again, and if I didn't get it together, the mission was going to suffer.

"Are you comfortable with that?" Lukas sat back.

I nodded. "I can do it. Circe?"

She swallowed, clearing her throat. "Yeah, it should be good."

She was completely closed off, her face like smooth marble. We parted in the hallway like we barely knew each other, but I felt Stephanie's eyes on my back. There was no way she hadn't heard Circe moaning earlier, but I would let Circle handle that.

I had problems of my own, one of them being Gretchen Hughes.

I'd missed my first therapy appointment, I hadn't filled out the paperwork, and I'd ignored three calls from her. Part of me regretted it. Part of me wondered why I needed therapy when I had Circe's pussy. I had my doubts that Gretchen could give me anything that worked better.

Merrick caught up to me in the parking lot. I paused, knocking my sunglasses over my eyes and throwing a leg over the Kawasaki.

"Gretchen called me yesterday," he said. "She was worried about you."

I sighed. To my surprise, he took a pack of cigarettes from his pocket and offered me one. Merrick smoked, but not often, and even less since he'd gotten married. He'd said something about health insurance once, but I knew it had more to do with what Clara wanted.

I took the proffered cigarette and let him light it. The wind was coming in from the coast, and it took him a few tries to get his going. When it finally lit, he blew a thin stream of smoke into the blue sky.

"When are you going to get it together?" he said flatly.

I winced.

"I've been kind, Caden," he said, his voice strained. "I've been so fucking patient with you."

My throat tightened. I inhaled, holding it in along with everything else.

"Just go to therapy," he said softly. "Swallow your pride for once in your life. You're thirty fucking years old. If you fucking can't do it for yourself, do it for me."

Merrick didn't swear this much—he really was at the end of his rope. There was a long silence where my father just stared up at the sky, a muscle in his jaw twitching.

"Why did you get here early?" I asked.

"I came because the person who has the most to lose is sitting upstairs in her office right now and no one, not even her own father, is looking out for her," he said. "Least of all, you."

That hurt. Not the words, but the tone. My brain went into overdrive, completing the sentence without my consent. *Least of all...you, you colossal fuck up.*

Merrick would never insult me like that. But my brain was so used to hearing it, it finished his sentence with what it thought I deserved.

What I used to think I deserved.

"How did you know I've been with her?" I asked.

"You didn't spend the night with us," he said. "So either you're magically cured, or you've been sleeping with Circe. Given that I saw her leave your apartment, I'd say it's the latter."

I cleared my throat and considered putting up my defenses. I could bite back, throw a cutting remark in his face that I was this way because other people had made me like this. That's what the old Caden would have done.

Instead, I nodded.

"You're right, it's risky," I said. "And I'm sorry I've ignored Gretchen. I'll call her."

He was shocked into silence. His cigarette burned down, seconds from his mouth.

"And I won't let anything compromise this mission. I swore to get you what you wanted, and I'll do anything and everything to keep that promise and complete the deal with Lukas."

"But you won't stop sleeping with his daughter," Merrick said.

I shook my head. "No, I won't."

"Why?" He took off his sunglasses and fixed his eyes on me. The emotion there caught me off guard.

"When did you know?" I said, my voice barely a whisper.

He leaned back, staring up at the sky like he didn't want me to see what he was feeling.

"When all the bullshit in my head went quiet," he said finally.

He might as well have nailed my coffin shut. If he'd intended on coming here to keep me away from Circe, it was having the opposite effect.

We finished our cigarettes in silence, and he threw the butts in the nearby trash. When he returned to where I still sat on the bike, he crossed his arms over his chest.

"Clara wants to meet her," he said.

I turned the key, making the Kawasaki purr.

"No," I said firmly. "We're just fucking."

"I know how 'just fucking' ends," he said.

"Oh yeah. Where's that?"

He laughed quietly. "It ends with you shelling out twenty to thirty grand for engagement jewelry."

I snorted. "I'm not that traditional."

His eyes narrowed. "I can't keep you from being with her, but you'd better give her what she deserves. She's organization adjacent, so you're bound by the rules."

"Is that why you're here? To make sure I'm compliant to engagement traditions?"

"Do whatever you want." He pulled open the Audi door. "Just wear a condom."

"Take it from someone who knows, huh?"

Merrick sighed and sank into the driver's seat. "I'm not the person to tell you to walk away from her if you have real feelings for her," he said. "I should have walked away from Clara, but I didn't. But as your commander, any fallout from this situation is yours to clean up. Understood?"

"Yes, sir," I said.

He drove off, and I took the Kawasaki to the training center. When I'd changed and arrived at the underground shooting range, I found Maelon already there. He was sitting on a bench by the door, boots dug into the sandy ground, staring into the distance.

"Where are the others?" he asked as I walked in.

"No others," I said, setting my gun case down. "I want to assess you."

He got up, cracking his neck. "I can't shoot. There's no point."

I unzipped the case and assembled the pistol inside. His eyes widened as I held it out grip first, pointing down. "Let's go."

He lifted it and I flinched, sidestepping. Right away, he caught on he'd fucked up.

"Down," I ordered. "Unless you intend to shoot someone, never point a gun at them. When you mean to kill, you point and shoot."

"Yes, sir," he said uncomfortably. "Can I ask you a question, sir?"

I pointed towards the first lane, and he moved ahead, waiting for me to step up behind him. "Sure, kid."

"Have you killed people?" he asked.

I felt my jaw tighten. "With a gun?"

His eyes darted over me, curious instead of horrified. "Yeah, either."

"Give me the gun," I said, taking it from him. "Now stand with your foot here, other foot here. You're going to want to feel pretty secure, and you're a tall kid, so make sure the recoil doesn't fuck you up. Make sense?"

He nodded, his face tight. I could tell he was nervous.

"You have a problem working with guns?" I asked.

He shook his head, eyes flaring up. "No, I'm just better with knives."

"You can show me that later. I need to know what your natural talent looks like. Now, put your arm up...like that."

222

He copied me, keeping his back straight. I circled him to check his form and was surprised by how good it was. He had a strong stance for a beginner, and his eyes were fixed on the target instead of bouncing around the room.

I laid the gun in his palm. "Close your hand. Like that."

He obeyed, curling his finger instinctively.

"No," I said. "Finger straight unless you intend on shooting. Control the urge to curl around the trigger. Understood?"

He nodded.

"That'll be a no sir or yes sir," I said.

"I meant, yes, sir, I understand," he said, ears going red.

"Good."

I moved behind him, locking my hands behind my back. "Shift your finger up and hit the button so that it shows red. That's your safety. You do not hit that button until you're ready to shoot. As soon as you're done, you hit that button again. The safety is not a substitute for trigger discipline. Guns can still go off when the safety is applied. Understood?"

"Yes, sir," he said.

He was learning fast.

"Hit the safety, point, shoot," I said.

"I...I don't know how to aim," he stammered.

"I'm not asking you to aim. I said shoot."

He faltered, and I narrowed my eyes, studying him. Maybe he wasn't as scrappy or ballsy as I'd initially thought.

"Maelon," I said, my voice even. "Hit the safety, point to hit the center of the target, and shoot. This isn't a test; it's an assessment of your raw talents. On my mark."

His spine tensed.

"Go," I barked.

He hit the safety, shifted the gun, and pulled the trigger. The bullet ripped through the paper target, three inches from the center. My brows shot up, and it took me a second to rearrange my face.

"Empty it," I said.

He obeyed, shooting five more times in a jagged circle around the center point. Then he lifted his finger, flicked the safety off, and pointed the pistol at the ground before turning around to face me.

"You never answered me, sir," he said, his tone controlled, like he was trying to stay respectful.

"About what?"

"Killing people," he said.

I took the gun from him, reaching for a loaded clip. "Yes, I have killed people. With and without guns."

He was staring at me with glittering eyes, like the curtains had finally parted and everything made sense. My throat tightened and my mouth went dry. My first day at the training center, when I saw Merrick step up to train me, I'd felt the same thing.

My very first sense of being a part of something.

Of belonging.

"Let's show you how to aim," I said, passing him the gun. "Then you can really tear shit up in here."

My ears were ringing by the time I dug the plugs out and headed to the showers. Maelon was quiet as he packed everything up and I showed him where to store it. The two other recruits showed up just as we were leaving, and they started talking together while Yale got the room ready for the next class.

I split off, feeling confused by the memories today had dug up. My chest was raw when I got back to my apartment and opened my computer on the countertop.

Gretchen had resent the assessment.

I ran a hand over my face, poured a cup of coffee, and hit the link.

CHAPTER TWENTY-SIX

CIRCE

When I got home, I found my father in the kitchen, having takeout sushi on the island countertop. For a second, I considered letting all my rage out and telling him he'd used me. But when he lifted his head, I could tell how this was going to go. He was going to pretend nothing was wrong, expect me to do the same, and leave me with a pat on the head for my troubles.

I pulled off my heels and dropped my purse, stomping in to grab a cup of water. He frowned, sending me a confused glance.

"What are you doing?"

"Eating."

His phone buzzed, and he glanced down. Then, quick as a flash, he flipped it over to conceal the screen. I stared, dumbfounded.

"What? Someone send you a nude?" I snapped before I could bite it back.

"Excuse me?" he said, brows rising to his hairline.

"Sorry, I just...got up on the wrong side of the bed," I said, backpedaling hard.

His shocked expression melted, revealing a flicker of something else in his eyes. I leaned in, studying his face, and immediately felt awful. He was tired, his eyes red like he'd been up all night.

"Are you okay?" I asked.

He nodded. "Going through some personal bumps. But it's fine."

Suddenly, I was a little girl, and it was just me and my father against the world. Guiltily, I took a beat to wrestle with my roiling emotions. We might be butting heads in business, but outside that, I still loved him unconditionally.

I chewed my lip. "Sorry, work has been stressing me out. Maybe we should take some time to talk. I definitely could use that...I'm a little hurt after—"

"No, you have a life," he interrupted. "Maybe we were too dependent on each other anyway."

I reeled back. "What?"

He sighed, crossing his arms. "Maybe we should talk about you getting a house. Or an apartment."

My poor, broken heart ached. "You want me to move out?"

"Circe, you're twenty-five," he said reasonably. "This isn't an unreasonable conversation to have at this point."

"Dad," I said, horrified. "You're dating someone seriously, aren't you? Am I making you uncomfortable being here?"

He lifted his hand. "No, it's just...well, maybe I am seeing someone. But I'm not ready for introductions."

"Why?" I was having a hard time keeping the pain out of my voice.

His eyes narrowed. "Are you ready to introduce me to the man you're seeing?"

My heart stopped. Had he seen Caden and I together?

"What?" I squeaked.

His lips thinned. "Honey, you're clearly seeing someone."

"We're just f—casual," I blurted out.

He gave a heavy sigh. "Let's talk about this like adults. It would be nice if I had a house where I could bring my dates home without making you feel awkward. I'm sure you would like to bring your dates home as well."

Did he want privacy...or did he just want me gone?

"Dad, I don't want to talk about that part of my life."

He sighed. "Alright, I'm heading out to sleep in a hotel in the city because you won't talk to me like an adult."

My stomach twisted. It was better he thought that was the truth, even though it wasn't. In reality, I was terrified that if I talked to him, I'd accidentally out the person I was sleeping with as Caden. It was better he thought I was just being immature, not sleeping with the man he'd ordered me to betray.

"Okay, that's fine," I said, throwing up my hands.

"Tell your boy toy I said hello," he called as I padded down the hall and up the stairs.

I slammed my door, heart pounding. I had to be more careful, or he was going to start putting pressure on me to meet Caden. And that couldn't happen. I'd gotten giddy and careless, intoxicated by all his tattoos and beautiful eyes and magic tongue.

I'd gotten sloppy.

Maybe deep down, that was what Caden wanted. He was, after all, on the opposing team.

I took a long bath with lavender salts to calm down and soothe my bruised feelings. I was chin deep in soapy water, my damp hair piled on my head, when my phone buzzed, revealing Caden's name. I scowled. No, he was not going to sweet talk me into his bed again tonight.

I hit the speaker button and set it on the edge of the tub.

"What do you want?" I asked.

He laughed softly. "You changed your tune since this morning."

"Kind of had a fight with my dad," I grumbled.

From outside, I heard my father's car door slam. Wheels rolled down the drive, and the gate screeched open and shut. I let out a small sigh.

"He just left," I whispered.

"Okay," he said, his voice low. "I'll come to you, butterfly."

"No, no, don't do that. We have security cameras."

"So shut them off. See you in ten." The phone clicked, and he was gone.

I gritted my teeth. All around me was a world I'd made for myself of pink and gauze. I'd erected barricades of the things that had kept me safe through my girlhood.

Silk, ribbons, fairy lights, fluttering curtains. All in the same shade of mauve, carefully color matched from my mother's wind chime.

Caden didn't fit into this world.

He'd probably think it was silly that I still had a canopy bed with gauze curtains and roses on the headboard. He was a fighter—and not the kind I knew how to deal with, the ones who fought through lawyers in crisp suits—he had blood on his hands and scars hidden beneath the ink on his skin. He was used to living an utilitarian existence.

There was no world where we melded together into one.

Wrathfully, I got out of the tub. For a moment, I considered putting on a sweatsuit to cover every inch of my body, but then I pulled on a silk slip instead. He'd already seen all of me, what did it matter?

My hand shook—why was I shaking—as I brushed on some mascara and lipgloss. I debated putting my contact lenses in and decided against it. It was alright not to look perfect for him.

The glaze over me was cracking, but it still held firm.

I heard the whine of his Kawasaki before I saw it. On my bare feet, I pattered down to the side door, flipped the cameras off, and hit the button to lift the gate. He appeared around the corner, looking so good that all my thoughts of making him go home disappeared. My breathing calmed, my heart slowed. A little piece of me that had felt lopsided since I'd left him this morning clicked back into place.

He pulled around the side and parked against the wall. I waited at the kitchen door, watching him take his helmet off and hang it on the handlebars.

My stomach swooped.

He'd cut his hair.

It was short, almost a buzz cut. Heat roared through my veins, and my jaw dropped. He was gorgeous, like a marble bust, a Roman statue in a museum, but in full color. Black lashes as soft as a feather on his cheek, bright blue eyes just like his father's glittering in the dark, unhindered by his hair.

I backed up, almost tripping on the kitchen stoop. He stepped inside, ducking so he wouldn't hit his head on the frame. Our eyes locked.

"Are you alone?" he asked.

"My dad's gone," I whispered.

His hand shot out, gripping me by the neck. For a second, all I saw was his wild, gleaming eyes before he pulled me against his body and his mouth came down on mine.

Kissing me like it was the last time we'd ever touch.

We were both panting when we broke apart. He brushed back a tangle of my damp hair and kissed the side of my neck in the same spot he always did. My bare toes curled on the cold floor.

"Why do you kiss me in the same place every time?" I gasped.

He nuzzled into the bend of my neck. "You have three little freckles there."

Guilt swept through me like a flood and made my stomach churn. I pulled back, gasping.

He frowned. "What?"

I shook my head, wordless.

"Talk to me," he ordered.

I couldn't tell him tonight, but in the last few days, I'd done nothing but reconsider my promise to complete my father's mission. When I'd agreed to it, I hadn't known my father's real plans.

I hadn't known I would fall for the *Brenin's* son.

I didn't know what it was like to sleep in Caden's arms, to feel his warm, lean body against mine. I didn't yet know that he dreamed of me in Aphrodite's temple in the cool of the morning, our bodies entwined on the stone ground, smelling of incense and sex.

My throat closed up. My eyes were sticky.

I wanted out.

That was the horrible truth of it. I wanted out, and there was no safety latch, no parachute to catch me if he let me fall when I finally told him the truth.

If I didn't betray Caden, I would betray my father. I couldn't have them both. I had to make a choice.

My father had made me responsible, but there was still a tiny fragment of me that longed for freedom, the kind Caden had spoken of that night at the koi pond, when he'd told me he dreamed of ancient worlds. When he'd explained the proper Welsh understanding of *Hireath*. At first, I'd dismissed it, but when I found the flaw in his story, it haunted me.

"No, a longing for what could have been. A place you'll always want, but never get."

There was no temple of Aphrodite at Ephesus; it was a temple to Artemis. I'd looked it up until my eyes went blurry from staring at my phone screen. I'd considered bringing this up to him, but I never had the courage to correct him on his mistake.

Now, I wondered if it was a mistake at all.

Maybe he dreamed of a place that had never been, that never would be, a pocket of space where we were together that was never meant to be real.

He dreamed of laying with me in a temple that had never existed.

Instead, we were heading into a very different story. I was going to be his real-life Brutus and bury my father's knife so deeply in Caden's back, there would be no bringing us back from the dead. That story would be real, visceral, and bloody.

Not beautiful like incense and stone.

I lifted my eyes. His beautiful face was half shrouded, half lit by the stove light. My heart ached. It didn't matter if I told him right now that I felt something more for him. Or never. It wouldn't change the outcome.

But I could give us just one more night in my bed.

My mouth shook as I forced it into a smile. "Take me upstairs."

He didn't have to be asked twice. He lifted me off my feet, one arm beneath my knees and the other securely around my back, like he was carrying me over the threshold on our wedding night.

"I'm assuming we head up the enormous marble staircase that way?" he said.

I nodded, slipping my arms around his neck. He carried me through the hall and up the curved staircase, hardly breaking a sweat. I watched the living room below fall away in a haze, wondering if this is what it felt like for people who had real feelings for each other. not rivals who had nothing but stolen nights and a tragic end.

"I'm at the end," I whispered, laying my head on his shoulder.

He paused before my door, and I turned the knob, letting it swing open. His eyes skimmed over the plush carpet, the flowery wallpaper trim, the lace curtains, and the bed surrounded by a cloud of gauze. A soft floral scent puffed from the diffuser, and the nighttime breeze fluttered through the cracked windows.

"Exactly how I thought it would be," he remarked.

Being in my room, my safest space, with him was chasing away the overwhelming guilt. I pulled my mind into the present.

We wouldn't last forever, but we did have tonight, and I was going to make the most of it. Tomorrow could figure itself out. Tonight, there was nothing but us, no business, no mission. No knife resting in my hands, waiting to be plunged into his back.

Just us.

Involuntarily, I leaned in and kissed him. Softly, then with intensity.

He moaned, long and deep in his chest, like he was starving. We sank down, the soft silk of my comforter meeting my back. His lips parted, consuming mine as his arousal pushed hard into my lower stomach.

He tasted so good. My fingers slid up and dug into his short hair. Our mouths broke apart, and I gasped, my head spinning.

"I need you," I whispered.

He shifted back onto his heels and reached to pull his shirt up, but I stopped him. He went still, watching as I climbed to crouch in front of him. His eyes were black in the dim light.

I'd never taken my time with his body like this. I slid my fingertips over the front of his pants where the hard ridge of his cock waited. It twitched, and warmth pulsed between my legs.

"Can I touch you?" I whispered. "However I like?"

His throat bobbed. "However you like, butterfly."

I peeled his t-shirt up, revealing the hard V of his Adonis belt. There were sharp swirls of ink disappearing beneath his belt. My core tightened as my toes curled.

My lip was sore from being pinned between my teeth.

His fingers flexed, but he kept his hands back. "You can unzip me."

I shook my head, pulling his shirt up over his head, revealing his lean muscles, scars, and dark, swirling ink. His chest heaved. I ran my fingers along the line in the center of his abs and traced the V until it disappeared.

"What was under this ink?" I whispered.

He cleared his throat. His lips parted.

"I got prison tattoos," he said, his voice rasping. "For things I did...things I didn't do. There were other shitty pieces I had done in garages, behind buildings. In other places."

"What kind of places?"

I kissed his Adonis belt, and he inhaled sharply. His stomach tensed. Feeling bold, I flicked my tongue out and ran it up to his shallow navel.

His pupils blew. "Jesus—fuck," he gritted.

I grazed him with my teeth. "You didn't answer me."

"I've been around," he breathed. "I slept wherever there was a bed. Sometimes that was jail, sometimes a hostel or a garage, sometimes home. Unfortunately."

I faltered, looking up at him, my mouth going still.

"I don't want sympathy," he said. "Don't you stop."

Obediently, I licked up past his naval. He tasted good—warm, firm, and clean...like Caden. He caught me by the back of the neck as I got higher and pulled me in to kiss my mouth, giving me a taste of his tongue before withdrawing.

"I need you," he said.

"Not yet."

He frowned, pushing me on my back. "Why?"

He looked so good, it made my chest hurt. He sank down on his hands and knees, crawling over me and pinning me to the pillows.

My thighs parted, and he slid between them, settling close enough that he could bend and kiss the freckles on the side of my neck.

My body tingled. My eyes locked on the ceiling, and it occurred to me this was the first time I'd laid in this bed with a man. My only sexual encounters before now had been at my ex's house or in the back seat of his car.

I'd laid in this bed, staring up at my soft, mauve ceiling so many nights. This was my sanctuary, and it felt so right that he was in it.

His mouth left my neck and moved to my ear.

"I think I might need to come first," he whispered.

"What?"

His mouth trailed to my temple. "If you want to be fucked tonight, I'm not going to last unless I come first."

His hips rocked, and I felt how hard he was. I knew not being able to last was something people poked fun at, but it felt like the biggest compliment to me, especially coupled with the way he liked to talk while he was inside me.

Praising me, telling me how good I felt.

I shifted to face him, our mouths brushing. "Do you want me to go down on you?"

He groaned. "Pull that slip down and jerk me off until I come on your tits."

My jaw dropped. "You're filthy," I whispered.

He started to say something, but then he bit it back. Still, I could tell what the first word was, and I had a pretty good idea of the next. *Only...for you.* That little slip up turned me on more than anything he'd ever said or done.

Only for me.

This gorgeous, lean body, his otherworldly mind that spun from dark to light faster than I could keep up, all his ink and scars. Those were all for me tonight.

To hell with what came tomorrow.

"Get up," I breathed.

He got to his feet, and I dropped to my knees in front of him and pulled my slip down. My breasts fell free, hard and tingling. I heard

233

the sharp intake of his breath overhead. My fingers trembled as I unfastened his belt and pulled his zipper down. His cock slipped free, hitting against his Adonis belt.

I wrapped my hand around the firm base and put the tip in my mouth, licking him to get him wet and feel him on my tongue. He jerked hard, and his hand slid over the back of my head, cradling me gently.

His heartbeat was in my hand, in my mouth.

"Fuck, butterfly," he breathed. "I can't wait."

My free hand dug into his thigh. My other hand pulled him free and worked him hard. His stomach tensed, and his lids fell, drenched in lust, glittering in the dim light. His head fell to the side, his eyes closed.

His cock jerked, spilling out onto me, covering my chin and breasts in his cum without any shame.

He didn't have to be ashamed.

He was beautiful.

His arousal was like a storm, shaking me to my core, sweeping through and leaving us both panting and drenched. Gently, he pried my hand off his dick and tucked it in his pants, crouching down before me.

"Let's get you cleaned up," he said.

I gripped his wrists. "Did...was that what you wanted?"

He tucked my hair back. "It was everything I've ever wanted."

"Then tell me."

He leaned in, gripping my head and pulling it in. His mouth came down on mine, tearing over me like the last throes of his storm, moving down until his tongue dragged the cum from my chin and brought it to my mouth.

Pushing the taste between my lips.

"Calling you a good girl isn't enough," he murmured.

My chest swelled with pride. He had no words. I'd made Caden Payne, the prince of biting sarcasm, speechless. He lifted me in his arms and carried me through the bathroom door, stopping short.

"It's very...pink in here," he said.

"Thanks, do you like it?"

"Add some more taxidermy, and it's perfect."

I couldn't help but giggle. He set me on the sink and reached for the washcloth. His cum was drying on my nipples and stinging my skin, dripping down to the slip bunched around my waist.

He was quiet as he ran the warm washcloth over my upper body—wiping, wringing it out, and wiping more until I was clean. Then, he dried me and pulled my slip up.

"Time to mess you up again, butterfly," he said, tapping my chin.

He made good on that. Back in my bed, I peeled back the silk sheets, and he slipped beneath them with me. Our bodies were naked and wound together in seconds. I was halfway through trying to remember if I'd taken my birth control pill when his cock slipped inside me, Caden groaning as he pushed to the hilt.

"I did," I gasped.

"What?" His abs tensed, hips thrusting.

"I took my pill."

He kissed me and licked down my neck. "I'll pretend you didn't say that."

I was about to protest, but he reached down and took his belt off the bedside table. Still inside me, he used one hand to slip the belt over my wrists and secure it to my mauve headboard covered in roses and ribbon.

His hand tightened on the pillow above my bound hands, and my heart fluttered frantically in my chest.

His hips slammed into me, and his eyes flashed.

"Gonna ruin you," he breathed. "Just the way you like."

CHAPTER TWENTY-SEVEN

CADEN

She was incoherent by the time we were done.

It was after midnight. I heard the bell tower clock strike in Providence, two miles over the trees. In the dark, I stood on her balcony in just my pants, my belt still bound to her headboard, and had a cigarette.

She watched me, naked and sleepy, propped up on the pillows with her sweaty hair piled in a messy bun on her head.

Down below, her koi pond glittered. Beyond it, the orchard moved in the gentle breeze. She lived in a doll's house made of beautiful things. I was the interloper, playing a game at being part of this glittering world.

Tomorrow, our next leg of this deal started, and we'd go back to being co-workers. Business rivals, even.

Never lovers.

I shook the inevitability of our demise from my mind. "Tell me something you've never told anyone."

Her brows arced. "Like a secret?"

I nodded.

Her eyes narrowed, going hazy. She nuzzled her face deeper into the pillow and sighed.

"Sometimes, I miss my mom," she said. "Which is weird, because I never met her. She died of heart failure. She had a lot of medical issues, and it was a few months after I was born. But sometimes, it feels like...you know how people feel a limb after it's amputated? Like that."

She didn't sound sad, just resigned, and maybe I admired that about her. Even in her pain, she was strong.

"Do you grieve for her?" I asked.

"Not the way you think," she said. "Maybe because my father was so insistent I go to therapy for it right away—that was his answer for everything from the minute I could talk."

"That was probably a good choice."

She nodded. "He was a really good dad growing up. He still is; things are just different."

"How do you grieve her?"

She rolled onto her back, her dark hair spilling like a river over her pillow. "The way you explained *Hireath*. Something I'll always want, something I'll never have. A pang in my heart that never...fully realizes but doesn't go away."

My own chest was tender for her. I took a slow drag from my cigarette, thinking hard.

"You're a very strong woman," I said.

She glanced over. "Do you think so?"

I nodded. "I like that about you. It was the first thing I noticed."

Her lips curved into a little smile. "You like strong women?"

"Very much," I said, stabbing out the cigarette and going to the bed.

"You're not like anyone I've ever met."

"Is that a good thing or bad thing?"

She beckoned me, and I slid down beside her, throwing my leg over her lower body so I could soak in her warmth. She pulled a blanket over us and snuggled deep in her plush bed.

"You're very capable," she said.

"Capable?"

She worked her jaw. "No, you're very...responsible."

"I sound a bit dry."

She giggled. "I'm trying to find the word; it's on the tip of my tongue. You're very...competent."

I stared down at her, unsure what she was trying to say. "Okay?"

"I think the thing that I noticed about you first was that you move through the world like you know how to do things. You get shit done, you take care of things. I know you're in charge of training a bunch of soldiers, and you get up and get it done. It's just...hot. I wish I could see you in action. I'd probably be drenched."

I laughed aloud, my head falling back.

"You think that me going to work is sexy?"

"Not going to work," she said, a little flustered. "You just handle shit, and it's so hot."

"Well, that's not what I expected you to say."

"What did you expect?"

I shrugged. "Maybe that I had a huge dick and that's the thing that turns you on the most?"

She blushed, rolling her eyes. "I mean, I do like your dick. But honestly, the fact that you run a whole training center is a lot hotter."

I bent and kissed her mouth, capturing that sweet little smile. "I'm glad I can get you drenched and collect my salary at the same time."

"I don't work around a lot of men who work with their hands," she said quietly. "Can I tell you something?"

She was serious now. I leaned in, nodding.

"Okay, when I first started at the company, I went to a big business convention, all really successful people like my father," she said, sighing. The memory clouded her eyes. "There was an outdoor party one night. We were all in a restaurant on the coast, and we got attacked."

"Attacked?"

She nodded, brows creasing. "There were some men trying to take hostages, basically, because they knew it was a group of wealthy people. They broke into the restaurant and held our table at gunpoint. My father had left to go to the bathroom a minute before."

She hesitated. I could see the blush draining from her face.

A deep anger settled over my chest. I had a pretty good idea of what came next.

"I was the only woman there, other than two of the men's wives," she whispered. "But they were at the back of the table. The man leading the group, he had a mask and a pistol. He pulled me from my chair and held me at the corner of the balcony."

Fuck, she was shaking. I cradled the back of her neck.

"You alright?"

"Yeah, I'm okay," she whispered. "It was just scary. He put the gun to my temple. Right here."

Her finger grazed her temple. Sick, I bent and kissed that spot.

"He said he'd kill me if they didn't get money," she managed. "Then one of his men said something about how I was just a wife, so I was worth less ransom money. So the leader started shouting that he would kill me right there if someone didn't step up to take my place, someone who was more important than me."

A tear slipped from her eyes, and I brushed it away.

"Not one person stepped up," she said. "Every single one of those men just cowered at the table. I'd have thought someone in that room of a hundred and fifty would have had a protective bone in their body."

She wiped her nose. I shifted onto my back and pulled her against my side.

"They should have protected you," I said.

She shrugged. "It was just a shock because my father would take a bullet for me. I thought that was the norm."

"It should be," I said. "What happened?"

"My father saw what was going on from the hallway. He got the hotel security, and they took the men out from the upper balcony," she said. "It was horrifying. They shot the leader while he was holding me, and his blood was everywhere."

She rolled and pushed her face into my shoulder. I held her for a second, trying to push back the anger in my chest.

"So that's why you were so scared at the rest stop," I said.

"Yeah," she said, muffled. "I just had a flashback and freaked out. I never thanked you for stepping in. I don't know how you knew so fast."

"It's part of my training to read body language," I said. "You were scared."

She looked up, her eyes puffy. "It was hot."

I frowned. "What?"

"It was really hot the way you just stepped in. That's what I'm trying to say," she said. "You just saw an issue, stepped in, and took care of it."

"Have you ever needed protected again, since then?"

She shook her head. "My father was protective before, but he kind of lost it after that. He had a tracker on my phone, a bodyguard, a driver, and security around our house every night. He had me wear a bracelet with a chip in it for six months until I finally broke down and begged him to stop. It was only recently that he started letting me drive myself alone."

"So putting you on this mission must have been a big step."

"Yes and no. You might have noticed everywhere we've gone is a safe place, surrounded by people he already knows. He let me out, but I'm on a short leash."

"He's afraid he'll lose you," I said.

She nodded. "He is, but that's not an excuse."

"I'm not defending him, but he likely struggles with a lot of guilt that he couldn't save your mother," I said, keeping my tone gentle.

"I know he does," she whispered. "That's why I didn't fight it until recently. But I can't live like this; he's suffocating me. I have to live my own life, risks and all."

"Yes, you do," I agreed. "Your father has done such a good job protecting you and keeping the world out that he forgot to let anything in. He made you safe, but he forgot to let you live."

Her throat bobbed as her dark eyes swam with tears.

"I'm ready to live, Caden," she whispered.

"You will," I said. "You are."

She pushed her face against me, and I held her in silence, feeling her blood thrum in her veins, feeling every breath. Her muscles relaxed slowly until we were both limp.

"You'd better stay here tonight," she murmured. "Can't have you wandering off in your sleep."

"I don't think I wander when I'm with you," I said, but she was already asleep.

CHAPTER TWENTY-EIGHT

CIRCE

It was so early when he woke me that the sun was still behind the orchard. He was already dressed, in a different shirt. An overnight bag lay at the end of the bed. He must have had it on his motorcycle.

I burrowed deeper into the blankets. He bent, stroking back my hair, and kissed my temple.

Guilt blossomed in my chest, heavy and cold.

I had until the end of the week to bug his apartment, or my father was going to start asking questions I couldn't answer. We just had to get through the next leg of the mission together and then...then, I had to betray him. My throat tightened. My eyes stung.

Fuck, the sun hadn't even risen yet, and I was already trying not to cry.

I pulled the comforter over my head, and he laughed quietly.

"You can sleep," he said. "I'll see you tonight at the hotel. I want you in my bed again."

His weight lifted. Everything in me wanted to jump up and go after him, but he couldn't see my tears. My body curled up tight, and I held my breath, listening to his footsteps move down the stairs.

His motorcycle hummed, then whined into the distance, leaving me in heavy silence. I rolled over and reached for my phone, setting the alarm for eleven. I took a sleeping pill from the bedside table and closed my eyes, blocking out the world.

Hours later, I woke bleary eyed and dragged myself through my morning routine. Quietly, I cried as I packed for the hotel, tears streaming down my face and dotting my shirt. My father was at work again. The house was quiet as I dragged my bags into the hallway and went back to grab my purse.

I wiped my face, sinking onto the bed.

He'd left his belt, tied around the headboard.

I couldn't do this anymore. He was falling in love with me, I saw it on his face. In his beautiful sapphire eyes. In the way he kissed the freckles on my neck. In the way he handled my body so gently, like I mattered to him.

This wasn't my knife to plant in his back.

This was my father's plan, not mine. I was just a vessel to get the job done. Resentment boiled, threatening to pour out of me at any moment.

I'd been a good girl and had done what I was asked for my entire life.

But Caden had changed me.

I wasn't satisfied with being obedient anymore.

Louis helped me load my bags, but I wanted to drive myself. It was only an hour up the coast, and it was a nice day. The sun was half shaded by clouds, the air balmy, and everything smelled fresh. Maybe it would help me get out of this slow, spiraling depression.

I went downtown to get a coffee and passed Caden's apartment. The blinds were drawn, and I did a circle around the complex and drove past the back lot. His Kawasaki was gone, so he must have already headed to the hotel.

Defeated, I parked on the street to wipe my face and blow my nose before heading into the cafe. It was almost empty.

"Can I just have an oat milk latte?" I sniffed. "No flavor. Thank you."

The barista sent me a fragile look. "Yeah, no problem."

She had a sweet smile, and I was making her nervous with my puffy face. I wiped my eyes again and swiped my card.

"Are you okay?" she asked, pushing my latte over the counter.

I laughed through the tears. "Yeah, just some guy. You know how it goes."

"Yeah," she said sympathetically. "I've been there."

I gave her a tip and headed out, not wanting more pitying stares on me. In the car, I settled down and reached for my phone to put on my road trip playlist. It wasn't in my purse.

I unzipped my suitcase, but it wasn't in there either.

I must have left it in the kitchen when I locked up the house.

Frustrated, I got back on the road and headed to the house. Louis's car was gone, and the garage doors were shut. I parked outside the door and let the engine running as I punched in the code. The door clicked, and I walked through, my eyes falling on my phone on the hall table.

The house was quiet. My sneakers had soft soles, so it was loud when I heard it, splitting through the hall and making me stop in my tracks.

A soft groan.

I froze. Who the fuck was in my house?

My hand slid down, but I'd left my pepper spray in my purse, and my purse was in the car outside.

I took a step back when a heavy moan came from the kitchen. My heart leapt. I glanced at the floor, and my eyes focused on a woman's sandal at the end of the hall. Before I could stop myself, I walked forward and picked it up.

I straightened and looked directly through to the kitchen at my father.

There was a woman in his arms, in just a bra and a short skirt. Her other sandal sat on the counter. He had his face buried in her neck, and she had her hand down the front of his dress pants.

"Oh God," I gasped, backing up and hitting the wall.

My father whipped his head up, pulling his zipper closed. The woman whirled, and my stomach dropped like a rock in deep water. Her eyes were wide, her pupils blown with fear. Her lip gloss was smeared beneath her septum piercing.

"D...Delaney?" I whispered.

Fear flashed through her eyes like a thunderclap. My father stepped back, trying to get her shirt untangled from her waist.

"Honey, it's not what it looks like," he said.

"Dad," I managed. "I don't...understand."

Delaney pulled her shirt up. Why? I had no idea. I'd seen her in her bra plenty of times. My father's lips thinned, and he started buttoning his shirt up, tucking it under his belt.

"Let's talk about this," he said calmly.

"Delaney," I said, voice vibrating with rage. "How long have you been fucking my dad?"

Her lower lip trembled. "I'm so sorry. I was going to tell you. I really was. I'm sorry."

"How long?"

"We've been together for almost a year," he said, his voice hoarse.

My jaw dropped, my ears ringing. "What?"

Delaney looked like she was going to vomit. She slid off the counter, adjusting her skirt and reaching for her sandal.

"I told you," she whispered. "I begged you to let me tell her."

I rounded on my father. "You're a fucking liar. Fuck you!"

His eyes blazed. "So are you. Do you want to tell me why I went upstairs to close the windows in your bathroom this morning and there was a shirt on your bedroom floor."

My stomach twisted. "A shirt?"

"Yes, the black t-shirt that Merrick's soldiers wear," he snapped. "When were you going to tell me you're sleeping with the fucking enemy? Who is it? Caden? Or is it the other one?"

The rage flooding my body was an uncontrollable torrent at this point. I wasn't telling him shit. I was going to gaslight and lie my way out of this because my father had been fucking my friend for a year, *and* he'd lied about it.

"I had a one-night stand," I shot back.

He cocked his head, pale eyes burning. "With who?"

"I have no idea. One of the Welsh organization's men."

"You brought one of them back here?" he said, his voice going flat, deadly calm. "When? That's a fucking security risk, Circe."

245

I threw the sandal across the room at the fridge. "I've fucked my way through most of Merrick's soldiers. If you've got a problem with that, take it up with him. I'm not stopping as long as they're willing."

That was a lie, obviously. I had no idea what I was saying, I just wanted to hurt him, and I'd hit the mark. Delaney's jaw was on the floor, her eyes enormous.

"Circe Johansen," he barked. "Enough."

I took a step closer, feeling all the rage I'd tamped down for years bubble up. "No, this is what you get for making me your puppet. You never asked me if I wanted to run your fucking company. You never gave me a choice about the Wyoming base. You just parade me around like I'm some kind of trophy and make me do whatever you want."

He stared at me, shocked into silence.

"And you never asked me if I wanted to betray the Welsh organization," I yelled, feeling the veins popping out on my forehead.

"Circe!" he snapped.

God, it felt so good to raise my voice at him.

"I hope it fucking burns you up that I let him fuck me," I shouted.

"Who?" he snarled, his palm coming down on the counter. "I know you, Circe, and it wasn't just anyone."

I wasn't telling him anything. I snapped my lips shut, glaring at him.

"Tell me," he said. "Or I'll go to Merrick right now."

"He already knows," I shot back.

His neck flushed and his eyes narrowed. "I'll put a gun to each of their heads if I need to."

"Lukas," Delaney gasped.

I rounded on her. "Don't use his first name."

She went silent, tears streaming down her face. My father circled the counter, getting closer, but I didn't back down. All my rage was out, seeping out of my pores, burning like fire in the tight veins in my neck.

"I'm serious, Circe," he said. "I'll tear this city up until I find the man who was in my house with my daughter."

My resolve snapped, but my desire to protect Caden's secrets remained. My father and I knew who he was, but Delaney didn't. If I told her, the word would spread. The last thing I wanted was to break his confidence.

"You know who it was," I whispered.

"Who?"

"The Welsh Prince," I said.

It took a second, but I saw the light bulb switch on as he realized who I was talking about. Part of me wanted to see his anger, but the other part of me was done with this entire mess.

I took a step back, my rage going from hot to ice cold in a second.

"I'm done, Dad," I whispered. "If this is what you want, you two go at it, but fuck you both."

Delaney was sobbing now, curled up on the floor with her head on her knees. Part of me wanted to relent, since this wasn't entirely her fault. She was so much younger than my father, and she probably had wanted to tell me. It wasn't like Delaney to keep secrets.

But I needed time to cool down and sort through my feelings before we spoke.

I whirled, phone in hand, and fled down the hall. My father's shoes clipped after me, following me out to the driveway. His hand curled around my elbow, and I wrenched it away, turning on him.

"Don't touch me," I snarled.

He was heartbroken; I saw the pain radiating from his eyes. In the faint lines of his face, in the hair falling over his forehead, in his clenched fists.

"Honey," he whispered. "Don't go."

Tears broke from my eyes, spilling hot down my face. "Dad, you really hurt me," I managed. "Delaney is my best friend, and you made her lie to me. And for what?"

He swallowed. "I...I'm not having a fling."

"What is this, then?" I asked, throwing my hands up. "Are you going to marry her? You're twenty-seven years older. She wasn't supposed to marry you anyway. She was supposed to marry Trystan."

His eyes flashed like a thunderclap. "I'll handle that."

"Dad," I barked. "What the fuck?"

"You tell me," he said, voice broken. "What the fuck happened to us?"

We stood there in the yard, faint breeze carrying the scent of green apples from the orchard. For as long as I could remember, it had just been my father and me in this huge house, surrounded by the trees, the stone fences, and the glittering koi pond. We'd spent so many mornings out in the garden. I'd driven down the roads with him, the car's top down, on the way to the office. I'd grown up doing my homework in his office, playing on the floor during board meetings.

It was just us, me and him against the world.

My tears came fast. My throat closed.

"I think I grew up, Dad," I whispered. "And I think...I think we need space. I'm not you. This isn't what I want anymore...I need to rethink some things."

He wanted to cry, I saw it in his glittering eyes, but he held back. He always did; he wasn't an emotional man.

"I'm going to finish this part of the mission, and then I'm getting a hotel in the city," I said, wiping my face. "We can talk about what comes next."

The lines of his face hardened. "You can't betray me."

I swallowed hard. "I won't. I just need time."

"Please call me tonight," he begged. "And, baby...."

"What?" I whispered.

"You're too good for him."

That pissed me off. He didn't know Caden, not the way I did.

I got in my car and slammed the door. Part of me wanted to run back and hug him to ease the pain in his face, but the bigger part wanted to haul back and deck him as hard as I could. My emotions freewheeled, jumping from anger to pain to sadness faster than I could keep up. I clicked the key fob and hit the gas even harder, pulling out onto the road and leaving rubber smears in my wake.

My heart thumped, my eyes sticky.

I turned on soft classical music and started counting my breaths. I shouldn't be driving when I was this upset, but I didn't have a choice.

Caden couldn't know anything was wrong until I'd gotten my story straight and decided what my next move was.

It wasn't as simple as a boy and a girl falling in love.

It was complicated. We were complicated.

A prince covered in ink to hide all his scars. An heiress locked behind bulletproof glass. We were never meant to meet or end up so deeply entwined.

From that first look across a crowded room, we were doomed for tragedy.

As soon as he found out that my father intended on betraying him and I was an accomplice, he would walk. At the faintest hint of pain, those walls could come up and shut me out.

And I deserved it. Even though I'd had no choice, I deserved it.

By the time I got to the hotel, my face was less puffy. I parked around the side and grabbed my bag, dragging it up the walkway with my face down. The hotel was a triple story building that sat right on the coast, overlooking the calm ocean. Everything was tastefully lavish, the lights in the garden and along the wraparound porch glowing in anticipation of the night.

The woman at the counter checked me in but didn't say anything about my red nose and sniffles. She handed me the key and politely averted her eyes. I was grateful.

My room overlooked the water. It was a big room with a sectioned off bedroom, a big bed with plush covers, and fluttering lace curtains. There was a welcome note, warm towels, and a glass of iced champagne waiting by the mantel.

I dropped my bag and peeled off my clothes, going to turn on the shower. The hot water poured over my head, soothing me. I was going to have to ice my face before I put my makeup on.

Hopefully, no one would notice how red my eyes were before I had to make an appearance downstairs. This was an important event, and I had to represent the Johansen name.

At least until I decided what my next move was.

I washed, dried, and styled my hair. My face was sufficiently depuffed by the time I put some full coverage foundation on and added a few lashes to make my lids heavier. Maybe that would cover the whites of my eyes. I brushed out the feathery bits of my hair to form a thin curtain bang and swiped on some red lipstick to draw attention down.

There, I looked fine.

Just to be safe, I slipped on a slinky black dress that showed more than a little of my cleavage. It left my legs bare from the midthigh down.

That should keep them looking anywhere but my sad, tired eyes.

It was almost seven when I left my room and headed to the dining room. It was a welcome banquet, and I had a mental list in my head of every person I needed to talk with. I'd be here until ten at least, working the room, making sure everyone knew there knew that while my father might not be involved with the hotel, he was connected to Merrick via the base.

My father never missed a chance to namedrop.

Outside the dining room, I paused and plastered a demure smile on my lips.

Then I sighed and walked in.

Pretty, perfect, with someone else's script in my mouth. Just the way I'd been raised.

My eyes skimmed the dim room, bathed in golden candlelight. There were suits every few feet, accompanied by women glittering with diamonds and gold. Hungry for the sight of him, I made a slow circle towards the bar, but he was nowhere to be found.

Then I saw him, and my heart skipped a beat.

He stood by the dark windows, his reflection double in the glass. He was deep in conversation with Vincent Galt, a graying businessman and the patriarch of the extensive Galt family. I saw him before he saw me, and I took a moment, breathless, just to soak in the sight.

He wore a tailored suit that fit his lean body beautifully. The jacket was gone—he always seemed to lose his jacket a few minutes into committing to a suit. The white sleeves of his shirt were rolled up, revealing his swirling ink.

It was no wonder that every woman who walked by gave him a second glance.

Something strange filled my chest, like I knew a sweet secret.

I swallowed the lump in my throat. I'd loved that body and felt that mind brush up against mine. I'd taken him into my body and soul and given him all the pleasure he could wring from me.

I'd loved him with my body, my lips, my tongue.

Even if he chose to walk away from me, I knew one thing for certain.

I'd never regret the nights I'd spent with Caden Payne, and I'd never regret that, for a fleeting moment I knew was doomed to end, I loved his mind and heart too.

CHAPTER TWENTY-NINE

CADEN

I knew the moment she walked through the door something was different. I saw her before she saw me. Her dark eyes fell on me, and I looked away. Forlornly, she turned and moved to the bar, lowering her eyes even when the bartender took her order.

Something was wrong.

I watched her, pretending I gave a fuck what Vincent was saying. God, she was devastatingly beautiful. She pivoted, and my scalp prickled as her eyes fell on me as I glanced away. I couldn't keep staring at her, or Vincent would notice. But I felt her, as acutely as her warm fingers and sharp little nails had dragged down my back the other night.

I glanced over for a second, and her eyes darted away.

"Excuse me," I said, dipping my head. "I just need to check something."

Vincent nodded. "I'll see you around. We're having cigars out on the porch later; you should join us."

"I'll be there," I promised distractedly, barely hearing him.

He melted away as everyone did. The entire room was a blur, and she stood at the center, in high definition. My feet moved without me realizing it. I drew up beside her at the bar, and she kept her face straight ahead, but she saw me. I felt the tremor of recognition.

"When did you get in?" I asked.

"Earlier," she said, her voice hoarse.

I assessed her, distracted by what she was wearing. It wasn't very Circe-like—she usually stuck to pastels, classy little skirts that hit her right at the knee and covered her figure.

This dress showed everything: her long, lean legs dusted with glitter, the outline of her breasts, the faint suggestion of her lace bra beneath. Her hair was pinned in a messy pile with her curtain bangs falling over her face. But the strangest thing of all was the deep red lipstick.

She glanced up, lashes heavy. Right away, I felt her energy, and it was chaotic. She'd been crying.

I eased closer, my hand sliding up against her waist. She dipped her chin.

"Don't touch me in public," she whispered.

Ignoring her, I leaned in. "What's wrong? Who do I need to kill?"

Her cheeks flushed, and she glanced up, biting her lip.

"No one," she said. "My dad is fucking my best friend. But it's fine, it doesn't even matter. I'm moving out anyway."

It took everything I had to keep my face blank.

"Who? The little blonde one?"

She rolled her eyes, wiping her nose. "Delaney. You know who she is. You're best friends with Yale."

My mind went into overdrive. This wasn't good—Merrick had been counting on arranging a match between Delaney and Trystan, who ran the Wyoming Project. Trystan had always had an interest in Delaney, and she was Yale's sister, which made her practically royalty in our world.

I ran a hand over my face. "Fuck."

She turned, brow arced. "Trystan's going to have to find someone else."

"Merrick won't be happy," I said.

She shook her head, downing the rest of her cocktail. "I'm horny. Can you fuck me in the closet or something?"

I gazed down at her, a little ache in my chest. She was in so much pain. Her beautiful dark eyes were puffy, and I could tell she'd been biting her mouth. Maybe making her feel good for a few minutes would help her pull it together, but I didn't want that.

I wanted to walk up to her father tomorrow morning when he arrived at the hotel and knock him the fuck out for making her cry.

But that wasn't my place. Yet, anyway.

"What if I just took you upstairs and we talked?" I said.

She shook her head. "There's nothing to talk about. My dad and my best friend have been sleeping together for a year, and they lied about it. That hurts, and it's going to hurt for a while. But I don't have a leg to stand on, because I'm fucking you and lying about it to everyone."

"It's different," I said.

That wasn't true, though. I wasn't a stranger in the way that Delaney wasn't just some random woman. We were all connected by complex threads. Did she know how complicated our relationship really was? Part of me wondered if she knew deep down that I was Merrick's son. She had to at least suspect it.

But I couldn't ask her, because then she would know for certain.

I wanted deep down to just say fuck it. Maybe it was time to let the world know who I was.

"Caden."

I blinked, looking down into her pleading face. "What is it, butterfly?"

Her lower lips trembled. "Take me somewhere. I can't do this tonight."

God, I wanted to hold her, but not here, where we would be seen.

"Do what tonight?"

"Raine Forge and the mission," she said, voice shaking. "Can that please wait until tomorrow? I'm just...a mess."

I set her empty glass aside. "Come with me."

She held out her hand, and I took it, holding her to my side as I slipped out the side exit to the back hallway. Our hands came together, her fingers weaving trustingly in mine.

"Where are we going?" she asked.

"Just out. Nobody has to know."

She was quiet as I guided her downstairs and out the side door. In the far lot, I'd parked my Kawasaki in one of the garages. I led the way and pulled my helmet down from the wall.

"I'm wearing heels," she protested.

"All you have to do is hold onto me." I dropped to one knee and unstrapped her heels, helping her out. They were delicate and beautiful, but there was something about seeing her bare feet that I liked more. The paint on her toenails was white, and she wore a thin silver anklet.

My dick twitched as my hand slid up her leg and pressed between her thighs.

Her eyes widened as she glanced over her shoulder. "This is a bit...open."

My fingertips trailed up. Her thighs tensed, but she didn't close them.

"Are you wearing panties?" I asked. "Your dress will push up when you sit behind me."

Her throat bobbed, and she nodded once. I rose and dropped her heels by the wall. She held still while I strapped the helmet on her and helped her mount the Kawasaki behind me. Her arms wrapped around my body and her cheek pressed warm against my back.

She started to speak, but I revved the Kawasaki and pulled into the lot. Inside the hotel, the windows glowed gold. The garden glittered, and the ocean roared softly in the background. The night was warm, the air thick with humidity and salt.

I pulled onto the road that ran up the coast. It was almost empty, so there was room to floor the gas. I heard her little gasp as we crested the hill and the dark cliffs lay stretched out below the curved road. We rose higher and higher, and I felt her fingers dig deep into my chest.

Holding me the way I wanted.

Part of me just wanted to keep driving, to disappear to another part of the world where no one could find us and never return. We could vanish and spend the rest of our lives in bed, on a tropical island somewhere.

But the part of me that had been honed by Merrick to see potential threats buzzed. Something else had happened since the night I spent in her bed. I had to find out what had happened.

She was listless and jumpy. She thought she was covering it, but I could feel the way her pulse picked up. Her eyes flitted over me, and a little bit of guilt passed through them.

She was keeping secrets.

But I was good at finding out secrets, almost as good as I was at keeping them, and I'd concealed who Merrick was to me for over a decade.

The ocean fell away beneath us as the road moved in a slow circle, bringing us higher into the cliffs. She held me tight, but I no longer knew what that meant for us come tomorrow. What any of this meant.

Time blurred.

We moved down the other side of the mountain until we got to my destination. It was one of Merrick's hotel sights, where the construction had been put on hold because of a disruption in the supply chain. The ground had been leveled, the stone walls and foundation laid down.

It looked like the remains of a temple.

I pulled the Kawasaki off the road and behind a cluster of bushes. She got to her bare feet, staying quiet as I unhooked her helmet. Her dark hair fell free, rippling down her back.

"Where are we?" she asked hoarsely.

"Hotel construction site." I hung my helmet on the handlebars and held out my hand. "Come on, butterfly."

The ocean rushed in the distance. We moved up the dirt path, and I helped her up the wooden stairs that led to the foundation of the porch. Here, the stone ground was smooth concrete. The walls hadn't been put up, and there was nothing but stone pillars surrounding us.

The view was breathtaking.

The ocean stretched out like dark velvet, the stars glittering through the sparse clouds.

She inhaled, sinking down to her knees, sitting back on her ankles. I knelt beside her, soaking in the view. When I glanced back over, there was a single tear falling down her cheek.

"Circe," I said. "Talk to me."

She shook her head, gasping once. "It's stupid."

"So what? There's no one to hear but me."

She shifted, hiking her skirt up so she could cross her bare legs. I sank down beside her, keeping one hand on her naked thigh. She wiped her nose with the heel of her hand.

"Did you know that the temple at Ephesus was for Artemis?" she asked. "Not Aphrodite."

It surprised me that she'd cared enough to look that up. I dropped my head, wishing for the first time that I'd kept my fantasies to myself.

I wanted to be tucked into a pocket of time and space that had never existed, to stay there with someone who didn't cast judgment, someone as sweet and gentle as Circe.

Yes, I'd dreamed of standing in a temple to Aphrodite in the cool morning, but that wasn't enough anymore. Circe had changed that; she'd made me brave enough to realize I wanted more than just a fantasy.

I cleared my throat. "Yes, I knew it wasn't a temple to Aphrodite."

"What did you mean by that?" Her voice broke.

It took me a moment to gather my thoughts.

"It was a place without the past, early in the morning," I managed, keeping my voice steady. "I was...the way I could have been if things had been different. And...also because consecrating a sexual relationship is Aphrodite's territory."

Everything felt heavier after the words left my mouth.

Her lower lip trembled. "Caden, is there something you'd like to say?"

I rose, unfurling my body, and moved to the edge of the stone slab. Down below, the ocean rushed over the sand, pulling back and leaving it flecked with foam.

Deep down, I knew I had to tell her the truth, and now was as good a time as any.

"I'm the *Brenin's* son," I said quietly. "Merrick is my father."

She was silent, but I heard her feet pad across the ground. Then, her soft hand slid over my lower back, and she rested her cheek against my bicep.

"I know," she whispered.

I turned. "That's what you fought about with your father. He knows you're fucking his rival's son."

She nodded, eyes glittering. "He knows."

Her head was on my chest, her hands on my stomach. I wrapped my arm around her body and buried my hand in her hair. I could smell her floral perfume, mingled with the salty ocean. Bending, I buried my face in her hair, and she sighed, sinking into me.

"I wasn't supposed to fall for you, Caden," she said softly.

"I know," I whispered. "I wasn't supposed to fall for you either."

We stood, wrapped up in each other, for a long time.

CHAPTER THIRTY

CIRCE

Guilt ate away at my insides. After a while, I pulled my face from the front of his shirt, leaving little makeup stains on the white fabric.

"Can I ask you a question?"

He nodded, gaze turning to mine.

"Why a temple to Aphrodite?"

He shrugged. "Because I prayed to Aphrodite."

I wasn't sure how to answer that. He had such a rough, scarred exterior, but below that, he was beautiful. He felt things deeply in a way I'd never experienced before. Despite everything that had happened to him, he still retained a sense of wonder.

He glanced over at me, lids falling. "You think I'm foolish."

"Why? Why is that any stranger than praying to God?" I pressed. "I know lots of people who pray. I think it's nice, human. Real."

He was quiet. Finally, he let out a soft sigh, like he was letting something go. His head tilted back, and the stars reflected in his eyes.

"I've never met anyone like you, Caden," I whispered. "I think you might have been born in the wrong time."

He shook his head. "I used to think so. Part of me wanted to live in a time where I could fight back...where I could have been a warrior. But now, I see why I was born here and now."

"Why?" My heart sped up.

He turned, brushing my hair back. "You know why, Circe."

I could feel the blood in my veins like a drumbeat. He bent his head, and his mouth brushed mine. He kissed me, softly at first, then more deeply, like he was laying his claim to me.

I pulled back, tears welling.

"I like to...think that if this doesn't work out, part of me will wait for you," he said, his voice rough.

My heart shattered. My lips trembled, and it took me a moment to regain my voice.

"You said you prayed to Aphrodite. What did you ask for?"

He tilted his head, his mouth thinning. "I asked for you. You are my only prayer that has ever been answered."

My body tingled like he'd held a live wire to it. This was the closest he'd come to confessing real feelings without saying those three words out loud. Yet, all I could think about was the day I'd come home and found my father standing in the kitchen with a horrible secret.

It hung around my neck like a heavy weight. I couldn't keep this secret anymore. I couldn't get to the end of the week and face my father and tell him I couldn't bug Caden's apartment and betray the organization.

So, between now and then, something had to give.

I dropped my head, rubbing my face. From the corner of my eyes, I saw his brows knit. His arms came around me and pulled me into the heat of his body. I nestled my head on his chest, lean and hard.

He was strong, but not in the way the men I worked with were strong. Caden's strength was raw, quiet. It didn't require an audience. It endured, and it hoped in a way I'd never dared to.

Maybe that was what I truly loved about him. I'd never met anyone who hoped even when there was so little to hope for. He was a survivor, an endurance fighter.

And yet, when he loved me, he was so gentle.

My heart thumped in my throat. My chest was raw, my eyes burned.

"We should go," I whispered.

He shook his head. "No, we came all this way. I'm fucking you, Circe."

My stomach swooped. "What?"

His hand slid up the side of my neck, turning my eyes up to meet his. The rough pad of his thumb dragged over my bottom lip, and I forgot how to breathe.

"We can deal with tomorrow when it comes," he said. "Tonight, I want you on the ground. In the open."

"Right here?"

His eyes tumbled over my face, fixing distractedly to my mouth. "Naked, on your back."

I stared at him, speechless. In the distance, the ocean thudded into the shore like the far-off beat of a drum.

"Lay down," he urged.

I hesitated, unsure where he was going with this. His lids were heavy, and the depths of his eyes burned soft. Hesitantly, my heart pattering, I shifted onto my knees so I could work my dress up over my hips. He watched as I dragged my clothes from my body, piece by piece.

Until I was naked, on my knees, on the cold stone.

His eyes flicked over me. Then, he pulled his shirt off and unfastened his belt. I expected him to push me onto the ground, but he slid to his back and beckoned me. Hesitantly, I rose and stepped over his body.

"What do you want from me?" I whispered.

"Sit," he said. "Let me warm the stone first, before you lay on your back."

I licked my dry mouth. "I thought the stone was supposed to be cold."

"For me," he said. "Not for you. For you...the stone is always warm when I'm here."

I wanted to sob, but I couldn't. If I didn't find the courage, this might be the last time our bodies were joined. Sinking down, I settled my sex against him, kept apart only by the fabric of his boxer briefs.

His rough palms ran up over my thighs, gripping my hips. I stroked my fingertips over his bare chest.

"If Merrick is your father, that makes you the Welsh Prince," I whispered.

He shook his head. "No, I'm his son. Not his heir."

"I don't know what the difference is," I admitted.

He let his head fall back, hands still on my body. "There's someone I think can replace him as the Welsh King, but it's not me. We don't believe in primogeniture. The founder of our organization believed it weakened our leaders. They thought that only the best, the bravest, the one who understood how much harm violence can cause, should be *Brenin*."

"I think that describes you," I said. "You're brave...and gentle."

His eyes were wide, reflecting the stars overhead.

"No, I was never meant to be king," he said softly.

"Maybe you're just refusing your birthright."

He sighed. "No, I know what I am."

"What is that?"

His lids flickered. "I'll let you know when I figure it out."

I leaned in, palms on his chest, until my hair brushed his face.

"You don't make sense," I whispered.

He was quiet for a moment before he cleared his throat. "When I know, I'll tell you." His hands tightened on my hips, his body tensing.

"What is it?"

"The stone is warm."

He rolled me onto my back easily, resting his lean body between my thighs. From here, the view was astounding. To my side, the ocean stretched out like dark velvet. Overhead, the stars hung heavy in the sky, bright white and gold. The warm stone pressed into my naked body, somehow softer than anything I'd ever laid on.

He spat into his fingers and worked them gently over my sex. I was empty inside, trembling with the anticipation of him filling me. I closed my eyes and felt the head of his cock, hard, hot, smooth, cool metal, pushing at the entrance of my pussy until my muscles relaxed.

He slid into me, to the hilt. My body hummed, my brain sparking.

I was whole, he was whole.

He felt it too. Face buried in my neck, hand on my breast. My lids fluttered open, and my arms slid up around his neck. He moved his grip down to my hip, holding my body as he began fucking into me.

Deep, slow.

Like he could fuck my soul instead of my body.

"Mine," he whispered, voice low and hoarse.

I wanted to say it back, to tell him that I was his forever, but that wasn't the truth. I was a liar, hopelessly in love with someone I was going to hurt beyond repair. All at once, I dropped from my high and into free fall.

Like Icarus, burned by the sun.

"Hurt me," I whispered.

He couldn't see my face or the tears sitting on my lashes. My hips sank down until my naked body was flush against the cold stone. His hard, lean chest and stomach pinned me down as he fucked me into the stone the way he'd fantasized about. Maybe the way I'd fantasized, too.

His breath came in short gasps, punctuated by all the things I longed to hear from him.

All except those three little words that would destroy me.

My head spun, drunk on the feel of his lean body taking mine again and again the way I'd imagined, but without the peace of the early morning in a sacred place.

Until he shuddered and went still.

He bent, his mouth brushing mine, and I turned my head away so he didn't taste my tears. I knew he felt my mood shift as he disengaged his hips and pulled me against him. His fingers stroked my hair back.

"Talk to me, Circe," he said.

I shook my head.

"Please, don't shut me out."

Desperation tinged his words, breaking down the last bit of resistance I had. Hot, roiling tears roared up my body and burst out, sending me spiraling with sobs. My body shook as my hands clenched, crushed between our bodies.

"Fuck, Circe," he said, his voice breaking. "If anyone hurts you, I'll kill them."

"I hurt you," I panted. "I hurt myself."

He went quiet. I pushed from his arms and sat upright, feeling so vulnerable.

"My father is going to take the infrastructure for the Wyoming Project," I said. My words sounded strange, like someone else's. "He's going to have his men take out yours and seize the base. Merrick will lose everything."

I heard his sharp inhale, but I didn't turn.

"I'm supposed to betray you," I sobbed. "My father ordered me to. The mission to get the shareholders to sign off was a distraction until my father had shipped out enough of his men to Wyoming. He's going to take the base and walk away a multi-billionaire, kill the competition. There's nothing Merrick or you can do about it."

I felt his rage; it swept through the space between us like the tides changing.

In a second, he was on his feet, his pants zipped, staring at me like he'd just been slapped across the face.

"Why?" he breathed.

"Because he wants more," I whispered. "And he doesn't know when to stop. He never meant to keep his word to Merrick. He told me after the first leg of the mission."

"No," Caden whispered. "Why would you let me fall for you knowing this? Are you some kind of sick, fucking sadist?"

"No," I said, scrambling to my feet. "Please. I didn't know until after we slept together at your apartment. I really thought our mission together was real."

"But you agreed to his real plan when you found out?"

I stuttered, but no words came. He didn't understand because he'd never had a father who'd loved me like mine did from my first moment, but I couldn't say that out loud.

His eyes flashed. "Because that's what you do, huh? Anything he wants?"

Anger sparked. My fists clenched, my arms wrapping around my body.

"I have no one but him," I snapped. "He's my father. He's all I had for years."

"And I had no one at all," he hissed. "Loneliness is no excuse."

"What would you know?"

"More than you," he said, reaching down to pick up my clothes. "You had everything you ever wanted. You could have been anything, Circe, and you chose to let him decide for you."

That hurt. I darted forward, making a grab for my clothes, but his hand shot up, gripping my throat with a firm, gentle grip, and pulling me in. My heart stopped even though I could still breathe. I'd never felt anything like the pain radiating off him before.

It was arresting. A tragedy.

"Do you love me?" he said, his lips barely moving.

My heart broke. It snapped, bleeding out in a rush as tears spilled down my cheeks.

"I love you," I whispered. "Now, please let me leave so you can hate me in peace."

His eyes narrowed. "Oh no, you're not going anywhere."

Fear blazed like a wildfire through my body. My fingers dug at his wrists.

"You hate me," I gasped. "Why do you want me here?"

"I love you," he spat. "And up until now, I've let everything and everyone I've ever wanted leave because I never felt like I deserved it. But I deserve you, Circe, you and all your lies. I'm going to fix this, and when I return, you'll be there waiting for me, even if I have to chain you by the neck to my bed."

My jaw dropped. Of all the ways I'd thought this would go, this wasn't even on the list. Shock moved through me like a storm and left me numb.

"You're not leaving me?" I whispered.

He cocked his head, a glint of something that made my hair stand on end in his eyes. "No, no one fucks me that hard and walks away," he said, his mouth inches from mine.

"Is this your idea of punishing me?" I breathed.

"No, Circe," he said. "I'm angry, but I won't punish you. I won't hurt you."

He bent in and kissed me harshly, giving more than a taste of his tongue. When he pulled back, it grazed my lips—a brush of heat that broke through the numbness.

Every part of me had assumed he'd walk away the minute I confessed.

But he hadn't. He was still here.

CHAPTER THIRTY-ONE

CADEN

I let her go, stepping back to put space between us.

I'd felt deep, emotional pain many times in my life. When the police came to tell me my mother had overdosed for the last time. When I was locked up for two years and not one person visited me. When I'd found out Merrick was my father and I had to grieve the life I could have had.

And all those times, I'd closed in on myself and grieved alone.

Not this time.

I was both livid and incredibly impressed. She had me hook, line, and sinker. She'd spent that night in her room with me, we'd bared our souls, and she hadn't cracked once. Maybe I'd underestimated her. Maybe she wasn't as inexperienced as I'd thought.

But I wasn't her victim, because I would have done the same exact thing in her place.

Of course she was loyal to her father. He was her only parent, and she loved him just as much as he adored her. There was a time when I would have jumped through hoops backwards just to get an ounce of parental love. It didn't shock me that she'd agreed to betray me.

No, what shocked me was that, ultimately, she'd chosen to betray Lukas, the man who'd raised her to adulthood.

The truth sank in slowly, then all at once, taking the breath from my lungs. She really did love me, enough to betray her father and spill the truth. I knew Circe intimately now, and she valued loyalty and honor. What she'd done tonight was the biggest sacrifice she could have made.

My eyes moved down her naked body.

"Hold still," I said, keeping my voice cool. "Spread your legs."

She bit her lip, dark hair falling around her face. A shiver moved up her spine, but she obeyed, shifting her feet out until her pussy was exposed. Part of me wanted to push my head between her legs and punish her by making her come until she begged for relief.

But not now. That could come later, after I'd handled this mess.

Instead, I knelt and slid her panties up her thighs, settling them on her hips. I was eye level with her pussy, and I felt her gaze following my every move. Gently, I leaned in and kissed her over the silk.

"Are you angry?" she whispered.

"No." I nuzzled into her, breathing in the faint sweet scent of her sex. "Anger doesn't describe what I feel."

"What do you feel?" Her voice broke.

"I don't know," I said.

That was the truth. A sob worked its way up, making her stomach shudder. "I'm sorry. I'm so sorry. I don't know what to do. I shouldn't have agreed to betray you."

I tilted my head, looking up at her from below. My chin rested on her pubic bone.

"I know."

She bit her lip, the tear tracks on her cheeks glittering. "How?"

"When was the last time you cried for someone?"

Her face froze, and her eyes darted like I'd put her on the spot. Her lip trembled, and her fingers hovered over my head, like she wanted to press it to her stomach.

But she was afraid to touch me.

"I don't know," she managed.

"But you're crying for me."

She nodded, wordless. I rose to my feet and picked up her dress, pulling it over her head. Her bra was somewhere in the dark, but she didn't need it. I took her face in my grip and turned it up to mine.

"That's all I need to know," I said.

Her throat bobbed. "I don't know how we can come back from this," she whispered.

"Neither do I," I said. "But I've spent my life running from good things. I never thought I deserved to be happy. Maybe I'm angry, but that's not important."

Her eyes were so big, like I could just fall right into them.

"I deserve you," I said firmly. "And I'm not giving up this time."

She was bewildered—we both were. I took her by the wrist and led her back to the motorcycle. Her cheeks were still wet, and her nose was running when I put the helmet back on. I wiped them on my sleeve and tucked her hair back.

"I'm so sorry," she whispered.

I got on the motorcycle, jerking my head behind me. "Get on."

She hesitated. "I mean it, Caden, and I meant the things I said to you that night in my room."

A flood of images moved through my mind from that night. We'd laid together, shared our bodies and our secrets. And in the morning, I ached to be joined to her again. I'd left her bed listless, longing for the next time I could touch her soft skin and kiss her mouth.

I glanced back over my shoulder at the stone structure overlooking the cliffs. I'd brought her here, desperate to feel the way I felt in my fantasies. We'd fucked it out on the ground, and it was nothing like I'd imagined.

Maybe because she wasn't just a dream.

She was real, flesh and blood, mired in messiness and obligations and pain the same way I was. The idea of us together came hurtling down to Earth, and I was so fucking grateful, because it wasn't just a fantasy anymore.

In my pain, I made a choice. I loved her, and I was going to see this through no matter how bad it got.

"Get on the bike, Circe," I said, my voice hoarse.

She obeyed this time, wrapping her arms around my chest. Her nails bit into my skin through my shirt as I kicked off the ground. The Kawasaki purred, and I guided it back onto the road and into the dark.

CHAPTER THIRTY-TWO

CIRCE

My entire body was in shock.

He parked the Kawasaki and guided me through the back entrance into the hotel. His hand was firm on my lower spine as we moved down the hall in silence. I kept my head down and my hair over my face, praying no one saw us.

We made it safely to the second floor. I turned to head to my room, but his hand shot out and gripped my upper arm.

"No, you don't." His voice was hard. "You're staying with me until this is over."

He threaded his tattooed fingers through mine, pulling me along with him. I wiped my face again, and my hand came away smeared with mascara. God, I was a mess.

"Until what is over?" I whispered.

"I have to make this right," he said. "Merrick told me that any fallout of us sleeping together was my responsibility, so I'm handling it. Then, I'm handling you."

"I didn't mean—"

He turned on me, pausing to dig his key card out. "I know, but it happened, and now it has to be dealt with."

He turned his back to swipe the card, hand still threaded through mine. My eyes trailed over him as I tried to absorb everything.

I'd misjudged him at first. I'd thought he was a player, that he wasn't serious. But now, I realized that Caden was deadly serious about his responsibilities in a way that not even I was for Johansen Enterprises.

The door swung open to reveal a room decorated just like mine. He pushed it shut, drawing the lock down.

We were alone. My heart thumped.

"I have about twenty hours to get to Wyoming and fix this," he said, "before your father notices I don't show up for dinner tomorrow. Can I trust you to stay in this room? Or should I handcuff you to the headboard?"

His tone shifted, going darker.

I took a step back. "I can stay put."

He cocked his head. "Can you? Because I like the thought of you cuffed to the headboard."

I nodded hard, but between my thighs, my pussy tingled. It was still wet from when he'd fucked me on the concrete. I glanced down, noticing the streaks where I'd dripped through the dust stuck to my skin.

"I won't move from this room," I said.

"Go sit," he said, jerking his head.

I crawled onto the bed and wrapped my arms around my knees. He started undressing to his boxer briefs and unzipped a black bag sitting in the corner. Inside, I could see a jumble of dark items. Something about his demeanor changed as he took out his uniform and pulled it on.

Fatigues, a t-shirt, boots. He strapped a canvas belt around his waist and pushed two pistols into the holsters.

He moved confidently, like an assassin. My head spun.

This was who I was in love with.

The Welsh *Brenin*'s son.

A broken man with blood on his hands.

A soldier made of steel.

He straightened, grabbing the bag and turning to me. "I'll make sure you're safe. Do not speak to anyone until I come to you, understood?"

Shivering, I nodded. "I won't leave the room."

He looked down at me through those heavy eyes. It hit me how much things had changed in such a short time. Not long ago, I was laying eyes on him for the first time. I was at war with myself, caught between wanting him and resenting him.

Now, the war was over, and my heart had won.

"Caden," I whispered, my voice cracking. "I'm so sorry."

He moved forward, boots heavy on the ground. His hand closed gently over my jaw, holding my face up so he could look down into it.

"I know," he said. "This isn't your fault."

"It...isn't?" My lungs were tight.

He shook his head. "My father told me you would be hurt, caught between the city's most powerful men. He warned me something like this would happen."

"He warned me too," I whispered.

His fingers were warm and gentle. I resisted the urge to push my face into his palm and close my eyes.

"My father is a good man," he said finally. "Your father...that remains to be seen when he finds out what you've done. But know that I will keep you safe."

My eyes overflowed. Hot tears etched down my jaw and neck, soaking his fingers.

"I know," I hiccupped. "That's what you do."

He nodded. "That's what I do, and I'll never stop doing it for you."

He bent and kissed me, long and slow, my tears staining his mouth. Then, he pulled back and grabbed his helmet from the end of the bed. Without looking back, he left the room and locked it behind him.

I lay still, listening as the clip of his boots disappeared until I was alone.

CHAPTER THIRTY-THREE

CADEN

The very first thing I did when I got back to Providence was call Yale and tell him to meet me at the training center as soon as possible. While I waited, I packed a bag of weaponry and got changed in the locker room.

Fatigues, boots, both pistols. A knife in the side of my boot.

Then, from my locker, I took my dog tag. Merrick's men didn't normally wear them, but we were required to take them into combat so we had some identifying feature on our bodies, just in case the worst happened.

I dragged my bag into the front hallway and sank to the ground in a crouch. The training center was dead silent. Someone pulled up outside, and a door slammed. I could tell by the boots crunching over gravel outside that it was Yale.

I wasn't taking him with me, but I needed him to know where I was going.

I'd gotten us into this. I had picked Lukas as our business partner for this project, and I'd fucked and fallen in love with his daughter, so I was going to clean up my mess without bringing anyone else into this or die trying.

And I wasn't dying tonight.

The door pushed open, and Yale entered. He faltered as he saw me in my combat gear.

"What's wrong?" he asked.

I rose, straightening. "Lukas is going to betray us."

His brows shot up. "How?"

"He never meant to keep his end of the deal. He was always going to have his men overthrow Merrick's and seize the infrastructure of the training base for himself."

There was a short silence.

"Fuck," Yale whispered. "Does Merrick know?"

I shook my head. "No, and he won't until it's cleaned up. We don't have time to brief him. I'm taking the plane and getting there tonight. I should be back tomorrow afternoon."

"I'm going with you," Yale said, no hesitation.

I shook my head again. "No, you have to keep Circe safe."

"What do you mean?"

I slung my bag over my shoulder, metal clattering. "Circe risked everything and told me what her father planned. We owe her protection."

Yale's eyes narrowed. "Why would she do that?"

I was tired of lying about everything, so I just shrugged, throwing up my hand.

"Because we've been sleeping together," I said. "She wanted to do the right thing."

Yale's jaw worked. For a moment, I thought he was going to give me a lecture. Instead, he just inhaled and let it out, slowly. "Alright," he said. "Are you sure she's not playing you? She could be sending you right into a trap?"

The thought had occurred to me for a fleeting moment. Before I saw her cry for me. Before I looked in her eyes and saw how desperate she was to keep me, so desperate that she was willing to lose everything. She loved me, of that, I was sure, even if, deep down, I still struggled to feel like I deserved it.

I wasn't sure what tonight or tomorrow would bring.

Or what we would do to get the funding for the rest of the Wyoming base.

But I did know one, solid fact.

Circe Johansen loved me, and I was never letting that go.

I shook my head once. "She isn't betraying me."

His eyes bored into me. "You love her," he said finally.

I stayed silent. I wasn't ready to spill all my feelings out for Yale in the training center tonight.

"Does she love you?" he pressed.

I nodded.

He sighed, his head falling back. "Fucking hell," he said. "Fine. What do you want me to do?"

"I need you to go get Circe and bring her back to my apartment," I said. "Lock her in, make sure she's safe. I don't know what Lukas will do if he's alerted that our trainees are attacking his. I don't think he'll go for his daughter, but he might."

"I can do that," he said.

He turned to go but stopped just inside the door. "Hey."

"Yeah?"

"Don't die, okay? I don't want to have to tell Merrick."

"I'll try not to," I said. "Oh, and...maybe you should sit down and have a talk with your sister."

His forehead creased. "My sister?"

"Just ask her why Circe's angry with her," I said.

"Uh, okay, but that doesn't seem like a priority."

"It'll make sense. I don't have time to get into it right now. We can talk more when I get back."

Still frowning, he turned slowly and disappeared. I stood there, realizing slowly that Yale probably knew more than I'd told him about my parentage. That shouldn't have surprised me. Merrick and I looked a lot alike, and Yale worked closely with us both.

It was, unfortunately, a secret that told itself to anyone who cared to listen. I'd just bet all my cards that no one was paying any attention to me.

I alerted the pilot for the private plane and took the Kawasaki out to meet him. He was quiet as I boarded the plane, and he only nodded when I told him where I was going and what I planned on doing.

"You'll have to walk to the base," he said as we rose into the air.

I nodded from the copilot's chair. "I know. I'll have to wake our people quietly, get everyone ready, and take it from the inside."

"The base is separated into two barracks?"

"They are," I said. "I can get our men together before his men are alerted."

We sat in silence for a long time. I leaned back, stretching my legs out as far as I could. The cockpit was small, and the sound of the engine made it seem smaller still.

"Caden," he said, after a while.

"Louis," I said.

He glanced over. "Sorry I didn't see this one coming, sir. I just drove Miss Johansen; I didn't see what Lukas was doing in his spare time."

"It's alright," I said. "You kept an eye on them. You're the reason I knew who I went home with the night I met her. You'll be compensated."

His mouth curved slightly. "How did you explain that one to Circe?"

"Facial recognition from the nighttime security cameras."

"Ah, that'll do it."

There was another long silence. Then, he cleared his throat.

"Do you want me to stay on with the family?" he asked.

"I'll talk to Merrick," I said. "He doesn't know you're a double agent. If I had to guess, he'll pay up with you and offer protection if you need it."

"I'm thinking me and my wife might skip town," he said. "Her family has a nice place down on the coast. I'd like a long vacation until my son's ready for school."

"Sounds nice," I said. "Get me there and back tonight, and you can vacation on the beach for as long as you like."

We were quiet for the rest of the flight. My body was ready to be out of the plane by the time we alighted on the landing strip, three miles south of the base. The stars were bright, and the mountains around us were so dark, I could barely see them.

Louis waited in the doorway. I jumped lightly to the ground, weaponry on my back.

"You'll wait?"

He nodded. "I'll wait."

I reached up, gripping his hand. "Thank you, sir."

"You're a good man, Mr. Payne," he said. "Good luck tonight. Come back alive. No one wants to tell Merrick you've gone and gotten killed."

His words echoed in my head, so reminiscent of Yale's, as I walked. The grass was long, but I had a small, circular light strapped to my ankle to keep me from stumbling. In the far distance, I could make out the training base—a quarter mile long and surrounded in steel wire paneling. The floodlights were on low, shedding a pale white glow over the steel rooftops.

Quiet, unsuspecting.

My mind wandered. Back at home, I knew Circe laid in the bed with tear stains on her face. Her future was uncertain. She'd given up working as the COO of one of the largest companies in the States and a father who loved her for me, the man she wasn't supposed to be sleeping with in the first place.

I admired her bravery.

I also respected it. She's jumped into a freefall with nothing but me as her safety net.

I had to come home.

I had to win, for her.

My heart was slow and steady. My senses were turned all the way up. My footsteps soft as I approached the fence and tapped my passcode into the gate. It creaked open, and I slid it shut.

Stepping on the edge of my feet, I made it to our side of the barracks. A coyote howled in the distance. Insects buzzed around the floodlights overhead. Otherwise, everything was silent as I unlatched the door and slipped inside.

It was time to see what I was made of.

If I would have lasted in the arena or died with everyone else.

That was never my path to take. But this, standing at Merrick's right hand and protecting my *Brenin*, that was what I was good at. Maybe what I was born to do.

I paused in the dark, rows of bed lined up on either side, as it hit me.

Merrick wasn't asking me to be him. He was asking me to be what Daphne had been for him—a kingmaker—because that was what he needed most. A guardian of the king who would replace him.

That was more important to our future than anything else.

My spine straightened. My shoulders went back.

Everything was falling into place, like it had been set up by some invisible hand. I was the kingmaker, and Circe Johansen was my wife.

It was that simple. All I had to do was believe I deserved it enough to take it.

CHAPTER THIRTY-FOUR

CIRCE

When the door opened at ten in the morning, it wasn't Caden. It was Yale, still in his training fatigues. I scrunched up against the headboard, pulling the blanket to cover my body. I'd put on Caden's t-shirt when I showered off my makeup and brushed my hair out earlier. It was all I had on—my panties were ruined, and my bra disappeared at the construction site.

"What are you doing here?" I gasped.

His eyes were guard, like he knew what I'd done. "Caden asked me to bring you to his apartment."

"But we have to be here tonight," I protested.

He shook his head. "No one will be here tonight when the news gets out."

My stomach dropped. "What news?"

His jaw worked. "Caden took out your father's men. Most of them were forcibly relocated, but some of them died."

My breathing came fast. Why had he used that word?

They hadn't died. Caden had killed them.

A sickly wave washed over my stomach, and I pressed my hand to it. Was I responsible for this? Or was this going to happen anyway? My father had planned to do the same thing to Merrick's soldiers, but that didn't lessen my guilt.

I wished I'd had a choice at the beginning, but nothing could have prepared me for how much Caden would change my life in such a short time.

"Get dressed," he said. "Let's go. Caden's concerned about what will happen to you when this gets out."

I faltered. "My father won't hurt me."

Yale's eyes remained hard as he backed through the door, pausing in the hall.

"I've seen stranger things than a father turning on his child over money," he said. "Power corrupts. Absolute power corrupts absolutely."

The door slammed shut. Hands shaking, mind whirling, I peeled myself out of bed. Caden had left me a pair of sweats that were too big in the bathroom. I pulled them on and gathered my hair, tying it in a messy bun on my head. Hopefully, no one would stop me in the hall.

I knocked on the door, and Yale pushed it open.

"My stuff is in my room," I whispered.

"I got it," he said, voice tense. "Let's go. The car's waiting."

My heart was pounding as he escorted me down the hall, using his body as a shield. It was right before lunch, and the hotel was empty, everyone sleeping it off or in the dining hall. My palms were drenched, my pulse fluttering.

Something terrible had happened last night. Caden had done what he was trained to do, and my father would be devastated when he found out.

My heart twisted in my chest.

Yale kicked the door open, scanning the lot before letting me out. The sun was shining, the sky was blue. I could hear soft laughter from the patio and ice clinking against glass. It sounded like my childhood, like parties with my father and lunches at the country club.

Would I ever go back to that world?

And if I did, what did that look like? Trying to work alongside my father with Caden lurking in the background like a vengeful angel?

And Delaney sitting there, having been promoted from my best friend to my stepmother?

I shuddered as I slid into the passenger side.

That sounded like hell.

We drove in silence. Everything felt too normal. The sun shone over the busy streets of Providence. I could hear children on the beach, laughing like nothing had changed. We passed by the turn off to my house, and the sunlight dappled the gravel like usual.

In the distance, I thought I heard the foundations of my perfect world collapsing.

My fingers twisted in my lap.

Yale parked around the back. He was right by my side, hand on my elbow, as we went up the stairs, like he was expecting me to make a run for it.

I wasn't. There was no going back now.

I stepped into the apartment, and Yale dropped my bags on the floor.

"I'm locking you in and setting the security system to my phone," he said. "I'll be at the training center with Merrick. If anyone crosses the threshold or windows other than Caden, I'll know right away."

I nodded, my mouth too dry to speak. He shut the door without making eye contact, and I was alone, standing in Caden's kitchen, in almost the same spot I'd stood when he'd gone down on his knees that first night.

My stomach churned as I went to the bathroom, flipping on the shower, and poured a glass of water. Hands shaking, I sipped it as I waited for the shower to turn warm. I had to get it together.

It helped ground me to stand under the hot water. It helped bring me back to scrub all the lies off my skin and let them swirl down the drain.

If I could have, I would skip to the end of this, the part where, somehow, I got Caden, and my father didn't cut me out.

My heart ached. Tears slipped hot down my cheeks and mingled with the water.

Around noon, I managed to drag myself from the shower, dry off and put on one of Caden's shirts before I crawled into his bed. It smelled like him, and there were still little stains from when he'd fucked me. The silky, expensive sheets were rumpled. I'd never understood that part about him. He was so particular, but then he'd go days without making his bed.

I rolled onto my bed, smiling despite my swollen eyes. I burrowed my face into his pillow and inhaled the smell of him, resting in the indent of his body on his side as I let my eyes close.

It was dark when I woke, and there was someone in the doorway. Heart pounding and sweat breaking out on my back, I blinked into the dark. Slowly, my eyes adjusted, and my stomach turned.

Caden stood in the entrance, in his boots and fatigues. His hair was matted, clotted with blood that streaked down his face and drenched his hands to the elbows. In one hand, he held his pistol. In the other, a flat box.

"Caden," I whispered.

He cleared his throat. "Circe."

My head spun. Maybe I wasn't as strong as I'd hoped, because the sight of blood was making me dizzy.

"Are you hurt?" I gasped.

He shook his head, stepping into the room and laying the gun on the dresser.

"It's not my blood."

He took another step, and the light from downtown Providence fell through the window and illuminated him. Something was different, not just that he was covered in sweat and blood and dirt.

He was taller somehow. His shoulders were straighter.

"My father is the *Brenin*," he said thoughtfully. "I am the Welsh Prince, but I'll never follow in his footsteps. I was never meant to be king."

I licked my dry lips. "What does that mean?" I whispered.

"Stand up, Circe," he ordered.

Legs wobbly, I obeyed. He set the box aside and pulled his t-shirt over my body, letting it fall to the floor between us with a soft thump. His eyes roved over my naked body, as if he'd never seen it before.

"I am the kingmaker," he said quietly. "In a way, I went through the arena. I paid my dues. I did my time. I spilled my blood. Now, it's time for me to mold the next king."

I wasn't really sure what he was talking about, but I could tell this was a pivotal moment for him. His restless, dark energy was still, like the smooth surface of a lake at dawn. He's always had an edge of chaos. I'd felt it from the moment I met him. But tonight, it was gone.

He was quiet. Focused.

Deadly calm.

His crimson hand lifted and touched my neck. The metallic scent of dried blood reached my nose, and my knees wobbled.

"I don't understand," I managed.

"You don't have to understand," he said. "All you need to know is that I've been searching for a long time, and now, I'm done."

Desperately, I wished I had his assurance, but I'd done this to myself. I'd chosen to betray my father for Caden, and now, my future was uncertain. My hands shook as I reached out and gripped his wrist.

"Do you still love me?" I whispered.

He released me, his eyes down, and picked up the box. The top snapped open to reveal a full set of amethyst and diamond jewelry— a bracelet, a necklace, an anklet, a little gemstone with a clip, and a ring with a stone that was easily three carats. My stomach did a somersault as my throat bobbed, trying to swallow.

"What is that?" I asked.

His fingers, dirty and stained with blood, lifted the bracelet. "In our organization, women are offered a set of jewelry. They accept it piece by piece until the final part. At the end, they're formally engaged."

"What...what?"

"You heard me, Circe."

My mouth hung open, and it took me a full minute to collect myself.

"Are you proposing to me?"

His gaze snapped up, and he took my wrist, clipping the bracelet one handed onto me.

"No," he said. "I think we're beyond proposing."

He fastened the necklace around my throat, adjusting it to hang between my breasts. The ring slid over my finger, exactly my size. Then, he knelt, and I felt his fingers between my thighs. My head fell back as he unfastened the stone there and replaced it with his own.

"You are mine, Circe," he said quietly.

I stared down at my naked body, covered in diamonds and little smears of blood and filth from his hands. Shock ebbed through my chest, through my body to the soles of my feet.

I'd fucked around, and now I was reaping the consequences.

"Caden," I said, my voice hoarse, disembodied. "How can you still want me? I betrayed you...or, at least, I almost did."

He stepped back, pointing out into the kitchen.

"The head of your father's commander is in a box," he said. "I'm about to hand deliver it to him tonight. How can you still love me?"

My knees gave way, and I sank to sit on the bed. Nausea washed over me, and my hands started shaking like I was in a strong wind. I was going to pass out or throw up.

"This is messy for both of us," he said.

"Caden," I cried. "I can't do this."

He was on his knees at my feet in an instant, gathering my hands and pressing them to his chest. Through my tears, I could make out the glitter of his cobalt gaze, and the emotion in it stopped me short.

"Circe," he whispered. "Let me love you, no matter what. If there was no place to love you but a temple that never existed, in a place we can never go, I would wait there. I'd love you there. Do you see why I have to have you?"

My hands came around his neck, and he laid his head in my lap.

"I love you," I said, throat catching. "And I think I love this part of you too, even if it scares me."

He looked up at me, my hair brushing his face. "Say you're mine then."

"I'm yours."

I'd never been so sure of anything except the new understanding that no one would ever love me harder than this man. He didn't do things by halves. He wasn't going to give up and walk out when things got hard. No, he'd taken that hit on the chin, strapped on his weapons, and cleaned up the mess.

Then, he'd come back to me and staked his claim.

"Say it the way I want to hear it," he ordered.

I hiccupped, wiping my face. "I want to be your wife."

He bent in and kissed my mouth, tasting of triumph and a deep hunger that excited and scared me. For a moment, I wondered why I felt fear, and then it hit me.

He was the first choice I'd made in my life. The first real choice, without anyone pushing me or assuming they already knew what I'd pick. Everything up until now had been chosen by my father, my therapists, my tutors, my business partners.

I pulled back. His lids had dropped, his eyes still distracted by my mouth.

"My eyes are up here," I whispered.

The corner of his mouth curled. "I know where your eyes are. They're very distracting...like the rest of you."

I parted my lips to tell him everything I'd been thinking. That he'd made me brave enough to stand up for myself. That I'd never met anyone like him. That I wanted to keep feeling the way I did right now, in his arms, forever.

Instead, I just brushed the wetness from my cheek. "You should really get cleaned up."

CHAPTER THIRTY-FIVE

CADEN

I left the head in the kitchen and fucked my wife-to-be in the shower. The hot water cleaned the blood from my skin, revealing scratches and bruises. She worried over me, tracing them. She was soaked and glittering with diamonds like a goddess.

A real goddess, flesh and blood.

No more dreams of incense and stone.

No more letting her turn to porcelain in her ivory tower.

I pulled her in, sliding my hand around her lower back, lifting her with my other hand and pushing my cock deep inside her soft, wet pussy. She moaned as her head fell back, her arms wrapped around my neck, her pointed nails digging into my shoulders.

"God, you feel so good," she gasped.

I braced myself and slammed into her, the wall shuddering beneath us as her moan turned into a yelp. My brain buzzed, and it hit me that I was truly, deeply satisfied.

For the first time in...maybe my entire life.

I hadn't faltered. I'd been presented with a situation that normally would have made me deeply question my worth or if I deserved love at all, and I'd held steady and forced myself to believe I could handle it and get what I wanted.

Maybe I could do this healing thing after all.

Maybe she gave me the confidence I needed.

Gently, I wrapped my hand around her throat and turned her face up. Our eyes locked, and her breasts heaved.

"I'm not angry with you," I whispered. "I could never be."

Her lower lip trembled. "How?"

"Because you risked everything to tell me the truth."

Her lips trembled. "I'm about to lose everything, right?"

I kissed her deeply, drawing her breath into my lungs. "No, no, you have me, and I'll take care of you."

She pushed her forehead against mine. "I think that would be alright."

"Yeah?"

"Yeah," she whispered, nodding. "I wasn't really comfortable being a billionaire COO anyway. At least not...not of someone else's company."

Her gaze was clouded. I drew back, thrusting into her gently.

"I do pretty well for myself," I said. "I'm not a big spender, but Merrick pays me very well, and I've got stock in most of his investments. You won't go without."

Her dark eyes softened, and my throat caught. I'd never seen her so vulnerable, so open. Even that night I'd fucked her in her bed, there had been a something guarded in her gaze. Maybe now, because the truth was out, she could finally be honest with me.

"I love you," she whispered. "Sometimes, you piss me off, but I love you."

"I piss you off?"

She rolled her eyes, wincing as I gave her a punishing little thrust, just to remind her whose dick she was on.

"I don't know... Maybe I was just so scared I'd fall for you," she said. "I didn't want to betray my father, but...I can't give you up."

I considered glossing over the part about her father, because I was balls deep in her and I wanted my dick to stay hard, but I could tell she needed a moment. I disengaged my hips, pulling out, and a line appeared between her brows.

"Your father was in the wrong," I said quietly. "I'm not just saying that because we're competitors. Merrick always fully intended on honoring their deal. Your father, I know you love him, but he intended on betraying us and going back on his word. Why, I can't guess."

She bit her lip, her eyes dropping. "I love him, but...he's always had a problem with power. He just wants to keep going, keep taking, keep consuming. He has all these charities, and he gives a lot of his money away, but that doesn't make it better. I think he thinks it'll balance out some of the things he does to succeed."

"It's better than if he wasn't." I shrugged. "But he has to live with himself. He could have had everything with Merrick. Now, he has nothing."

Her chin trembled. "Not even me."

I took her face in my grip. Her eyes were full of tears, and my chest ached, hating seeing her so broken.

"If it's possible, I will fix this," I said.

She sniffed. "I know you hate my father."

"I won't have my wife upset," I said firmly. "If you need to repair your relationship with him to be happy, I'll swallow my pride. But if he so much as looks at you wrong, we're done. No one disrespects you."

She sighed and pushed her face into my chest. I pulled her in, stroking her wet hair.

"There's no need to worry," I said gently. "I swear, I'll handle everything."

She gave a little, shaky laugh. "You shouldn't have to handle my bullshit."

"It's my bullshit now."

She was quiet after that. I dried her off and laid her in the bed. Her hands came up and pulled me in after her, drawing the sheets up over our bodies. This time, when I pushed my cock into her, she was relaxed. Her eyes were hazy as we fucked, and her pleasure spilled out like water.

Overflowing, like she couldn't hold it back anymore.

I fucked her thoroughly and ordered food for when she woke up. When I left, the box from the kitchen under my arm, she was fast asleep with her head on my pillow.

Good. It was better if she slept through the day.

The drive to her father's house felt long. I pulled up out front and, to my surprise, his car was in the driveway, idle, the engine on. I parked on the street and took the box out, walking up the drive, my gun easily accessible on my hip.

The door opened. Lukas stepped out in a seersucker suit. Judging by the relaxed look on his face, he hadn't heard the news yet. He saw me as he reached the car and froze, glancing around.

"What are you doing here?" he said.

"You don't need to go to the hotel," I said. "There's no deal."

It took him a second, but he collected himself. His eyes narrowed. "What are you saying?"

I dropped the box on the ground with a wet thump. "It means you betrayed us. I cleaned every one of your men out of our training base. Here's what's left."

He went pale, his eyes dropping. There was a long, shocked silence.

"Don't reach out to your daughter," I said. "She's under my care now."

I saw him connect the dots in real time, and I waited, because what he said next would decide if I chose to reach out to him when the dust was settled and strike another deal, or if we were done forever.

Rage swept through him, quickly followed by horror. A muscle in his jaw twitched and his pupils blew. Then, his shoulders sank, and he lifted his chin, fixing eyes brewing with hatred on me.

"Where is my daughter?" he said. "I swear, if you hurt her, I will end you."

Goddamn it, I was really hoping I could kick this man to the curb. Sighing, I turned to go.

"She's safe," I said. "She's sleeping, in my bed."

I heard his anger, heard his fist dent in the roof of his car, but I didn't turn around to look back. I had more pressing concerns. Lukas could rage all he wanted. He was beaten before he'd ever had a chance to turn on us.

The Kawasaki hummed as I pulled back onto the main road and headed out to Merrick's house. He would likely be packing up to head out to the hotel right now. I increased my speed, getting off the highway and heading down the country lane that led to my father's house.

It felt different. Last time, I'd been desperate and afraid.

Today, I was sure of what I would do tomorrow, even if it was difficult. Even if it took years.

I parked and went to knock on the door. It swung open to reveal Clara in an enormous hoodie and sneakers, dragging her suitcase.

"Caden?" she said, frowning.

"If you're heading to the hotel, might want to hold back," I said. "Can I come in? Is Merrick home?"

"He's in the kitchen," she said, pushing her suitcase aside. "Why? I wanted to go to the hotel. Did it burn down?"

I stared at her as we walked down the hall, trying to follow her train of thought. "No, the hotel didn't burn down."

"That's good. Merrick had a bunch of trouble with the wiring," she said. "He spent weeks last summer on the phone with contractors. It would be the worst if the wiring caught fire or something."

"No, wiring is good," I said.

We entered the kitchen, Clara at my heels with a concerned expression on her face. Merrick stood at the counter, two thermoses before him. Coffee trickled through the pour over, smelling faintly of hazelnut. As soon as he saw me, he froze, and his brows rose.

"What is it?" he asked.

"Lukas was going to betray you and seize the infrastructure of the base," I said. "I flew out last night, and Trystan and I cleaned house. You're safe out there, but Lukas isn't friendly anymore."

The silence was so loud, it rang in my ears. Merrick's eyes narrowed, his mouth thinning. Clara clapped her hand over her mouth as she looked back and forth between us, waiting for us to react.

Merrick cleared his throat. "How do you know this?"

I swallowed. "Circe. She was in on it."

Merrick's eyes narrowed. "Where is she now?"

"In my apartment," I said. "She's asleep."

There was a long silence. Merrick glanced at Clara, and she sent him a look, like she was reminding him to be kind.

"Can we trust her?" Merrick asked.

"She gave up everything to tell me," I said. "She's devastated. Her relationship with her father was already on the rocks because he's fucking her best friend, Delaney, and this was the nail in the coffin. She's torn up about this. I think she deserves our trust for what she sacrificed."

"Delaney? *Our* Delaney?" Merrick's eyes flashed.

I nodded, and Clara gasped.

"I thought she was supposed to marry Trystan," she whispered.

"She was," Merrick said grimly. "I'll have to handle this later. Did we sustain any casualties last night?"

I shook my head. "We took them by surprise. They only lost a dozen men. I tried to run them out with minimal loss of life. Their commander was an exception."

"What happened to him?"

"I brought what was left to Lukas. Thought he might need to hear the message loud and clear."

Merrick opened his mouth, and I gave him a hard look. Our last plan to get funding for the Wyoming Project had been through Clara's former fiancé. Then, he'd put his hands on her, and Merrick lost his shit and beat him to death. So he didn't have a leg to stand on, and if he said one word to criticize what I'd done, I was going to remind him of that.

Instead, he sighed and dipped his head.

"I see you've handled this," he said.

"I have," I said firmly. "You told me if there was fallout, I had to handle it, so I did."

Merrick did that thing that made me more uncomfortable than anything else—he looked at me like he was my father. His eyes were soft, and I almost wished he was angry. I knew how to deal with negative feedback, but I still struggled to accept love. Approval was just as bad.

"Good," he said quietly. "I'm proud of you."

I looked away.

Clara cleared her throat, backing up. "I might go unpack, let you two have a moment."

The last thing I wanted was for Merrick to have an opportunity to get emotional. After the night I'd had, all I wanted was for things to go back to normal.

Except I wanted Circe to be part of my new normal.

"Wait," I said.

Clara leaned in the doorway.

"Could we...all go out tonight?" I asked, feeling awkward.

Clara's jaw dropped. Not once had I gone out to dinner with them since their marriage. The only time Merrick and I spent time together was for work.

"Yeah, of course," she said quickly. Her eyes darted back to her husband. "Right?"

"Uh, of course," he said. "Is Circe up for that?"

"I think it would be bad for her if she stays in bed," I said. "She's having a hard time, and I think maybe letting her know she's not alone would help."

Merrick nodded. "Of course. Do you want to meet at the steakhouse?"

"Isn't Circe vegan?" Clara asked.

I shook my head. "She doesn't eat a lot of meat, though. She eats like a lot of healthy shit."

Merrick laughed. "I have a feeling we'll get along. How about the new sashimi place that Clara helped me outfit last year? It's only thirty minutes from downtown."

"Sounds perfect," I said. "Now, I'm leaving before you say anything embarrassing."

Merrick shook his head, following me out to my Kawasaki. He paused at the bottom of the stairs and crossed his arms over his chest. I swung my leg over and settled in the seat.

"Just so you know, I took the evaluation," I said.

I'd thought it would feel nails on a chalkboard to talk to Merrick about this, but it felt more like...relief. My shoulders were straighter, less bogged down by invisible burdens.

"And?" His brow furrowed.

"Gretchen diagnosed me with the same shit as you," I said.

He didn't say I told you so. No, he just nodded. "What's the plan?"

I considered hiding the truth, but maybe it was time for some secrets to come out. Maybe I was done hiding all the pain. My eyes found anywhere that wasn't my father's face, settling on the rose garden around the side.

"I kind of have a problem with meds," I said.

"As in?"

"Like...I've abused every medication I've ever taken. So, I'll try therapy first."

"Addiction isn't the same for us," Merrick said. "Your brain wants more and more, and if you don't get a handle on it, it'll consume you. I used to have an...an issue with substances before I did therapy with Gretchen."

I had a vague idea that he'd had a different life before me, but it felt like such a relief to hear him say it out loud. I'd come a long way, and I had a long way to go, but there was hope for normalcy. Sometimes, it was right in front of me, and I was just too stubborn to see it.

"You don't have to choose medication as your treatment plan," Merrick said. "It worked for me when I needed it, but it may not work for you. What's important is you work with Gretchen closely and let her monitor you."

"I know. I'll talk it over with her," I said, putting my helmet on. "See you tonight."

CHAPTER THIRTY-SIX

CIRCE

When I woke, Caden was gone. There was sushi in the fridge, so I nibbled on a few pieces and curled up on the couch. The world felt too calm, and it was making me jumpy. Was my father about to show up and demand I go home with him? Or was he so angry, he never wanted to see me again?

I logged into my bank account, the one he'd had his name on since I was a child. To my surprise, the amount in it had almost doubled, but his name was gone from the account.

My stomach twisted. I knew what it meant.

He still loved me, and he was still protecting me, even when we were at odds. That only served to make me feel worse, but I wasn't ready to reach out. Truthfully, I wasn't sure how long it would take to feel ready. I turned my calls and texts on mute, because Emmy was blowing up my phone, begging me to contact her. Then, I put the phone away in the bedroom.

Caden returned in the middle of the afternoon. I was in bed, watching TV, when he tossed something through the air. I looked down, and my brows shot up.

"A credit card?" I said.

"Yeah, I wasn't sure if you had money or if your father cut you off," he said.

I swallowed past the lump in my throat. "I have my own account. He took himself off this morning, but he left a bunch of money in there."

His jaw worked. "Alright, it's up to you, but take my card just in case."

I slipped out of bed, putting the card in my pocket. "Do you want me to use yours?"

He kissed my forehead. "Maybe. Go out and buy yourself a dress, makeup. Whatever you need."

I slid my arms around his neck. It felt so good to force the events of the last few days out of my mind and pretend everything was fine. Maybe he was right; I should do some retail therapy.

"Why do I need a dress?"

"My father and Clara are going out for dinner tonight," he said.

"Oh?"

"I'd like it if we joined them."

My mind went back to the day Merrick had come to my office. We hadn't had a great conversation, but I didn't resent him for it. He'd been right to warn me, because everything he'd said had come true, but that didn't mean I felt completely comfortable going to dinner with him.

But, if I was going to be with Caden, I needed to at least put in an effort. I nodded, standing on my toes to kiss him.

"I'll go get some things at the shops," I said. "I'll be back in an hour."

Retail therapy was the ticket for putting some distance between now and last night, but it still felt lonely without Delaney or Emmy at my side. And that loneliness made me rack up a weighty bill at the boutique downtown. When it was time to pay up, I found I couldn't use Caden's card.

Maybe when we got married, we could have an account we shared, and that would feel alright. But for now, before I understood how much he made, I wasn't going to use his money.

He was in the kitchen, working on his laptop, when I got back. For a second, I stood in the doorway with my bags and took a deep breath. This felt so good, like home—walking in and having him waiting for me like we were a normal couple.

Maybe now, we could be.

I set my bags down and slipped up behind him, wrapping my arms around his waist and laying my head on his back. He smelled so good...like my home, my future. He turned, swiveling the stool, and slipped his arm around my body to pull me in.

His mouth moved over mine, kissing me thoroughly. When we broke apart, his lids were heavy.

"I've got something for you," he said, kissing the side of my neck.

My toes curled. "What?"

"My dick," he said.

I laughed aloud, even though part of me had anticipated that response. The heaviness that had laid over me since we arrived home was slowly disappearing. I would have to face it tomorrow, but for tonight, I could forget my father and Delaney.

Losing my father and my best friend in one day hurt.

"I might have a glass of wine tonight at dinner," I said. "Or five."

He nipped my neck. "Don't drink your feelings. I've been down that route."

"You know I don't drink like that."

He was quiet, resting his face in my neck. I slid my arms around his neck and let him hold me for a second before he pulled back.

"We should get going," he said.

I nodded. "I'm a little nervous."

His lids fell. "Want me to fuck you and take your mind off things, sweetheart?"

I laughed and he smirked like he'd won a prize. "Believe it or not, there are some things that even your dick can't fix."

"What about my tongue?"

Playfully, I pushed his face away. "Down boy."

He let me go and slapped my ass hard as I turned to go. For a second, I stood shocked. Then, I whipped around, and he gave me the dirtiest look I'd ever seen, one that promised he'd make good on his threats tonight.

"If I can't fuck you now, I'll be fucking you when we get home," he said.

Speechless, I ducked into the bedroom and went to shower and get dressed. Part of me wanted to pretend I was indignant. The other part of me loved it. That much was evident between my legs.

My heart hammered as I pulled on my dress and heels. Meeting Merrick and Clara seemed like a big step.

"You're alright with this?"

On cue, he appeared behind me in the doorway. His eyes dropped and dragged up my body. Over my cream heels and pale blue sundress that clung to my body and left my shoulders bare.

"Fuck," he said quietly.

I could have said the same about him and his nice pants and shirt. His hand tensed in his pocket, like he was holding himself back.

"I'm sure," I said.

"How sure?" His eyes glittered.

I took a step closer and leaned up to kiss his mouth. "Maybe I've been sure since you fucked me at the lodge."

"Was that when you knew?"

I shook my head. "I don't think I knew until you slept in my bed."

"That's when I really knew."

He slid his hands around my waist, cradling me like I was made of glass. "I love you," he said.

My lashes were wet. I blinked hard, trying to keep my mascara from running.

"Please don't make me cry."

He kissed me, gently so he wouldn't smear my lipstick. "Say it back."

My throat felt dry when I swallowed. "I love you," I whispered.

His lids fell, wavering like it took him a moment to believe me. Then, the light stayed on, burning steadily.

"We should go," I said. "And can we please take your car? The Kawasaki will ruin my hair."

He laughed, releasing me to take my hand and guide me from the apartment. I stood quietly while he moved through his rituals.

Tapping lightly, checking the locks. Pausing and shaking his head once.

"It's fine, it's good," he said softly.

I caught his hand, and he looked up. "It's locked. I can vouch for it."

His shoulders loosened, but he didn't speak. Instead, he guided me down the stairs and into the garage, opening my door like the gentleman I knew he wasn't and helping me into the seat.

Spellbound, I watched him pull out and get onto the main road. This gorgeous man was mine. All his flaws, his scars, and the ink he'd covered them with—it all belonged to me.

That made my head spin.

He laid his hand on my thigh, gripping it. His touch burned like fire all the way to the restaurant. I'd never been to this part of Providence, it was fairly new, having been built up over the last few years. Caden helped me from the car, and I smoothed my skirt, glancing around for Merrick's Audi. It sat by the door in a reserved spot.

"Are you sure this is a good idea?" I asked.

He took my hand. "My father is a good person, and Clara is too. She's going to be over the moon. Maybe a little *too* excited."

"So when we get married, she'll be my mother-in-law?"

He led me to the door. "She doesn't like being called my stepmother, so she'll like being your mother-in-law even less. I'd think of her more as just family."

I followed him down the front hall to one of the back rooms. The restaurant was quiet, everything bathed in candlelight. Soft laughter, voices, and the clinking of glasses filled the room. In the dining area, Merrick and Clara sat at a round table. I was glad I'd decided to dress up, because Clara was glittering in a tight, berry pink dress and a full set of diamond jewelry. Merrick wore a plain black suit.

Caden pulled out my chair and I sat, awkwardly.

"Hey," Clara said, offering me a sweet smile. "You doing okay?"

I nodded. "Yeah, all things considered."

She glanced at Merrick and back at me. "For what it's worth, I think you're very brave."

Inside, I melted. My chest ached, but not in a bad way.

"Thank you," I whispered.

Caden's hand squeezed my thigh under the table. "Let's get some drinks."

Merrick passed me the liquor menu, and our eyes talked. There was a softness in them that hadn't been there the last time we'd met. I offered him a small smile, and he returned it.

"For what it's worth, Circe, I agree with Clara," he said.

I dipped my head, wiping my eye delicately so I didn't smudge my makeup. "Thank you," I said, clearing my throat.

"Anyway, what's everyone having?" Clara asked brightly.

"They have an aged whiskey that's very good," Merrick said.

"I'm not much of a hard liquor drinker," I said. "I'll just have a glass of the merlot."

Our waitress appeared and took our orders. The first few minutes were incredibly awkward, but then everyone got their wine and whiskey, and the atmosphere relaxed. Clara couldn't hold her alcohol at all, so she started chatting about anything and everything after a few sips of wine. I threw caution to the wind and did the same. It had been so long since I'd truly let myself relax.

The night moved fast. We all had steak and seafood and more drinks. After a while, the hostess invited us to sit outside while they lit the outdoor fireplaces. Clara curled up against Merrick and sipped on her drink while Caden sank down on the other side of the fire, stretching his long legs out.

I glanced over at him. We were on a bench; I could lean into him, but we'd never been physically affectionate in public before.

It felt like a big step.

He reached out and slid his hand around my waist, drawing me close until my side pressed against his. I glanced up and he brushed my temple with his lips.

"You okay?" he whispered.

"Yeah," I said softly. "I think I might be kind of happy."

He smiled, turning back to the fire. We finished our drinks, and Caden said he wanted to get back home because he had to be at work early. Merrick left Clara curled on the bench a few feet away while he walked us to the car. He opened my door, and I offered him a tentative smile.

"Thanks," I managed.

His eyes were kind. "I'm glad you're alright," he said. "The organization appreciates what you did, and you'll be protected and provided for no matter what."

I swallowed, throat tight. "Thank you."

Caden was already in the driver's seat, so I couldn't say anything more, but before I could duck into my seat, Merrick tapped my arm.

"You're good for him," he said, voice low.

I settled in the seat, unsure how to answer him. He shut the door and stepped back, hands in his pockets, to watch us drive away. Caden's hand drifted to my thigh, and I glanced over at him, studying his handsome profile.

All I could think about was how good this new normal felt, how vast the world was without the restraints of my father or my work. Tomorrow, I got to wake up and decide what I wanted my future to look like. I was free of a cage I'd never been able to see until he came along and opened my eyes.

He'd given me that, and I would never be able to thank him enough.

CHAPTER THIRTY-SEVEN

CADEN

Steam rose in slow drifts from the tea kettle.

My pour over dripped in the kitchen.

Directly across from me, looking perfectly posh in a flowing dress and heels, sat Gretchen. I was in my training fatigues, already dressed for my first class after my appointment. Early morning pigeons swooped over the city, and the sun shed golden rays over the beach in the far distance.

"How was your first week?" Gretchen asked, flipping her pad open.

I thought back. My first week learning about myself had been tough. It felt like untangling a mess of threads. I'd spent my nights staring up at the ceiling and running over every memory I had, trying to understand what was my fault and what was just part of how my mind worked. The conclusion I'd come to was that I'd never know the answer to every question, but I had to forgive myself before forgiving anyone else.

That was the hardest part.

I'd never wanted to be a victim, and yet, I was.

I opened my mouth to tell Gretchen it went fine, and everything spilled out, all my realizations that not everything bad in my life was my fault. She listened without moving, giving me every bit of her attention.

When I was done, she cleared her throat.

"You never deserved your childhood," she said. "And that's the hardest thing for people to grasp. For some reason, we're all wired to be ashamed when it's the people who failed or abused us who should feel shame."

I turned, staring past her head, unable to meet her gaze anymore.

"I should have been cared for properly," I said, keeping my voice steady. "I was just a kid."

"Yes, you should have."

"I didn't deserve abuse and neglect."

"No, you didn't."

My chest hurt so fucking much. I cleared my throat and forced my eyes back to hers. "I'm getting married, and I want kids. I've always wanted kids. But now that it's actually going to happen, all I can think about is...how could the adults in my life be so negligent? I can't imagine looking at my child and just...choosing fucking drugs over them. I know it's an addiction, but I can't fucking imagine it, even at my absolute lowest. And my fucking stepdad...what kind of monster looks at a kid and decides to beat the fuck out of them?"

She smiled and her eyes softened.

"You're breaking a terrible cycle, Caden," she said. "All of your thoughts are very normal things to struggle with at this stage."

"The realization is hard," I said flatly.

"But it's necessary for forgiveness."

"I don't know if I can forgive the people who were supposed to raise me."

"No, I mean forgiving yourself is hard, but it's necessary. For not knowing, for needing time to heal. It's called grace," she said, setting her pad aside and folding her hands.

"Grace?"

She nodded. "It's a word often associated with religion, but you'll find that it's just as necessary outside of that. Your path to healing yourself won't be easy or linear, but you have to just keep giving yourself grace, even when you don't feel like it."

I swallowed past my dry throat. "How many times?"

"I've found you never really stop needing to give yourself grace," she said.

"I'm not sure if I deserve that," I said.

"Would you give Circe the same grace?"

I didn't hesitate. "Of course."

"Then give it to yourself too. You're the person she loves most in this world, so be kind to that man," she said, getting to her feet. "And you don't have to forgive the people who hurt you. Some people don't forgive and forget. They just walk away and heal themselves."

I ran a hand over my face. "I don't think I can anymore. Forgive them, I mean."

"That's your choice," she said. "Whatever you choose, it serves only to help you move forward. Now, let's talk about Circe."

She went to open the balcony door, letting the warm morning air pour through. I stayed where I was as her heels clicked around the kitchen. In a few minutes, I heard a frying pan hit the stove and a steak sizzle. My stomach growled.

"What about Circe?" I asked finally.

"How's the sex?"

My brows rose and I got up, joining her in the kitchen. "A bit bold, no?"

"I'm your therapist, darling," she said, dusting off her hands. "But it's up to you how intimate you want to get in therapy."

I thought it over and decided I didn't care that much. "The sex is great. Why?"

"Good. Best you've ever had?"

"Yeah, it is."

She flipped the steak and went to get eggs from the fridge. "That's good. You two seem like a good match."

"Do we?"

She returned. "I know on paper you don't, but you have very compatible traits. And I think it works out for you that she's very well adjusted mentally. She seems competent, driven, but unsure of what she wants."

"That's a solid assessment," I said.

Gretchen pulled the steak off the stove to rest and started cracking eggs. "Is she reconciling with her father?"

"She wants to," I said.

My mind went back to the other night when I'd gotten home late to find Circe already in bed. She was asleep, and her phone screen was still on. I'd picked it up to set it aside, and my heart sank as my eyes moved over the unsent message meant for her father.

She missed him. She missed Delaney.

"I'm going to speak with her father," I said. "I think I can make a deal."

Gretchen set my steak and eggs down before me and handed me a fork and knife. "What kind of deal?"

"One where I talk to his daughter and help them reconcile, and he writes a check for what he owes us so we can fully fund the training base," I said.

Gretchen leaned on the counter, crossing her arms. "You think he'd be amenable?"

"I think he loves his daughter," I said.

"And you'd use that against him?"

I shook my head. "No, but I think a part of him loves her enough to realize that betraying our deal was his fuck up, and he needs to make up for it if he wants a good relationship with his daughter and grandchildren."

"What if he doesn't agree to it?"

"Then we reevaluate," I said. "I'll give her anything she wants."

Gretchen's face softened, and she leaned across the table and patted my arm. "Eat your breakfast, and we'll wrap this session up. I know you have to be at work at nine."

I left her office thirty minutes later feeling raw but hopeful. Part of me wished I could just skip ahead to the part where I was fixed.

When I got to the training center, the gun range was empty. I checked my phone, but I definitely wasn't late. Frowning, I did a loop down the hall, but Maelon was nowhere to be found.

That was strange. From his first day here, he'd been nothing but punctual.

I was just passing the hallway that led to the arena when I saw a black pile on the floor. I paused, frowning. Was that a jacket? Stepping near, I kicked at it with my foot, and a silver mug rolled out from beneath. It was definitely Maelon's jacket and thermos.

Quietly, I moved down the hall and stairs, entering the cool, underground tunnels. At the end, I could see the gates to the arena were open. When I drew near, I saw a lanky shape hunched at the center, arms wrapped around his knees, chin down.

"Maelon," I said quietly.

My voice echoed. He lifted his head and turned.

"What are you doing?" I asked, stepping into the arena. "We have practice this morning."

He nodded, getting to his feet slowly. He tucked his hands behind his back and dropped his eyes.

"I just wanted to look, sir," he said.

I drew up beside him, scanning the stone sides of the arena. "At ease. You can speak."

He relaxed, balling his fists, rubbing his knuckles. "You're training me for this, aren't you? Sir?"

Into my mind flashed an image of everything Maelon would go through if he chose this path, everything I'd go through at his side as his kingmaker. Merrick had spoken to me of his path in the arena, and I'd heard Daphne talk about how hard she'd trained him.

Years of blood, sweat, tears. Years of longing for glory, only for it to end in one day.

Was it worth it?

How much suffering and death did it take to produce a gentle king? A king who had tasted pain so thoroughly, he would do anything before he let one of his people feel the same?

And was Maelon that king?

Could I stand at his side and watch him suffer?

Part of me wanted to roll those questions around in my head forever so I didn't have to make a final choice, but I was over deflecting. Truthfully, since meeting Maelon, I'd known deep down that I was in the presence of someone who would shift our world on its axis, perhaps just how Daphne knew by looking at Merrick that he would be the next *Brenin*.

"There was another boy like you, once upon a time," I said, sinking down to a crouch in the sand.

"Are you talking about Merrick?" he asked.

I nodded. "Daphne believed he could be king, that he could be the one to lead us until another man took his place. But Merrick believed it too, and now, he'll go down as the greatest *Brenin* in our history."

"Why? Why do it?"

My eyes moved over the stands, over the stone benches. "Because when he's gone, when I'm gone, our organization will still stand. Because he secured a future for not just my generation, but my children's children."

Maelon ran a hand over his face, wiping his nose.

"Merrick will never reap the crops he sows," I said quietly. "But they're worth planting all the same."

Maelon glanced up, meeting my eyes. "I want this," he said. "All my life, I've felt like I was different, like I was made to do more."

"I felt that when I met you."

"But I can't do it alone," he whispered. "I'm not brave enough."

I straightened, reaching down to offer my hand. He grasped it, and I pulled him to his feet.

"If you want to be king, I will make you a king," I said.

He lifted his chin, and I saw it flash through his face—a thousand years of kings and a thousand years more to come.

"I'm going to break you down and make something of you," I said. "Some days you'll hate me for it, but someday, you'll stand in this arena, and Merrick will lift your arm for the crowd. Trust me that I'll get you there."

He nodded once. "I trust you."

"Good, let's begin," I said.

I was halfway to the gates when I noticed he wasn't with me. When I turned, he still stood at the center, but his chin was lifted, and his eyes were quiet.

"I'd like to see my mother this weekend," he said.

I dipped my head. "You may."

He cleared his throat, and his feet moved this time, carrying himself out of the arena at my side. "She's going to cry when I tell her," he said finally.

"That's her right," I said.

"Sir," he said, his voice tight.

"Yes?"

"Do you believe I can do this?"

"Yes," I said without hesitation. "I do."

He nodded. We were both quiet as we moved up the hallway and entered the training center. There was an aura of finality around us that day, one that sobered us both. I pushed him hard and left him still working when the buzzer sounded to signal midday.

Tomorrow morning, we would start in earnest.

CHAPTER THIRTY-EIGHT

CIRCE

I wasn't prepared for what living with Caden would actually be like. I was used to structure and working hard, but not the way Caden was. He moved through life like he was powered by a relentless motor. His body was strong and could go for hours. His mind was brutally sharp, wickedly dark, but still so soft for me when it was just us.

He moved fast and hard.

Unexpectedly, I ground to a halt.

From my first moment, my father had pushed me to succeed. I'd jumped out of bed every morning eager to please and went to bed at night feeling like I hadn't done enough. Now, there were no expectations of me. If I chose to stay in bed all day and read, Caden didn't care as long as I was happy.

All my drive dissipated. I found myself getting listless.

I missed my office, missed my friends. Delaney hadn't reached out to me, and I was ignoring Emmy's forty-eight phone calls a week. I didn't want to bad-mouth Delaney to our mutual friends, so I just shut down. Maybe I just didn't understand. After all, I'd fallen for someone I wasn't supposed to have.

Why was she any different?

But the wound still hurt, especially when my father was texting every night, begging for me to call him back. I didn't tell Caden, but I could tell he knew. He saw me turn my phone off and tuck it into the bedside table when he got in from work.

The only solace I found was with Caden.

When he wasn't working, he took me out of the apartment whether I liked it or not. We met up with Clara and Merrick on the weekends for the next month. I'd never experienced the kind of luxury they lived—we'd always had money, but we never used it for anything enjoyable. We'd rarely gone out except to network, but Merrick took Clara out for pure pleasure.

I was fascinated by them. It was clear Merrick was hopelessly enamored by his wife, and she was in awe of him. He kept her glittering with diamonds, and she looked at him like he'd hung the moon and stars.

A few weeks later, Caden and I started going along with them. We took the sailboat out, ate at restaurants along the coast, stayed in Merrick's new hotels. Clara and I connected easily. She was sweet and cheerful, and we spent a lot of time together while Caden and Merrick conferred in low voices at the bar.

That was one part of the Welsh organization that ground my gears.

I didn't want to be infantilized, and these men didn't believe in letting women into the business side of their operation.

"Does it bother you?" I asked Clara one day.

We were staying at a hotel on an island off the coast. It was scorching hot outside, so we'd both sought refuge on the shaded balcony of the restaurant. Clara was curled up in a berry pink bikini with matching sunglasses and, for some reason, her entire set of engagement jewelry. That was another thing I was getting used to. Apparently, not wearing the jewelry often enough was seen as strange.

I wore only my engagement ring. I wasn't quite acclimated yet.

"Does what bother me?" Clara asked, glancing over the rim of her margarita.

I glanced across the restaurant to where Merrick stood with Caden, both speaking quietly in Welsh.

"Being on the outside," I said.

She shook her head. "I don't care to be on the inside of the organization's operations."

"Why?"

She shrugged. "It's not interesting to me; it's a bit boring, honestly. And I don't feel the need to know just for the sake of knowing. That's not my concern, even as Merrick's wife."

I took a sip of my drink—a fruit punch flavored blended drink with sweet rum. "What is your job? What's my job supposed to be after I marry Caden?"

Clara sighed, pushing her sunglasses up. "I manage Merrick's social schedule outside of work. He's incredibly busy, and I know him better than anyone, so I know what's important to him."

"I love Caden, but I don't think I can do that for him," I said slowly.

"That's just what I chose," she said. "I'm social. I enjoy being his wife."

I stayed quiet, trying to wrap my head around her confidence. All my life, I'd been told that my value was in business. How much money I brought in was a direct result of what I was worth as a woman. But here Clara was, telling me that meant nothing to her.

"Do you ever feel...anxious? About not having your own money?"

She let her head fall back, laughing. "Oh, I have money. My job is to manage Merrick's home, his schedule, and his personal image. He pays me for that, and I have a separate bank account that's in my name only."

My brows shot up. "Really?"

She shrugged, like it should be obvious. "Of course, I don't work for free. Being the Welsh *Brenin's* wife is work. On weekends, he spoils me like it's his full-time job, but during the week I do a lot of management and networking for him. It took a lot off his plate when we married."

"What do you mean exactly?"

She waved a hand at the restaurant. "This chain of hotels was one of Merrick's biggest business investments in the last year. I met the woman married to the builder at a party. We went out to lunch the next day, and by the end of the week, I had a deal for Merrick."

"Oh, that makes sense," I said slowly. "But I don't think I can do that for Caden."

"Caden's not a businessman," she said. "He's a soldier."

I chewed my lip listlessly. "I don't know where that leaves me."

She leaned in, setting her empty cup aside as her dark eyes fixed on mine.

"Wherever you want to be," she said. "You have money, you have experience. Start your own company or go work for whoever you want. You're Circe Johansen."

My brain had been turning a mile a minute since the night I told Caden my father was going to betray him. In a single second, it ground to a halt. All the boiling emotions I'd kept tamped down stopped bubbling.

She was right.

I didn't need my father or his business.

I was my own person.

A smile broke over my face that I couldn't bite back. Clara's brows lifted, and she gave me an expectant look.

"Did it just hit you?"

"Yeah," I said, sitting up breathlessly. "I have the resumé. I can take care of myself."

Clara reached out and took my hand, squeezing it.

"You can," she said. "But I just want to remind you, you don't always have to. You've got someone who's happy to take care of you when you need a break."

She patted my arm and got up, padding across the room in just her bikini. I smiled, wishing I had that kind of confidence. She moved past the bar, and I caught her glance back at her husband and the subtle shake of her hair. He dropped his conversation with Caden instantly, turning on his heel to chase after her.

Impressed, I got up and leaned on the railing. It didn't take long for Caden's presence to fill my space and his hand to rest on my lower back as his mouth grazed the freckles on my neck.

"You look good," he murmured.

I glanced down at my modest one piece. "Thank you."

"Want to go upstairs? Maybe take a nap?"

I turned in his arms, looking up at his heartbreakingly handsome face. His eyes were obscured by dark glasses, but I knew he was gazing into mine. "Why do I have a feeling there's no sleeping involved?"

"Because we're still in the honeymoon phase, butterfly," he said.

"Is that a bad thing?"

"Not to me." He shrugged. "I want to honeymoon with you before and after the wedding."

"Is it appropriate to honeymoon while on a weekend vacation with your father and his wife?"

He wrapped his arm around my waist, pulling me off the balcony. I barely had time to grab my purse from the table before he was ushering me into the hall. The minute we were alone, his hand came down on my ass, sending a shock of pain and arousal through my hips.

"Hey," I yelped, darting ahead of him.

"You fucking love it," he growled, catching up to me.

We didn't resurface until dinner time. The four of us ate at the restaurant in the outdoor seating overlooking the beach. The sun set, casting long shadows over the tables. The staff lit torches, and the air filled with the sharp scent of citronella, mingling with the fried food and beer. We ate until we were full and drank until our heads spun. Even Clara and Merrick, who weren't big drinkers, indulged themselves.

Upstairs, Caden was ragingly horny. Clara and Merrick were staying in the room next to ours, and there was nothing more horrifying to me than my future father-in-law hearing us. We fucked in the bathroom because it was the furthest point from their room, but the minute our bodies touched the bed, he was sliding between my thighs again.

"Caden, you have to be quiet," I begged.

He pushed his cock into my aching pussy, filling me until my eyes rolled back.

"Maybe I'll switch rooms tomorrow," he groaned.

"No, that's so obvious."

He drew back and slammed into me, sending the bed thumping into the wall.

"Caden!"

"Do you think that people don't know we fuck?" he panted.

"Please," I begged.

He pulled his dick out of me, rolling onto his back. "Please, you know they're on the other side of wall doing the same thing."

I jumped up, scowling. "That's enough. I'm getting some water; do you want anything?"

He shook his head, watching me with a smirk as I padded out of the room and into the kitchen. I was filling a glass with ice and water when I heard it: a soft thump, followed by muffled laughter. Then—thump, thump, thump.

Oh God, that was the bed hitting the wall in Merrick and Clara's room. Horrified, I grabbed my glass and scurried into the bedroom. Caden took one look at my shocked face and smirked.

"I was right," he drawled.

"Okay, you win this time," I said, setting my drink aside and straddling his waist. "And you can fuck me however you like. Apparently, no one has any shame."

He bucked me off and flipped me onto my stomach, pushing a pillow under my hips and thighs. His cock pushed between my legs, entering me in one, slow thrust, filling me with his hard warmth.

"I've spent my life drowning in shame," he said. "Not anymore."

He dug his hands in my hair and closed his fist, holding my head back. His teeth grazed my shoulder as he slid out and thrust back in, dragging his piercing over my inner muscles, making me clench.

"Fuck, that's right," he rasped. "You take the whole fucking thing, butterfly. I want you to feel it when you sit down tomorrow."

He made good on his promise. When we went to join Merrick and Clara for breakfast along the beach, I had to bite my lip to keep from gasping when I sank down. Caden didn't look at me, but I saw his smirk. He knew I still felt him inside me, and he was proud of it.

I took my hat off, fanning my face.

"Late night?" Clara asked cheerily.

"No, we fell asleep pretty early," Caden said, stretching his legs out under the table and crossing his arms.

"We did too," said Merrick. "Vacation does that to you. Ready to head home tonight?"

"I am," I cut in. "I think I'd like to get moving on some work in the city tomorrow morning. I'm ready."

Caden took off his sunglasses, fixing his cobalt eyes on me. "What work?"

I glanced over at Clara, and she gave me an encouraging nod.

"I was thinking about doing something independently of Johansen Enterprises," I said, surprised by how good the words sounded. "A new job or company."

"Doing what?" Merrick asked.

"Consulting," I said. "When I went into Johansen Enterprises, they had a horrible turnover problem. I came up with a new employee handbook, set up a new system so employees felt like they were getting what they put into the job, and our turnover dropped by eighty-six percent in the first year."

"That's impressive," Merrick said. "How about you work for me? I have turnover problems for some of my businesses that could be looked into, and I need someone with management experience for the operational side of the new hotel chain."

"I don't know about that," Caden said.

"Actually, that might not be a bad way to get my feet wet," I said. "Send me the job description, and I'll send in my resumé."

Merrick laughed. "I don't need your resumé; I know your work history. You're hired if you want it."

Caden's brows shot up, but I ignored him. "Done," I said, leaning forward and shaking his hand. "But only for a year or so. Then I get to branch off and do my own thing."

"Fine by me," said Merrick.

On the way home, I turned to Caden. "Would you rather I not work for you father?"

He glanced over, putting his hand on my thigh. "No, I don't mind as long as it's purely business. I don't want you getting caught up in anything that could hurt you. Organization business is off limits."

I rolled my eyes. "Yes, sir."

He squeezed my leg. "Good girl."

We drove down the coast in silence, the golden light streaking over the ocean. The radio droned softly in the background. Everything smelled like summer, and I was deliciously sleepy, worn out by the weekend.

"Do you want to have a baby?"

My eyes shot open. "What?"

His face hadn't changed, and he was still staring ahead. "I'd like to have kids, but I get it if you don't. I understand it's hard to work and be pregnant."

His voice was casual, but I felt a tremor of deep longing in it.

"Can I think about it?" I whispered. "I think I do, but there's a lot of logistical planning to work through if I'm going to work too."

He nodded. "I understand it's a lot to ask."

I slid my arm over his shoulder, stroking the back of his neck. "I think it's kind of hot that you want to have kids with me, but we still have to be smart about it."

The corner of his mouth jerked up. "For now, we can just practice."

"I'd like that," I teased. "But here's a better question for this stage—when are you planning on making an honest woman out of me?"

He shrugged. "I'll take you to the courthouse tomorrow morning."

All my life, I'd assumed I'd have a huge wedding with all my father's friends and business partners. That was what everyone in our world did, but it felt distinctly wrong for Caden and I, especially after what we'd been through together. I'd never looked forward to my wedding, and now, I realized why. It was always going to be a networking opportunity for everyone else involved.

"Okay," I said. "That's fine."

"Really?"

We pulled up outside his apartment, and he cut the engine. He shifted in his seat, reaching for my hand.

"Don't do it just because that's what I want," he said.

I shook my head. "I just don't want to be anyone's spectacle. Maybe later...maybe when I sort through everything with my father, we can throw a party with everyone. But I'd like to get legally married before then. I want something that's just for us."

His throat bobbed, and he leaned in to kiss my mouth briefly. "I won't tell anyone. We'll get up and go as soon as the courthouse opens tomorrow. Fuck work, this is more important than anything."

"Thank you," I whispered.

We were quiet as he led me inside. We'd only been together in his apartment for a few weeks, but we already fell into a routine. He went to check his work emails. I wandered into the bathroom to take off my jewelry and makeup. We both met up in the bedroom to get undressed.

I glanced over my shoulder as I unzipped my dress. He was unbuttoning his shirt, slipping it down, revealing his muscled, tattooed shoulders.

"Caden," I whispered.

He turned. "What is it, butterfly?"

"I have to make this right," I said, voice wavering. "These last few weeks have been so good, but everything is bittersweet."

He crossed the room, cradling my face. Sometimes, I forgot how tall he was until he was directly over me. I had to tilt back to look into his shadowed face.

"Do you mean your father and Delaney?"

I nodded.

His lips thinned. "Alright, but I'm going with you."

I shook my head. "No, let me go alone. I'll go to the country club tomorrow at lunch if he can make it. I just don't want him to think we got married at the courthouse because I was trying to avoid him. I want a clean slate, no baggage, for us."

He bent, lips brushing my forehead. "Whatever you want, you can have. We'll get married Tuesday instead."

The next morning, I waited until Caden had left for work. Then, I pulled my phone from the drawer, scrolled back to the last time I'd called my father, and tapped his number. Hands shaking, I set it down and hit the speaker button.

It rang once before he picked up.

"Circe," he said.

"Hey, Dad," I whispered, throat hoarse.

"Are you alright?" He sounded frantic, not angry.

"Yeah, I'm with Caden," I said, squeezing my eyes shut. "Dad, before you say anything...I want to talk first."

He cleared his throat, like he was tearing up. "Okay."

"I'm not sorry I told Caden, but I'm sorry if you were hurt by what I did. But I fell in love with Caden, and I couldn't let you hurt him like that. And you were wrong. I'm sorry, but you were wrong to go back on your deal with the Welsh organization."

There was a long silence. He cleared his throat again.

"Thank you for being honest," he said. "I'm not going to lie and say I wasn't hurt, but I understand that I hurt you too, and for that, I'm sorry."

I opened my mouth, but my eyes stung. Tears welled over, and I wiped them away furiously.

"Does Caden love you?" His voice cracked.

"Yeah, Dad, he does," I gasped.

"Will he take care of you?"

"Yeah, he takes really good care of me. He really does."

I heard him blow his nose, and it took everything I had not to break down. There was a moment of silence when I knew he was gathering himself. Part of me wanted to bring up everything else that had made me betray him, but suddenly, I didn't care anymore.

He'd never tried to harm me; he'd just suffocated me. It wasn't out of maliciousness, probably more out of his own desperation not to lose another person he loved.

He loved me, that I knew for certain.

"Dad," I whispered.

"Yes, honey?"

"If you want to be with Delaney and she wants to be with you, that's not my business," I said. "I don't think I'll ever be comfortable being close friends with Delaney in the same way again. It just...feels so strange. But I want to be on good terms with both of you, and I do want you both to be happy."

"Thank you," he said, voice cracking. "I'm sorry again. I shouldn't have lied."

"I'm sorry too, for hurting you."

"Please come see me," he said.

I took a deep breath, forcing my voice to steady. "Have lunch with me and bring Delaney. I'll meet you at the country club at noon."

"Really?"

"Yes, we need to break this ice."

I could hear him start pacing his office. "Bring Caden too."

Into my mind burst the image of Caden, lounging at the country club with all his tattoos on display, giving my father an ice-cold stare over a mimosa, lip curled like a Doberman standing over me, ready to bite at the slightest provocation.

"Is that a good idea?" I asked.

"We need to break the ice too," he said, laughing weakly.

"Okay," I said, taking a deep breath. "I'll meet you at the country club at noon. With Caden."

I set the phone aside, hoping I wasn't making the whole situation a lot worse.

CHAPTER THIRTY-NINE

CADEN

It was eleven when my phone rang from inside my locker. I'd just finished showering after training when I heard it buzzing against the metal door. I swiped the screen, my fiancée's name popping up.

That felt good. Somehow, I'd made Circe Johansen mine, and it felt like winning the lottery. Every morning, I got up and had to resist the urge to congratulate myself in the mirror.

I tapped the speaker button and reached for my clothes. "Hey, butterfly."

"Hey," she said, her voice hesitant. "I changed my mind."

"About?"

"The country club. Both my father and I want you there for lunch."

I narrowed my eyes, fastening my belt. "When?"

"Today. Is that okay?"

Part of me wanted to say I didn't think it was a good idea, but my heart couldn't deny her anything.

"Of course. I'll be there in fifteen."

When I got back to the apartment, the old Circe was firmly in place. She stepped out of the bathroom in a tight seersucker dress with delicate purple flowers all over it. Her long legs ended in a demure pair of heels. The only thing that was different was the jewelry.

A little anklet on her leg. Her ring weighing down her finger. Her neck and wrists glittering with my jewelry.

My dick woke up, thinking about the only piece that wasn't visible. Between her thighs, under her silk panties, was the diamond I'd given her to wear on her pussy.

She stood on her toes and kissed me discreetly so she wouldn't ruin her lipstick.

"Thank you for coming," she said. "I know it's not what you want to do."

"I'd rather do you," I said, taking her hand and spinning her so I could get a good look. "But it's eleven thirty, so I'll wait for tonight."

She rolled her eyes, but she was smiling. "Wear something nice, please."

"I was going to wear my uniform."

Her eyes widened. "Could you not?"

"I'm joking, sweetheart." I spanked her ass as I walked by and went into the bedroom. I had a nice, light gray suit that worked well for summertime. She lingered in the door, arms crossed, while I put on the pants, shoes, and white shirt. That was as good as it was going to get. Not even her father could get me to put a suit jacket on.

"Good?" I asked, smoothing back my hair.

She bit her lip.

"You look really good," she said, her voice breathy. "Roll your sleeves up a little. I like it."

Her eyes followed my every move as I obeyed, rolling them to just below my elbow. Then, she went to the dresser and slid open the top drawer. I couldn't keep my eyes off her either, watching her felt like a gift I couldn't get enough of. She was everything I would never be, and I was fine with that now.

We were two different people from two different walks of life, but when it was just us, stripped back, we fit together perfectly.

Her body was made to lay beside mine.

She returned, this time stopping when our bodies were inches apart. Then, she lifted my hand and put something in my palm. It took me a second to drag my eyes from her face to look down.

It was a silver watch. I didn't know much about expensive watches, but I could tell this one was worth something. I shifted it, flipping it over, and my heart stopped.

To my love, Caden Llwyd.

My throat was dust dry. I glanced down at her, and she was waiting, her eyes wary, clearly worried about my reaction. When I didn't say anything, she reached for the watch, but I closed my hand over it.

"I'm sorry. I shouldn't have had that engraved," she said. "I just...I looked you up and found out that Payne was your stepfather's name. And...I felt awkward having it engraved. So I just put your family name there. I'll have it fixed."

I shook my head. "No, don't."

She chewed her lip hard. "What's wrong?"

I flipped the watch over and over. "Nothing. It just never occurred to me that I could drop his last name. It's something I'll need to give some thought to."

She reached for it again. "I'll have it removed."

I let her take it but kept my hand extended so she could secure it for me. She hesitated and then slowly slipped it over my wrist and tightened the strap.

"Don't remove it," I said. "I'd rather it be my Welsh name, even if I don't change it. And this will be our children's name unless you disagree."

She shook her head, smiling shakily. "I'd like my children to have your family name. It's really lovely."

"It is," I agreed quietly. "And my father is a good man. His family are good people."

"I've never met his aunts, Daphne and Ophelia," she said. "I'd like to."

"I'm sure they're begging Merrick to meet you already." I bent and kissed her forehead. "Let's get married first. And before we do that, let's go fix all this shit with your father, alright?"

She nodded, tilting her head back. I kissed her, taking my time because my throat felt oddly lumpy. When I pulled back, I'd gotten it together. She offered a sweet smile, and I tapped her on the chin.

"Thank you," I said.

What I didn't tell her was that this was the first real gift I'd ever been given. My mother and stepfather never celebrated birthdays or holidays, and Merrick wouldn't have dared to give me anything when I was in my denial phase. Somehow, it made it mean even more that she was the first person to give me something, especially something made custom.

I kissed her again then spun her around and spanked her ass so she wouldn't see how I really felt.

I was still getting used to sharing the vulnerable parts of myself.

She wanted to take her car, so I helped her into the passenger side. To my surprise, she didn't ask me to roll the top up. I drove feeling like the luckiest man in the world, unable to keep my eyes off her. She was gorgeous, dark hair whipping in the wind as we cruised down the road.

I hadn't realized it until today, but she was different since everything had fallen apart.

Her shoulders were more relaxed. Her skin was suntanned, her eyes sparkled. She laughed, smiled more. Even though the future was unsure when it came to her career, her entire being was lighter.

A slow realization sank in. My hand gripped her thigh.

For the first time in my life, I was good for someone.

Which meant...I was healing.

"You okay?" she asked.

I glanced over, glad I was wearing sunglasses. "Better than okay."

We pulled up outside the country club a few minutes later, and my mood had done a one-eighty. This wasn't my scene. It was my father's world, at least the one he showed to the public. Clara fit in here, with her jewels and ability to talk about nothing for hours, but I didn't look or sound like any of the people here.

But she had crossed into my universe. I could do the same for her.

I opened her door, and Circe let me help her out. She had a little mauve handbag that looked like it wouldn't fit anything, and she held it primly in her hand, her other hand tucked in mine as we headed up the walkway.

"It smells like hyacinths," she said.

"Does it?"

She nodded. "One of my earliest memories is that smell. My father took me here every Sunday after church."

I glanced over, surprised. "You go to church?"

She shrugged. "We did for a while, but it was more of a social status thing for my father. Then, the church we went to shut down."

I stroked her knuckle with my thumb. "I feel like there's a lot we don't know about each other."

She smiled. "We've been busy."

I pulled open the door, my hand on her lower back. "Starting tomorrow, I have a lifetime to learn everything else."

She gave me a look, a sweet smile and a flutter of her lashes. I noticed when she felt safe, she let herself be softer. It felt like a privilege that she was soft with me.

Inside came the gentle flurry of iced tea glasses clinking and soft laughter. Fans whirred overhead, the air sweet like hyacinths and salty like oysters. There was a distinct scent of money, of boredom. Of everything I wasn't.

Her hand tightened, and I followed her eyes to the table on the far side, in the golden glow of the afternoon sun.

Her father sat on the left side of the four-person table. On his left was Delaney, wearing a demure linen sundress. She looked older, and it took me a moment to realize that she'd taken out her septum piercing.

"I don't know about this," Circe whispered.

I bent, my mouth by her ear. "I've got you, sweetheart. Just tap my leg if you want me to take you home. I won't let anyone disrespect you."

She nodded, sending me a grateful look. I led her across the room as her father rose. There was an awkward moment where they looked at each other before her father stepped forward and pulled her into his arms, and I saw her shoulders quiver. They hugged for a long time. I sank down and gave Delaney an awkward nod.

Lukas murmured something to her, and she laughed weakly. They broke apart, and I pulled Circe's chair out, helping her to sit next to me. Her father sank down, and everyone looked away while he wiped his eyes.

"Hey," Circe said, looking directly at Delaney.

"Hey," Delaney whispered.

There was an awkward silence. I cleared my throat.

"Maybe we should get some drinks?" I said.

"Yes, of course," Lukas said, pulling the menu from beneath his napkin. He held it out to me. "They've got a great Japanese whiskey."

"I'd like an Aperol Spritz," Circe said.

The server appeared, and it wasn't long before everyone had drinks and the atmosphere eased. Not a lot, but enough we all got to the end without an argument. I wasn't sure why I was here or what the point of this was, except to prove we could all make small talk together. I stayed civil with Lukas in the same way I had before. Delaney and Circe chatted about Providence and their mutual social scene.

An hour later, Lukas stretched and sat up. "Well, I'd better get back to the office. Before we go, I'd like to have a private word with you, Caden."

I caught a strain of ice in his voice. "Fine by me."

Circe stared after me with perfectly round eyes as I followed Lukas to the bar. He leaned on the counter and released a short sigh.

"I don't like you, Caden," he said. "I never have. You're not who I want my daughter to be with. But for the sake of keeping her in my life, I can be civil with you."

"The sentiment is mutual," I said. "I've got no interest in being your friend."

"Good," he said.

"I'm glad we're in agreement."

He let out another sigh, like he was trying to swallow something particularly bitter. "Circe will remain my sole heir. However, she texted me on the way here and let me know she is resigning from Johansen Enterprises, which is for the best. I can't have her working in my company when she's with the son of my competitor."

"She intends to strike out on her own," I said. "I think she'll do well."

"She does well at everything she attempts."

"She does."

The corner of his mouth turned up. "We have some common ground. We both love her."

"That's true," I said. "I might not like you, but you love your daughter. That's enough to afford you my respect."

"That's all I'm asking for," he said, his mouth returning to a grim line.

"That's not all I want." I squared my shoulders. "I want the deal back, but this time, without the shared base. You owe it to me."

I'd expected to get angry, but he sighed. "I thought you might ask for that. I just hope you're not using my daughter as leverage."

"This has nothing to do with Circe," I said, annoyed. "This is about honor."

His jaw worked, eyes narrowed. "Fine," he said. "But I want something."

"You're not in a position to bargain," I said.

"I'm a businessman. Of course I'm bargaining. I want you to train the men who train my security. If you do that, I'll enter into a non-compete agreement in the areas where we both work, and you will receive the funding you need."

I frowned. "Why? You want me working with your men?"

He ground his jaw, like it hurt him to speak. "My men have never been trained the way you had them training. Share that with us, and you get what you want."

I studied him. I knew he wasn't going to sign the check without getting something in return. I didn't want to get myself into another deal with Johansen Enterprises but, this time, I did have the protection of being his son-in-law, the father of his future grandchildren. There was only so much he could do to me without angering Circe.

"Alright," I said. "So long as Merrick agrees, I'll do it."

He held out his hand. I hesitated and then shook it. We both let go quickly.

"I think you should speak with your daughter alone, later," I said. "I want her to feel this rift is fully healed so she can move forward."

"I will," he said.

We didn't have anything else to say to each other. Despite our differences, it was clear to me we understood each other. We would be cordial when our paths crossed, but we'd never be close.

But he had gained a bit of my respect today. Not much, but I knew it took a lot for him to swallow his pride and meet with me. In many ways, we weren't so different. Maybe, in another life, Lukas would have led an army too.

Circe and Delaney stood by the window, less than a foot from each other. I could tell they were both trying not to cry. Circe kept shaking her hair back and blinking, laughing awkwardly. To my relief, when they parted, it was with a quick hug.

In the car, I passed her a tissue. "Are you alright, butterfly?"

She sniffed, nodding. "Yeah, I just...don't want things to change. I mean, I do, but I didn't want it like this."

"Are things fixed with Delaney?"

She looked down at her lap. "They're fixed, but it still feels weird. I think we just moved on from what we were before, but if she's happy with my father, I don't want to stand in the way of that. I don't think she meant to hurt me."

There was a long silence before she intertwined her fingers with mine.

"I don't have a grudge against anyone," she said, sinking back into her seat. "We all just grew up. Things changed."

"You don't resent her? Some people might hate her, in your shoes."

She shook her head. "No, I couldn't hate Delaney."

There was a quiet ache in my chest as we drove home. Circe was strong, resilient and resourceful, but she was also kind, much kinder and sweeter than I deserved.

That night, after she was asleep, I lay awake for a long time. Sitting up against the pillows, moonlight a pool over the bed. She slept soundly, naked and half covered by the sheet.

We'd slept together after I got home from work, after we'd had takeout at the kitchen table.

It hadn't been like the sex I'd had before knowing her. It was familiar, casual, like the quick kiss she gave me when she was going to be late. I had slid into bed beside her, she'd pushed her ass into me, and we had a quickie without speaking. Then, we both passed out.

It was wonderfully domestic.

I woke up fifteen minutes later, stirred by someone driving a motorcycle down the street. In a flash, the sound woke a sudden realization in my heart.

I hadn't sleepwalked since that night, not since she started sleeping in my bed. I got up to make a note in my phone to mention that to Gretchen, even though I wasn't worried about it.

There was a lot I'd previously worried about that no longer bothered me.

Having a woman who loved me, a name for what was going on with my brain, and a future had given me stability. I had hope now.

But more than that, I had people to lean on who cared about me.

It took me a while to fall asleep, but not because I was upset. When I finally did wake in the early morning, my heart was still pumping hard. I rolled onto my side to find her side of the bed empty. The shower ran from the other side of the bathroom door, and everything smelled faintly like hyacinths.

I smiled, deeply satisfied in every way for the first time in my life.

Today was my wedding day.

CHAPTER FORTY

CIRCE

THE FOLLOWING SPRING

When we got married, Merrick asked Caden what he wanted as a gift, and he said the site of the hotel where he'd taken me that night, where he'd told me who his father was, where I'd revealed my father's plan. Confused but thrilled to finally be allowed fatherly behavior, Merrick gave it to him.

It turned out, Caden had a lot of money saved up, and without telling me, he used it to build the most beautiful house I'd ever seen, overlooking the sea.

It was simple, minimal like his apartment, but beautiful like my childhood home. When he brought me there for the first time, he took my hand and led me from the car. He walked me up the driveway, through the garden planted with purple hyacinths, over the porch where a little wind chime hung, the metal butterflies clattering, past the stone pillars on the porch and into the front hallway.

Our bedroom overlooked the sea. Caden bought a boat and built a dock down below. He called it *The Aphrodite* and took me out on it on long weekends when he wasn't at the training center and when I wasn't at the office Merrick had rented for my department in Providence.

We both took breaks now. Life was slower, and we enjoyed everything so much more.

I woke one Saturday, the beginning of May, feeling good. He'd come in late the night before, and I barely remembered him getting into bed before he was already gone.

My back cracked as I sat up, resting against the pillows. I'd spent all Friday at the office, combing through the reports for the spring quarter. Everything looked better than good, and I was proud of the work we'd done. Last night on my way home, I got a text from Merrick expressing his thanks at how well we'd hit the goals he'd laid down.

I enjoyed this new job. It fed my need for challenge, but it gave me the freedom I craved.

Downstairs, the door slammed, and I stretched out, letting the sheet fall into my lap. The sun coming through the window was deliciously warm on my bare skin, my body relaxed except for between my thighs, where I felt the tension of not having the time to sleep with my husband for the last few days.

His boots rang up the steps before he appeared in the doorway, bathed in sweat from his run. He stopped short, his brows rising.

"Don't move," he said.

"Um...why?"

The corner of his mouth jerked up. "I just want to take good look at you. Nice tits."

I rolled my eyes—he was so full of shit, but way too charming for me to care. Soaked with sweat, he crossed the room and knelt over me, bending and kissing my mouth.

Heat moved through my veins as desire fluttered between my legs.

He pulled back, and I followed his mouth with mine. He brushed my hair back, and the look in his eyes was so gentle.

"I'd like to have dinner with you tonight," he said.

"Where?"

"Here." His lips brushed my forehead as he straightened and moved to the other side of the room.

I relaxed into the pillow, enjoying the sight of him pulling the wet shirt from his lean, tattooed torso. He'd finally gotten the tire irons covered with a chest piece that blended in with the rest of his ink, a collection of Greek statues—exactly what I thought he would get. I'd gone to one of his therapy sessions with Gretchen, and she explained ADHD hyperfixations. Some of his obsession with ancient cultures was due to that, and some it was, well, just Caden. I loved him for that, for his quirks, his passions.

He was wonderfully, beautifully complex.

Our brains worked differently, but in those differences, I'd found so much happiness. We were so happy—I hadn't realized it was possible to be this at peace before meeting him.

"Is that what you want? Dinner here?"

I pulled myself to the present as he stood in just his pants, waiting for an answer.

"I'd love to have dinner here with you," I said. "Are we cooking or ordering in?"

"I ordered the things we need to make dinner tonight," he said, tossing his clothes in the basket and moving into the bathroom.

It was two parts, with the toilet and sink in a separate room for privacy, but from the bed, I could see right into spacious front area where the open shower was. The wall came up to my waist, and the upper portion was glass. He stepped in and turned on the water, letting it pour over his head.

I settled in to enjoy the view. The glass came down to just above his groin, giving me a hint of the delicious trail of hair that led to his cock.

My thighs pressed together. I was horny, but why get up when he was going to come to me anyway?

Instead, I lay in a sleepy haze and watched my gorgeous, naked husband without a care in the world, my mind completely empty.

And the best part was, I wasn't thinking about work on my day off.

He finished and left the shower, naked and cock hard, dark tattoos glistening. I slid onto my back, and he crawled into bed, hovering over me before dipping his head to lick my hard nipples as I moaned, spreading my thighs.

"Want something, butterfly?" he murmured.

"I'd like your tongue," I sighed. "Please and thank you."

He laughed, kissing down my stomach. Sending tingles of pleasure through my body. I ran my hand over his head, over his short, dark hair, and pushed him down. He went obediently and I let my eyes roll back as he slid his tongue over my pussy.

My entire body turned to water as he moved his palms up my upper thighs, gripping the underside of my knees and flipping me. There was a rustle, and then he slid his head between my knees. Surprised, I reeled back, but he gripped my hips and pulled me down onto his face.

"Oh God," I gasped.

His tongue slid over my pussy, slow at first, touching everywhere but my swollen clit. My palm pressed against the wall for balance as I glanced over my shoulder, and my thighs shuddered at the sight of him, fully hard and pierced, the tip of his cock wet with desire.

Pleasure moved like lava through me.

My toes curled hard, and I came on his tongue, on his face. He lifted me down while I was still shuddering and pushed me onto his cock, forcing me to take all of his hard, hot length the way I craved.

It didn't feel like just pleasure anymore. It felt like the part of me that had never had a chance to be whole fit into the broken bits of him. Between the two of us, we made something beautiful.

It was home.

His hands gripped my body and guided me through every movement, rising, falling, my head back. The ceiling swimming overhead. Finally, he couldn't take being beneath me anymore and flipped me to my knees, pulling my head back so I had to look at him fucking me in the mirror across the room.

He finished inside me, and I fell onto my back, warm and satisfied.

"You're so beautiful," he murmured.

I smiled at him, closing my eyes as he kissed my forehead. "You're so handsome."

We spent the whole day together, the way we did every Saturday. I went outside and lay in the flower garden. Caden had a koi pond put in, and my fish swam lazily under the lily pads as the soft, spring air teased my hair and made me sleepy.

So I slept, because I had nowhere to be and nothing to do.

When I woke a while later, I wandered inside and found him in the library on the first floor. Despite having little to no formal education, Caden read more than anyone I'd ever met. Now, I found him stretched out on the couch, flipping through a textbook.

I leaned over, squinting. Was he reading about the history of...building materials in ancient civilizations? That checked out.

I sank down, and he glanced over.

"Ready for dinner?" he asked.

Nodding, I slipped down to lay on his chest. He set the book aside and stroked my hair back, his heart slow and steady in his chest.

My throat felt lumpy. How had I wasted so much time being so busy doing nothing at all when I could have been doing this?

"What time is it?" I murmured.

"About five."

I yawned. "Sex or dinner?"

"Hmm," he said. "Let's make dinner, sleep it off, and have sex."

"Sounds perfect."

We lay together for another half an hour before we made our way to the kitchen. It was one of the most beautiful spaces in the house: white stone, a fireplace shaped like a thin rectangle, and a window that looked up at the backyard where the orchard grew.

He'd ordered ingredients for fresh spaghetti. I put on quiet music, and we worked our way through making the sauce, buttering the bread, spreading it with fresh garlic. It turned out, cooking together when there was nothing else to do wasn't the same as trying to cook after a long day of work.

I dipped the spoon into the sauce and put it to his lips as his brows lifted.

"Very good," he said.

I licked the spoon. "Caden."

"Yes?"

"How happy are you?"

He sobered, his dark eyes glittering in the dim firelight. "I don't think there's a scale I can judge happiness like this on."

I slid my hand up his chest. "All I want is to make you happy."

"All I want is to make *you* happy, butterfly. It sounds like we both got what we want."

The sauce bubbled over at that moment, and I was glad for it. Dipping my head to hide my tears, I pulled the lid free to let it breathe. His hand lingered on my spine, his mouth on the back of my neck.

We ate on the back porch. Then, he took my hand, and we walked, both buzzed on wine, up the hill to the orchard. I'd planted every kind of fruit tree that could grow in Rhode Island, and they were sprouting quickly. By the end of next summer, we would have early fruit.

Hand in hand, we walked through the new growth to the other side, where he'd built a stone gazebo, supported by smooth, white pillars.

In the center sat a white marble statue, its beautiful face grave. Incense rose from the bowl at her feet—Caden must have been here earlier. As I gazed up at it, the memory of him telling me I was what he'd prayed for resurfaced. I knew now that wasn't all he wanted.

"Caden," I whispered.

"Yeah?" he murmured.

"I think I'm ready to start trying," I whispered.

His body stiffened before his strong arm snaked around my waist and pulled me into his side as his lips brushed my head.

"Thank you," he said.

"I love you," I whispered, biting back happy tears.

"I love you," he murmured, voice rough. "Now and always."

A deep sense of calm settled over me as I gazed at the spiral of smoke drifting into the dark sky. I think I understood what this meant to him. He'd dared to hope, to ask for something better, and some benevolent force had granted his prayer.

He took me by the waist, pulling me against his body, reminding me that we'd both gotten everything we wanted. Happiness was no longer a dream, but a real place we existed in together.

"You were here earlier," I said. "What did you ask for?"

He ran his hand from my throat, down between my breasts, to my stomach. "I asked that when you were ready, we would have a family."

I closed my eyes and wound my fingers through his. He'd come to the temple in the early morning to light incense, and knelt on the cool stone.

And this time, he had found peace.

THE END

OTHER BOOKS BY RAYA MORRIS EDWARDS

The Sovereign Mountain Series
Sovereign
Redbird (an epilogue to Sovereign)

Unreleased
Westin - September 2024
Jack - 2025
Jensen - TBA
Deacon - TBA

The Welsh Kings Trilogy
Paradise Descent
Prince of Ink & Scars (May 2024)

The King of Ice & Steel Trilogy
Captured Light - Lucien & Olivia
Devil I Need: The Sequel to Captured Light
Ice & Steel: The Conclusion to Captured Light & Devil I Need
Lucien & Olivia: A Christmas Short

Captured Standalones (currently in print)
Captured Desire
Captured Light
Captured Solace
Captured Ecstasy

Made in United States
Troutdale, OR
06/26/2024

20822999R10210